Book of Death
and Madness

Book of Death and Madness

The Book of Ancient Evil

Book Two

John Haas

WFP
WORDFIRE PRESS

EBook ISBN: 978-1-68057-401-2
Trade Paperback ISBN: 978-1-68057-400-5
Dust Jacket Hardcover ISBN: 978-1-68057-402-9
Case Bind Hardcover ISBN: 978-1-68057-403-6

Cover design by Janet McDonald
Cover artwork images by Adobe Stock
Kevin J. Anderson, Art Director
Published by
WordFire Press, LLC
PO Box 1840
Monument CO 80132

Kevin J. Anderson & Rebecca Moesta, Publishers
WordFire Press eBook Edition 2023
WordFire Press Trade Paperback Edition 2023
WordFire Press Hardcover Edition 2023
Printed in the USA

Join our WordFire Press Readers Group for
sneak previews, updates, new projects, and giveaways.
Sign up at wordfirepress.com

CONTENTS

PART THREE

DEDICATION

To my buddy Greg Neill. If not for him bugging me to write a Lovecraft story, this series might never have been written.

PREFACE

"The oldest and strongest emotion of mankind is fear,
And the oldest and strongest kind of fear is fear of the
unknown."

—H.P. Lovecraft

PART ONE

LONDON

THE LONDON EVENING NEWS
No. 349
London, Tuesday, December 15, 1885
Price one penny

In which Shaw and Singh return to England in pursuit of Ananya
and the book of evil

DECEMBER 15, 1885

S haw paced their sitting room, as best he could. Every second step gave a hollow double thump as his cane impacted against the thin Turkish carpet.

"Three weeks, Singh." He fumed. "Three weeks and still no clue to Ananya's whereabouts."

"Almost four," Singh corrected, not looking up from the day's newspaper spread before him.

Gas lamps shed enough light for reading when there wasn't sufficient from the broad windows. The lad's hands disappeared into the opposite sleeves of his white linen robe. His turban, an addition to his wardrobe since departing India, moved with his scanning of each article.

Shaw gave a huff of frustration and sat on one of the matching florally decorated chairs, gesturing toward Singh's reading material. They'd been keeping a close eye since returning to England, but there'd been no mention of any Indian princess in London. Likewise no mention of any activity which could be considered Thuggee related. No mysterious deaths or disappearances. It was as if Ananya had stepped off her ship from India and simply disappeared.

All they knew for certain was that Ananya had come to

London. They'd known as much before leaving India in pursuit of her. Both her ship and theirs—arriving a full month apart—had moored in Southampton to disembark passengers. From there they'd followed her trail to the train station where the ticket agent and a porter both remembered her vividly. She'd purchased two tickets for London. After that, nothing. She'd travelled across as an Indian princess in a style which befit her station, but on reaching this shore she and her Thuggee servant had somehow vanished. Shaw assumed she hadn't left the train before Waterloo Station, where everyone disembarks, but had no proof of that.

Nothing.

It was maddening.

Or, at least for Shaw it was. As usual Singh viewed the entire situation with his exasperatingly calm and logical perspective. The lad—perched on the edge of manhood just as he perched on the edge of his seat—leaned back to sip his post-lunch tea. He was six feet in height now, maybe a touch more, and had shoulders which dwarfed Shaw's. The traditional Indian robes Singh wore did little to hide the muscle underneath, though they did give an air of the exotic, the mysterious. All in all Singh cut quite the imposing figure ... unlike himself. Shaw was slighter of build, thin without being scrawny. At five foot eight he had to look up at Singh most times.

Almost four weeks since they'd returned to England, and another four on top of that since Ananya had arrived. Somewhere in London she was holed up with that book.

Who knew what her plans were?

Outside the steady clip-clop of a passing horse and carriage filled the silence. Inside the room a wood knot popped inside the fireplace.

"No information from your contacts?" Shaw asked.

Since arriving Singh had made contact with several of his fellow Indian transplants, people working for the well-to-do in the city's heart. Another wealth of knowledge, Singh maintained, were the newsboys, children ignored as much by society as Indian servants were. Both had the opportunity to see and hear what others might not, often before that news became an article in the paper.

"No."

Of course he hadn't. If Singh had any information, he would have already shared it and they would have their first real clue. Shaw had exhausted all of his own contacts, going to fellow graduates who had established medical practices while he'd chosen to go into the service of Her Majesty's Army. Each of his old classmates had met varying degrees of success, though all were able to walk without assistance from a cane.

None had any useful information.

They had, however, helped Shaw set up in his own practice, one knowing of a lodging with sufficient space on the ground floor for a medical office. This place, in South Kensington, had come furnished as well, though they'd needed to find proper medical equipment. His fellow doctors had then referred patients in an effort to get him started. Though Shaw had yet to meet all of those referrals it was already clear the quality of these patients. Hypochondriacs. Chronic nuisances. The borderline demented —just a hair too much on the sane side for committal, but close enough to be unsettling.

Those suffering from nightmares interested him most, but so far these were in the realm of paranoid ravings rather than from outside influence ... at least as far as he could tell.

In any case the medical practice kept enough money coming in and allowed them the time to search. More than that, it provided some level of normality to their lives. It wasn't all murderous cults and evil books.

God! His own thoughts sounded like those of his patients, though he wished it were a clinical madness. A madness rooted in reality wasn't paranoia but potential annihilation.

Normality. He was afraid that word would mean less for them each passing day. Already he struggled to remember a time when the shadow of this evil didn't influence their days. What choice though? Shaw knew if it came to choosing between the life he wanted and sacrificing it all to save the lives of many he would do what needed to be done.

What kind of life was that for Singh? Considering it made Shaw want to weep. The lad deserved so much better, and Shaw's paternal instinct toward him was frustrated by his inability to provide that better life. Singh, of course, had his own ghosts to deal with.

When this was over, he promised. *When this was all done he would provide a real life for this boy.*

Shaw glanced at the paper then got back to his feet, trying to pace again. It was important to work his leg and not let it atrophy, but there were times when each step caused a bright spike of pain. Pain which was already becoming an old friend, less noticeable with time. Was that desirable, to become desensitized to one's own pain ...

"There's an article on a second museum break-in," Singh said.

Shaw stopped. "A second break-in? Same museum?"

Singh shook his head.

"Where was this one?"

"Someplace called the South Kensington Museum."

He would need to take Singh around to these museums, take in the exhibits. It could be a continuation of their education. More normality.

Yes. Plenty of museums in London to visit.

Plenty.

A sweat broke out over his body and the hand not clutching his cane shook at the thought of visiting the British Museum. He cleared his throat.

"Where was that first one?"

"The Natural History Museum."

Yes. They should go to each of these, see what clues this thief had left behind. Surely it wasn't connected to the idol in any case ... No. That was a supposition Shaw found he couldn't convince himself of, not in the least. Not with a second break-in.

No, there was a thief and he ... or she ... was searching for some specific item. Unless ... "Was anything stolen?"

"Not at either museum." Singh continued to leaf through the paper. He'd come to almost the final page. "Hmm."

Shaw stopped in his movements and turned to the lad with one eyebrow raised. Singh seemed to sense it and continued.

"Sailors saw some sort of creature along the Thames."

"A creature?"

Singh shrugged his thick shoulders, eyes locking on Shaw's. Both knew what this meant. Ananya had raised another monster.

"Where was this?"

"Near Limehouse."

Shaw leaned onto his cane with practiced ease, ignoring that ever present pain. "We should investigate."

"No."

"What?" Shaw stared at his youthful friend. "Why?"

Singh's eyes bore holes into him and Shaw felt the weight of that gaze.

"It is time we visited the museum, Doctor Shaw."

Shaw took a step back, gave his head a shake.

"Two break-ins," Singh said, tapping the paper with splayed fingers. "Did you tell Ananya where you sent the idol?"

"I don't think so." Shaw cast his mind back to his last encounter with the woman and shook his head. "No. Just a museum."

"She is searching."

Shaw wanted to argue, to say this creature lurking around Limehouse was of greater importance, would have more chance at leading them to Ananya. He couldn't. It would come out as weak and pleading, and it would also not be true.

"We have put off checking on the idol too long, Doctor."

Too long? Why, they'd been back in London less than a month. Establishing their office and home, hunting for Ananya, questioning his society friends, making contacts. This had all taken a certain amount of necessary time, and the idol was safer there than it would be in his desk drawer.

That last was true ... or at least it *had* been. Now ... now it needed to be hidden somewhere better.

Only, he didn't want to see that repulsive thing again, was afraid to. It had affected his mind last time, making him sleepwalk. Oh! Those nights of waking, standing over the crate which held the idol. He'd been no better than an opium addict without any control. That had been after less than a day of exposure to it. It had taken his friend Lassiter over, wormed its way into his consciousness. No, he didn't want to see it ... and at the same moment undeniably wanted to see it again. His palms itched to hold it.

"No."

He wasn't sure if he'd said it aloud or to himself. It didn't matter. *He* was the master of his own life, not some fetish. He refused to lose control of his own person in such a manner ever again. He refused!

Singh stared at him, fingers continuing to tap the newspaper. No judgement lurked inside those eyes, no concern, just patience. The message was clear: Singh believed in him, and his ability to resist.

Shaw hoped that faith was not misplaced.

"Two break-ins," Shaw repeated. "These people are searching for something in any case."

No, not *these people*. Ananya. To believe this was anyone else was just a resistance to accept the facts. Even if it wasn't her, the possibility was enough. The idol would be better off in their possession.

"Fine."

"Should she recover the idol," Singh said, "she will use it to suck the will out of people, as she did in India. She has more British to choose from here."

"Yes, yes! I've already agreed to go. No need to belabour the point."

Singh tried to raise one eyebrow in question but was only able to raise both. It had the effect of making him appear surprised. The boy inside the man was evident when he made such gestures and it reminded Shaw of years earlier when Singh had been just a child. It also dissolved Shaw's annoyance.

"I apologize, Singh. The idea of seeing the idol again makes me snappish."

"I do not want to see it again either."

That brought Shaw's attention back around to his young friend. No, of course Singh didn't want to see it. His exposure to the effects of the idol were much greater than Shaw's own, though Singh had never been allowed to touch it, thankfully.

Shaw sighed, looking toward the floor. He should tell Singh to stay here, that he would take care of this. Only he couldn't. He needed his friend's assistance in getting around too much ... No. Another flimsy excuse. The fact was he couldn't do this alone, couldn't trust himself to do this alone.

"The idol frightens me," Singh continued, "as it did when I was a boy. At least now we know what to expect."

Another thing Shaw hoped to be true.

December 15, 1885

Winter in London was dull and grey, the sun hidden behind perpetual clouds while the air carried an almost metallic scent. Damp as well, a dampness which got into the bones and made Shaw's leg ache more than usual. In the cab, being jostled by the sway of the coach, Shaw watched the world outside go past, enveloped inside a dreary, foggy day. One thought chased all others away inside his head.

The idol.

"Meditation helps to hone one's thoughts."

Shaw turned toward his companion and, being able to do so, raised one eyebrow. Singh lay one hand against their satchel bag on the seat.

"With your thoughts focused," Singh continued, "the idol may have less influence."

Singh fell silent, looking in his direction with a calm which Shaw could only envy. Meditation. Shaw had hesitated asking for details, judging it to be more of a private observance than something to be shared, much like a person's religion. If he were being honest the concept was odd to him, to simply sit and breathe.

The influence of the idol. Could anything affect or alter that?

"I …" Shaw cleared his throat. "Well, bit late to be any benefit today I'm afraid."

"Focus on your breathing," Singh said like the most patient teacher in all of history. "On the way your body moves with each inhalation and exhalation."

Focus on your breathing. Shaw replayed the words in his mind, absorbing the concept while waiting for Singh's next instruction. In a few moments it became obvious none was to come. "Is that all?"

"For now, yes."

Simple enough. With a shrug Shaw closed his eyes and focused all attention on his breathing. The inhalation and how he shifted to his right. The exhalation and a repositioning of his bad leg. Again. The movement of his chest, up with conscious slowness, then down.

An unexpected calmness did come over him, lasting all of two or three seconds before ideas and thoughts once again crowded in on his mind, demanding attention. If stray thoughts could derail his calm what use would it be against the idol insisting its way into his mind?

He opened his eyes to a satisfied nod from Singh, as if he'd accomplished some monumental victory on his first attempt. Not for the first time he felt less like the fatherly figure he hoped to be, and more like a child.

"Singh …"

"Yes?"

"Why do you suppose she didn't break into the British Museum first?"

"Why should she?"

"Why, it's the most sizable museum in London. The most important."

"Is it?" Singh considered. "Perhaps, like me, she wasn't aware."

Yes, Shaw could accept that.

"Or," Singh added after a few moments thought, "she could be progressing geographically from wherever she is."

"Hmm, Natural History Museum was first, then South Kensington Museum. Working her way inward? Could she have settled into Kensington too?"

Singh shrugged and turned toward the window, no theory to contribute. Shaw did the same, considering. Outside the world of London passed by: Street vendors hawking roasted chestnuts, pedestrians with scarves across their mouths against the day's choking yellowish fog. A man on a penny-farthing passing in the opposite direction, tipping his hat to their driver. Always in the shadows were the unworried movements of rats.

They rolled to a stop at the museum. Singh descended first, a hand out to help and guide Shaw, a process which he detested for its very necessity, though he drew the line at Singh taking his arm while they walked, no matter how much agony he felt. They crossed toward the museum's front door, passing through the fog, then through the front door and into a spacious, bright foyer. The museum was calm and silent, the lunch crowds having come and gone. A scent of aged paper hung in the air, joining the silence in library-like atmosphere. Shaw removed his top hat to hold in his free hand as they crossed the open room toward an enthusiastic man gathering people for a tour.

"Would you be able to direct me toward the curator?" Shaw asked.

"Which one?" the man asked.

"There's more than one?"

"Yes, sir. One for each of the major departments. One for Egypt, one for—"

"Ah, I see. I am looking for the curator of the entire museum. The man in charge."

"Oh, you want the director then. I'll send someone to see if he is available."

The man did so and turned back to his tour.

"Perhaps you should speak with this director alone."

Shaw turned toward his friend, surprised. He wanted to say that he needed Singh with him, that he didn't want to confront the idol alone, didn't even want to see it ... but Singh was correct. He was an impressive figure and unintentionally intimidating with his stature. They didn't want to threaten this director.

"I'll be fine, Singh," he said, and demonstrated the breathing exercise which Singh had taught him.

Satisfied Singh stepped away to view nearby displays.

"Good morning, you wished to see me?"

Shaw turned to find a thin man, taller than himself and younger than expected. The man wore an impeccable suit which would have cost as much as Shaw's practice made in a month.

"I am Nigel Kinkaid," the man said, holding one hand toward Shaw. "Director of the museum."

"Doctor Archibald Shaw."

The two men shook and Shaw wondered the best way for getting around to the topic of the idol.

"Pleased to meet you, Doctor. Are you one of our donors then? Come by to see what your investment has brought the museum?"

"No, I'm afraid not. I'm inquiring about an item I shipped here while with the army in India."

"Ah, a different breed of donor then."

Shaw smiled at the joke and the easy way with which the man made conversation. "Yes, I suppose I am."

"Not everything gets displayed, I'm afraid, and a good deal ends up in storage. What was the item?"

"An idol."

The man's friendly expression faltered and his weight shifted, as if ready to step back. "An ... idol? We have many idols of course."

"Yes, of course. This was a hideous sculpture about seven or eight inches in height. Would have arrived seven years ago, in a crate from Hyderabad."

"Seven years ago ... Hyderabad ..."

The man appeared somewhat entranced, as if remembering a fantastic experience. The smile all but slid away from Kinkaid's face but returned as his focus snapped back to Shaw.

"Yes, I know the shipment you mean. As I said, still somewhere in our storage and has been for years." The man started back toward the entrance, Shaw following in his wake. "No time or inclination to unpack those crates I'm afraid, and no place to put them anyway, you understand."

"I could look through the storage if that—"

"Afraid that would be out of the question. Only employees of the museum you understand."

"Yes, but—"

"I have much work to return to now if you'll excuse me."

They'd arrived at the door and the director gestured toward it as if Shaw were no longer welcome on the property. He could see Singh coming along behind the man but keeping a discreet distance.

"Yes, I—"

"Don't worry, Doctor. If I should come across your idol I shall let you know."

With that the man turned and headed deeper into the museum, sparing one glance back over his shoulder as he went. Singh came up beside Shaw and watched the other man's retreat.

"He seemed rather eager for you to leave."

Shaw looked to his friend and nodded. As usual, Singh cut through to the center of the matter. The two wandered out of the door in silence, Shaw staring back over his shoulder. His great concern had been in seeing the idol again, so much so that it hadn't occurred to him it might not be that simple.

"He knows the idol," Singh said.

Shaw turned toward the door again, replaying the conversation inside his mind as if watching two players on a stage. Yes. Of course he did. Kinkaid had not even asked about his interest in the idol. "Still, what can we do about it?"

What indeed. Was that an honest question or mere words to

cover the relief felt at not having to encounter the idol? Certainly it was safe enough where it was. Safer than back in their rooms.

"That is a good question, Doctor," Singh said as they passed back into the fog and headed toward a waiting cab. "What can we do?"

Shaw stopped, his mind following Singh's insinuation that there was some action they could do. *Should* do. As much as he wanted to forget the idol existed, he couldn't. Ananya wasn't about to forget and should it fall back into her hands ... Yes, it was safer here for the moment, but it was also a known location. The safest place for an item as dangerous as this idol was somewhere fewer people knew, and had access to. That was logical.

"What are you prepared to do?" Singh added.

"Quite right, Singh. Quite right. We need to retrieve that idol, before someone else does."

But how?

Off to their right a newsboy—one of many who dotted London's street corners—called the headlines of the day.

Shaw's mind returned to those days in India, to the idol and the book. To Ananya and the cult, and the deaths of Lassiter, Walsh, and far too many others. Circumstances which could repeat here, and in much greater numbers. So what *was* he prepared to do to prevent that?

"And ..." Shaw took a deep breath, let it back out and forced some calm into himself in a way he thought Singh could have admired. "I am prepared to break into the museum to retrieve it first."

Singh considered the words a moment before turning back toward the cab. A moment later Shaw followed. The lad appreciated directness to a degree which made him uncomfortable. It forced him to examine events more closely, and himself even closer. Shaw much preferred to close off his thoughts and allow them to solve problems.

Still, Singh was right. They needed to get that idol, before someone else did ... or find Ananya first, which was not about to happen. It was frustrating that they couldn't go directly to her. They had no clue on what section of the city she'd disappeared into and until she revealed herself that was a dead end.

Shaw looked up from his contemplations to find Singh purchasing a paper from the newsboy. The two spoke as if they knew each other, and probably did. Singh had taken to the papers as a source of information rather without hesitation, and was even better at getting insight from the boys themselves. They found him fascinating, exotic, and Singh, for his part, listened to them with interest which was uncommon from adults.

Singh returned with the paper in hand, a earlier copy of which already waited on their table at home. "A body was found along the Thames," he said. "Near Limehouse."

"More work of this monster?"

Singh gave one quick nod. The two stood staring at each other, unspoken communication passing between them. Shaw glanced back at the museum but any possibilities there would have to remain until later. In the absence of other activity they would do what could be done.

December 15, 1885

L imehouse," Singh told the cabbie while Shaw made his slow climb into the cab's interior. "Down near the Thames."

"This body—" Shaw began as Singh took his seat opposite.

The young man folded the paper and placed it on the seat next to him. "A stevedore. One who works along the shore, helping boats unload. A man known for violence and drinking. The police aren't taking it seriously."

No, of course they weren't. This was Limehouse, a part of London's East End where life was abundant and cheap. How had Dickens phrased it? The surplus population? The police wouldn't concern themselves about occurrences in Limehouse or Whitechapel, not until it threatened to affect those better off.

"The man was attacked by something with sharp claws."

Shaw recalled the long dangling fingers of the creature in Hyderabad, the people torn apart by its mindless thralls.

"A maut?" Shaw suggested.

Singh shrugged.

"Why would she raise another of those creatures?" Shaw said. "They stopped obeying her commands back in India."

"Perhaps she expects better results without her brother nearby. Or ..."

"Or?"

"Or this is some different creature."

"Hmm ..."

"Playing a game of guesses is without value."

"True." Anything was possible when dealing with Ananya. Shaw laid no claim to understanding how the woman's mind worked. She had murdered, called up foul creatures, all in an effort to bring ... No! He couldn't—*wouldn't*—consider that name. He knew it though. Oh yes. It lurked inside his mind like a rat inside the walls.

The cab jostled Shaw from side to side, the roads in this part of London being less well-maintained. He did his best to brace himself between the use of his good leg and the ever-present cane. It was a skill he was getting better at, though it still was far from pleasant.

At least Limehouse wasn't *too* far from the museum.

As if in answer to his thoughts the cab rolled to a halt, the cabbie knocking on the roof to let them know they'd arrived. The man took payment and was on his way, not wishing to stand idle in Limehouse any longer than was necessary. It was a rough and dangerous area, though Shaw was unworried with Singh by his side. The lad had proven his ability to take care of himself, and looked dangerous to boot. With any luck that would be enough to keep the more dangerous characters away.

Often he would forget that Singh was only a lad of fifteen. He didn't belong here, chasing monsters. Neither of them did. They should be back in their comfortable rooms, going over lessons of mathematics, science, and history. There were times when he wanted to cry out at the unfairness of it all, to strike something with his cane. The weight of humanity's survival rested on their shoulders, and it was a crushing burden.

"Doctor?"

Shaw came back to the here and now with a shake of his head.

He pulled his coat tighter against the cold and damp, worse here so close to the water. "Right. Lead the way, Singh."

A smell of damp stone drifted to their noses on a breeze which cut through their clothing. The cries of gulls and lapwings hunting for food filled the air not too distant from where they stood. At least the fog was thinner here.

Nearby a group of sailors tended their ship, a smaller three-masted schooner. Shaw and Singh approached these men, aware of the immediate change in their attitudes. Each of the sailors pulled their slickers tighter around them, their caps lower to obscure all features. Several returned to their ship and disappeared belowdecks. One man crossed his arms and scowled at the approaching pair.

"Stop there."

Shaw came to a halt, Singh taking one more step to ensure he was between his friend and danger.

"What you want?" The voice was guttural, like trying to speak around a mouthful of liquid.

"We are looking for where the man died," Shaw explained, wishing he'd been able to exercise better diplomacy. "We are ... working with the police."

"Ia!" the man spat, then pointed up the shore. "Half mile. Go."

For a moment Shaw caught a glimpse of dry, scaly skin. Not uncommon among those who work in a salt atmosphere, surely. More uncommon was the quick flash of face, the bulging eyes and rubbery lips. A moment later it was gone, the sailors standing with all attention on them. Shaw opened his mouth to ask a second question when he felt Singh's hand on his shoulder. The lad gave a quick shake of his head, a gesture in the direction the sailor had indicated.

"Our thanks," Shaw said, allowing Singh to lead him away.

No sailor moved while Shaw and Singh moved away, deeper into the fog.

"Are they following?" Shaw asked, voice low.

Singh listened for a moment then shook his head.

No. Those men merely wished to be left alone. Such physical deformities—assuming they were all similar to their leader, if not worse—had resulted in people who shunned contact with their fellow men.

Shaw wished he could return, to help these men if possible, but knew it to be impossible. Were they diseased, like the lepers? Was the warning to come no nearer for Shaw's benefit as much as their own? He would never know.

Following the man's direction along the shore led them to their target, the place where man and monster had come together in the night. The police had been there and gone, taking the body with them and spending no more time than was necessary. Little was left behind except for traces of blood and too many footprints in the mud.

"Hopeless," Shaw mumbled.

Singh had hunkered down, inspecting the softer earth close to the water. He stood and headed inland, toward the furthest edge of the shore. "It is big."

Shaw shuffled closer, being careful not to step where Singh was investigating. The lad was finding clues which were invisible to his own eyes.

"See." Singh pointed.

It was half of what could only be called a paw print, longer than a tiger's but clawed in a similar fashion.

"What is it?" Shaw asked, knowing Singh would have no better idea than he did.

"Not a maut," Singh replied. "The maut's feet were clawed, but human sized. These are much longer."

"They are?"

Singh nodded, pointing out a second partial pawprint close to obliterated by the traffic of people. Shaw cast about for some lair where the creature could have gone and found no possibilities. There were no caves or tunnels, nothing that wouldn't be disturbed by the activity which would occur around it at all hours. No, this—

"And whatta we got 'ere?"

Shaw and Singh both turned toward the sound of the voice and found five dockworker types, stevedores, appearing from the fog like ghosts. They stood, twenty feet distant, staring, wearing the typical cloth caps and canvas trousers of their ilk. One in the back chuckled, as if at a joke only he had heard. They were not there for any friendly reason, that much was certain. Shaw glanced to Singh who shifted a step forward, ready to once again get in front of danger for him.

"We're investigating the death," Shaw said, trying for an official sound. "I'm a doctor."

"A doctor, eh? Well, la-di-da," a different man said.

"Ha! I gots a pain for you to look at," the one who'd chuckled said.

So, these weren't ones to be intimidated by Singh's appearance or impressed by Shaw's assumed authority. Another glance at his friend, who had both eyes on the dockworkers. The lad made no move, no expression showed he had any worry or concern though these men obviously meant them violence. Belatedly Shaw's thoughts went to his service revolver in the drawer of his nightstand, where it had sat since their return to England.

The five moved closer, the odor of their stale sweat drifting across the gap.

"Now, why would a doctor care about the death o' one man here in Limehouse?" another man spoke, and when he did the others all looked in his direction. Their leader. "What with the body already gone. Police came and cleared him away quick as you please. Didn't look around much."

"They don't know what to look for," Shaw said.

The chuckler. "That sounds like the bobbies, a'right."

Shaw switched tactics. "You men are in danger here, especially at night."

Another chuckle.

"Not as much danger as yer in right now," one who'd been quiet until now chimed in.

The leader looked at this man as if he'd overstepped his bounds, taken *his* job of making clever threats. He turned back to Shaw and Singh. "He ain't wrong. Hand over yer money and maybe yuh won't get hurt too badly."

"Maybe," Shaw observed.

Singh's muscles tensed under his robe, prepared for the inevitable. Shaw shifted all his weight to his unimpaired leg, gripping the head of his cane in the other hand.

"Maybe," the leader repeated, a smug grin telling the likelihood of that.

"How about, instead," Shaw said, "you go your way and we go—"

One man who'd been silent up to then rushed forward with a yell, perhaps spurred on by the fact he hadn't gotten a word in. He headed straight for Singh, who stepped to the right and shot out his right fist to collide with the man's upper jaw, an inch or so below his eye. The man went down, face first into the mud.

"He dropped Charlie!"

The leader waved a hand to quiet his partners and pointed at Singh. "Get him. I'll see ta the good doctor."

The other three converged on Singh but Shaw had his own problem to focus on. The leader came toward him and Shaw hopped back a step or two. They were left with little choice. Handing any money over would not prevent a beating at this point and in all likelihood never would have. He knew the type, and to be honest he didn't want to surrender. He'd had quite enough days without control over his own life. No. One option left then, the cane which Singh had purchased for him in Bombay. As a weapon it didn't look like much, but it held a secret.

Shaw gripped its head and pulled, freeing top from bottom. A sword, concealed in a sheath. Without waiting for the man to register surprise and come up with a response Shaw thrust it forward, skewering him through the meaty part of his upper leg. The blade missed the bone, as intended, and came out the far side.

"Ahhh! Oh, God!"

The man went over backward, pulling free of the blade and holding his wound while he writhed in the mud.

Shaw stepped closer and pressed the tip of the blade to the man's throat, getting his wide-eyed attention. The chuckler was down in the muck, holding a bleeding, and most likely broken, nose.

The remaining two would not be defeated as easily. Each had drawn a simple wooden-handled blade and approached Singh with more caution, ready for the next trick. This was a losing battle about to turn deadly.

"Call them off," Shaw warned, giving the sword extra pressure.

"Ow! Hey, yeah. Sure, sure."

The leader whistled at the remaining two. They stopped, looking back at the scene of Shaw with his sword.

"Knock it off boys," the leader said.

"Tell them to grab their two friends and go."

"You heard 'im, get outta here."

The two looked at each other, then at Singh. A quick glance at their knives and doing the simple math of two blades against one unarmed man. Shaw tried to appear unworried as he held a blade at a man's throat and waited. Singh, unruffled, positioned himself for the next attack, unsure if it would be theirs or his.

"They're still here." Shaw pressed the blade against the stevedore's throat, dimpling the skin.

"Go, I said!"

The two still upright grumbled and shrugged at each other, perhaps acknowledging to themselves that they'd gone from five down to two in as many minutes. With some effort they got the others to their feet. Chuckler was under his own power, holding his nose, eyes wide and teared with pain. The other two grabbed their final, now semiconscious friend, and got him vertical.

The four retreated with frequent backward glances, muttering to each other.

Singh came to stand beside Shaw, ready to catch him if his balance should go.

"Shall we kill him, Doctor?" he asked, knowing full well the answer to come.

Shaw let the idea sink into this man's mind. "Hey, we were just gonna rob you. Rough you up a bit at most. We weren't gonna kill you."

"No?"

"No, I swear."

"Hmm." Shaw withdrew the sword, making sure to move sideways as he did to give a small nick. He kept the sword pointed in the man's direction, the threat clear. "Perhaps you'll answer some questions before you go."

"Yeah. Yeah. Sure."

Shaw found himself enjoying the control of this situation. He, Archibald Shaw, had someone at a physical disadvantage. He wiped the blood from his blade and returned it to the lower part of his cane, using it to keep him upright once again.

"What happened here?"

The dockworker tried to sit up but gasped with the pain and held his wound tighter. After a couple of deep breaths he shrugged. "Bart was out here at night. Stupid."

"Stupid because ...?"

"Because yuh don't go anywhere 'round here alone. Not at night. That's just lookin' for trouble, even without ..."

His eyes darted aside. What he'd been about to say sounded deranged and he avoided that. Shaw said it for him.

"Without some monster lurking?"

The man jerked, startled. "You know about that?"

"Some. How many days has it been here?"

"I ... 'bout a week I guess, from what I hear."

"You haven't seen it?"

"Me? Nah. Stories are enough for me."

"Stories?"

"People seein' it from a distance."

"What did it look like?"

The man huffed out a breath. "A monster, like yuh said." Both Shaw and Singh stared at the man until he decided to add to it. "Yeah, yeah. Heard one sailor name of Old Willy tell it. Saw it from his ship. He was the first and we all thought he was drunk."

"Until someone was killed?"

The man shook his head. "Disappeared."

"Disappeared," Shaw repeated, as if trying the word on for size.

"Didn't think mucha that first one. People disappear. People run off. The second one was supposed ta ship out a day later but never showed."

"Go on."

"Didn't find but scraps 'a the jacket he was wearin'."

"How many?"

"Four, so far as I know. This was the first time a body was left behind."

"So, two disappeared, and two killed it appears," Shaw wondered to himself.

"Me, I'm gonna head ta Southampton or Dover fer work soons I got the train fare."

"You were telling what Old Willy saw," Singh prompted.

"Right, yeah. So, Old Willy saw it close to sundown, movin' in the shadows. It was grey or maybe black. Thin with long, clawed fingers."

The man stopped.

"Is that it?" Shaw asked.

"That ain't enough?"

"It will do." It didn't in fact, but it was all this man knew. Shaw wanted details on whether the creature moved fast or slow. Did it exhibit any intelligence?

"Willy always got shifty-eyed at the end, mutterin' whatever came next."

"Where do we find Old Willy?" Singh asked.

"Where you find any sailor waitin' for his ship ta leave. The Ox and Crown."

"Where is that?"

The stevedore gave directions and Shaw shrugged at Singh to say he was out of questions. They both looked back at the man who held up his hands.

"That's all I know. I swear!"

"Fine," Shaw said, retrieving the satchel bag from Singh. "Now, pull your trousers down."

"What?"

The man's gaze went sullen, ready to fight whatever strangeness was about to happen.

Shaw fished around inside of his bag. "Oh, for God's sake. Pants down or pull it up past the wound if you can." He pulled out a roll of bandage and approached the man. "Or, you can hobble all the way home. You might not bleed to death."

The dockworker's eyes went to the bandage, then to Shaw's face. His mind worked out what was happening and he pulled the pant leg up, exposing a thin, straight wound which continued to bleed.

"Raise the leg a bit."

The man tried but without much luck. Singh grabbed it around the ankle and held it up, the way he would have with any paying patient back at their office though with much less gentleness and a tighter grip. Their patient sucked in a gasp of pain. Shaw ignored it as he set about wrapping the man's leg with the bandage. When he was done Singh dropped the leg and the man gasped again. Shaw gave instruction on changing the bandages and keeping the wound clean. Advice the man was unlikely to follow.

"On your way," Shaw said.

A glance at both his and Singh's face to be sure he'd heard right, then the stevedore was on his feet, backing away. Once a sufficient distance he turned and limped away at the quickest pace he could manage. Shaw and Singh left in the opposite direction, hoping that the man wouldn't consider coming back once he found his friends. No, Shaw was sure they would cut their losses and go elsewhere in search of extra money.

A sudden hand on his arm caused Shaw to jump and try to swing around at this fresh attack.

"It is only me, Doctor."

Shaw relaxed, allowing Singh to provide him extra balance without admitting he needed it. The fight had taken too much of his stamina and moving in a straight line had become quite the task. He would need a seat soon, and for some time, to recuperate. He considered a low stone wall running alongside them, but resolved to make it to the Ox and Crown.

"So," he said, seeking to distract himself. "Old Willy."

"Hmm."

"You sound doubtful."

"The distance from ship to shore, the dimness of light. How could he see that much detail?"

Shaw thought about it, nodding.

"I want to know the ending," Singh added.

"The part he would only mutter? Yes, I agree." They were silent a dozen steps before Shaw spoke again. "Four disappearances."

"Yes?"

"It seems that this one, and the one which left bloody scraps behind, could be separate from the other two."

"Ananya?"

"Maybe. Maybe—"

The sound of voices came from deeper in the fog, off to their right and getting closer. Shaw's heart sank at the idea of another skirmish. This time around he would be less useful, exhausted as he was. Still, the element of surprise and his concealed sword could help again. He looked to Singh, hoping to pass all of this to him unspoken but stopped at the strange look on his friend's face. He wore an expression of recognition and called a greeting to these voices in his native language. The conversation stopped, a pause before a return greeting and three Lascar sailors came into view. The Indian men glared at Shaw suspiciously before greeting Singh with instant ease and comradeship, speaking in low tones. Singh nodded to something in agreement and the other three laughed, one clapping Singh on the shoulder. The four looked back and Singh made a comment, gesturing. From that moment all made a point of ignoring Shaw.

Shaw limped to the low wall, brushing away the layer of coal dust. All too often this dust would fall in a filthy snow to coat everything in London. Shaw sat, taking the pressure off his bad leg. For a few moments he revelled in the pleasant sensation, a bit of a rest, but the leg never gave him that much respite before reminding Shaw of it being overworked.

The Lascar sailors and Singh continued their conversation as if Shaw were not there, speaking back and forth too rapidly for him to follow. Even after his years in India and being able to speak the language he couldn't follow such rapid-fire conversation. These men spoke a rougher dialect, too, the equivalent of what English sailors spoke he supposed.

Shaw passed the minutes going over what they knew about Ananya and this monster, about the idol and the book. It took less time than expected, reinforcing how little useable information they'd learned.

After another five minutes Singh looked back at Shaw and spoke once again to the sailors. The three said their farewells and continued on their way. Singh returned to his side and watched them leave.

"I don't think they liked me much," Shaw said.

"They did not, but no more than any Englishman."

That was not surprising and Shaw accepted it. He wasn't as naïve as when he'd first arrived in India, thinking the British people were making everywhere they landed a better place by their very presence, some sort of saviour race. He was getting the idea that there were few places in the world where Englishmen were welcome ... even in England.

"The sailor, Old Willy, left on a ship this morning."

Damn it! Shaw doubted this man would have told them much more but there would have been some minor detail. "So that's the end for any information. At least until this monster strikes again."

"This Old Willy spoke about the encounter but most thought he'd been drunk. The Lascars did not, they believed from the first."

"And ...?"

"Since the Lascars listened Willy did more than mutter with them." Singh paused, turning toward Shaw. "Old Willy thought it was coming to attack him."

"Why?"

"It looked at the man, then unfurled two wings and flew into the sky."

Shaw came to a halt, quickly looking above.

Definitely not a maut then.

DECEMBER 15, 1885

Ananya could be in the Limehouse area."

Singh considered. "Perhaps."

Once again the two rode inside a cab, jostled with each lurch. Given the sun had set and the fog remained this carriage at least moved somewhat slower, though not by much. The cabbie called to a second driver in passing, their words indistinct.

"If she's calling up new monsters then we will need to move quicker on discovering where she is."

Singh nodded, the point an obvious one and needing no verbal response. Of course they needed to discover her quicker. She had obviously deluded some poor fool into reading from the book to summon this creature. Probably the Thuggee she'd escaped India with, unless those two sailors who had disappeared had become converts or captives instead of food. Who knew how many others had disappeared in the area. No, they would need to investigate this area more.

"We can return tomorrow, in the daytime."

Singh turned to look out the window, into the dusk. They lurched through the early evening toward home and dinner.

"Doctor?"

"Yes, Singh."

Singh didn't respond, but continued staring out the window. Shaw followed his gaze and saw the British Museum which they'd visited hours earlier.

"What the deuce?"

A dozen bobbies shuffled around outside of the museum, looking here and there, inspecting the door and the bushes. The streetlamps surrounding the building lit the area in flickering gas flames, creating an aura around each in the night's thinner fog.

"Something has happened."

For the first time, as far as Shaw could recall, Singh had made an unnecessary statement. He let it go and hammered on the roof for the cabbie to stop. They descended from the cab once again and stood on the edge of the museum's property.

"Whatever has happened," Shaw said, "it looks like they're concluding."

Indeed, most of the dozen police that had been milling around outside as Shaw and Singh's cab pulled up had gone in separate directions. Back to their individual beats? Only two of the bobbies were left behind, one at the front door as an obvious sentry and a second who went around one side of the museum. The one at the door had his gaze locked on the two of them.

"We are attracting attention, Doctor."

"Inevitable, I suppose."

The two started forward, intent on reaching the front door while the policeman shifted toward them.

"Can I help you, sirs?"

The bobby's tone was pleasant but the message was clear. They were not getting to that front door without first going through him.

"Ah, yes," Shaw said, slipping into his best non-threatening doctor's voice. "We are here to see the director."

"Not tonight I'm afraid, sir."

"Oh?" Shaw aimed for a mildly interested air. "What's happened here?"

"A break-in of sorts."

"Of sorts?"

The bobby glanced from Shaw to Singh and back again, apparently sensing no danger from either. "Well, sir, the museum's door was unlocked but they'd closed for the day. Someone decided to enter anyway and when they were spotted rushed deeper into the museum."

"Goodness! Did they catch ... him?"

"No, sir. He was chased but got away."

"How exciting."

The bobby shrugged. It may be fascinating for some but hardly exciting compared to what the man saw on a day-to-day basis.

"Anything stolen?"

"Don't think so, but not sure yet. The museum director and one inspector from the Yard are looking about inside." The man came to a realization, eyes narrowed. "You ain't the press, are you?"

"No, no. Just a doctor and his friend hoping to drop in on the director."

"You a friend?"

"Mmm, more of an acquaintance I suppose." Shaw turned, as if preparing to leave, then returned to the police officer. "What was this thief after, I wonder?"

"Well, we ain't sure he's a thief yet but he headed straight for the India section."

Shaw gave a quick glance at Singh who stood implacable, eyes on the policemen blocking their path.

The India section.

Of course it was.

Only the idol was not on display. Kinkaid had tried telling him that it remained in the same crate it had arrived in, abandoned and relegated to the most forgotten corners of museum storage. Forgotten. That was a lie, a story to hasten Shaw's departure. No, Shaw remembered too well his friend Lassiter and the effect that thing had on him, how twitchy and possessive he'd become. Kinkaid exhibited the beginning of those same signs.

The idol had come to absorb Lassiter's every waking hour except those spent in his duty as a doctor. Even then, when the ward got slower Lassiter would start to fidget like an opium sot and look for reasons to leave. It wasn't a simple addiction but something more sinister, more insidious. The idol wore down the mind, eroded a man's sanity and made it more susceptible to the influence of Cthu ... No! He couldn't, *wouldn't* think that name!

"You a'right there, Doctor?"

Both the policeman and Singh had their attention focused on Shaw and he didn't wonder why. He could sense the sweat on his brow and heard the struggle to get his breathing under control. His heart hammered inside his chest. What had Singh said? Focus on the breathing with each movement.

A shuddering breath in and a slight movement of his good leg. A breath out as he leaned more heavily on his cane. With gradual, grudging effort, his breathing came back under control.

"I'm fine," he said. "Too much rushing about today is all."

The bobby nodded as if understanding what Shaw meant. An expression of sympathy crossed the man's face and he glanced behind him at the doors. "Shame for you to come all this way for nothing."

Singh stepped closer and Shaw leaned against him, giving relief to his leg while increasing any potential sympathy he might be receiving.

"The detective inspector was just wrapping up, sir. He and the director should be along—"

As if in response the door opened to reveal a man in a cheap suit and bowler hat, thin and shrewd in appearance. His only affectation was a walrus-thick moustache. Behind him stood Director Kinkaid who looked as if he wanted nothing less than for all the people around him to be on their way.

"Who's this now?" the inspector asked, gaze narrowed. The

eyes of a hunter who missed no detail, like a hawk which had somehow become human.

"Doctor Archibald Shaw, sir."

Kinkaid exhaled a short breath.

"I've come to see the director."

"You know this man?" the inspector asked over one shoulder while keeping both eyes on Shaw. His eyes drifted toward Singh, as if the massive lad were prime suspect.

"This is my ward," Shaw supplied before it was demanded. "Singh."

Depending on whom he spoke to, and what was expected, Shaw selected diverse introductions for Singh. Ward. Friend. Son, once or twice when annoyed at the attitude of a particular person. Assistant in relation to the medical practice, but partner when talking about any circumstance of real importance. Inside his own mind Shaw most often considered Singh his confidant, his friend, and if not his son by blood then assuredly in spirit.

The inspector looked away with a shrug, the momentary suspicion having received a pardon.

"I know him, Inspector," Kinkaid admitted, "though I've no more to say now than I did earlier."

The inspector's curiosity was rekindled and he looked from Shaw to Singh then back at the director. "I might be missing part of the story here."

Kinkaid waved it off as unimportant. "The doctor came to inquire about seeing some items he had shipped back to the museum during his days in Hyderabad."

"India?" the inspector said. "Isn't that interesting."

"Not particularly," the director answered. "The items are still crated and stored in our archives for that very reason."

"In storage then?"

Kinkaid gave one nod to the inspector though both eyes remained on Shaw and Singh. "I told the doctor I would contact him when I had the time to open those crates."

"Hmm." The inspector considered the problem a moment

longer before deciding that no real interest lay in it. "We'll keep a closer eye on the museum for a few days. Step up patrols and all that."

With a tip of his bowler to the director and another toward Shaw the inspector descended the steps, the remaining bobby following in his wake. The inspector gave the man instructions before crossing to a police wagon. Somewhere in the distance the clip-clop of horses' hooves carried through the night.

Without a word Kinkaid started to close the huge door, no interest in either of those standing on the doorstep. Singh moved, ready to shove the door inward, but Shaw raised one hand in a caution to wait. The police were not so far that they wouldn't hear noise of a scuffle.

"The thief will return," Shaw said, stepping closer. "This one, or others like him."

Or her.

Had the door slowed?

"They're after that damned ugly idol," Shaw spit out, "and whoever is in possession of it."

An inch left of interior still showing the door paused, as if that barrier itself were considering Shaw's words. One heartbeat passed. Two. Singh's muscles bunched, ready to leap. The door opened again, Kinkaid's face appearing in the gap. The director scowled at Shaw.

"You may come in." The gaze shifted to Singh. "Alone."

Shaw shook his head, not wanting to abandon Singh out here in the cold night. "I—"

"My sole offer," Kinkaid said.

"I shall remain here, Doctor," Singh said, leaning against a column in his most nonchalant manner.

The lad looked at Shaw's cane and raised both eyebrows in a warning to *beware* before inclining his head toward the door and Kinkaid. Shaw nodded. He would be ready to defend himself if this man should turn out to be more threat than appearance suggested.

Shaw shuffled through the open door, moving slower than was necessary at the moment. He could use a seat but was far from incapacitated. Still, if this man thought him more helpless than was fact this wasn't a bad thing.

Director Kinkaid kept an eye on Singh as he closed the door, slipping the lock into place. He turned to Shaw, scrutinizing him. The man's eyes were lucid and knowing, like Lassiter in those periods when he wasn't mesmerized by the idol.

In no possible way was this man in possession of the idol for the last seven years.

"You were not director here when the idol arrived."

Kinkaid's eyes widened, one eyebrow raising. "No. In those days I was assistant curator for the India section."

"But you were there when the idol was unpacked."

"Oh, yes. It came wrapped inside a coat."

"My coat."

"Sir Kenneth Martin, head curator for India, unwrapped it. The idol tumbled onto the table and sat there, staring at us."

Shaw nodded his understanding.

"We examined it, both Sir Kenneth and I knowing this to be something special. Unique."

"Unique. Yes."

"He decided to take it to his office and I didn't see it again," Kinkaid said, "but I didn't forget it."

"It is not something one forgets."

Director Kinkaid gritted his teeth and glared at Shaw, fists clenching. "This was no treasure you sent, and you knew it."

Shaw retreated a step, opening his mouth to claim his innocence. Instead he closed it with a snap not able to look the man in the eyes.

Deep breath in. Deep breath out.

Kinkaid's gaze shifted to stare up the museum passage, as if his name had been called. "Shortly after that Sir Kenneth became director, and I filled his previous position."

"How do you come to be in possession of the idol now?"

The man's focus returned to Shaw. "I found the idol in Director Aaronson's desk after he ... died."

"Aaronson? I thought you said Martin."

"Neville Aaronson took over from Sir Kenneth. I took over from him."

Director Kinkaid gestured and headed deeper into the museum, in the direction he'd looked a moment earlier. He moved at a pace which Shaw was able to keep. The hollow sound of their footsteps against the marble echoed back at them.

"What ..." Shaw hesitated, afraid of the answer to this next question. "What happened to Martin, and Aaronson?"

Kinkaid chuckled, a quick sound out of place for the topic and pushed aside a moment later. "Nothing you would find in the papers, detail all hushed up you understand. Still within the museum it is whispered that there is a curse." Kinkaid stopped and turned toward Shaw, glaring. "How right that rumour is people will never know."

Shaw stared back at the man who forced a grim, humourless smile onto his face. He continued on, while Shaw considered the presence of his concealed sword once again.

"Neville Aaronson died two months ago. He went up to the roof and threw himself off into the great courtyard."

Suicide. Another death attributed to this idol, another one on his conscience. "And Martin?"

"Sir Kenneth closed up one evening, went home and ate dinner." Kinkaid paused, took a breath. "After dessert he murdered his entire family."

Several deaths then. "No."

"Oh, yes."

"How long—"

"He'd been in possession of the idol for three years. Aaronson didn't find it immediately on becoming director. No, Sir Kenneth had hidden it away someplace and it wasn't found for two years after his death. That's when Neville changed, becoming more erratic. He started to forget his duties and spent lengthy stretches inside his office with the door closed. In all he possessed it less than two years."

They continued along a hallway and out of that part of the museum open to the public, past a sign which stated No Admittance—Staff Only. One door faced them at the end of the hall, the name Director Kinkaid etched onto it, which the man opened and passed through.

The room was as neat and tidy as any office Shaw had seen. Cabinets and shelves lined either side with books and smaller artifacts filling them. A wide oak desk positioned at the center with one chair behind and two in front. The scent of old paper, ancient wood, and worn leather. Newer papers in two uniform stacks waited for Kinkaid's return with pen and ink. A blotter. A bronze statue of an elephant off to one corner which would have taken both hands to lift. On the far side was a closed door which would lead to other offices or storage.

"Now I am in possession of it," Kinkaid said, starting across the room.

"Yes."

"And what is it I am in possession of?" The director stopped and turned back toward Shaw, gaze boring into him. "Not merely an idol, that much is certain."

"It's ... a long story."

"A long story." Kinkaid repeated each word as if they were a sentence of their own. Without another word he sat in one of the two chairs before the desk, gesturing at the other. With a mutter of appreciation Shaw took the offered seat, placing the cane between his legs, right hand resting on the head of it.

One deep breath to focus his thoughts, followed by a slow exhale. "It started before I'd even arrived in India."

Shaw told of Lassiter meeting him at the ship, and how they'd become friends, Shaw's first in India. The story of the idol and how Lassiter had found it among the belongings of a murdered doctor took longer.

"He showed signs of addiction as early as that train ride, but it rapidly descended into the idol absorbing his every waking hour."

Kinkaid nodded, fingers rubbing against the arm of his chair.

Shaw continued on, telling of the maut which haunted the wilderness around their outpost. To anyone else he would have been branded a madman with such a tale, but Kinkaid understood, accepted it without question. Lassiter's murder. The cult which had done the deed. Their obsession with finding someone to read their book.

"The book!" The volume of Shaw's voice had risen, his eyes wide and taking on a raving tone. "Do you know about the book?"

No. Calm.

Deep breath in. Deep breath out. Deep breath in. Deep breath out.

When he focused on Kinkaid again the man gave his head a shake, answering his last, frantic question. Thoughts once more under control Shaw told of Walsh's murder and his own laming, of how the cult was determined to force *him* to read their book. Of his subsequent dismissal from the army and final encounter with the cult in Bombay.

Kinkaid jumped to his feet and Shaw's left hand shot to the lower part of his cane, prepared to free his weapon. The other man didn't notice, stalking around the other side of his desk and leaning heavily against it. He stood this way for several moments before standing erect.

"I see." Kinkaid tapped the fingers of one hand against his desktop. "I see. I see. Obsession and addiction, that is what I can expect."

Given the man's current demeanor, his willingness to lie about the idol to the police in an effort to keep it hidden, Shaw was sure the obsession had already begun. He recalled the idol's effect on himself, and that after less than one day being in his possession.

"Shall I become violent as Sir Kenneth did, a danger to those around me, or merely suicidal like Neville?" His gaze returned to Shaw. "I knew both of them well. They were respectable men. Smart. Learned."

"Yes, you—"

"And you killed them by sending that thing here."

Shaw wanted to protest, to explain why he'd done it, to justify his actions. He couldn't. "Yes."

A nod from Kinkaid as if that acknowledgment was acceptable. He sank into the chair on his side of the desk, leaning forward. "Sir Kenneth. Neville. Both dead for a cult which never came to bring them to the next stage."

"No! *Not* for this cult!" Shaw struck his cane against the wood floor with a resounding thump. "Both idol and book are more ancient than any cult. The Thuggees serve their master using those as tools to bring him back. The idol's sole function is to soften men's minds and make them more susceptible, more ready to accept that dread, sleeping god Cthu—"

No! he warned himself. *Do not say that name!* He had been well on his way to raving and that was not the way to convince this man.

Shaw held one hand out in a halting gesture. He cleared his mind while Kinkaid looked on. "Madness of some sort is in your future I'm afraid. Unless you allow me to take the idol away."

Kinkaid leapt up from his chair as if jabbed with a knife. He bared his teeth at Shaw, giving the impression he would flip the heavy desk over. "Take it away?"

Shaw said nothing, made no move.

"No! No. I don't think so, Shaw. It may well be in my best interest but ..."

The man trailed off.

"Yes, I know," Shaw filled the silence. "You want it, but you don't. You wish you'd never seen it but can't be without it."

"Madness," he said, voice low. "How were you able to send it away?"

How? It had all come down to a promise he'd made Singh on

their first night. A promise to get rid of the idol. "I had a greater influence."

"A greater influence. Hmm." Kinkaid considered a moment before giving his head a shake. One deep breath, a smoothing of his suit and the man was back to his officious self. "In any case Shaw, the idol is safer here than hidden inside your own home."

A consideration which Shaw had already had himself. It was true. The museum would have security, a guard patrolling the halls at night, many places where an idol could be hidden.

But those were convenient excuses.

Ananya knew where the idol was, or at least knew the British Museum was a place to search. She'd come once and would come again. No, the idol needed to be removed from the museum. It needed to be his burden, not someone else's ... at least until they had destroyed the book.

How easy it would be to stand and draw his sword, to run this man through and take his precious idol. Kinkaid wouldn't even anticipate it. The death of one man against what evil could be unleashed should Ananya have both idol and book in her grasp once again. The imbalance of those two options makes the choice obvious.

Shaw gripped the head of his cane. Ready to spring, and pain in his leg be damned.

What? No. No!

The inspector would remember him, as would the bobby. Both had heard his name and it wouldn't take much time before he was behind bars and the idol was free again. No, there must be a better way.

In all those considerations Shaw realized he hadn't even considered the weight of taking a human life. That concerned him ... or rather, it concerned him how little that concerned him. He was a doctor! He saved life, he didn't take it.

Singh's words came back: *What are you prepared to do?* Remembering the deaths of Lassiter and Walsh, and considering what would happen if he didn't get that idol and book back into his possession, a better question might be: What is he *not* prepared to do? What wouldn't he do to preserve all of humanity? Should there be any limit in such a matter? As a doctor he has sworn to do no harm, but what if inaction caused more harm? What if a refusal to do a lesser harm resulted in a greater one? Would he sacrifice who he was and all he believed in?

Shaw gasped.

The sinister thoughts, so unlike him. As if he were being influenced. "The idol is in this room, isn't it?"

Kinkaid made no effort to deny it. "You want to see it."

Now it was Shaw's turn to jump as if stabbed. The words hadn't been a question, more of a statement bordering on accusation.

Shaw *didn't* want to see it, didn't even want to be in the same room as the damned thing. No. He would demand Kinkaid keep the idol in whatever hiding place he'd chosen—*The desk. It's in the desk.* Shaw opened his mouth, words of rejection on his tongue.

"Yes." His voice came out hoarse, a whisper, unrecognizable. "Oh, yes."

The director's eyes darted to the desk and back, more confirmation of the idol's position. The man's eyes glared a full minute before standing. Shaw expected to be hustled out of the room, out of the museum. Instead Kinkaid's hand went to the drawer on his right, looking surprised at his own actions.

Here was a conflicted man. He held a secret, wanting to share it, needing to not be alone in the knowledge he held, yet unable to confide in anyone. Much the same as Lassiter.

Kinkaid drew a key from his pocket and unlocked the desk, giving a quick warning glance across the distance. He pulled the drawer and retrieved a heavy, ominous item, placing it on the desk, facing toward Shaw. The gaze of that dread sculpture landed full on Shaw and he began to hyperventilate. His palms had gone clammy, and he wanted to run, to flee from the museum, pain in his leg be damned. A whimper caught in his throat and he reached one grasping hand out.

"No," Kinkaid said.

Shaw dropped his hand back to the head of his cane, once again contemplating how simple it would be to draw the concealed sword.

Kinkaid wouldn't see it coming.

No!

"Put it away," Shaw said. "Please."

Belatedly he remembered the instructions on breathing and worked on calming himself. Kinkaid took the idol and deposited it inside the drawer once again, though Shaw could still perceive the pull.

"You see it is safe here." Kinkaid locked the desk and deposited the key into his pocket. "Hidden."

"Safe," he repeated, heart hammering inside his chest. Breath in. Breath out.

"I will not allow *anyone* to take this from me."

Until you lose your mind and kill yourself or your entire family ... but there were no words he could say to this man to impress on him the danger of keeping the idol. The hold was stronger than any logical argument.

The director gestured toward the door and Shaw stood. One last glance at the desk, as if he could see through solid wood, then he turned and made for the door, Kinkaid close behind him.

"Have you found any detail on it?" Shaw asked as they made their way back along the hall. Each step a greater relief than the last. "What it's made of? Where it came from?"

Kinkaid hesitated before his natural instincts as a historian took over. "Nothing. There are vague mentions of statues which could mean this or a million others. No sketches or descriptions. No stories. No history."

It was what Shaw had expected.

"I want to throw it away, you understand?" Kinkaid stared straight ahead. "I want to, but know I won't."

Yes, that was quite understood. This idol was a treasure. Not the sort of item to display on a shelf but rather a secret shame hidden inside of a drawer, because it was also a drug. It had absorbed Lassiter, and Middlemarch before him in all likelihood, had corrupted these two poor men in the director's position before Kinkaid.

At the front door, ready to be shown out, Shaw stopped. Kinkaid wouldn't listen to any reason but maybe another warning would help.

"There will be others coming for the idol."

"Your Princess Ananya."

"And whatever followers she has gathered."

Kinkaid nodded.

"Hide it, down in your storage far away from those who may come looking."

The director stared back and Shaw knew he wouldn't be moving it far from that desk drawer. With resignation Shaw said his farewell and departed. Outside Singh leaned in the same spot, as if he hadn't made any move in all that time. The lad didn't ask if Shaw had gotten the idol, the reality of the situation being obvious. They walked back toward the street edge to hail a passing cab.

"I found a staff entrance," Singh said. "The easiest way to get in after hours."

"Good," Shaw said, watching the passing bobby who would be keeping a closer eye on the museum tonight. "Tomorrow night then."

Singh glanced at the policeman and shrugged an acknowledgment. The unspoken statement being that he would remove that obstacle if necessary. Singh had asked him what he was prepared to do to retrieve the idol. No need to ask his friend the same question.

While Singh had a sense of peace in who he was, he also had a pragmatic soul. The idea of the ends justifying the means was a belief which Singh embraced instinctively. Back in Kinkaid's office Shaw had contemplated what he was prepared to do back, weighing the death of one against the deaths of many, but Singh had made that calculation long ago and decided the correct path. It was simple math to him.

Shaw considered that old saying about choosing the lesser of two evils, realizing that the lesser evil was, in fact, still evil.

He couldn't do it, couldn't take a life. Murder was where he drew the line.

"Tomorrow," Shaw repeated, watching the form of the bobby disappearing into the night.

They would have to hope Ananya or her followers didn't come back before then.

DECEMBER 16, 1885

Last night's newspaper sat to one side on their dining room table as they started breakfast. Familiar news in those pages but Singh would go through every one of them page by page, article by article, looking for clues on Ananya or any other strange occurrences.

"A thought has occurred to me, Doctor."

"Mmm?" Shaw shifted focus from his cup of tea.

"The attempted break-in came after we visited the museum."

Shaw waited but no more was to come. As usual Singh had connected the information and assumed Shaw would do the same. He considered the problem, needing a distraction from his thoughts in any case. After a moment he saw it.

"You think we were followed there."

"Yes."

"I'm sure we would have noticed Ananya."

"No. One of her Thuggees."

"One of? She only left India with the one."

Singh stared back patiently until Shaw put the pieces together for himself.

"Yes, yes," Shaw agreed. "She would have started recruiting replacements after arriving here."

"Or found some on the ship."

"Why would she need to follow us? Surely she could figure out where the idol was on her own."

"You are British and still believe the choice of museum obvious."

That was true. A person would need to be familiar with London to know the British Museum was above all others. How would Ananya know that the treasures sent back from Hyderabad would go there? He looked back into his tea, long since gone cold and unappealing.

"You are quiet this morning, Doctor Shaw."

He gave a distracted nod and continued his tea gazing.

"You are having second thoughts on entering the museum tonight?"

"Hmm? Oh, no, no. You've convinced me on that point, especially if our moves have been watched."

"Then?"

Shaw placed his teacup into the saucer, his hand shaky. "Aaronson and Martin, the two directors. They're dead because I sent this hideous idol to the museum, as are all of Martin's family."

Singh remained silent, giving Shaw the opportunity to get his thoughts out.

"Now Kinkaid is likewise consumed by the addiction. What will become of him?

"All the more reason to remove it from his possession."

For a moment Shaw brightened, then he remembered the director's reaction when he suggested taking the idol from him. "No, the damage is already done where Kinkaid is concerned."

"It is."

Shaw wished his friend had contradicted him on that point. "I became a doctor to heal people, but death chases wherever I go."

When Singh spoke again his voice was calm but earnest. "If you had never gone to India you would know nothing of this. Life would have gone on for you."

Shaw wished that blissful concept could be true.

"Lassiter would still be dead. His fate was sealed when he took the idol."

Yes, Lassiter was already in possession of it when they'd met. Marked by the Cult of Kali.

"Walsh too may have still died."

Walsh? Yes, it was possible he would have died at the cave. So many maybes.

"I would also be dead."

Shaw jerked his head up. Singh nodded agreement to his own statement but went no further in his details. *Is that true? Yes. Singh would either be dead or deeper into that cult. A living death.*

"We make our plans, Doctor. We have our desires. Meanwhile life throws obstacles in our way."

"This is more than a mere obstacle, Singh."

"It is. Much more. This is a calling."

"I don't want it."

"Being desired is not necessary for life's calling. Its nature is to be arduous and require difficult choices, sacrifices. A calling forces us to endure."

"A calling."

"Just so."

That didn't make any of this easier, and in many ways it was worse. Singh would tell him that too was in the nature of a calling. Calling. Purpose. Quest. No matter how Shaw dressed it up this was like some malignant disease come to settle into his body.

The bell rang and both looked through their dining room doorway, past the sitting room and to the main door beyond. Shaw couldn't quite see it from his place.

"A patient?" Singh suggested getting to his feet.

The most likely explanation, though the hour was still early. A chilling premonition hit Shaw that nothing lingered on the other side of that door which he wanted to see. Talk of purpose and cults, death and old friends had colored his perceptions.

Singh seemed to agree. One hand slid into the opposite sleeve, to the blade concealed there. Ceremonial and ornate but also wickedly sharp and pointed, quite functional. A side effect of all the previous day's excitement. On returning home Singh had gone directly to his room and withdrawn the knife from a drawer. When asked about it Singh shrugged and said London was a more dangerous city than Bombay.

Did he carry it more to protect himself, or Shaw?

Singh went through the sitting room toward the door while Shaw started rising to his feet. If this was a patient he would need to explain firmly that they were to wait for regular hours, and to use the entrance to his office below, not their living quarters.

An emergency?

Shaw heard the murmur of Singh's voice and a second masculine one drifting through the open door. He made his way around the table and into the sitting room, gripping the head of his cane in one tight grasp.

"Archibald."

The voice brought him to a halt, eyes narrowing at the man in their modest entry space. He had aged since the last time they'd spoken, and was heavier, too.

"Doctor Shaw, this man—"

"Quite right, Singh. This is my father."

"I'd heard that you were back in London, my boy. You could have come to pay your respects."

"Why would I do such a thing?"

"Isn't being family enough reason?"

"No." In all the list of necessary actions to complete on his return to London, a visit to his father had not even crossed Shaw's mind. "You didn't come see me off when I left for India."

"Pshaw! Far too busy, I'm afraid. Just not—"

"What do you want?"

The other man gritted his teeth at the rudeness and picked at some unseen lint on his overcoat. "Why, to say a simple welcome home."

"Welcome home?" Shaw mused, turning the words over in his

mind. "Welcome home. In all my years at boarding school you never once said those words."

"What do you—"

"What I mean is you never wanted me home as a child, never had time for me, never had the slightest interest in me. Why now?"

"Now that you're an adult perhaps you're more interesting."

"*More ...?*"

"Look, do we need to do this in front of the help?"

Shaw turned to Singh then back. "Singh is not *the help*. He is my ward, and my friend."

No, confound it! Their relationship encompassed more than that. Singh was family, as much a son to him as any flesh and blood could have been, but those were matters the two of them needed to discuss without a third party in the room.

"I shall go purchase the morning paper, Doctor."

"Only if you want to, Singh."

Singh gave a nod and departed through the still-open front door. Shaw wondered if the lad would pause outside and listen, to ensure he would be safe ... No, if Singh sensed any danger he wouldn't have left in the first place.

"He—" his father began.

"Not another word about that boy." Shaw had a finger up, pointing toward his father.

The man raised both hands in a calming, surrendering gesture. "I didn't come to fight." Shaw opened his mouth, prepared to give his father exactly what he didn't go there for, but the man rushed his next words before Shaw could begin. "I see you were hurt."

Shaw looked down at his leg and cane acknowledging the fact.

"In battle?"

"Of a sort."

His father raised one eyebrow in question, a trait they both shared. The similarity irked Shaw.

"I fell down some stairs if you must know."

"Stairs? By Jove, Archibald, I do hope you have the sense to embellish that story when you tell it."

"I should lie? Tell people I was shot?"

His father gave him a knowing wink. "Turn every negative to an advantage."

Shaw gripped the head of his cane tighter. His patience for this man and his unwanted fatherly advice had reached the limit. This visit was done, but his father didn't seem to agree. The man glanced toward the sitting room, an unspoken hint that he should have already been invited in. Outside a horse clopped past, its driver calling out his business of repairing umbrellas. The other man shrugged when no invitation came, giving a look around and raising his eyebrows in judgement. These surroundings were no more or less opulent than what Shaw had grown up in, but for the first time he noticed how much better dressed his father was. Black silk top hat. Expensive coat. Somewhere along the line the man had come into money. His import business had shown results in the years since Shaw departed apparently.

So what did this man want with him?

"Unfortunate you couldn't have been here for your mother's funeral."

Shaw gritted his teeth and said nothing.

"It would have meant—"

"Enough! I don't want to hear you talk of Mother either."

"Hmph, no wonder when you deserted her to go to India."

"Deserted ...?"

The thought had occurred to Shaw more than once. He *had* run off to India, and left his mother with what? A man no better at being a husband than he had been as a father, though Shaw hadn't realized it at the time. A person's home life becomes normal, for want of a better word. It wasn't until after he'd left, looking back with a clearer perspective, that he was able to see how contemptuously his mother had been treated.

"Did she at least have a nice funeral?"

"Oh, I suppose, though the point of spending good money

on a person beyond caring is ridiculous. Still, have to maintain appearances."

Shaw pictured swinging his cane in an arc toward his father's head.

"I'm remarried now."

The wind left Shaw's sails, though he couldn't say why. What did he care if his father had married again? He scrambled for some response to hide how this news had affected him. "I hope you treat her better than you did Mother."

His father shrugged, as if the point was irrelevant to the topic. He pulled a card from an inner pocket of his coat, handing it to Shaw. It held his father's name and an address which Shaw had no intention of ever visiting.

"It's not far from my first factory. Empty now." A wistful expression crossed his face. "You remember it?"

Shaw remembered. His father had taken him exactly once, when Shaw had been six or seven. They'd gotten separated while touring the lower basement and he'd panicked, rushing along one passage and down another until he'd come to a metal door leading to the outside. There he'd stood wailing until his father found him. Instead of a hug or any show of compassion, Shaw had earned a scowl of disappointment and an order to compose himself. He hadn't been taken anywhere of importance by his father again.

"Stop in some time and meet Emily." A pointed glance at the sitting room. "I'll invite you in to sit."

Shaw held the card in one hand, willing the man to leave.

"Still have your head in the clouds I see," his father said. "Only half in the conversation. Do try to live more in reality."

"Reality?" Shaw laughed, a trifle too forced. It wasn't a frantic sound, but closer to that than either humour or the scorn he'd been intending.

His father took a step back.

"Reality," Shaw repeated. "You should be happy you are so

blissfully ignorant. If you knew half of what I'd seen you would go mad."

A snort of derision from his father. A roll of the eyes. He pulled out his pocket watch—solid gold of course—and *tsk*ed at the time. "Must be off, I'm afraid. Don't be a stranger."

With that his father was through the door and gone while Shaw seethed. He moved to the couch and sat, wondering on the true purpose of that man's visit. Was it to rattle the bars of his cage, as it were?

Singh stepped into the room, the paper in one hand at his side. A look of concern covered his face.

"I'm fine, Singh. Sorry you had to see all of that."

Singh came closer. "I have heard some information, about an Indian woman. Recently arrived. Working with the poor in Whitechapel."

"What? Yes!" Shaw struggled to his feet. "That must be her."

He paced as best he could, thoughts of his father pushed to the back of his mind. It could be some other Indian woman, he supposed, but ... No. No, this was her. He felt it.

"Do you have an address?" Then before Singh could respond, "Why would she be in Whitechapel? She had better resources than that."

"Doctor Shaw."

He looked at Singh and noticed at last the distressed expression on the boy's face.

"What? What is it?"

"Ananya has been murdered."

December 16, 1885

M urdered!" Shaw repeated for the third or fourth time, this time inside a cab heading for Whitechapel. It was the only word he was able to get out.

Singh did not respond or comment. It was unnecessary and he was content to allow Shaw his outbursts, knowing it was how he coped with absorbing unexpected information. And what information it was, little more than an hour old. The newsboys were aware Singh was looking for information on any Indian woman and so they'd gotten it to him as promptly as possible.

"What was she doing in Whitechapel?" Shaw said. "Searching for replacement Thuggees? The people are poor and desperate but are they potentially fanatical? Murderers? Yes, beyond doubt some would be."

"This area is like Limehouse?"

"Yes and no. Limehouse is where sailors came off boats and decided not to return home. It houses Chinatown and a fair amount of opium dens. Whitechapel holds brothels and flop houses. Both are rough, brutal areas, overcrowded to the extreme, holding much of the city's poor people."

The cab rolled to a halt and the driver knocked on the roof. "Far as I go."

Shaw looked out the window and saw they were not yet at their destination.

"We're only on the edge of Whitechapel."

"Yuh, and if I get me cab in there I'll never get back out with them crowds."

Little point in arguing. From where they had stopped it was plain the cabbie knew his business. People milled about everywhere in greater concentration than any other part of London. Shaw descended from the cab and prepared for an unwanted stroll. At least the address was nearer the side they were on.

The smell approached them in a wave before they'd even entered the streets of Whitechapel. The stench of urine and sewage. Shaw raised a handkerchief to cover nose and mouth while Singh moved forward, stoic and unyielding, though his eyes did water. They made their way up the first street, past decrepit housing, avoiding the refuse which lined the streets, blown up against the buildings where rats mingled in the shadows. They kept a distance from the street's tenements to avoid buckets of urine carelessly emptied from windows above. Shoes scuffed against the rough cobblestones as they turned at one corner and continued along the next street. No one accosted them, though all eyes were on the strange pair, and they were often jostled by the crowds. That was impossible to avoid. Singh didn't blend in with his height, robes and turban, though his manner of moving, his air of danger, and emotionless expression fit. Sikhs, as Singh's turban suggested, were intimidating, with a reputation for violence and mysticism which afforded a slight berth around them. That small space lessened Shaw's stress at being surrounded, while simultaneously offending him for Singh.

"If stereotypes must exist," Singh said in a low voice, "let us use them to our advantage."

Shaw turned toward his companion. "How ...?"

"Your expression."

His expression? Had he been glaring at those around him?

Yes, he supposed he had. With effort Shaw softened his expression.

Crowds lined both sides of the street, passing here and there, some standing aimlessly, leaning against a lamppost or brick wall. The hems of every woman's skirts were smeared from the coal dust which deposited on every surface. Children rushed in groups, playing games identifiable only to them. More than once Singh took Shaw's arm to prevent him from tumbling to the urine-puddled ground, other times he led the way to press through the crowds of people.

On their left Salvation quarters, where meals were available for a penny. The prayer that came with it was free for those who believed prayers were listened to. On the right a butcher shop displaying unidentifiable cuts of meat in the window. The occasional woman selling radishes or other hardy root vegetables.

A decrepit woman with a clay pipe clamped between her teeth squinted and told them to get out of Whitechapel. Leave the poor alone.

In all they travelled two blocks though it felt like twenty. Competing smells of damp stone, urine, and the occasional whiff of opium fought for their attention.

"I've read of the crowds here," Shaw said in a low aside. "Most parts of London have fifty people per acre. Whitechapel has eight hundred."

"This reminds me of Bombay."

It was true. Shaw recalled his first day in India and the crowds he'd had to get through from ship to train. They'd pressed in on him, making him claustrophobic. Perhaps if he'd grown up in Whitechapel the crowds would not have bothered him so much ... but then it was unlikely any doctors came out of this area.

The common lodging house where Ananya had lived and died had much the same appearance as the buildings surrounding it. Rows of filthy windows and brick on a dirty, crowded street. A building where a bed could be had for the night if one could come up with three pence Hardly the quality Ananya was accustomed to.

Inside curious people stood about in a cloud of acrid sweat and unwashed clothing, glancing up the stairs to the second floor and the bobby standing there with crossed arms. This dour-faced man turned any people back who dared to climb those stairs. Naked floorboards and cracked plaster walls were the main style of this building. No carpets. No pictures on the walls. Not even cheap wallpaper.

"We do not look as though we belong here," Singh said.

They did not. Should they wait? Come back later once the police had departed? By then any sign of the book could be long gone, if it wasn't already. They needed to know if the book was in the police's possession, or someone else's.

A grim weight pressed on Shaw's soul. If retrieving the idol was important, keeping this book from the wrong hands was nothing short of paramount. At least before this they knew Ananya had the book. Now ...? He started toward the stairs but felt one hand on his shoulder and turned toward Singh.

"You remember the inspector's suspicion of me last night?"

Yes, if Shaw had not been with him the boy would have been detained and questioned just for being in the area, and for not being white.

"I shall remain down here."

Shaw nodded though he didn't like it in the least. He hated that Singh should be treated differently for the simple fact of being Indian. He also hated the idea of leaving the boy behind here, knowing what he did of the area.

"Be careful. Don't go anywhere with ..." Shaw stopped himself. "I apologize, Singh. I don't intend to treat you like a child."

"I understand."

Singh was no longer a child, and truth be told, even at eight Singh was more resourceful and wise than Shaw was today. "I'll return soon."

Shaw moved to the stairs and made a greater deal of climbing than he felt. It was a fresh ploy in his arsenal for getting others to believe him more infirm than he truly was ... not that the leg didn't hurt with constant, throbbing pain. It just affected him less than he allowed others to believe.

"Sorry you came all this way, sir," the bobby at the top said, stepping forward to allow no possibility of passage. "The inspector isn't wanting anyone through."

"Ah, I understand. I was in the area and thought I would offer my assistance as a doctor."

"Much appreciated, sir, but the body's already gone. On its way to the morgue."

Shaw nodded and didn't move away. That wasn't unexpected. London police tended to clean up crime scenes without delay to avoid the sort of scene happening downstairs. Shaw let out a short sigh and played the last card he had. "I ... knew the victim."

"Did you, sir?"

"Yes. Back in India, we'd ... met ... once or twice."

"I see. Yes, Inspector Abberline might indeed find that useful. Wait here a moment."

The bobby moved down the hall to an open door, keeping an eye on the stairs lest someone quicker than Shaw snuck his way through. He mumbled a few words and listened to a response before returning to Shaw.

"Yes, sir. The inspector would be interested in seeing you. Go on through."

Shaw gave his thanks and started toward the room, wondering how much of a mistake it had been telling he knew Ananya. He needed to see inside that room though, needed to know if the book was there, needed to hear what details this inspector had. At the door he stopped and knocked on the frame.

"Inspector, I—"

"You!"

Inside stood the same shrewd-faced, walrus-moustached inspector he'd met at the museum.

"Ah," Shaw said, at a loss for other words. He took a step back in surprise then moved as if it were a matter of imbalance, replanting his cane in front of him and leaning on it. He tried for an air of casualness.

"You certainly do get around, Doctor," the inspector said, moving to stand between Shaw and the entry into the room. "You knew the victim I hear."

"I did. Met her back in India once or twice."

"A friend?"

"No, not a friend."

"Suppose you tell me why you are here then, visiting someone who is not a friend."

"I ..."

What could he say that wouldn't make him sound suspicious at best, a lunatic at worst? Why was he truly here? To get information, of course. To find out about ...

"She had a book, from her days in India."

"A book?"

"Yes, I was coming to purchase it."

"I see."

"I'm a collector, you see."

"A collector. Yes, that sounds plausible." The inspector scrutinized Shaw. "Do you believe in coincidence, Doctor?"

"Well, I—"

"Because I do not. Twice we've met in as many days. First for a break-in, and this time in relation to a murder."

"Surely you don't think I—"

"I discount nothing. Tell me about this book."

"It ... was old. Leather bound with inscriptions on the cover."

"Valuable?"

"I would say so. To some, in any case."

"To you?"

Shaw thought about it and agreed that it would indeed be. "Is it here?"

"I have not seen it." The inspector looked over one shoulder then back. "But I was not specifically searching for a book either." He made no move to go back into Ananya's rooms.

"Inspector, do you think—"

"That you could come into the murder scene and rummage around? Certainly not. You'd like to head to the morgue next and give the body a once-over, I suppose."

No matter what he said this inspector would treat him with suspicion. Understandably so. No, Shaw had no interest in Ananya's corpse, but he saw how all of this must appear. Did the inspector think him some sort of ghoul? Or worse, a suspect? Situations reversed Shaw would have the same reaction ... but only because he wouldn't know the greater danger. Oh, how he wished that were true. Ignorance is truly bliss.

Shaw drew himself erect as possible, looking the inspector in his eyes. "I merely thought I could be of some assistance in identifying if the book were here."

The inspector softened a touch. "Hmm, yes. In that case, if I should come across it I will be sure to consult you on it. For identification purposes, you understand, not so you can take possession of it."

"Understood." Shaw shifted weight. His bad leg was starting to call for attention. "How did Ananya die, Inspector?"

"Beaten to death." Another glance back, as if the body were there to see. "Not a good way to go."

"No way is."

"Some are better than others. Personally I'm hoping to die in bed as an old man, if not in service to Her Majesty before then."

Shaw appreciated the brief insight into the inspector's interior workings just as the man realized he'd gotten too personal. In a blink he was back to all business.

"This Ananya is in the morgue now, identified by one of the ... ladies"—the inspector raised one eyebrow to emphasize what type of *lady* he meant—"who live downstairs. Yet the deceased was not one of these working girls, was she?"

Shaw shook his head, unable to consider any circumstances

which would bring Ananya to that state. It was *not* within her character. She was the user, not the used.

"Why would she settle in Whitechapel then? Given her background I would expect her to be in Limehouse with the rest of them."

At the word *them* Shaw gritted his teeth. He'd witnessed enough *us and them* to last a lifetime. Still, at the heart of it the inspector asked a vital question, the same one he'd been asking himself. Why *was* Ananya in Whitechapel?

"I'll take your card this time, Doctor." The inspector had one hand out, palm up. "If I find this book *or* have further questions I'll come around to see you."

Shaw handed over his card with address and name on it. The inspector glanced at it before sliding it into a pocket and giving him a nod of dismissal. The interview was at an end, and Shaw was free to go. With effort he turned from the rooms where Ananya had died and headed back along the hallway. Returning to the stairs the bobby there gave Shaw a more amiable farewell than the inspector's.

Step by step, one hand on the banister, Shaw descended to the next floor. He felt the policeman's eyes on his back, and the inspector's judgement on him as a person. A strange sensation. He felt like a criminal though he'd done nothing wrong.

Halfway down he scanned the crowd for Singh. The boy should have stood out but was nowhere to be seen. A cold sweat broke across Shaw's forehead, a tingling up his spine.

"No," he whispered, increasing his speed. "No, no, no."

Where was he?

At the bottom Shaw took the turn and started up the hallway, squeezing between people as best he could while scrutinizing those he couldn't see from the stairs. Singh was here somewhere. Shaw hoped for a person in the crowd who would appear likely to respond to questions, but all appeared sinister, colored by his fear for Singh.

"Doctor," a voice called from his left.

He spun toward it and found Singh standing in an open door leading to one of the rooms. Shaw forced himself forward, wanting to hug Singh with relief, but knowing that would embarrass them both.

"What are you doing in there?"

Remembering what ladies lived down here from the inspector's comments one answer was obvious, which he immediately discounted in relation to Singh.

"I have met some interesting ladies."

"I ... see."

Singh gestured him through the door and into a cramped, shabby room with six beds in it. The floors and walls matched those of the hallway for lack of comfort. Austere. Functional. Was this the surroundings which Ananya lived in upstairs as well? A difference of one floor would not have made a better neighbourhood. Inside the crowded space stood three women, dressed in the shabby clothing common to the neighbourhood. Drab colors and worn fabrics with coal dust–stained hemlines. One wore a shawl across her shoulders which came low enough to keep both hands from view.

"This is Miss Mary Ann Nichols," Singh introduced the one with a shawl.

"Everyone calls me Polly."

"Polly," Singh amended. He gestured at the second then third woman introducing each in turn. "Miss Mary Jane Kelly, and Miss Martha Tabram. Ladies, this is Doctor Shaw."

Tabram gave a clumsy curtsy, and a coy half smile. "Pleased ta meetcha, Doctor."

"The pleasure is mine, madam."

"Ooh, madam and ladies, is it? Nah, we ain't that posh."

"Yer a friend of Singh here?" Kelly asked.

This final lady, younger than the rest, had an Irish lilt which was quite charming. From her manner of speech it was obvious that Miss Kelly had a bit more education than her friends. Shaw acknowledged he was indeed a friend, wondering where this was going.

"We pulled the boy in 'cause he's obviously from the same place as Miss Ananya."

"You knew her?"

"I did." Nichols glanced toward the others.

"They dragged poor Polly here upstairs ta identify the body," Tabram added.

Nichols made a disgusted sound.

So this was the woman the inspector had cast his judgement on with the raise of an eyebrow. Just another of London's castoffs, left to make her way however she could in the East End and be judged for it meanwhile. All likely alcoholics, trying to get enough each day to cover the cost of a room and gin.

"Anyways, I knew I could trust Singh here 'cause he ain't a rich boy," Nichols said, and stopped, staring from him to Singh and back.

It became obvious that something was expected but Shaw couldn't determine what. Singh cleared his throat and tapped where a pocket would be on his robe by way of a clue.

"Oh!" Shaw reached into his own pocket and drew three coins. "I assure you I'm not a rich boy either, but I may be able to help."

He held one toward Nichols which she took, her left hand darting from under the shawl and disappearing just as quick. The second and third went to Kelly and Tabram who took it each with a nod. He drew three additional coins from his pocket, hoping the unspoken promise of more to come would not be lost on them.

"Much appreciated, Doctor," Nichols said. "Nah, we can see you ain't like the others with money what come aroun' here at night."

Shaw took the compliment with what he hoped to be a disarming smile. "Do you have information about Ananya?"

"Yuh. She showed up 'bout two months back, helpin' us poor folk though she obviously wasn't one'a us."

Kelly added with her lilt, "The girls all liked her, and even the boyos running this house thought she was a'right."

"She was your friend?"

The women glanced at each other but Kelly spoke.

"Nothin' so grand as that. More an acquaintance. Ananya helped us girls, good fer a coupl'a bob whenever we were short for rent."

Tabram jumped in, eyes on the coins and wanting her chance to earn one. "Mos'ly she kept to herself. Didn't come aroun' ta chat fer the sake of chattin', though she had lotsa questions 'bout London."

Of course she did. She would have been trying to become acclimated as quick as possible. What was her endgame though? She would be looking for someone to read the book. Was she looking for the idol to find a subject to ... No. No. Shaw reminded himself that Ananya was dead and all such questions had ceased to be of consequence. They were not here for Ananya, they were here for that book.

"You were in her room?"

Kelly shook her head. "Not me."

"Had one ta herself up there," Nichols said. "Not like this. Musta been payin' a pretty penny fer it."

She gestured to the room with its many beds. A place to sleep for the night but no home any of the women could call their own.

"This is very important, Miss Nichols." Shaw made sure to clink the coins in his hand together, reinforcing the promise of payment. "Did you ever see an old book in her room?"

Nichols took a step back without seeming to realize, eyes widening. The amiability on her face slid away before coming back, but not without effort. She pulled the shawl tighter, as if a great chill had passed through her.

"Oh yeah, I saw that. Only the once, but once was enough fer me, y'know."

"Did you ... see inside it?"

Nichols shook her head with great vigor. "It made my head feel funny jus' lookin' at it. I didn't want ta look any further."

Confirmation that the book had been here, as Shaw knew it must. Was it still? He should have kept quiet about it when talking with the inspector. Now if the man found it he would be sure to take it with him.

No. The inspector was no idiot. If he saw the book he would know it was special.

"Some rich boys came aroun' a few days back," Nichols continued. "Three of 'em ta see Miss Ananya. They went upstairs an' after a few minutes they was all shoutin' at one another. Brought us runnin', includin' the guys what look after this house. These rich boys was tryin' ta steal her book. Well, our boys stopped 'em and told 'em ta shove off."

"Rich boys," Shaw mused. "Anyone you recognized?"

"None o' the regulars," Kelly said. "No one I ever saw before and not nice types, but what rich boy is?"

Nichols stepped a bit closer. "I'll betcha that's who did Miss Ananya in though. They came back fer the book and gave her what for in the process."

A fitting theory, and one which Shaw had already considered.

So that was it then. The book was gone and in the hands of the rich once again, as it had been in India with Ananya's brother Kanwar. In his hands it had been dangerous but at least he understood the dangers of what he held. He hadn't wanted to raise this ancient evil, but only wished for some minor monster to control and free his country of the British. Still a danger. Every use of the book weakened the veil between worlds, and who knew if that veil could build up again once gone.

What did these "rich boys" want with it?

They would be much like Kanwar, playing with a power they didn't understand. They would have resources, manpower, followers, money. Much more difficult to get to than Ananya. They were an unknown quantity. Perhaps they understood less about this book, but that wasn't anything which could be depended on.

Nichols huffed. "I tol' the copper this information but they don't care about no dead Indian woman, any more'n they care about the whores she was helpin'. Not over live rich men in any case. They won't look no further now they identified the body an' all."

Shaw nodded, seeing she was probably correct. He handed each of the ladies a second coin with his thanks for the information. He and Singh turned to go.

"Miss Ananya was always talking about the power o' women," Kelly said. "Behind closed doors, y'know. Said we could better ourselves."

Women. Yet another segment of the population discriminated against and repressed. You would think with a queen on the throne this would change. The ladies had moved closer to the room's one filthy window, huddled together over their newly acquired coins. Kelly spared them a wink as send-off.

Outside Shaw turned toward Singh. "Ananya was about power but not for these poor women."

"For Kali."

"I thought you understood it wasn't Kali in the book."

"Does the name matter?"

Shaw thought on that. He could shout Kali a hundred times, but that other name ... No, even thinking that name felt too much like calling to it, and that elder god's attention was not something one would want.

"Names have power."

"Who took the book?"

"I have no idea, and worse, I have no idea how to find out."

DECEMBER 17 TO 20, 1885

I n a black mood Shaw brooded in the upstairs office, staring at the passing day through the room's one window. Not so different from the room where they'd met those ladies, though the window was larger and cleaner.

They'd planned on returning to the museum but with Ananya dead—and danger of the idol being stolen gone—there was little point. The idol was now as safe there as anywhere, and the whereabouts of that book had become the greater concern, if they had the slightest hope in hell of finding it. The ticking of the room's clock mocked him, reminding him of how rapidly time was passing. Would there come a day when he wasn't ten steps behind?

What options then? Could the idol lead them to the book?

Oh, but how deeply would one have to embrace the madness for that to be possible?

"Could your father help in finding these men?"

Shaw jumped, startled. He hadn't noticed Singh enter the room, so involved in his own thoughts. A cloud of anger crossed his face. Not anger at Singh so much as anger at the thought of his father. To seek the man out? Unthinkable!

Singh persisted. "He may know the correct people to question."

It was an argument which made sense except Shaw was looking from an emotional perspective while Singh used logic.

"No, before going to that man there are others I can speak with."

Yes, the same people he'd gone to in scouting for Ananya, but perhaps they would have better insight, better knowledge and connections in their search for these so-called rich boys. Maybe one of those frantic hypochondriacs that had been referred to him as a patient would have information. Without doubt one of those would drop in soon enough.

There were other friends ... or acquaintances at least. Former schoolmates. People who had gone on to business and banking and would associate with a better crowd now.

Shaw explained to Singh and that easily they had a plan. Not much of one, but better than being in this room and staring out the window.

Two more days passed while Shaw went from doctor to doctor, friend to friend, acquaintance to acquaintance. One would suggest another, who would suggest a third and so on until he'd come full circle. He phrased his questions as an antiquarian might, a collector in pursuit of a specific vintage book, bringing the subject around to others who may also have an interest. Inexpert questioning at best, no discretion involved. In all honesty Shaw would have admitted it was an act of desperation, an attempt to stave off the inevitable visit to his father.

Shaw had taken to asking everyone he met about rich men interested in a rare book, or recently come into possession of one. The nervous man in Shaw's examination room widened his eyes.

"Why? What have you heard, Doctor?"

Shaw stopped in the process of a physical examination the

man didn't need—a superfluous task performed with the aim of setting the other's mind at ease. Something about being examined by a doctor soothed him and who was Shaw to deny that?

"I've heard nothing, Willoughby." Shaw took a step back to focus on the man's face. "That's the problem."

Harrison Willoughby's lips worked at words only he could hear. The man was tall and rake thin. Brown hair had already started to recede though the man had not yet left his twenties. His prominent Adam's apple bobbed as the man swallowed.

"There is a club, catering to interesting activities. Not the sort I would belong to, you understand. No, no. They wouldn't allow one such as I through the door." Bitterness in his voice and expression were plain. "My younger brother, Richard, is a member. Bored, disaffected men, just as you described."

"A club?"

"They call it the Hellfire Club."

"I've heard of it. Hardly a secret."

"There are ... levels within the club. A more elite club within the club, as it were."

Shaw raised one eyebrow. "Your brother—"

Willoughby jerked his gaze around to Shaw, as if realizing he'd said more than was prudent. "No. No, no, no. Forget it, Doctor. I shouldn't have mentioned it. In fact, I didn't."

Harrison Willoughby was on his feet and out the door before Shaw could do much more than process the information. A secret group of young, disaffected men with money, hidden within another group. That sounded like the sort of organization these rich boys would be a part of.

Now ... how could he hope to get near them?

"Archibald."

Shaw stood in the doorway to the office, gritting his teeth. Just being here froze his soul.

"Father," he said.

The office was huge, as big as their sitting room. Sizable desk. Leather chairs.

"You've met Emily?"

Shaw looked back over his shoulder at the woman standing in the door. Her eyes darted to his father and back, giving a brief smile before leaving. Emily reminded him of his mother, in the same beaten-down and stuck in a loveless marriage fashion.

"How is your ..." A vague wave of one hand, as if searching for the correct word. "Boy?"

"Singh is well."

"Still trying to show you're a better father than I am?"

"I beg your pardon?"

"Isn't that why you adopted this orphaned Indian boy?"

Shaw gritted his teeth. How and why he'd taken Singh in was none of this man's affair. "I did not come to discuss Singh with you."

"To what *do* I owe this pleasure?"

"Information." Shaw jumped right past all of the social niceties which the situation demanded and straight into the true purpose of his visit.

"Oh, yes? Information on what? The import of brandy and gin?"

Shaw crossed the room, stepping closer to the desk. "The Hellfire Club."

"The Hellfire Club?" His father placed the papers he'd been perusing into a neat pile, his pen in a holder next to the inkwell. He leaned back in his chair. "Not your sort of club, son."

Hearing the word *son* from the man's mouth made him want to shout, but in the interest of his mission Shaw kept that impulse under control. "I agree."

"Hardly a difficult club to find either, Archibald."

"No, but I'm not interested in the club itself. I am looking for some within the club."

"Oh?"

"A group within a group." Shaw waved one hand vaguely. "An inner circle."

His father raised one eyebrow and once again Shaw was struck at the similarity between them. It irked him beyond reason. "And why are you looking for them?"

"It's about an item. A book."

"A book."

"An old one which I came across in India."

"Sounds more like something a book dealer could help with."

"This book is rare, one of a kind."

His father stared back at him, assessing. "There is more to this book than you've said, something which makes it special."

"I—"

His father waved one hand, dismissing the information. "Doesn't sound like anything the Hellfire Club would be interested in. They're mostly rich hedonists doing what they please."

"Mostly?"

"Some are more ... focused."

"Are you a member?"

"No. I've no interest in that foolish fancy."

Shaw wasn't certain he believed that, but wasn't prepared to call him a liar.

"I don't know much more than that," his father said, returning his attention to the papers.

Shaw knew when he was being dismissed. This wasn't unlike what he'd experienced as a child. At least today they'd exchanged a dozen sentences.

"Leave it alone, Archibald. These aren't the type of men to antagonize."

Shaw took another look at his father, wondering on how he could still be made to feel like a ten-year-old boy. With a sigh he headed back to the street. Another dead end. Another frustrating meeting that went nowhere. Each passing day took the book further from them.

He hoped Singh was having better luck with his newsboys and contacts among the richer people's servants. Those last tended to see more than was considered but they were also tight-lipped. None wanted to chance losing their employment. Still, it couldn't have netted less than what his own efforts had.

DECEMBER 20, 1885

S haw stepped through the bottom door, standing at the entry for a minute. To his left were the professional office and examination room. No patients were scheduled for the day, and it appeared none had arrived for any emergency call either. He headed up the stairs toward the rooms he and Singh shared. It was slow going and not for the first time he wondered if they should have set up living quarters downstairs and the office on the upper floors. Basic walking wasn't too bad, if he didn't overdo it, but stairs were not his friend.

Seeing his father had been exhausting. Not in any physical sense—getting there and back hadn't been too monumental a task. No, it was his mind which was weary, his soul. Meeting his father's new wife—he refused to call a woman younger than himself his stepmother—was a more pleasant experience than he'd expected. She gave the impression of being a lovely if quiet woman and not for the first time he wondered why she would marry a man as odious as his father ... Though, in truth, it wasn't all that difficult to fathom. A woman in English society had few avenues to secure her future security. His mind turned to Miss Kelly on that point.

He pushed all thoughts aside, his mind focused on the end of this journey. A quick afternoon nap would do wonders.

No sound of movement came from the floor above and he didn't bother calling out. Most likely Singh was still out making his own enquiries, though it wasn't uncommon for the lad to make no sound for hours when in meditation. All the more reason not to disturb him.

Reaching the upper landing brought a sense of accomplishment and pride. Shaw continued on through the door to stand in their entry, jostling the umbrella holder by the door as he passed it.

A step further in brought a warning sensation. Something was off. The day's paper lay sprawled across the table. Unlike Singh to leave a mess. If he left, or went to meditate, he would have tidied up first.

"Singh?" he called.

Then the world went black. "What?"

A sack shoved roughly over his head, the whiff of burlap drawing a gagging reaction from him as the rough material scraped his skin. Vague shapes danced in the dim view he was afforded through the sack.

"What is this?" he demanded.

"Do be quiet."

The voice was the soft, refined English of an educated man. For emphasis the side of Shaw's head was slapped, but without much force. Enough to be taken as warning.

Shaw's arms were grabbed on either side as he felt himself propelled across the floor, leg screaming in agony. He wanted to tell them he would walk but couldn't catch enough breath to do so. A moment later he was dumped into a chair, gasping while ropes were tied around and around to keep him in place.

"Is he secured?" the cultured voice asked.

"Yes," came a second, deeper voice. Accented. Russian?

"Fine. Remove the sack."

"Right."

The sack was whisked from his head, scraping the right side of his neck and face. Friction burned his skin there and elicited another gasp. He wanted to raise a hand to press against the spot but found himself as secured as they'd claimed.

Before him stood three men, aligned in a row, all dressed in top hat, pants, jacket, cloak and shoes that were black as a train's engine. The only differentiating items were the masks covering their faces. The ones on either end wore traditional theatre masks, one comedy, one tragedy. The man in the middle wore a simple white mask, a green and blue butterfly decoration on its left cheek—the sort of mask worn at French masquerade balls.

Beyond them Singh lay on the floor, hands and feet bound behind him then to one another. Hog-tied. The lad didn't move and Shaw felt the icy hand of panic grab at his heart.

"Singh!"

"Calm yourself, Doctor," the man in the butterfly mask said. "He is merely unconscious ... for the moment."

Shaw spun his attention back to the three villains, glancing about for others hidden in the shadows. No, only these three. Like the stevedores in Limehouse, Comedy and Tragedy deferred to Butterfly in their manner, in their glances. That man was the unspoken leader.

"What do you want?" Shaw demanded of him. "Who are you?"

"Second question first. We're who you were looking for, Doctor."

Who he was looking for? The ones who stole the book! "The Hellfire Club?"

Butterfly gave a curt nod. "Now, suppose you tell us why."

"Why?" Shaw said. "You know why. The book."

"Mmm-hmm," Butterfly agreed. "The book. Good."

The man pulled a second chair closer to Shaw and sat, coming eye to eye. A faint flowery scent crossed the gap to Shaw. He crossed his legs and placed both hands on the knee in an almost effeminate manner. Just two cultured friends having a conversation, his demeanor said.

Behind his two associates stood with arms crossed. Each of them were average height with Comedy being the heavier and more muscular. Shaw bet neither of them smelled of flowers.

"Where is it?" Butterfly asked.

"Where is what?"

"We had a look about your rooms of course but couldn't find it."

"Couldn't find ...?"

"You are looking to sell it?"

"Sell ...? What? No!"

Butterfly cocked his head to one side while Shaw's mind whirled with the implications of those confusing statements. These men thought *he* had the book. But then—

"A pity," Butterfly said. "We'd hoped to handle this in a civilized manner."

"But I—"

"Kill the Indian."

He said it as if asking for more tea, not even focusing attention toward his two companions. Comedy and Tragedy moved for Singh, the former drawing a five-inch hunting knife from some place of concealment, a blade used for efficiently gutting a kill.

"No!"

Butterfly raised one hand and the two halted, all of them staring at Shaw.

"I ... I don't have the book," Shaw said, eyes darting to Singh then back.

Butterfly lowered his hand and the two resumed moving.

"No, wait," Shaw said. "Please. Please!"

Another gesture, another stop. Comedy and Tragedy looked at one another, the latter shrugging while the former gave a slight giggle. Was this all theatre? A show for his benefit? Or was this merely a cruel man who enjoyed the task? Shaw couldn't decide which was true. He needed something to convince these men, to keep them from Singh.

Butterfly tapped one finger against his knee. "Why did you kill the girl?"

"Ananya? I didn't."

The man uncrossed his legs and leaned forward, scrutinizing Shaw's expression. Behind the mask clear blue eyes showed confusion, uncertainty.

"I swear," Shaw continued. "We thought you killed her."

"Now, why would we do that?"

"She had the book and you wanted it. She wouldn't give it to you."

Butterfly leaned back into his chair, considering a moment before turning to the others. With another gesture they returned to stand on either side of their leader.

"That business between us and Ananya was only that, business. We offered a price and she refused. We tried to take it and she countered." Butterfly chuckled. "It was simply a matter of finding the right price or circumstance."

Shaw thought of Ananya and knew that price would be far outside what these three would be willing to pay. Butterfly cocked his head to one side and viewed Shaw with a questioning eye.

"You were at the scene of her murder."

"Yes."

"Why?"

Did it matter what he said? They were here for the book which was something he couldn't give them. Even if he was in possession he couldn't give it to such as these.

"Come now, Doctor. It's a simple question."

Comedy brandished his blade, like a theatrical villain. "Should we kill the Indian now?"

Definitely a Russian accent.

Butterfly kept his gaze on Shaw. "Should he?"

"No." Shaw sighed. "We were looking for the book as well."

"Obviously. Why?"

"To keep it out of the wrong hands."

"Hands such as ours."

"Yours. Ananya's. Anyone who would use it."

"Use it how?"

"To read it."

"Isn't that what one does with a book?"

Shaw saw he was being played with. Pieces of the puzzle were known to these men, but not all. They searched for information with slightly better skill and style than Shaw had gone about his own investigations. Perhaps if he was able to satisfy them on that point it would keep Singh safe.

"Reading this book will call ... creatures. Evil, monstrous beings that should stay buried."

Comedy and Tragedy glanced at each other with Comedy giving a brief giggle. This was information they already had but the confirmation excited them.

"An ancient sleeping god," Shaw said, low. "One which must stay sleeping."

"The book can do all that now?"

"Yes," Shaw said in a quiet voice.

"What else can it do?"

"Isn't that enough?"

Shaw's mouth was dry, his head pounding. The burlap's smell lingered inside his nostrils. He shook his head once, trying to clear it. These three fools had no idea of what powers they were attempting to deal with. Shaw's eyes locked onto those of the leader.

"This book is an abomination," Shaw said, voice quiet but steady. "It must be destroyed."

"Destroyed?" Butterfly leaned away from Shaw. "Are you *mad*?"

Shaw gave no response.

"Destroy an item of such untold power?"

"Untold power, yes. It doesn't give power, though, it takes."

Butterfly scoffed, a quick sound behind his mask. "Oh, I

believe I can control some pathetic Indian goddess."

"It's not ..." Shaw narrowed his eyes at them. They knew some details, believing what the Thuggees had. "How did you learn of this book?"

"Oh, we had inside information, Doctor." Butterfly chuckled again but less with humour than an affectation. "The princess brought a servant with her, only he lost faith in her ability to lead, had started losing that faith before they'd left India. He found us."

Servant? The Thuggee who'd come with Ananya? It didn't seem likely that he would even be able to communicate ... No, of course he could. Shaw remembered the man who'd left with Ananya, the one who translated for the rest. That man knew English quite well, like Ananya and her cousin, Suresh, who had lost his mind piece by piece with each glance into those pages.

"The fellow was erratic, paranoid," Butterfly continued, as if reading Shaw's thoughts. "He was able to get his point across to one of my brothers." He gestured at Tragedy on his left. "Who had the foresight to bring the man to me."

Shaw noticed the use of past tense in regard to the Thuggee, as well as the fact that the story only held this group of three. Butterfly did not speak for the Hellfire Club, was probably not even a part of that inner circle. No, if this concerned the entire club then he and Singh would have been brought to them.

"You're acting alone."

Butterfly straightened, glaring at Shaw a full minute before speaking. "For now. For now. Once we have the book the others will fall into line."

Then he was making some bid for power. "You ... You're not a high-ranking member of the Hellfire Club, are you?"

Butterfly tapped Shaw's bad leg to the right of his knee and Comedy stepped forward. One fist shot out, punching the area Butterfly had indicated. Shaw gasped a half scream and struggled against the bonds.

"Manners, Doctor. Remember who is in control here."

From behind the trio Singh struggled against his own bonds, making angry noises into his gag. Shaw was relieved to see him moving.

"Tell your manservant to be calm, Doctor."

"He isn't my—"

"Again."

Comedy gave another punch, to the same area.

When Shaw got his gasping under control Butterfly gestured toward Singh again.

"It's all right, Singh," Shaw said. "I'm ... I'm fine."

"We are no closer to the book," Tragedy said, speaking for the first time. His voice came through similarly cultured to Butterfly, but younger.

Their leader agreed and refocused on Shaw. "If we don't have it, and you don't have it, then who does?"

"That ... that's a good question."

Butterfly's fingers drummed against one knee, staring off past this room.

"I entreat you," Shaw tried. "Forget about the book. You don't know what you're searching for."

Butterfly's attention returned to Shaw but the man had sagged in his seat somewhat, not knowing what their next move was. Shaw well understood that sensation.

"Power? Oh, I think we know."

"Not power. Dependence. Subservience. Death and destruction to all you care for. This book is no different than the ..." He shut his mouth with a snap.

"Than what, Doctor?"

"Than ..." Shaw closed his eyes against it. He'd made a mistake and cast about for another comparison, coming up with no possible diversions. "Never mind."

"Oh, no, we insist."

Shaw kept his eyes shut until the impact, third time in the same spot, shocked them open. He cried out.

"That is painful, isn't it?"

Shaw glared at the man.

"How much more painful will it be when we start doing awful things to your friend there."

Shaw's eyes darted to Singh and back. He pressed his lips together tight. Butterfly gave a shrug and the two men in theatre masks started toward Singh, Comedy once again withdrawing his wicked blade.

"No! Please!"

Butterfly looked at Shaw but didn't signal for the others to stop. Both continued toward his boy.

"Better speak quickly, Doctor. Neither move all that slow."

"The Museum."

"Yes. And?"

"An idol sent there from India seven years ago."

"Hmm, and this idol does what exactly?"

A glance toward the two who crouched in front of Singh, Tragedy grabbing the boy's head and holding it still. Comedy placed the blade against his throat and looked back toward Shaw and their leader.

"It's ... it's ... it's connected to the book, to this monster, this god it will call back. It softens the mind and makes the holder more in tune with it all."

"Connected. It can lead to the book?"

"I ..."

Tragedy pulled Singh's forehead back, presenting better exposure to the throat.

Shaw nodded. "I think so."

Butterfly waved the other two away from Singh once again. "Which museum?"

"British Museum, isn't it?" Tragedy said.

Shaw looked away.

"Yes, I thought so. Connected to that break-in?"

Butterfly stood, giving his companion a respectful nod. "Well done."

"My family donates money. I can get in there and find it."

Butterfly chuckled again and headed toward the door, his two accomplices in step behind him. Neither looked toward him or Singh. Shaw jerked against the rope holding him. It wasn't so tight as to cut off circulation, but tight enough to allow no real give.

"What about us?" Shaw demanded.

Singh lay on the floor, eyes closed and controlling his breathing, making testing movements against his own bonds, which had the same effectiveness as Shaw's. They could be trapped this way for days.

Butterfly stopped at the door and paused this way for several seconds before turning back, Comedy and Tragedy stepping aside. "You? Oh yes. My appreciation for the information."

"Untie us!"

Another pause. "Do not get in our way again, Doctor."

With that Butterfly turned and left, the other two close behind. Comedy touched the knife to his forehead in a mocking salute before following his friends through the door.

Shaw jerked at the bonds holding him to the chair, trying for some slack in the rope and finding none.

Half an hour passed as Singh worked himself into an upright position, balancing on his knees. He walked toward the front door in this manner, his bound arms pulling him in the opposite direction. Each time he toppled over the process would begin again.

"I know you have something in mind, lad. I wish I could help."

Singh made a noise of agreement, or at least Shaw interpreted it as such. With the gag still wedged into his mouth the boy couldn't communicate his thoughts or what his end intention was. At the door he toppled to one side, his hands questing for the cane which Shaw had dropped.

Of course! The sword concealed there was their best hope of getting free without some chance visitor stopping by. The concealed blade hidden inside Singh's sleeve would be of no help the way he was tied, and Shaw wouldn't be able to reach it, even with his hands in front as they were.

"To the right," Shaw suggested. "Yes, a bit more."

Singh rolled and came up again with the cane gripped in his right hand. Several deep breaths then he started back. Another fifteen or twenty minutes passed to bring it across the room and place it into Shaw's hand, dropping it several times in the process. With his eyes Singh told Shaw what to do next, staring until understood.

"Grab the hilt?"

"Nnn-hnn."

"Right."

Shaw moved his hand until only holding the cane by the top. Singh pivoted, fell, rose again and grabbed the bottom part of the cane. With a couple of jumps forward he was able to free cane from sword.

More eye gestures told Shaw to place the tip of the cane against the floor.

"Like this?"

Singh made a noise of agreement and turned his back to the sword. Shaw saw the place where rope and blade would meet.

"A little further back, Singh. Left. A bit more. There!"

Singh had his ropes pressed against the sharp edge.

"Careful, Singh. Don't cut yourself."

It was probably the last consideration Singh had, and Shaw only said it because he needed to say something. A few movements from Singh as he worked out the best way to rub his bonds against the blade. Only one instance where he fell over and needed to reposition. Soon the ropes had started to fray and split until, without fanfare, they separated and Singh spilled to the floor again. His hands were free and with slow movements he brought them around, working circulation back into the numb limbs.

"Take your time, Singh."

In truth they both knew it was a race against the Hellfire Club to the museum, and those three had a head start of at least an hour.

"Well done, my boy."

Singh reached up and pulled the gag free from his mouth. He rolled over to look at Shaw. "That was unpleasant."

"Indeed."

Singh forced both legs under him, wobbled as he made his way around Shaw with the sword and severed the knot holding him in place. Shaw leaned forward and rose from the chair, using the lower part of his cane as a brace. Singh returned the sword and soon top and bottom were reunited.

Unpleasant. Yes. Shaw had experienced a strange sense of claustrophobia being secured to the chair as he was. At the end it felt as if the walls were closing in though he sat inside a spacious room. At least he was left ungagged to spew his ire while Singh did all of the work.

Shaw hobbled around the room, forcing circulation back into his limbs while Singh controlled his breathing.

"Are you ready, my boy?" Shaw asked, grabbing the satchel bag with his medical supplies. They would need it for the idol since Shaw had no intention of touching it. "I'm afraid we must get to the museum."

Singh nodded and got to his feet. Neither were recovered from the ordeal but something needed to be done, and once again they were behind. Their only hope was that Tragedy had not been able to get in to see the director yet. Perhaps Kinkaid was not even at the museum.

"The man in the butterfly mask posed a valid question," Singh said.

"Question?"

"If they don't have the book, who does?"

"Yes, I see." Shaw shrugged, crossing to the door. "A third

party is at work? Aren't there enough players in this pantomime already?"

They made their way outside, intent on finding a cab to transport them. Afternoon had given way to evening since Shaw returned home. One lamplighter neared, intent on his trade but giving them a tip of the cap in passing.

Shaw glanced at his watch. "The museum will be closing soon."

Singh waved at a passing cab which rolled to a stop before them. Neither spoke as they settled in. All they had were worries and it seemed bad luck to give voice to them. Instead Shaw focused on their hopes. Hope that Tragedy had been delayed. Hope to get in to see Kinkaid themselves. A wild hope to convince the man to part with the idol and bring the damned item back home.

No. One hope wasn't too much, but several was unlikely. He did not have the kind of luck they would need.

So far behind. Again.

All for an idol Shaw didn't even want. The thought of possessing that thing made him feel unclean. Could they drop it in the Thames then? Or in the ocean? Possibly. Before they did that though, the question of whether this idol could lead them to the book and its current holders needed to be answered.

The book!

Compared to *that* this idol was nothing. Nothing! A flea compared to a wolf ... Unless it *could* lead to the book. Then it was a clear threat indeed and better in their possession than in the hands of the Hellfire Club, or this unknown third party.

They had to get that idol, *had* to! But to do that they needed to get to the museum, and hopefully before Tragedy ... Shaw found he had come back to where he'd started and groaned. Around in circles, like the hapless dog which chases its own tail.

Around and around and around.

Shaw cursed himself for not returning to take the idol as they'd planned.

December 20, 1885

On reaching the museum they found those few last visitors leaving and the night guard starting to close up.

"Wait!" Shaw gasped, the two rushing for the entry. He stopped a couple of feet away, one hand gripping his cane, the other his doctor's bag.

The guard stopped and reopened the door a quarter of the way, enough for his head to view the two of them.

"Sorry, sir, museum's closed," he said and pushed on the door.

"We must see Director Kinkaid."

The door halted again, the guard's weathered face filling the gap. "The director is busy with another gentleman. I'm afraid you'll need to return in the morning."

The door closed with a thud, like judgement proclaimed from on high in a crack of thunder.

Shaw gritted his teeth and stared at the closed door. "We have to get in there, Singh. Kinkaid's visitor must be the man in the tragedy mask, if not all three. By morning the idol will be long gone."

"The staff entrance," Singh said.

Shaw nodded and followed his friend, heading around one side of the museum. Out on the street a carriage passed going one way while a costermonger pushed his cart of wares in the other. Pots and pans banged together as he rolled through the streets toward home.

What are you prepared to do?

Singh's words returned to Shaw, as they had more than once. Already he had accepted the idea of breaking into the British Museum after hours. He'd been half ready to run Kinkaid through the other night. He *had* run that dockworker through. What would come next?

Down a back lane to a door marked as *Private*. Singh reached for the handle, pulling on it with a grunt. "Locked."

"Of course it is," Shaw grumbled. "Nothing can be simple."

He hated the whiny sound of despair and defeat in his voice. He took a deep breath and pushed it away.

"We have to get in there, Singh."

Singh listened at the door for a second or two then straightened, pulling Shaw to one side and pressing flat against the wall. One hand had snaked up his sleeve, gripping the knife he kept there. A second later the door swung toward them and a man rushed out, headed for the street, looking at the watch held in his hand. For a moment Shaw thought it was one of the Hellfire Club escaping in a rush, but it was just some harried museum worker, late leaving and in a rush to catch a cab home. Singh grabbed the edge of the door and skirted around while Shaw followed.

What would they have done if the man had looked their way? Would Shaw have allowed Singh to kill him? To keep the idol from the wrong hands? To destroy that book and keep that monster sleeping?

What *was* he prepared to do?

Did the ends truly justify the means? He was afraid that they might.

The two stood in the dimness of the museum, allowing their eyes to grow accustomed to the change in lighting.

"You know where the office is," Singh said.

Shaw nodded though Singh couldn't see the gesture. "Go straight."

Entering from the front door the path would be short and straightforward, not needing any conscious thought. From here, and in the gloom, Shaw found a need to reorient himself as they moved along the dim hall.

Singh shot out one hand, stopping Shaw. Both made not a sound as the museum guard passed by, not ten feet from where they stood. The man whistled a tune, paying more attention to the sound of his music than the surroundings. Obviously he didn't expect any trouble, even with the museum break-ins that had been happening and one such attempt on this museum. A true believer in the power of a strong door lock.

Singh stared at the retreating back of the guard, as if daring the man to turn around. One hand disappeared into the opposite sleeve, ready once again. Shaw placed a hand on his friend's arm, a message that this guard was not their enemy, nor even an obstacle at the moment. The whistling receded with the guard. Singh led them in the opposite direction.

With the lights dimmed and all the visitors gone home the museum was a contrast to the daytime version. Silent, like walking through a graveyard at midnight. Graveyards *should* be silent though, mournful. A museum should be full of life and knowledge. The murmur of patrons. Children seeing wonders for the first time. The silence and darkness had a weight to them, pressing in on Shaw who felt like a tomb robber.

Would this tomb have a curse on it, like those in the Penny Dreadfuls? What mummy's curse could be worse than the curse he'd already discovered?

They crept along the halls, shoes making the occasional soft scuffing noises against the marble flooring. Each willed themselves to make less noise, less—Shaw in particular being vigilant with each placement of his cane, each shift of the contents within his doctor's bag. He guided Singh by pointing for direction with his cane. Singh followed without comment, eyes focused on the blackness ahead. Step by step they crept their way through the still museum, through the libraries with their priceless manuscripts, the smell of their musty pages filling the air. Past oak-lined display cabinets holding untold treasure from the Royal Geographic Society and Richard Francis Burton's explorations. Had that man encountered any sign of elder gods in his adventures?

Shaw was certain that any moment a voice would call out, demand what they were doing there. If caught they would be branded as those who'd been breaking in to museums. How could they prove otherwise? That would bring their mission to an end. No. Being caught at this point would likely be a death sentence for the guard. Would Shaw be able to stop Singh? Would he try?

They crept forward with great care and silence.

Into the entrance, so spacious and bright during the day, warm and welcoming, now only filling them with a great sense of exposure. As if they were gazelle crossing the open plain, possible lions hiding in the tall grass. They passed into the Roman exhibit, Shaw wishing they could stop and examine each display. Forward. Forward. A balance between moving with as much speed as possible against their ability to stay silent. Several minutes later they arrived at the hall and started toward the director's office.

Voices. A conversation from inside the director's office. The voices were more intense than a normal conversation. Not quite an argument but moving in that direction.

Singh's eyes narrowed. This time he shot one hand into his sleeve and drew the knife. It glinted in the scant light. Singh looked toward him and Shaw gave a wave to continue on. As they crept forward the voices grew in volume and anger. Would this draw the guard back? Or did he already know not to disturb his employer?

"No, no," a familiar voice said. "My good man, I know you have the idol from India. I merely wish to see it." Yes. Though he hadn't spoken much the voice was still recognizable. The man behind the tragedy mask.

"I've already said I have no idea what idol you are talking about." Kinkaid speaking.

"But you do."

"I'm very busy and—"

"Look, my family's donations pay your salary, Kinkaid. I demand you show me this idol."

"I won't."

Shaw and Singh crept closer to the door, closer, until Shaw was able to see around the edge and into the room. Taller than he, Singh peered over his head and onto the same scene. A young man, still dressed in the black clothing he'd worn to their home, lifted his arms and let them slap against his sides in a frustrated gesture. This would be Tragedy judging by the voice and lack of accent. The director stood to the side of his desk, one hand resting against the wood, the other tapping against his side. His eyes darted here and there, as if enemies lurked in every corner. He would take a step back in retreat, then one forward as if ready to push the enemy from his office.

Tragedy took a deep breath and started again in a more amiable tone. "We got off on a bad foot. That is my fault, and I apologize."

The director's eyes narrowed. The hand tapping against his side stopped while the one on the desk twitched, as if searching for some object.

"I truly only want to see the idol," Tragedy said. "I've heard it is quite a curious item."

"You want it," Director Kinkaid hissed.

"No. I—"

"Yes! Yes, you do!" The voice was rising, frantic. "You want it for yourself."

Tragedy retreated a step, head cocked, as if finally hearing the strange tone of Kinkaid's voice. Did he hear what was obvious to Shaw? That the man he spoke with was not in his right mind, not by a long jump.

"You can't have it. It's mine."

"I don't—"

Kinkaid's left hand darted out and grabbed the bronze elephant statue resting on his desk. "MINE!"

He bolted forward, statue raised in both hands, plunging it down in a lethal arc even as he reached the other man. Shaw could feel it, that sick need to keep the treasure to himself. It came off of Kinkaid in waves, like a fever. The elephant impacted Tragedy's head with a sickening crunch, the flat base caving the man's forehead inward. Tragedy hadn't even managed a second step back.

"MINE!"

The young man sunk to the carpet as Kinkaid swooped the statue upward again and brought it down. This time to a more squelching crunch.

Then a third time.

"Mine," Kinkaid said once again, but without as much vehemence. "Mine."

December 20, 1885

S haw found scant sympathy for the dead man. He and his friends had chosen to play with a danger they couldn't begin to comprehend and now this one had paid the price. Kinkaid had killed for the idol, and would kill again until he could no longer live with it. Shaw wanted to turn away from all this, from this room, this museum. Flee and forget he knew any details about idols and books and gods.

Tragedy's head and face were an unrecognizable pulp, leaking across the floor. It would take someone who knew him well to identify the body. Shaw glanced at Singh who stood, wary eyes narrowed on the director.

Yes, the man was dangerous and more resourceful than Shaw would have thought. If he had pulled his sword while meeting with Kinkaid would the man have been so easily killed? There would have been a struggle and perhaps surprise would have given him the advantage, then again he might have been the one left lying on the floor in a pool of blood.

One thing was certain, whatever the director did after this his life was ruined, and he would be arriving at that same conclusion once rational thought returned ... *if* it returned. One director had killed his family, one had killed himself. This one had killed a man in the Hellfire Club, a man of some influence.

"Who's there?" Kinkaid's voice demanded. "Who?"

Had they made a noise? Shaw and Singh glanced at each other, both shrugging in answer.

"I said: Who. Is. There?"

Shaw gestured at his friend to stay put and was answered by Singh's two raised eyebrows. He made the gesture to stay put again, an expression of pleading on his face. He was a much less threatening figure and had a better chance of talking to the man without the unspoken threat of Singh standing behind. Singh gave one nod but raised his knife and refocused on the room beyond. Yes, Shaw could go alone but Singh would not be *that* far behind.

Shaw stepped from his cover to stand in the doorway, making another show of needing the cane more than he actually did.

"You!"

"Yes, me, I'm afraid."

Nigel Kinkaid gripped the bronze statue tighter, ready to use it as a weapon once again which Singh wouldn't allow. Shaw raised one hand.

"You don't need that. I didn't come here to take your idol."

A necessary deception, but not an outright lie. Yes, the idol needed to come with them but they'd arrived in pursuit of the Hellfire Club. Had he ever split hairs so finely before?

"You're with him!"

Kinkaid raised his bronze weapon and Shaw imagined Singh in the hallway, gripping his fist tighter around the knife, ready to pounce. He didn't want this man dead, hoped it wouldn't come to that, but they needed to take the idol. Shaw had to convince Kinkaid of that, somehow, but first he had to prove they were on the same side.

"No, I'm not," he said, keeping his voice even, calm. Shaw eased his way into the room a half step at a time. "I sent the idol away from India to keep the damned thing from people like this."

The director's gaze darted to the dead man and back again.

"This man," Shaw continued, "and his friends."

"Friends?"

"Yes. I'm afraid there are several others."

Kinkaid looked through the door as if these others were right behind. He gripped the elephant statue a bit tighter, eyes narrowing. Shaw placed his doctor's bag on a chair and refocused on Kinkaid, unsure what to say next. This was complete improvisation and he wasn't sure he was up to the task.

Kinkaid's eyes went to the statue in his hands as if seeing it, and the blood which coated his hands, for the first time. "What have I done?"

"Defended yourself, I would say."

Kinkaid stared at Shaw. "Yes. Yes, I had to do it. You see that."

Shaw made a sound of agreement, though the director was only half talking to him.

"Yes. Yes, I had to," Kinkaid repeated, words rushing together. "He would have taken the idol. Stolen it. He can't have it. No one can. It's MINE!" The volume increased with each word until nearing a shout.

Shaw didn't move or react until Kinkaid's attention had returned to him. "There will be others."

Tragedy's friends would come after the body was discovered and this poor man found himself dragged away for murder. With luck Kinkaid could convince the police it was self-defense, it all depended on how influential the dead man's parents were.

"What will you do now?" Shaw asked.

Kinkaid thought about it then shook his head, taking a step away from the body and his crime. "I ... I don't know."

Shaw raised a hand in a calming gesture, even gave a thin smile which he hoped conveyed the idea of *it's not that bad*. "I can help."

"You? What can you do?"

Shaw looked down at his leg. Perhaps he had made his helplessness too believable. "Me, and my friend. We can both help."

"Friend?"

"He isn't here to take the idol either," Shaw said, speaking in the same calming voice which he used for his more agitated patients. "May I call him in?"

The director's gaze darted to the door and back. His breathing rate increased. Another glance at the body and he nodded.

"Singh," Shaw said, at a conversational level, not taking his eyes from the man gripping the bronze elephant, fingernails pressed tight against the bronze.

Singh stepped into the room, though not so quick as to startle the man. The knife was once again concealed and he kept both eyes on Kinkaid while remaining close to the door.

"This is my friend, Singh."

Singh gave a gentle inclination of his head, a slight bow of respect which calmed the other man somewhat, even receiving a nod in return. Singh turned to look out the door, giving the unspoken message that he was acting as guard for those in the room. Through it all he kept one hand discreetly inside his robe.

"We will help as much as possible," Shaw said. "This man will be missed though."

Kinkaid's eyes went to the dead man then back again.

"Someone is coming," Singh said, voice low, unalarmed.

Kinkaid jerked, his eyes darting to the body once again. "That should be Faraday, the night guard."

"Hmm," Singh said.

The lad returned to the hall, then just as quick backed into the office again, both hands halfway up. He retreated further until coming to stand between Shaw and the door. Shaw looked around his muscular friend in time to see a man enter the room.

He expected the man in the butterfly mask, or his other accomplice. Maybe the night guard as Kinkaid had said. Instead, standing in the open doorway was a man he'd met twice, and each time he'd felt off-balance in the conversation.

"Inspector Abberline," Shaw said.

The man held a gun, pointed toward Singh, the most obvious

threat in the room. The inspector closed the door, leaning back against it so nobody could sneak up behind him. His eyes darted around the room taking every detail in. Singh. Shaw. The body. Kinkaid.

"Ah, I have you now."

Eyes continuing to take in more details. Kinkaid holding the blood covered statue.

"I have someone in any case."

"What are you doing in here?" Director Kinkaid demanded.

"I am an Inspector of Scotland Yard and I go wherever I bloody well need to."

That shut the director down. Shaw felt a sudden irrational impulse to tell this man all about the book and the idol, to explain every facet of what had happened here. He would be in Bedlam before the clock struck midnight.

"One of my patrolmen saw you two." The inspector pointed a finger first at Singh then at Shaw. "Skulking about. Saw them enter through the back door and all. They called for me."

Another glance at the body on the floor. An expression of confusion as he tried to put all the pieces together. It would have been much more convenient if someone other than Kinkaid held the murder weapon.

"You'll all have to come with me."

Shaw couldn't allow himself to be locked away. Without him the book would work its malign influence over whoever held it, as would the idol. The contact with that person's skin would already be driving them mad, whispering to them, demanding certain actions. Beside him Singh's muscles had tensed, all attention on the inspector, ready to jump the man. Shaw placed one hand on the lad's arm.

"Inspector, please," Shaw said. "Let's be calm."

Shaw would need to tell the man all he knew, or at least enough of it, but how to do that without sounding like an utter lunatic. Evil idols. A book of even greater evil. Secret cults. Ancient gods. Any concocted story would have a better chance of being believed. He could throw Kinkaid to the wolves, the man would come off as erratic enough, but the three of them in agreement would add a touch more believability. If only the director would follow his lead.

"Inspector, this man on the floor—"

A shout of warning came from somewhere out the door and down the hall. A demand to stop.

"*That* is Faraday," Kinkaid said, then to the inspector, "the night guard."

"No!" Faraday's voice came. "No!" Followed by a short, blood-chilling scream.

Quick glances were exchanged while the inspector's gun remained levelled in their direction, ready to swing toward any one of them.

"You have another conspirator in the museum," he accused.

"We do not."

The inspector's face became incredulous. "I would hardly expect an admission of guilt."

"How many did your man see enter the museum?"

"Hmm, perhaps that is not your doing," Abberline conceded, cocking one thumb toward the door behind him. "But I told you once that I do not believe in coincidence."

The inspector's mouth drew into a grim line as he processed the information, apparently coming to the conclusion he couldn't allow the night guard to be murdered. "Nobody. Moves."

One point of the gun at each in turn for emphasis before shifting to one side. He reached out and opened the door toward him. A step and he was in the hall, gun still aimed into the room. He glanced at them then back up the hallway, considering his options.

The gun faltered, his gaze staring back the way they'd all come. "What in the hell?"

A slow distant sound of tapping against the marble floor. Something sharp.

Click. Clack. Click.

A chill raced up Shaw's spine. *It* came closer.

Click. Clack.

"Inspector, I suggest you come back inside this room."

Singh now stood at the door, peering down the hallway, seeing what the inspector saw. The gun had swivelled away from the room, those inside judged a lesser threat.

Click.

Abberline's gun rose, aimed at whatever approached. "What in the ...?"

Click. Clack.

A low growl.

The inspector fired off his revolver, answered by a shriek of outrage. Singh muttered something and grabbed the inspector by his overcoat, yanking him into the room. He slammed and locked the door while Abberline looked from Singh to Shaw, the eyes of a man who'd gazed on unspeakable horror.

"What the devil is that?" Abberline demanded, pointing toward the door.

"The stuff of nightmares, no doubt," Shaw said. "Singh?"

"Not a maut. The Limehouse monster I would guess."

Shaw gritted his teeth and glanced around for options.

DECEMBER 20, 1885

"D octor Shaw." Singh moved to stand in front of him. "It is time for us to leave."

"You can't leave," the inspector said, glancing at the dead man lying on the floor. It was an automatic response, more instinct than intellect. A way for his shocked mind to tether itself in reality once again. Still, the man appeared embarrassed for it. He looked over his shoulder at the door moving away from it. "Right. What do you suggest then?"

"The back door," Shaw said, turning toward what he hoped was another exit. It stood open, and Kinkaid was gone. Shaw cursed under his breath while exchanging glances with the others. They could do little but follow.

"Hey, you," the inspector said to Singh. "Help me push this desk in front of the door."

"My name is Singh."

The inspector grabbed one side of the desk and spared a look at the door. Singh went to the other. Too heavy to lift, they slid it across the room and into place.

"Thank you, Singh. You think it will slow that creature down?"

As if to emphasize the question the first blow came to the door. The sound of wood cracking filled the room.

"No," Singh replied.

A second blow and items on the desk rolled to the floor under the impact. Shaw had started for the open door while the other two moved furniture. He'd passed into the next room, a storeroom of sorts, then turned back.

"The idol!"

Singh herded him forward. "There is no time."

"Damn it! That's the only reason we are here."

"It will do no good if we die obtaining it."

A third impact and the door itself grew a crack up the center. Shaw gritted his teeth and allowed himself to be ushered back into the storeroom. Another open door at the far end. The director had escaped through there, leaving them to die.

"Kinkaid," Shaw called. "Wait!"

No response. How far had the man gotten in those couple of minutes? Shaw stared at the door and hoped it didn't lead to the same hallway that monster stood in. Behind them another, final impact as the door was splintered. The inspector slammed the door between rooms.

"No lock!"

"Hurry!" Singh said, hustling Shaw forward.

More splintering as the beast made its way through the now-destroyed first door. The inspector passed Shaw and Singh in a rush for the door.

"Kinkaid," The inspector hissed. "Kinkaid!"

Abberline popped back into the room, looking at Shaw, then the door behind them. If he was hoping for greater speed the man would be disappointed.

"Go," Shaw said. "Kinkaid may need help."

Especially if that creature didn't come alone.

The inspector hesitated a moment longer, struggling against the idea of leaving people in danger. Instinct is hard to overcome. He nodded and disappeared through the door.

When Shaw and Singh reached the next entry they found a meeting room of sorts. A rectangular table surrounded by chairs, enough for ten people. Beyond that they could see the museum through another open door. Singh once again closed the door behind them, just as their pursuer assaulted the second door.

"That one is not as thick as the first," Singh said.

"No." Shaw continued his best version of hurrying which resulted in greater speed and force being placed onto his healthier leg, and the other with aid of the cane taking the weight for a second at most. Almost a skip.

Silence behind them. Then a howl and another creaking-cracking noise as the door behind them was assaulted. One more hit and the door would be finished. Shaw felt himself scooped into Singh's strong arms and carried at a brisk pace forward, through the next door and into the museum. This method gave them better speed than if he continued to hobble under his own power.

"Which way?" Singh asked.

To their right was the Roman exhibit they'd come through, and the front door. Straight ahead held a trip through Egypt.

"Kinkaid!" Abberline shouted from somewhere down that second route. "Kinkaid!"

The final assault had started against the last door.

"No time," Shaw said. "Leave me and go."

Ignoring Shaw's protest Singh hurtled forward, stumbling as he tripped over the shredded body of the guard. He was able to catch his balance and continue forward, losing only a few seconds.

A second hit to the door. Wood cracking and splitting.

"We need a place to hide," Singh said, continuing into the Roman section.

"There!"

Shaw pointed to a space between two displays of Roman armour. With most lights inside extinguished for the night there waited a deeper dark there. Singh made no response, taking them into those shadows. He placed Shaw's feet on the ground and pushed him back against the wall, the unspoken statement that Singh would defend Shaw with every ounce of his being made plain.

The smells of leather and bronze came from either side of them.

Final door destroyed, the beast was through, back into the museum. Which way would it go?

A howl raised the flesh in fear bumps.

Click. Click. Click.

No. No! Go the other way! Please!

Each display held a weapon. On the right a sword, on the left a cestus. Singh's eyes darted to each, knowing he couldn't grab either without making more noise than they were worth. Still, the lad's hands twitched with his desire for a weapon and pulled his knife free once again.

Shaw had no idea on the nature of this monster but doubted that knife would slow it more than the doors had.

Click. Clack.

It was close.

Around the corner which led to the director's office. Coming closer.

A grunt of displeasure.

More nails on tiles.

Closer still.

Movement from their right as the beast made its way into the Roman section. Step by step until it stood before them. The sight of it made Shaw's mind want to shy away in terror, to gibber and sob in one corner. In that it had a similarity to the maut. The mere sight of such a thing made him want to flee.

It moved on two lengthy, clawed feet. Grey in colour with patches of midnight. The limbs were thin, like a greyhound's, giving the impression of great speed while its body was solid and scaled. Two leathery, bat-like wings lay folded across the back and a whiplike tail twitched from behind. Its face was devoid of features. No eyes. No nose. No mouth. Just a blank smoothness which ended in two horns.

How did it howl without a mouth? It ... It ... had an odor of damp earth, like a fresh grave.

The world around Shaw went grey, heading toward white. With a supreme effort of will he forced his attention back to this creature. Singh's muscles tensed, ready to launch himself at this creature. Shaw held no hope of escaping if he did. Once this beast finished with Singh it would be on him moments later. He gripped the head of his sword cane. With luck, while Singh distracted it, he would be able to drive this blade into the monster's skull.

Judging by the stonelike appearance of the head he didn't hold an abundance of hope for that.

Without nose it sniffed at the air.

Could it smell them?

Oh, God! Why hadn't he considered that?

Indeed the monster sniffed again. Another clack of nails on tile as it swung the horned head left and right. Both Shaw and Singh readied themselves for what would likely be a last stand.

Kinkaid and Abberline would get free at least. It would appear they made the right choice in heading the other direction. Neither of them knew the danger of the book though, not to the extent they did. Neither had taken the quest to find it, or the vow to keep it from the wrong hands. No! He and Singh needed to get free of this museum.

The beast emitted another low growl then turned and bounded deeper into the museum, back toward the Egyptian exhibits.

December 20, 1885

Singh released a pent-up breath. Shaw did the same, but it came out as a whimper.

"All right," Shaw whispered. "We're fine, Singh. We're ... fine."

The words were as much, or more, for his own benefit as for Singh.

"For now," Singh agreed.

Yes. For now. They were not home free yet.

"We can reach the front door," Singh suggested.

Shaw nodded, ready to leave the museum and that monster far behind. When he spoke it surprised him as much as Singh. "The idol."

Singh looked back the way that monster had disappeared then to Shaw. Without another word they headed toward Kinkaid's office.

Somewhere deeper into the museum a scream shattered the silence, drifting through to their ears. It lasted as much as ten seconds before silence returned.

"Kinkaid," Shaw confirmed.

The beast had found him.

Ten seconds later there came a gunshot, then two more in

rapid succession.

"We should hurry," Singh said.

Shaw was able to step through the shattered doorway by turning sideways while Singh stooped to avoid the higher parts left behind. The desk had been flipped aside, landing on its top with the unfortunate dead man underneath.

"That's where he kept it," Shaw said.

"Will that not be locked?"

Shaw gritted his teeth. Most likely, and the key would be inside Kinkaid's jacket. Still, they were here and he needed to try. Upside down as it was he got the sides reversed in his mind and pulled on the opposite drawer. It gave some but became jammed with what was inside.

The idol?

No. He saw his mistake with the reversed drawers. There'd be no getting either drawer open this way.

"Singh, help me flip this back over."

Both knew that Singh helping him flip the desk meant the lad would be doing the work. He was considerate enough to say nothing and leave Shaw his dignity while approaching the desk. Singh crouched at the knees, sliding his fingers under one edge where the dead man kept it from lying flat against the floor. Singh put his back into the task and even his muscles were strained to right the heavy, solid desk. It flipped onto its back side with a muffled thump that sounded deafening in the once again quiet museum. The two looked at each other, then toward the shattered door, listening for the click of nails on marble.

"Once more," Shaw said.

He ran through an imagined series of events, purely supposition and hope. Tragedy arrived, knocked on the door—or perhaps barged in as someone rich and entitled would. Kinkaid put the idol away but the other man couldn't have seen that or he would have known where the idol was. No, it had to be in the drawer.

This time Singh pushed the desk forward while Shaw did his best to ease it to the floor and make less noise. They were marginally successful, but the noise was still greater than either cared for. Still, the desk was now back to its natural position, though one leg rested on a book give the entire setup a wobbling manner.

Shaw rushed to the drawer, sure that it would be locked but needing to confirm the fact. He yanked harder than necessary and was surprised when it slid open smoothly.

The drawer was empty.

"No."

Singh looked over his shoulder. "Kinkaid."

"Kinkaid," Shaw agreed. How had he thought the man would leave it behind?

"I'll get it," Singh said.

"No!" Shaw spun toward him. "You can't touch it."

Singh stared back a moment before giving a nod. Shaw may not be able to keep Singh from this life but he wouldn't subject him to touching that abomination. It was too late for him. The idol knew him.

"We'll go together."

Neither moved, both steeling themselves for what came next. A stroll through the museum with that monster loose. Was this lunacy? It was why they'd come.

But why had the monster come?

The idol?

Kinkaid?

Himself and Singh?

Singh pulled his knife free again. "Ready?"

Shaw took a deep breath. He turned for the door then stooped and retrieved his doctor's bag which had survived the monster's assault better than the room's furniture. They headed for the door and through it, making their way up the hall and into the actual museum.

"I shot it."

Both jumped at the sudden voice. They whirled, Shaw drawing his sword while Singh stepped in front of him. The inspector came from the shadows leading to the Roman exhibit.

"I shot it three times. Each a hit. Either the noise of the gun or the impact of the bullets scared it off, but they didn't cause any lasting damage."

"Is it ... still here?" Shaw asked, taking in the gloom around them.

Abberline shook his head. "Escaped through the front door, and with hardly more effort than it took to get through the office door."

"Escaped," Shaw repeated. As if they somehow had the creature trapped instead of the other way around.

The inspector looked embarrassed. "I got turned around, lost Kinkaid. Truth is he gave me the slip. Heard him scream and arrived in time to shoot at that thing."

"Where is he?"

Abberline hooked a thumb over one shoulder. "Front door."

Shaw started back that way as fast as he could and found Kinkaid lying in a patch of moonlight just inside the museum. One of the front doors had been smashed through where the monster had escaped.

How had it gotten in?

Kinkaid's expensive suit had been shredded as had the skin beneath. Bone showed through in several spots and the man stared at the ceiling with lifeless eyes. Shaw crouched and started to search the man.

"Here, here, Doctor," Abberline said. "Leave the man be."

Ignoring the inspector, he continued. Abberline appeared in a state of shock, but recovering. At the moment the man didn't have it in him to stop Shaw.

It didn't matter. Kinkaid didn't have the idol.

"Damn it."

"It is gone," Singh said.

Shaw nodded.

"What's gone?"

"Something I need to take with me, though I don't want it in the least."

"Cryptic," Abberline said.

"Nothing you'd truly want to know about."

"Try me."

"Inspector, there are things in this world ... things that once you know about them you can't go back to not knowing."

Abberline glanced at the dead man, then the front door. "I can believe that."

"Be glad you only know this part of the story."

The inspector considered that, slipping his sidearm back into its holster. He shook his head. "Won't do me any good. I have the kind of mind which fixates on a problem and wants to know every detail."

"Even if it's something you won't want to know?"

The inspector waved a hand at the surrounding carnage. "Often I learn things I wish I didn't know. Comes with the job."

Shaw looked to Singh who shrugged.

"Very well." Shaw sighed, collecting his thoughts. "It began in India ..."

It was the most abridged version he could give, keeping to cults and murders while staying clear of idols and cursed books. It came from reflex, a knowledge that no one in their right mind could believe such fantastic stories, that telling all would have him branded as a lunatic and a fool.

At the end Abberline said one word. "No."

"No?"

"Oh, I believe every word. That something like the Cult of Kali can exist in these modern times is repugnant." He pointed toward the destroyed front door. "But none of it explains that monster."

"No. No, it doesn't, does it?"

The two stared at each other and Shaw noticed the man had sweat across his forehead. He dipped one hand into his coat pocket.

"Nor does it explain ..." The inspector cleared his throat. "Doesn't ... explain ..." His teeth were gritted, struggling.

"Doesn't. Explain. This!" With a cry of despair Abberline pulled out the hand inside his pocket and slammed whatever was there onto a nearby table with a resounding clunk. An item far heavier than its size suggested. It was wrapped in a blue cloth which fell away as if the material did not want to touch what was within. "Nothing explains this!"

Shaw's gaze fell on that thing he never wanted to see again. There was no joy in this, no sense of victory, no satisfaction at reaching a necessary goal. His heart sank at the sight of it and Shaw found himself muttering over and over the word *no*, until Singh placed one hand on his shoulder.

"Oh, Singh. I don't want it."

"No, Doctor."

"I stumbled over it while chasing Kinkaid, fell headlong. When I looked to see what I'd tripped over it was that ... thing. I didn't even realize I'd put it in my pocket."

"No. You wouldn't have."

Had Kinkaid dropped it? Or had it escaped Kinkaid's pocket, ready to be found by another? As it had been left for countless others while in India.

"Why was it so difficult to pull from my pocket?" The inspector's right hand twitched, as if about to reach out and take it back. Singh would have stopped him, but the inspector forced his hand to one side first, backed away a step, two. "There is an ... influence."

Abberline's eyes held a haunted quality. He cleared his throat again, set his jaw and stood taller, taking a step forward. Singh turned toward the inspector, ready to intercede.

"Doctor," Abberline said. "This is the item you need but don't want."

"It is." His voice was far away to his own ears.

"Take it. It is yours." The man turned his head, taking the idol from his line of sight.

Shaw sagged against the words. He held his leather satchel out to Singh who took it, held it open. Shaw tilted the idol into it using his cane. The idol stared up at him from the confines of the bag and Shaw closed it again.

Could this thing lead to the book? And if so what would be the cost? Using the idol, even in an innocent and helpful way, it was still a path to evil. That was how it started.

"Now," Abberline said. "Tell me the rest of the story."

"Inspector, are you sure—"

"I'm sure I *don't* want to know … and at the same time I need to."

"Tell him," Singh said.

Shaw looked to his only friend then back. With a sigh he began again, filling in the missing parts from his earlier telling. The idol. The maut. The book and elder god. How the cult used this idol to weaken the minds of British people, prepare them to read the book. He ended with what would happen if they failed, the weight of human existence resting on the shoulders of a half-lame ex-army doctor and a fifteen-year-old boy.

Abberline nodded, the horrible craziness helping make sense of tonight's carnage.

"And that book is out there," Abberline said. "Somewhere in London."

"Yes. In the hands of God only knows who."

The sound of a police whistle cut through the night.

"Blast!" the inspector said. "One of the bobbies has found that front door."

Shaw and Singh looked to each other. The inspector had seen awful things tonight, circumstances he couldn't tell another soul, but he was still a police inspector. What was to become of them? What would Singh do if the man tried to arrest them?

"Give me five minutes," Abberline said, "then go out the way you came. I'll organize them all in front, give you enough time to leave."

"We can go?"

The inspector looked as if it went against every instinct he had but nodded. "I'll be in touch. I have a connection which may be helpful—"

Another blast of the police whistle, close and approaching the door. Abberline turned and headed for that sound. "You there! Officer! Do not make a mess of my crime scene."

"Inspector Abberline, sir. I didn't realize—"

"No, no. No reason you should. Come with me and keep blowing that whistle, we'll need all the help we can muster."

Another blast, receding, and another. They allowed five minutes to pass then headed back to the staff entrance, going a few blocks before stopping to hail a cab. On the ride home Shaw leaned forward in his seat, the weight of that idol already pulling at his soul.

"So much death, Singh."

Singh nodded.

"The sailor. All three curators. That guard. Ananya. The man from the Hellfire Club."

"It has only just begun, Doctor."

"I'm afraid you're right." Shaw looked down at the satchel, resting on the floor of the cab. "This horrible god continues to swallow people's souls."

"There is a question you have not considered."

Shaw followed the change of topic, considering all that had happened, his mind in a whirl. A shake of his head when no thoughts would come.

"Why did that monster leave without the idol?"

Shaw again looked at the bag between his feet then back to Singh. True, Kinkaid had possibly dropped it but that shouldn't have stopped the creature from retrieving it. Hadn't it sniffed at the air, following its quarry? Unless ... "It was there for another reason."

"Yes."

"Kinkaid?"

"Possibly."

A chill crept through Shaw's body. Would this monster come

for them next? As if the idol on its own was not enough. He noticed Singh continued to stare at him, waiting. "What else am I missing, Singh? I don't think I can take much more tonight."

"Only this." Singh's gaze travelled to the idol then back up to meet Shaw's eyes. "With Ananya dead, who sent this creature?"

PART TWO

KENSINGTON

THE LONDON EVENING NEWS
No. 208
London, Friday, July 27, 1888
Price one penny

In which Doctor Shaw is profoundly
affected by the idol

July 27, 1888

Whitechapel lay around him, the streets dirty and narrow as he remembered from the brief visit years earlier. Tonight they were quiet, deserted. No children ran past in the midst of some unidentifiable game. No layabouts slouched with back against the nearest wall, waiting for some adventure to happen. No women stood gossiping with their neighbour or regaling them with stories of children and husband.

Quiet. Deserted.

Shaw turned, looking back the way he'd come. He was alone.

Why was he in Whitechapel by himself?

He was searching for something but had no idea what, or of where his final destination might be. What was more Shaw couldn't remember travelling here.

Where was Singh?

He looked down at his left hand, finding a scalpel where his cane ought to be. Blood coated that arm to the elbow, bright and reflecting the moonlight just as the metal blade did.

What had happened? How the hell had he gotten to Whitechapel without his cane?

From a distance came the throb-throb-throbbing complaint

of his leg. A warning that it had been overused. He groaned and the sound came from far away.

Another damn dream.

With that realization his eyes fluttered to reveal their dining room. Shaw swayed, sweat drenched his night clothes the way blood had in the nightmare. His hands were empty. No bloody scalpel. No cane.

Sleepwalking.

Again.

With awareness came the full agony of his overtaxed, abused leg. Another groan as he shifted weight to his right leg and started a hopping movement toward the nearest chair. He grasped the back of it, jerking the chair out from the table and collapsing onto the seat moments before he would have spilled to the floor.

Even his strong leg was wobbly. Lucky he awoke so near the chair.

Shaw leaned forward onto the table and groaned a third time. Through the doorway separating dining room from sitting room he could see light streaming in from the windows there. Early morning. Singh was certainly out or he would have steered him back toward the bedroom, as he had on previous occasions.

The idol had called to him.

Reaching into the pocket of his housecoat he found the office key, as he knew he would. The office, where that idol was stored, hidden, locked away inside the desk drawer. Shaw carried the key to the room, but Singh retained the one for the desk. A failsafe to ensure neither was manipulated into freeing the damned thing ... not that Singh was ever the idol's target. He would have passed the office to get here which meant he'd been searching for some tool to open that drawer.

Again.

Past nights he had woken in the office to find himself pulling on the drawer. Other times standing outside the office door with a kitchen knife or other implement in his hands.

No, the idol had found Singh to be unassailable because of his skill at meditation and clearing his mind to outside influence. All Shaw had was a stubborn refusal to give in and the occasional self-administered shot of morphine when he could no longer resist. Last night he had denied himself the drug and felt wretched at the result of it.

What could he do though?

To take morphine all the time would reduce him to a hopeless addict, and once that happened his mind would be softened and easier prey for the idol. And if he *didn't* take the morphine then he was susceptible in his sleep, and would awake unrested and miserable, an easier target through exhaustion.

Damned if he did, damned if he didn't. It had always been some antiquated parable which meant little to him, but now it applied to his life with galling accuracy. Misery from the idol or misery from the morphine, and both options left him too numb and tired to learn any further meditation techniques which Singh tried to teach him.

Was he already addicted? Would an addict realize?

He should hobble his way back to bed before Singh returned, yet the thought of that task was too great at the moment. What was the actual point? Sleep would just bring him under the vicious sway of the idol once again.

What was the point of anything?

They held the idol in their possession, in hopes of it leading to the book, but even that appeared hopeless. They'd looked. For two years now they had looked for the damn book and found no trace. Even Abberline with all of his resources couldn't pick up the scent. He'd questioned Harrison Willoughby's brother, Richard, about the Hellfire Club and found out little. The two surviving members, Butterfly and Comedy, were either lying when they claimed to be of that club, or they were so minor in the organization that the younger Willoughby knew no details about them.

Of the book? Nothing. No sign of it. No visitors who were in possession of it wanting Shaw to read it. No supernatural sense of its existence or position. No way they'd been able to discover on forcing the idol to guide them to it either.

Nothing.

Nothing.

Nothing.

No hopes.

None.

Yet if they didn't find a way then all of London would pay the price, and soon after all of the world. Close to three years since Ananya brought that book to the city, and was subsequently murdered for it. He was no closer to preventing this than when he'd first encountered the cult in Hyderabad.

The ticktock of the mantel clock in the sitting room drifted to him, emphasizing the passing of time which was not their ally. It felt like mockery.

Shaw rarely left the rooms anymore, consenting to go as far as his downstairs practice to treat patients and no farther. Two years ago they would receive the occasional visitor, but now only Inspector Abberline came. All his Doctor friends had given up, avoiding his increased moroseness and withdrawn behaviour. His father had stopped by unannounced twice, the last time storming out in a frustrated anger. He had not returned in more than a year which suited Shaw fine.

The wooden chair pressed against his back and buttocks, feeling more like bare boards than padded cushions. With a sigh he got to his feet. Better to lie in bed than here, if he was in fact able to make the journey without his cane.

Standing was accomplished with help from the tabletop and the chair back for support. Once up he questioned the value of this effort. Better to just sit and wait for Singh ... but he was already standing and his stubborn nature took over. Using the furniture as temporary support to take his weight Shaw began the interminable task. It was slow going. He was able to make his way to the sitting room door, but from there was forced around the outside of that room to maintain use of his makeshift canes. At the couch he stood, left hand gripping the padded arm, staring at the hallway leading back toward his bedroom. The walls could provide support, but to get there he would first cross a three-foot open section without any assistance.

Might as well be three hundred.

Belatedly Shaw realized he could have brought the dining room chair with him, used it as a four-legged cane. Now he'd come too far to go back. If he returned he would remain at the table, perhaps even sleep there ... if he even made it.

No way forward and no desire to go back. The couch made his best option for way point. Shifting his weight Shaw turned, the support now on the wrong side. It forced him into hopping steps to make progress.

He groaned.

And cursed.

Behind, the clock continued to tick, mocking him once more. He would speak to Singh about letting it wind down. Another hop. Sweat broke out on his forehead. Hop. Hop. Why hadn't he stayed at the table? After long minutes of arduous shuffling the couch seat waited behind him and Shaw allowed himself to drop onto it. Like all of the furniture this couch was provided when they moved in. It was previously well used, though still service-able. Still, the couch was less padded than the days when it had been new. Shaw hit the seat, heard a creak of the wood under-neath, but no crack. His back hit the padded back of the couch and stopped with a painful impact.

Done. He was done for now.

Shaw rested, watching the sun make its way across the floor as it rose higher in the sky, his only other company the clock's constant ticktock which threatened to drive him as mad as Poe's "Tell-Tale Heart."

The front door opened and Shaw shifted focus as Singh came into view. At seeing Shaw out of his room the lad smiled—a lad who wasn't a lad anymore and had in truth been one only in age when they'd left India. Shaw tried to return the expression but his inner misery wouldn't allow it.

"Sleepwalking?"

"Somehow without my cane this time."

Singh tossed the morning paper onto one end table beside the couch and came closer. "Nightmare?"

Shaw nodded, more miserable for the admission.

"Rest," Singh said. "I shall get your cane, and then some tea."

Singh headed for the kitchen to start the kettle, then went to Shaw's room. Movement from the corner of his eye called Shaw's attention. He turned to find shadows at the edge of the room, no movement. Further influence of the idol? Or was imagination and exhaustion turning his senses against him too? Again from his other side with the same result, shadowy shapes which resolved into nothing when he focused on them. He pressed both hands against his eyes, falling back upon the one meditation technique he'd been able to absorb. Deep breath in, focus on the motion of his body as he did so.

"Go away," he whispered.

Not long before he would be a raving paranoid like Harrison Willoughby. No, that was an unfair assessment. True, Willoughby was paranoid, but far from raving. What fortune when the patient is in a better state than their doctor?

The light sound of an item being set on the coffee table made him jump. Opening his eyes again he found the promised cup of tea, the faintly spicy aroma drifting out to his senses. His friend took the seat to Shaw's right, one of two on either end of the couch. He sipped from his own cup. Shaw's cane had been deposited next to him, leaning against the seat cushion. The two sat like this, Shaw picking up his cup but not drinking while doing his best to ignore the shadowed movements.

"Doctor," Singh said, "perhaps it is time we consider disposing of the idol."

"We've been through this!" With a grunt of displeasure he set his tea back on the saucer, some of the liquid sloshing over onto the table. "I am convinced this idol can lead us to the book."

"It has not led us anywhere except to nightmares."

Shaw closed his eyes and took a deep breath. He heard the snappish quality of his words and felt guilty for them. Lack of adequate sleep and the idol's influence affected him, but being short-tempered with Singh was of no use.

Another deep breath while Singh waited patiently.

Always so damned patient.

No. That wasn't his thoughts.

He truly did believe the idol could lead them to the book ... though where that conviction came from he couldn't say. His own mind? From without?

He opened his eyes again and lifted his tea, staring into the liquid. "Would you have us drop it in the Thames?"

"Yes."

Shaw had already considered the idea, several times, knew his thoughts well on this subject. "It wouldn't stay there, don't you see? Sooner or later the idol would come back, into someone else's hands. Someone unaware of what they'd found."

"As you were."

"Yes." The word was low.

Shaw had never been one for self-pity but if anyone had earned it ... He made eye contact with Singh for the first time since the lad came in. Neither said a word, but the truth lay in the boy's eyes. Neither would wish this onto another person.

"Like it or not, Singh—and I most definitely do not—we are stuck with this burden. Maybe once we have resolved the danger of this book we can consider dropping the idol into the ocean."

"In a locked box."

"Yes."

Even then it wouldn't stay down forever.

They sat in silence for several minutes before Shaw cleared his throat and changed subject. "What news from your investigations?"

It was a struggle to ask when all he wanted was to return to his bed, but for Singh he would force that effort. The lad had been heading out each day, looking for any sign of the book. Anything to bring hope to this hopeless situation.

Hopeless.

Singh tapped the newspaper. "A university professor has gone missing."

"A professor?"

"One week ago."

Shaw found it a labour to bring his focus around more than he already had. "A professor of ...?"

"Linguistics."

"Linguistics?"

The study of how languages work. Yes, whoever has the book would be wanting some sort of Rosetta Stone, some way to translate an unfamiliar writing. Shaw shivered at the remembrance of those few words he'd been forced to look at years earlier. Even now he could close his eyes and recall the mortal dread that went alongside them.

Singh opened the newspaper to the article, ten pages in and no more than brief paragraphs of information. A simple story: the professor had gone into his study that night and was gone come bedtime.

Familiar. Similar to what had happened in India. Had someone taken this man to read the book? Possible, but what could he and Singh do with the information?

Nothing.

The article gave no possible leads. This professor could have just as easily disappeared for personal reasons. If it had been foul play Abberline would be more capable of finding details from the scene than they were.

"Next time the inspector comes we will ask about this missing linguist." Shaw rose to his feet, tea untouched and mind already on bed.

Morphine.

Yes, morphine was the key to it. Just this time, to get some true rest.

He'd made it to the head of the hallway leading back to his bedroom when a ringing came from their doorbell.

JULY 27, 1888

S haw halted, staring down at his slippers. Would he ever be allowed to return to his bed?

"Will you see a patient?"

"I suppose."

Singh headed toward the door.

Yes, he would see patients, no matter how little he felt like doing so. Money was money, and it was needed to continue on. He refused to reduce Singh to poverty again, not for such a minor reason as him not feeling up to the task.

Perhaps it would be Abberline coming by to check on them. The inspector came by every so often, dropping in without any advance warning, asking further questions about the whole affair while having little in the way of leads in his investigation.

The first such visit came days after the affair at the museum. Inspector Abberline stopped by with the mysterious connection he had mentioned. Connection. A sure understatement if ever there was one. Prince Albert Victor, grandson of Queen Victoria and second in line for the throne after his father. The man who would one day be king. It was unbelievable. Abberline was the prince's man inside of Scotland Yard, the man who brought any information of interest to the prince. Womanizer and gadabout he may be but Albert Victor had a serious side. Shaw and Singh had told the prince every detail, back to their first meeting in India. The man had listened, on their couch which was, in all likelihood, the cheapest fabric to ever touch his skin. The expected incredulousness and scorn didn't come, instead Albert Victor had given them his sympathy for sacrifices made, and for those which were to come in the future. In his travels he'd seen many strange occurrences, enough to know the world was not always what it suggested. There were threats to the British Empire out there and he was determined to keep them away from the shores of England. He'd pledged a monthly stipend to help Shaw and Singh in their battle; however, money which came with ease had the ability to end in the same way.

"Yes," Shaw repeated in a voice only he could have heard. "I should see my patients."

Singh opened the door before a second ring could come. He said good morning to whomever stood on the other side. A mutter of indistinct voice in response.

"Head down to the office," Singh said. "I shall be there in a moment. Doctor Shaw will follow shortly."

Another murmur then Singh closed the door, going to the nearby end table and retrieving the downstairs office key from the drawer. Resigned to the fact that he would need to interact with this patient Shaw had already continued toward his room, each step a full journey. He didn't ask who the patient was, nor did he care.

What if he just went back to bed?

Singh would come back after perhaps fifteen minutes and find him asleep. The lad would usher the patient out under some pretense, or tell him the honest truth and that person would leave with even less confidence in Shaw's abilities as a doctor. No. No, he wouldn't do that. Not today in any case.

With a sigh that came from the bottom of his soul Shaw started to change from his night clothes. The pants were always slow going but he could bend his leg if he did so gradually. He'd become quite efficient at getting dressed, yet another act he had always taken for granted, and something he did less and less these days. In a few minutes he was ready to see the patient. A quick stop at the great mirror between hall and sitting room to confirm he was presentable. This ornate monster had hung on the wall when they'd moved in, three-quarters his own height it showed from just below the waist up to a foot over his head. Right now it reflected a stranger. The man staring back was thinner and wore haunted eyes, the hair uneven, the face unshaved. Was that what he looked like these days? How much time since he'd cared enough to take a glance? A sad shake of his head and he turned toward the door.

Not quite so quick was his walk down the stairs. Going up was easier. On the way down he needed to take each step one by one, the way a child might. Frustrating, but whatever this patient's problem a few extra minutes wouldn't make the difference.

The practice was a set of two rooms. A waiting area equipped with several chairs and a desk, large enough to hold as many as six people ... not that they ever had so many arrive at once. Beyond that another room for examinations with a table and medical equipment. Another desk inside where Shaw could make notes. He supposed the entire setup was unconsciously modelled on the hospital back in Hyderabad. In this outer waiting room Singh already sat at the desk, newspaper to one side in anticipation of being alone. Pacing the room was a most unexpected Harrison Willoughby.

Hadn't he been thinking of the man less than an hour ago?

It had been months since he'd last seen Willoughby. In that time the man had lost a great deal of weight, and deep circles ringed his eyes. At this quick glance Shaw diagnosed that Willoughby had not been sleeping or eating with any regularity, something Shaw recognized from personal familiarity.

"Good morning, Willoughby."

The man started at the sound of his voice, a look of relief

coming to his expression before being covered once again with misery. Closer up Shaw revised his initial assessment. The man had always been whip-thin and couldn't afford to lose any of the weight he'd had. Now he showed signs of approaching starvation. He was frail, fragile, and his balance was off, evidenced in the manner with which he swayed.

"Doctor Shaw!" Willoughby headed toward him, one hand out to shake Shaw's own. "Oh, Doctor. I fear I am losing my mind."

The hand was clammy, cold. The man's eyes darting, trying to see in all directions at once.

"Steady on, Willoughby." Shaw gestured toward the examination room beyond. "Let us see what we can do."

"Would you like my assistance, Doctor?" Singh asked.

This was a surreptitious code they used to ask if Shaw felt he didn't want to be alone with a patient. Harrison Willoughby was about the least threatening man to visit Shaw. A stray breeze would likely knock him over.

"Thank you, Singh. I think we'll be fine."

Willoughby perched on the examination table, then jumped back to his feet at the click of the closing door. His eyes scanned about the room in panic before sitting again. Shaw made no move to start an examination, knowing from past experience that Harrison Willoughby came more for talk than anything medical.

"What seems to be the problem this time, Willoughby?" Shaw asked, a trifle on the abrupt side.

Willoughby didn't notice. "Dreams."

Shaw shivered, a reminder of his own, covered in blood and holding a scalpel. "Dreams?"

Willoughby shook his head. "Nightmares."

"Yes, I guessed as much."

This close it was evident that Willoughby's eyes weren't just ringed with exhaustion. A haunted look filled them, a knowledge of things seen which cannot be unseen.

A short, humourless laugh. "I'm afraid to sleep. The dreams wait for me, pulling me down. Each night is worse than the last."

"What sort—"

"It watches me."

The words were so low to be almost unheard but Shaw caught them.

"Calls to me."

Willoughby reminded him of Neufeld back in Hyderabad, how that man got when being affected by outside influence. How his painting became corrupt and macabre in those times. Only Neufeld was affected to such a degree because of his artistic sensitivities.

"Are you an artist, Willoughby? A painter?"

Willoughby gave a shrug. For a moment Shaw considered that this man might be affected by outside influences, rather than just being a sad man with mental problems.

"A writer."

"Sorry?"

Willoughby sighed, a sound which strangely brought him closer to sounding normal. "I ... write stories."

"I see."

"It is a passion which my family does not appreciate, you see, and so I keep it to myself."

Willoughby had found some calm in talking of writing, though he still looked ready to bolt at the slightest sound. Yes, Shaw knew the upper-class sensibilities would not be supportive of a writer in the family. Painting? Sculpting? Certainly. These were the more noble pursuits of a gentleman. Even poetry would be acceptable, but fiction?

"They've changed lately. Become sinister."

"Sinister?" Again a memory of Neufeld and his paintings.

"Bleak. Oppressive. Macabre." Willoughby stared off, as if no longer in the room. "The ideas come, too hideous to contemplate, too insistent to ignore. They must be written."

Shaw leaned forward, drawn into the man's words. Willoughby spun his focus back toward Shaw.

"It's the dreams! They've changed too, becoming more horrible, keeping me from sleeping until the story is finished. Only then am I permitted to collapse, exhausted into bed to be woken by some other nightmare the next night." Willoughby's face contorted as if about to burst into tears. He continued in a whisper, eyes darting as if they might be spied upon in the closed room. "Now ... now I am seeing things while awake."

A chill coursed up Shaw's spine.

"What sort of things?"

"The kind which might actually be there." Willoughby giggled, then raised a hand to his mouth at the fragile sound of it. "Do you ever see movement from the corner of your eye but when you turn nothing is there?"

Shaw nodded, recalling all too recent incidents. Was Willoughby truly affected by external influence, or was it unjustified paranoia? Shaw sifted through the information, returning to the memories of Neufeld's paintings. So violent, visceral, compared to his normal paintings of nature. How would those sensations manifest in a story?

"I shall prescribe a medication for dreamless sleep," Shaw said. Walking around the other side of the room's small desk he dipped his pen into the inkwell and scribbled on a slip of paper. "Ask the pharmacist for this."

Willoughby took the paper and slipped it into a pocket, not even glancing at it. The man was exhausted. Hopefully the laudanum would give him the necessary sleep. What next if that didn't work though? Opium? Sleep at a cost.

Shaw wondered if he was thinking about Willoughby or his own sleeping problem and self-prescribed solution.

"Eating will also help your body build the strength needed."

Willoughby focused on the floor, dejected, and Shaw felt a flare of annoyance. What did the man expect? A miracle cure held in this room? He'd given sound advice and a prescription.

Deep breath in. Deep breath out. Focus on the breathing.

What else? Some clue in the man's art? Yes.

"In the meantime," Shaw continued, "I'd be interested in seeing how your stories have changed—"

"My stories?" Willoughby jumped to his feet, a snarl on his face. "No! No, no, no, no! Those are mine. Mine!"

A rage lurked behind those eyes and for a moment Shaw wondered if he should have accepted Singh's offer to be here.

"Willoughby," Shaw said, in a calming tone.

"Mine!"

"It's fine, it's fine. Yes, the stories are yours."

The other man backed toward the door, eyes on Shaw as if expecting to be tackled. He spun and grabbed the knob, throwing the door open, slamming it against the inside wall.

"Willoughby!" Shaw called again.

But Harrison Willoughby was gone. Shaw took a step to give hopeless chase, even thought about calling for Singh, but what right did he have to force treatment on the man? Willoughby was distressed, but hardly a danger ... he didn't believe so anyway.

Singh's huge shape filled the doorway and Shaw focused on him for the moment, returning to sit behind his desk.

"Nightmares," Shaw explained.

Singh raised both eyebrows and glanced over one shoulder at where the man had exited. "What sort of nightmares?"

"The kind which may be something more."

Singh returned his attention to Shaw. "The book?"

"Perhaps. Perhaps."

Shaw found his attention waning, his body exhausted from the less than complete night's sleep. He leaned back in his chair and closed his eyes, trying to force his attention toward what this could mean, but finding his mind drifting further. No, thoughts of Willoughby and the book would need to wait until he could refocus.

"Just, give me a few minutes, Singh. Please."

Too short. Too snappish. Shaw could hear it in his tone but

was unable to prevent himself. He heard no movement but when he opened his eyes again Singh was no longer there. He would apologize later.

Yes, the thought of returning upstairs was overwhelming at the moment. A few minutes rest and he may be able to consider it. There were no scheduled appointments for the day, and for that Shaw was grateful. All they would have are the patients who drop in, usually in some state of emergency and panic.

Though Harrison Willoughby may be a special case after all.

Enough. For the next ten minutes he would focus past all facets of evil books and idols and ancient gods. For ten minutes he would think about himself and how he felt. With eyes closed he reached down and massaged the muscles of his left leg. The sleep-walking had taken its toll. How the hell he had managed to get that far without his cane he couldn't imagine ... No, that wasn't true. In the dreamworld he was able to ignore that pain, force his leg to take the weight and support him no matter the cost. That damned idol—

No.

No thoughts of evil for ten minutes.

What other subject could he think about? Singh? Yes, that would do. The lad was growing up to be a strapping young man. At the age of eighteen he was taller than Shaw by close to a head, and wider in shoulders too. Not the sort of person to meet in a shadowed alley, though Shaw knew at the center of the lad's soul was a purity, a force for honor, which others could only pretend to have. It was this purity which forced Singh to accompany him across the ocean to England in pursuit of ...

With a sigh Shaw leaned forward and opened his eyes. All topics led him back to the same subject. A subject which weighed upon him like a boot on an insect.

"Oh!"

Shaw jerked forward in his chair at the realization that he was not alone. A man stood a few steps inside the examination room, off to one side. Almost in the corner. Middle-aged, thinning hair and wire-rimmed spectacles. Overweight by at least twenty pounds for his five-and-a-half-foot stature. He wrung his hands and stared back at Shaw, unmoving except for the hands.

Another damn patient. How had this man gotten past Singh in the outer office? Perhaps the lad went back up to get them some tea as he sometimes did.

"Come in then," Shaw said, waving the man toward the chair opposite him. "Don't just stand in the doorway."

The man did not come further into the room, did not sit as offered. He'd still made no sounds or movements other than the hands. Wringing. Wringing.

Odd.

Shaw cleared his throat, leaning forward onto his desk and controlling his annoyance. "How may I help you?"

The man's eyes moved left, right, back to center, widening with each movement. He gave his head one shake then cocked it to one side, lips working but making no sound. The appearance of someone who was terrified. Shaw began to wonder if he was in more mental than physical distress.

Another shake of the head then the man opened his mouth, widening into a silent scream. His eyes stretched open in an accompanying expression of horror and hopelessness.

"I say, man! What—"

Brackish liquid poured from the man's mouth, coursing down his chin and continuing along the body. It pooled around his feet in an ever-growing puddle. Still the water came. An impossible amount.

"What in the hell?" Shaw managed, pulling himself to his feet.

The man made no other movement, and still no sound.

"Doctor Shaw?"

Shaw's eyes darted to the door. Singh stood there, a puzzled look on his face.

"Who are you talking to, Doctor?"

"Why, to ..."

No one else occupied the room. In the two seconds he had

focused on Singh the man had disappeared. Shaw could see the entire room from where he stood, and it was obvious that the man had not passed Singh. He had simply ... gone. Not even a trace of the brackish liquid remained on the floor.

Gone.

If he'd ever been there, like those movements he kept seeing.

No, this was different. This man had been in the room, Shaw knew that. It wasn't hallucination or illusion. Someone, or some*thing*, had visited him.

Shaw returned to the office chair. What meaning did this visitation have? The man was not anyone he knew, or anyone he'd met even briefly. He had a fair memory for recognizing faces. A vision of something to come? No, that didn't come across as true somehow. Had this already happened then?

Perhaps.

Vision or visitation? Or was it yet another assault against his sanity from the idol? More torment. As tricks go this one proved superior in its ability to be unnerving. If this were a regular occurrence it would take its toll. Not being able to know if a person he spoke to was real or nightmare. No, he couldn't abide that long. They would find this book soon or be forced to discard the idol, no matter the repercussions. Either that or go mad.

Singh continued to stare, with an expression of concern now.

"Never mind, Singh." Shaw waved a hand, getting to his feet again. "Just more nonsense from our treasure upstairs."

Singh scoffed at the idea of the ugly idol being any sort of treasure.

"Let's head back to our rooms, my friend. If any other patients come they can knock on our door."

JULY 27, 1888

S haw made for his room, nothing on his mind except for the hope of catching up on sleep. No, that wasn't quite true. He wanted the sleep but his mind was at least half on the strange visitation he'd received, and what the meaning of it could be.

Movement from the corner of his eye caught his attention once again and Shaw stopped. Another vision, or just shadows? If he didn't look directly at it would he be able to glean some information on what was there? Was this the same as Willoughby was experiencing?

The movement had stopped with his own, yet he knew it to still be there, just on the edge of his perception. Waiting. With a casualness he didn't feel, Shaw allowed his eyes to drift toward it. Still there. A vague shape to his left.

Yes.

The hall mirror.

He'd allowed himself to be spooked by his own reflection, and though the reflection had not been what he'd expected earlier it had hardly been the stuff of nightmares.

A rare sense of good humour flickered within him and he completed his turn toward the mirror, stepping closer.

"No," he whispered, any good feeling sliding away.

That ... that wasn't him. Couldn't be.

The stuff of nightmares.

His reflection wore a wide, hideous grin. A lunatic. He reached one hand up to reassure himself that he was not in fact wearing such a grimace. No, if anything it was a mask of horror. His mirror image likewise raised a hand, but this one held a bloody scalpel. The one from his dream.

It lunged toward him and Shaw took a step back, averting his gaze from the horrible reflection.

"Not real," he muttered. "Not real."

More tricks of that damned idol.

Shaw leaned against the opposite wall, refusing to look into the mirror again. While he stood this way another ring came from their bell. Reality or another trick?

No. This was real.

"God!" Shaw spat. "Can I not be left alone?"

Singh returned from the kitchen, passing Shaw and heading for the door. He turned back both eyebrows raised in question.

"Yes, yes, Singh. I'll see whatever damned person is there."

Singh opened the door. "Inspector. Come in."

Shaw gritted his teeth against this intruder. He didn't want to visit with Abberline either. For a moment he considered continuing on to the bedroom and visitor be damned.

"Good to see you up and about, Doctor." Abberline did not try to hide the surprise in his voice or expression. His shrewd eyes homed in on Shaw, examining him in the same way he examined everything.

Shaw grunted by way of greeting.

Last time the inspector visited Shaw hadn't even risen from bed, under the influence of morphine as he was. He'd listened with barest interest from his room as Abberline and Singh spoke about their worry for him. Abberline had obviously not expected any different of today's visit.

The inspector tossed his bowler onto the rack before

stomping into their sitting room, a folder of papers in one hand. "You've heard of the missing linguist?"

Shaw turned toward the man, taking in the shrewd face and perceptive eyes. He gave no reply and Abberline didn't need one. The man had a habit of controlling every conversation, a skill which came from years of police work, or so he said. It was meant to intimidate, as it had so effectively when they'd first met. This skill often made its way into conversations which were not interrogations though. Shaw found it annoying, all the more so for it being logical, understandable.

"We have," Singh said.

Abberline settled onto the couch without being invited, vest riding up until he pulled it back into place. Were they truly at that place in their relationship where the inspector made himself at home? Shaw thumped his cane all the harder making his way to the couch. If Abberline noticed he gave no indication, waiting for Shaw to reach his seat. Singh took one chair positioned at a right angle to the couch.

"We investigated the man's disappearance of course, found no reason for him to just up and leave. No mistress. No money owed. No enemies."

The inspector took a photograph from his folder and placed it on the table before them. "The good aspect of investigations into people of some minor importance is the existence of photographs." He puffed up with progressive pride at using such modern methods as photography in his investigations.

"Yes," Singh said, tapping the folded newspaper still on the table. "Poor people only get their photo taken after they are dead."

Against his will Shaw's eyes went to the picture and the familiar face there. He reached out and grabbed the photograph from under Abberline's fingers, eyes narrowing at the sepia toned representation. Yes, familiar, but not as he appeared in the photograph. Here the linguist looked straight forward, wistful smile on his face as if enjoying the novelty of a photograph.

"Professor Moore disappeared from his house last week. His wife saw Moore at his desk after dinner studying papers, but come bedtime he was gone. He hadn't passed anyone to go out the front door, and could only have exited through the open window, as improbable as that would be."

"Not on his own," Singh said.

"Quite right, but it is equally improbable someone could have forced him without making a great deal of noise."

Shaw placed the man in the photograph, the thinning hair and rounded spectacles. This was the man he'd seen downstairs. "You've found his body, haven't you?"

"Humph," Abberline answered, unused to being interrupted while delivering a monologue. "You astound me, Doctor. Yes, I'm afraid we have. Found him floating in the Thames."

The inspector withdrew another picture and placed it on the table where the first had been. Both were of the same man but at opposite ends of a lengthy hallway. Life at one end, death at the other. Professor Moore's eyes bulged, staring, mouth hanging wide as if trying to scream even in death. Last Shaw had seen the professor wore a face exactly like this one, only spewing brackish water. So, he'd been visited by a dead man then. Why? Was it a warning, or a plea for help?

"Professor Moore is only the first," Abberline said.

Shaw looked up. "What makes you say that?"

"Over the past week, since Moore went missing, others have followed. A museum curator, a journalist, a librarian, a musician and a vicar." Abberline placed a picture of each as punctuation to naming their professions. "All missing, all well educated in some way or another. One missing man can be explained, but this many is beyond the possibility of coincidence."

Shaw sifted through the pictures, face by face, afraid he would be seeing one of these men next. Had they been taken by the new holder of the book? It appeared the most plausible answer, especially given the death expression on Moore's face. Now each of these others would be forced to read as much as possible before succumbing to madness. How much could they manage? A word or two? A page? Time continued to pass by with increasing speed. How much time was left to find these people before they chanced upon a reader who didn't fall to immediate lunacy?

Abberline leaned back on the couch, arms crossed, and huffed out a breath. "I had hopes of finding clues to follow at one of these fellows' homes."

It was obvious he had not. If he had Abberline would have been chasing the next clue instead of invading their home uninvited.

Deep breath in. Deep breath out. Shaw closed his eyes and repeated, knowing none of his current annoyances came from the inspector's presence. Another deep breath. He could focus for five more minutes.

"Do the men have anything in common?" Singh asked.

"Other than their level of education, no." The inspector shook his head. "It's possible these are only the men we know of. There could be others who have disappeared without anyone noticing."

"What is this?" Singh asked, tapping the death photo of the linguist, the man's neck.

Abberline gave a quick glance. "Moore's throat had been cut."

"Cut?" Singh's gaze jumped to the inspector's face then returned to the picture. "This is not the way of Thuggee!"

"No? I suppose the book's current owner is not Thuggee then."

"The book is not owned," Singh said. "It owns."

Abberline shrugged to say that was all the same to him. The inspector had seen strange occurrences, and heard even more, but the finer points escaped him. Perhaps that was his defense against strangeness.

"Well," the inspector said, getting to his feet. "The investigation continues." He swept the pictures back together and replaced them in his folder, then crossed the room and retrieved his bowler hat. He turned it in his hands.

"There is more." Singh stated, rising.

Abberline rolled his shoulders, as if limbering up. "The prince is returning home."

Shaw attempted to recall the last piece of information Abberline had told them of the prince but had no idea what it was.

"His ship will dock within a few days and he will have what information he has gathered from his travels abroad."

"And the prince will want to see us," Singh said. "You are here to ensure we are not an embarrassment."

He glanced at Shaw still seated on the couch who looked somewhat in their direction. "The prince believes you and wants to help. I just thought it best to give you the chance to ..."

"Clean up?" Singh suggested.

The man nodded and placed the bowler on his head, somewhat off kilter. After a quick farewell he was out the door and gone. Singh closed the door behind the man then returned to his seat.

They sat in silence for several minutes before Shaw found the strength to rise and head toward his bedroom. "I need to sleep, Singh."

"If the bell rings—"

"Unless it is Queen Victoria herself tell them to bugger off."

July 30, 1888

T
hree days passed without any further word from Abberline, either on the impending visit from the prince, or with an update on the missing men. Life went back to their bleak version of normal. Shaw would sleep as much as possible, through horrific nightmares and a repetitive influence to sleepwalk. Spectral visitations were thankfully contained to that one from Professor Moore days ago, though Shaw had no illusions about whether it would happen again.

Awareness returned and Shaw found himself at the desk in the upstairs office, the key to the room still held in one hand. The door itself stood open and against the inside wall. He shook his head, trying to clear the fogginess of sleep from it.

What was he doing here?

But of course, Shaw already knew. On the desktop in front of him gleamed a kitchen knife, one of the longer ones with a thin blade. Had he already tried to force the lock?

Certainly, the impulse to come here had not been his own, but without Singh's drawer key there could be scant hope of getting to the idol. The desk and drawer were solid oak. The one lock had been changed to the most rigid, serious one available, a present of sorts from the prince. Forcing the drawer would take more tools than what were available in these rooms and a great deal of noise.

No danger of the idol getting free, though attempts were made on a continual, nightly basis.

He could sense the loathsome thing in the right-hand drawer and glared at it.

Had he used morphine last night? He couldn't remember, though if the idol had gotten through to him he had to assume not.

Shaw leaned back in his office chair, staring at the ceiling as if an answer to all his problems would be written there. Certainly, he wasn't looking for help from a god he'd never believed existed. No, the only god he believed in was not one to pray to.

All the words he'd told Singh two days earlier were true. He didn't want to damn some other person with this idol by discarding it, and he knew quite well that it would make its way back whether it took days or years. Evil did not stay lost.

Could the idol lead them to the book or was he deluding himself? If it could he had no idea how, not on the fair side of sanity. Perhaps when he inevitably went mad he would see how. No, the book and idol were connected, he felt it in his soul. Though whether that connection was the already known one of the idol softening the mind, or something more he couldn't say. This all signified precisely nothing and left them in the same position they'd been in the past two years.

"A smaller evil is better than the greater one."

Shaw started. Had he said that aloud? Those words he'd thought while visiting Kinkaid. Hadn't he considered drawing his sword and running the man through to take possession of this idol?

Why think of that now?

The idol was pushing at his mind again, searching for better control over him in these waking hours.

"The end justifies the means." He considered the thought then cast it aside as appalling. "No. No."

Didn't it though? Wasn't locating this book and destroying it worth any price? If this horrendous god was allowed to wake would he not wish he'd taken any step, made any sacrifice? What do people wish for when it was too late to make wishes?

Which thoughts were his and which came from the influence of the idol he couldn't say. Where did he end and the other begin? He could never be entirely certain of his own thoughts. The closer his proximity to the idol the worse the thoughts, and the idol was secreted away next to his knee at the moment.

He should leave.

He didn't.

"Why?"

No. He knew why.

Shaw needed to know that his mind, his motivations, were still his own. The sleepwalking cast doubts, but if he could sit here and resist the thing, despite its probing influence, then he was still right in his mind. At least while awake.

The idol chipped away at him, bit by bit, wearing him down the way wind erodes a mountain over vast ages ... but Shaw knew he was no mountain. Still, he knew this idol, but the idol did not know him. Not yet. *The end justifies the means. A smaller evil is better than the greater one.* Yes, Shaw believed much of these words but would not be driven to any action without knowing the reason why.

Murder?

That thought burst into his mind, startling him. He shook his head firmly. That was the line he'd drawn and would not cross. Did those others who had possessed this idol have these same thoughts, hear these same words? Lassiter? Middlemarch? Kinkaid and the other directors?

He closed his eyes, focused on his breathing, trying to implement the meditation techniques Singh had shown him. They helped in pushing the darkness back some days.

Some days.

Deep breath in. Deep breath out. Focus on the breathing.

The smells of the office broke through to his consciousness. The faint lemony scent of wood polish, the leather of his office chair.

Focus past the—

You've missed something.

Shaw halted mid-breath, eyes opening.

Missed something? What could he have missed? When? Not as far back as India. No, if he missed some piece of information back then it was too far in the past and too many miles distant to make a difference. From before they possessed the idol then? Some vague clue he had missed in all of the rushing around? He tapped one finger against the desktop. Possible. Or was it something since then? Had he missed a vital clue to lead them toward the book?

Where had that thought come from? The idol trying to influence him or his own inner thoughts? Both were plausible.

So difficult to focus, to think. His mind always felt in a fog.

Deep breath in. Deep breath out. Focus on the breathing.

Yes. Yes. There was something. It lurked at the back of his mind, nagging at him. He *had* missed something. Shaw went over the information. Abberline had questioned Willoughby's brother in hopes of tracking Butterfly and Comedy. Dead end. They'd followed every clue, questioned every collector of rare books. Dead end. They'd wandered the streets of Whitechapel hoping for some sensation, anything, to reveal itself to them. Dead end.

All dead ends.

Singh placed a cup of tea on the desk in front of him and Shaw looked at the lad. He stood in his robe, well composed as always. The one constant, dependable, positive piece of Shaw's life.

"What have we missed, Singh?"

"Missed?" Singh moved to the chair opposite and sat. "In regards to what?"

"I don't know! Do I have to come up with—"

Shaw closed his eyes. Deep breath in, deep breath out. Repeat.

"Forgive me, Singh. Being this close ..." He gestured at the drawer.

Singh nodded, understanding.

"There is some piece of information we have missed, but I don't know what. Something about the book, or the idol, I think. But what? What?!"

Shaw felt himself becoming more agitated and questioned once again whether this idea was an internal or external influence. If external, what was the idol's motivation? To play with his mind some more, the way a cat plays with a mouse before growing bored and pouncing on the hapless creature?

Singh sipped from his tea, thinking for several seconds and presumably going over inside his own mind every path they'd already followed to dead ends. "I cannot think of anything."

"No." Shaw sighed. "Nor I."

Shaw placed his head in his hands, looking toward the desktop, eyes drifting to the drawer with its hateful hidden *treasure*.

Hidden treasure.

Hidden.

Hidden.

Yes, to some this idol would be a hidden treasure. The book as well.

Something about hidden—

"Yes!" He turned back to Singh. "You hold the key to the drawer, and I hold the key to the office. Neither of us can get to the idol alone."

"Correct." Singh looked to one side, as if he could see through the oak of the desk.

"Kinkaid kept the idol hidden in his office."

"Also in a drawer."

"Always at hand but hidden from all other eyes."

"Yes."

"Ananya and the book, she would have kept it close as well."

"She did. It was the cause for her death."

"What if ... what if, it's still there?"

Singh cocked his head to one side, questioning.

"What if she hid the book away, Singh? Perhaps that's why we haven't found it, or seen any signs of activity. What if no one has it? What if it's still hidden inside that room?"

A dubious expression crossed Singh's face. "You think this is possible?"

The sudden energy of that idea deserted him as Shaw considered its likeliness. "No. No. I don't know. I don't know what to think anymore."

Singh opened his mouth to reply then shut it again, his gaze resting on Shaw, taking him in. Shaw's interest waned further and he waved the idea aside.

"Forget it, Singh."

A cock of the lad's head, his eyes remained levelled on Shaw, his mind working. "This thought may have some merit."

"It does?"

"I think we should investigate."

"Us?"

"Just so, Doctor."

Shaw's eyes darted. Leave these rooms? To go further into the outside world than his downstairs practice? It was unthinkable.

"But Abberline ..."

"The inspector investigates the missing men."

"I ... I can't ..."

"Very well, I shall go alone."

"No!"

Was he so ruled by this idol and his own morose thoughts that he would send this lad back to Whitechapel by himself? Not under any circumstances. He thought earlier how murder was where he drew the line, but Singh's well-being was the true line.

"Do we wish to find the book?" Singh asked, pulling Shaw's attention back around. "To be able to dispose of this ... *thing*?" Singh leaned forward to tap on the desktop to his right.

Shaw's tongue darted out to moisten lips which had gone dry.

Was it possible? It wasn't likely, but a possibility was better than nothing. Wasn't it? "When?"

"Today, after you wake."

"Wake?"

"Yes. If we are returning to Whitechapel you need rest first."

"But ... what if I sleepwalk again?"

"Then I will guide you back."

Shaw nodded, accepting Singh's nursemaiding. On the way toward his bedroom he wondered once again if this idea had come from his own mind.

July 30, 1888

Whitechapel had changed since the last time they'd visited these streets. Then it had been unbelievably overpopulated and miserable, but vibrant as well. People had crowded the streets, walking, talking, living. Children ran and played. Now those streets were quiet. What inhabitants were out skulked more than strolled. Silent, dark and furtive, bundled up as if against great cold though summer hung pleasantly in the air. These shapes moved from view, glaring suspicion at Shaw and Singh as they passed, cloth caps pulled down to obscure their faces.

Urine, damp stone, and opium once again assaulted their nostrils. That much had not changed. Making their way through the dusk-shadowed streets they once again kept to the road's edge to avoid chamber pots being emptied on them. The streets themselves conveyed the impression of being more narrow, the buildings closer together and slanted inward.

Imagination, surely.

The lack of people had more to do with nightfall than any sinister explanation. Weren't the streets in any area changed once night came? Decent people retiring inside for dinner, children preparing for bed. People closed their curtains against the approaching night even as they passed.

Shaw found a lightness in his step, even the regular pains of his left leg did little to dampen it. Step by step two years' worth of fog had begun to lift. He could think again, and those thoughts turned to Kinkaid and how he'd kept that idol hidden. It whirled inside of Shaw's mind, round and round, like a dog chasing its tail.

Did the idea have merit? Or was it as ridiculous as he was coming to think? The book. Hidden inside these past two years. Was it possible?

Maybe.

Maybe.

Not probable, but just barely possible.

Hidden beneath a floorboard perhaps?

"A floorboard?" Singh asked.

Shaw turned toward his friend, one eyebrow cocked.

"You said, hidden beneath a floorboard."

"I did?"

Singh came to a stop, facing Shaw. "You still consider this a possibility?"

"I ..." Shaw shrugged, focusing on the direction they were headed. One street further. "I don't know, Singh. I ... I ... Well, what do you think?"

"I believe this is a dream. An unlikely hope."

Shaw nodded. Singh was right. What the devil were they doing in Whitechapel?

"However," Singh added, "we are here now, and we have no better ideas to follow."

Shaw understood now. "Your motivation was to get me out of our rooms."

"Just so. I am pleased to see you outside again."

"It does feel ... good."

A weight had been lifted from his back. Shaw had not felt this lucid in a year. Longer. Was this all it took? Remoteness from the idol? He'd wanted to bring it tonight, but Singh had refused to open the drawer. The argument which had ensued was enough to convince him it must stay behind.

Should they dispose of the idol? Could they? Shaw questioned the advisability of even returning to their rooms tonight.

It would not be that easy.

They arrived across the street from the two-floored common lodging house where Ananya had died. Rats scurried through the shadows behind them like thoughts through a man's mind. The idea that the book may indeed be inside that building still clung to Shaw's thoughts and refused to fully go away, and, as Singh said, they didn't have any better ideas at the moment.

"How do we get in?" Singh asked.

Shaw hadn't thought that far ahead, hadn't thought much past the basic idea to be honest. They didn't belong here, not the sort to come and rent a bed for the night. "We could offer to rent the entire room, pay extra."

The plan was rubbish and they both knew it. The rough men operating these houses would be as inclined to take their money and boot them back out the door. Well, maybe not with Singh there. The lad gave one nod of agreement, which was enough, and they took their first step toward the shabby lodging house.

"You shouldn't go in there," an accented voice said from behind them.

Both spun toward the speaker of those words, Singh placing one hand in front of Shaw, ready to act. A disheveled man stared back. Wild uneven beard and uncombed hair. His clothes were dirty and tattered, cloth cap askew on his head. He twitched, eyes darting. His tongue snaked out to lick at dry, chapped lips. This man fit into Whitechapel better than either of them.

"Why do you say that?" Shaw asked.

The man's eyes shifted away then back. "That building would be dangerous for two men who do not belong in this neighbourhood."

The accent was mid-European. Polish? Slovakian?

"I imagine that could be said of every place in Whitechapel."

The man laughed, with more amusement than the comment warranted. Just a shade over the line into manic. "True. True. True."

Singh took a half step in front of Shaw, always on alert for a threat. "Thank you for your warning, but we are not unfamiliar to danger."

"True, true. You and the doctor have seen much."

Another laugh, this time at their expressions of surprise.

"You know us?" Shaw asked.

"Doctor Shaw and Singh," the man said, pointing to each in turn.

Shaw saw the muscles tense underneath Singh's robe as the young man peered around for hidden ambush.

"I am alone," the man said. "Always alone, always alone ... unlike you two who have each other, and the friendship of a certain police inspector."

"Abberline?"

"Abberline. Abberline. Yes. He knows more than any other copper. Too much for his own safety." The man changed topics in a blink. "Why are you thinking of going in there?"

Shaw opened his mouth to give some plausible reason.

"It's not in there," the other man spoke first.

Shaw and Singh glanced at each other. Singh raised both his eyebrows.

"What's not?" Shaw asked.

"The Necronomicon."

Shaw sucked in a breath of horror while Singh stepped back, hand remaining in front of Shaw as protection. Neither had heard the book named before, but without doubt this was its true identity.

"Necro ..." Shaw couldn't finish.

The man cocked his head, staring at each of them in turn. "A book of spells, rituals, and information on ancient, evil gods."

"Gods? Plural?"

"Oh, yes. Azathoth. Dagon. Yog-Sothoth. Nyarlathotep. Cthulhu."

Each name was a punch to the soul. The streetlamps dimmed in response, the gas inside flickering. The air itself surged with a charge of energy, a faint scent of sulphur accompanying it.

"Stop," Shaw raised a hand. "Stop, please."

"Names have power, Doctor Shaw. Yes they do. Names can call to that which should not be called."

"You just called several."

"Did I?" The man looked thoughtful, as if unsure of what he'd said. "I suppose I did."

Shaw and Singh stared at the man. Singh's fists clenched and he appeared ready to strike. Shaw changed his assessment of the man to lunatic.

"I have little left to lose," the man continued, "except my life which is a paltry, wasted thing."

"Who *are* you?" Shaw demanded.

"Oh!" The man hit the side of his head, as if dislodging a memory. "Aaron Kosminski."

Kosminski held out one hand and stepped forward, his rank odor reaching them first. The man had not bathed or washed his clothes in some time. Singh planted his feet firmly between this man and Shaw, an unspoken threat.

Kosminski gave him a friendly clap on the shoulder. "Pleased to meet you, too."

"It's fine, Singh." Shaw placed one hand on Singh's upper arm, easing the lad aside. He stepped forward to take the offered hand. "What do you know, Mister Kosminski?"

"Ha! Too much." The man took a deep breath and let it loose in a foul cloud. Any trace of humour slid away from his expression. "Too much. I was living in Poland when I first encountered the book. Just a child of fifteen. I loved to paint and play violin. Do you know artists are more affected than others?"

He thought of Neufeld and his paintings. "Yes."

Kosminski frowned. "I learned this too."

"Wait," Shaw said. "What book? The one we search for was in India when you were fifteen."

Kosminski's focus had shifted, staring past them and into the distance, as if seeing through years. "The Necronomicon, was written by a madman. An Arab named Abdul Alhazred." He stopped, whirling his attention back upon them with a shout. "No!"

Singh's right hand clenched into a fist at the exclamation and Shaw once again placed his hand against the lad's upper arm.

"No, no, no, no." Kosminski continued, as if this were not a one-sided conversation. "You're right! Alhazred didn't write it so much as transcribe it. Certainly those words and symbols did not come from a human mind, not even one so deep in the grips of madness. He *transcribed* it, and paid the ultimate price."

"And you claim to have seen this book?"

"Saw it? Oh, yes." Kosminski scratched at a spot on his forearm. "Saw it. Looked inside."

"No," Shaw whispered.

"Oh, yes. Oh, yes." A pause, then. "Touched it. Read from it."

Shaw took a step back from the man and this claim. That explanation explained Kosminski's state of mind, but it was still impossible.

"No," Singh said with a gasp. "No, it isn't possible."

"What's not possible, Singh?"

"No!" the lad repeated, directing his words at Kosminski. His teeth were gritted, eyes wide. Fear? Anger? "There is more than one?"

"Yessss," the man hissed. "Very good, Mr. Singh."

"More than one?" Shaw asked. "More than one of what?"

"How many?" Singh demanded.

A shake of Kosminski's head. "Not many. Too oppressive to copy when a man loses his mind at one word."

The horrible truth dawned and Shaw shuddered, almost collapsed. "More than one *of this book*?"

"More than one. Yes. Yes. Yes." Kosminski's head bobbed.

"No!" Shaw stepped back again, both hands raised and pulling at his hair. "No! This isn't possible. This isn't right."

"No," Kosminski agreed, his eyes mournful. He looked to be carrying the weight of the world. "I was surprised when the music started again here."

"Music?" Singh asked.

"Yes, yes. The music. It plays without end inside my head, or perhaps not. Do you hear it now?"

Shaw forced his attention back, shook his head.

"Ah." Kosminski's eyes focused toward the street, disappointed. "The music drifts across the night on summer breezes and down the chimney in dead of winter. It plays like the Piper of Hamelin calling to me. The music of the book."

"How many books?" Singh repeated. "How many to destroy?"

"Hmm." Kosminski got a faraway look. "One, written in Greek, was destroyed long ago, by a monk. John Dee, the magician, was translating it to English." He shrugged, dismissing the thoughts. "The one in Poland was destroyed ... though it nearly cost me my mind." He tapped one temple with a vigor which must have caused pain.

"Nearly?" Singh asked.

Kosminski spun his attention back toward the Indian lad and stared for a second before smiling. "Oh, yes. Not quite. Not entirely. I still know a hawk from a handsaw." He gave Singh a wink. "Others are hidden away, secure, safe, unreachable."

"You destroyed one?" Shaw asked. "Then ... this book *can* be destroyed."

"Oh, yes. It is possible, possible. With certain rites, certain rituals. It is not easy and there is a cost." Another tapping at the side of his head. "Still, better to destroy this book and pay the cost than allow one of these gods to return."

"Rites and rituals?"

"Yes! The book is powerful but it also holds the key to its own destruction. A certain spell, on a certain page ... But, how to find the correct page without becoming crazed first?"

"You've already found it once!" Shaw said.

Kosminski voice went lower, more conspiratorial. "It doesn't remain. The spell is done and then gone from the mind, like smoke. The book must be searched."

Shaw shook his head. "I saw inside that book, saw how it affected others."

"You saw—" Kosminski came close to examine Shaw, foul breath making him wince. "Yet you are still sane?"

Shaw shrugged, not so sure on that fact.

"Saw inside the book," Kosminski mused. "Saw inside the book. Yes. Yes."

Singh watched the man warily while Shaw found himself drawn in, hopeful.

"And now you are looking for this book," Kosminski said. "Even though you know what is inside."

"No, it is *because* we know what is inside."

"Quite right." Kosminski nodded. "I knew you were special when I first saw you. Knew it."

"And when was it that you first saw us?" Singh said, arms crossed and glaring at Kosminski. "How exactly do you know us?"

"Oh, I've been keeping an eye on you since the morning you visited the Museum."

"You were there?" Shaw said. "Why?"

Singh answered. "He was the one breaking into the museums."

Kosminski's head bobbed again. "I knew an item of power was hidden in a museum, could hear it singing its own song to me. I couldn't determine which museum though, and the police chased me away."

"*You* were looking for the idol?" Shaw said.

"An idol? An idol? Yes." He drew the word out into an extended hiss. "Yes, yes. The idol of Cth—"

"Please!" Shaw raised a hand to ward off that word.

"Quite right." Kosminski agreed. "Quite right. Names can call attention to yourself."

"Yes, you mentioned as much," Singh said.

"Did I?" The man gave a grin which displayed teeth in desperate need of cleaning, then it was gone, the intense focus back on Shaw and Singh. "I was here the morning you came, when the princess was murdered."

Singh's eyes narrowed again, his distrust for the man growing. If Kosminski saw that distrust it was ignored.

"A few nights later when you returned to the museum I was there as well."

"You saw—" Shaw began.

"Oh yes. I saw. Saw you go around the back and that inspector come and follow. Saw that monster break down the door and escape. Saw the other police come but you were not arrested."

"You saw that thing?" Shaw demanded. "What was it?"

Kosminski shuddered. "A night gaunt. A creature that cannot exist for any length of time outside of the dream world ... but long enough."

"Night gaunt," Shaw repeated, shivering at the memory of the creature.

"It flew into the night and afterward I couldn't hear the music of the idol anymore."

"Yes, we—" Shaw began before Singh placed one hand on his shoulder. A warning to silence. Shaw shut his mouth with a snap.

Too late.

Kosminski's attention came back to them. He inched forward, sniffing at the air around Singh, then Shaw, as if he were a human bloodhound. One eye squinted in examination. One of Singh's hands reached for the man before Shaw gestured to stop.

"Ahhh, yes. *You* have it. The idol. It affects you, influences you ... haunts you. Oh, it is wearing you down, dream by dream, vision by vision."

Shaw kept his silence, though he didn't need to say a word for the confirmation to be written on his face, he was sure of that.

"The idol. The idol. This is a powerful artifact. It must be guarded closely."

Shaw felt his stomach drop. He didn't *want* to guard it. He wanted to be rid of it. "Can the idol ... can it lead us to the book?"

Kosminski considered it before nodding. "Yes. Book and idol are related. Linked."

"I see," Shaw said. A glance at Singh. "I see."

Singh turned toward Shaw, speaking in a low voice. "I do not trust this lunatic. For all we know he killed Ananya and took the book."

"No. No, no, no. I do not have the book."

"Would you admit if you did?"

"If I had the book I wouldn't be here. I'd be trying to destroy it."

Shaw gave Singh an expression to say that it did make some sense, to him at least.

Kosminski clapped his hands, startling them both. He glanced at the lodging house then back again. Shaw followed his gaze, a distinct embarrassment bubbling up at the weak idea they had followed here. How ludicrous the thought was now, but without it they would not have met Aaron Kosminski.

"An item like this book would not stay hidden," Kosminski said. "Not for two years. It would call out until minions of one god or another came calling."

"You said other copies were hidden," Singh prompted.

Kosminski started to swat at the air, as if a cloud of insects had come to buzz around his head. "Yes, yes, yes. Those are different."

"Different. How are—"

"So you said. What—"

Kosminski stopped swatting at imaginary bugs and levelled

his gaze on them. "Did I not say? This book is the original from which other copies were made."

"The original?" Shaw asked.

"What does that mean?" Singh followed.

"It means more power, more danger. The copies hold spells and rituals. The one I encountered had words which could steal a man's mind. The first though ... it could protect itself."

Shaw could believe that.

Kosminski turned to Singh. "Don't be glum. It isn't hopeless. Never hopeless."

That, Shaw had greater trouble believing.

"To destroy the original would also destroy all copies."

"All of them," Shaw repeated.

"*That* is why it must be found."

"Are you able to bring us to the book?" Shaw asked.

The smile drifted from the man's face. "Not now. No! Not now."

"Why not?" Shaw said.

"To follow the book, to call attention to oneself before being ready is dangerous." He took a step back from the two, eyes widening, darting left and right. "I couldn't take you now. No, no. Not now. The eyes are on me and I am not ready to be seen. Oh, Gods! I cannot do it. Can't. Can't. Can't. Can't." He turned to Shaw. "Tell no one that you saw me."

With that Kosminski turned and bolted up the street, much like a wide-eyed horse fleeing a barn fire. Singh moved to give pursuit but Shaw placed one hand on his friend's shoulder.

"Let him go, Singh. He is too agitated and dragging him back here won't help. I suspect we will see him again."

Singh grunted, eyes still on the madman about to disappear into the yellowed fog.

"Mister Kosminski has information," Shaw said.

"Mister Kosminski is not right in the head."

Shaw wondered how many steps behind the man he was at the moment.

They turned, headed back the way they'd come.

"How many lives it would take to copy this Necr—" But Shaw couldn't finish.

"It is obscene," Singh agreed.

"An apt word, Singh. How many lives ruined, how many minds devastated."

They continued the rest of the way in silence.

JULY 30 & 31, 1888

They did not return directly home. Shaw couldn't. He'd found some semblance of who he used to be. He couldn't go back to being under the idol's sway.

"Please, Singh. Don't make me go back to the rooms. Not yet." Shaw could recognize his mind dying in those rooms. All the more apparent now while being free of it these past hours. He looked to Singh then away again, embarrassed by the compassion and sympathy on his friend's face.

"I will gladly dispose of it before you go back."

"You know I can't do that."

The lad said nothing further. What was there to say? It was an insanely heavy burden to bear, but Shaw could have turned away from it at more than one point. Even now he could throw the idol in the Thames, as Singh had suggested, and let it wash up some other place, to be someone else's problem.

A problem he wouldn't wish on anyone.

This is a powerful artifact. It must be guarded closely.

"Kosminski said it was linked with the book," Shaw added. "It could lead us to it."

"Kosminski is a lunatic."

"Yes. He is," Shaw agreed. "Please, Singh, let's ... let's put off our return a while longer."

"A walk then?"

Shaw nodded. The idea of walking outside, even in the foggy pollution of London, sounded splendid, no matter how much his leg complained afterwards.

They wandered the streets of Kensington, speaking of what they knew and what they hoped, comparing ideas they could come up with. Frequently they would stop to rest until several hours had passed and either late night or early morning greeted them, depending how one looked at it. They returned to their rooms to face the inevitable.

The idol's influence hit him like a train ... no, that wasn't quite right. More like ocean waves, washing into him again and again, threatening to drag him back out, away from the safety of all he knew.

He was drowning in the idol's influence. For now though, he tread water. Barely. Soon he would return to his depression and refusal to leave these rooms, but for now he would resist.

"I will need morphine to sleep."

Singh held no judgement in his expression, only compassion, and a wish that he could take this burden from Shaw. Shaw reached up and patted the young man's shoulder.

"Thank you, Singh."

"You are welcome, Doctor."

"I am sorry, my friend. Sorry for all the bad-tempered words and every time I've snapped at you." He looked into Singh's face, just for the moment. "And for everything I will say in the future."

"No apology is necessary."

Shaw hustled Singh off to bed, promising to follow soon enough. Hours later he still occupied one of the chairs, staring out the window at a sun which was close to fully risen.

He refused to sleep.

In dreams he was more vulnerable, more susceptible to the idol. The previous night's excursion had given him a short relief, cleared his mind of the depression and the nightmare of this situation. The idol had been pushed back, at least for the moment, but Shaw could perceive its grasping fingers, pulling at the edges of his being. It was only a matter of time. He struggled against that influence, holding on to what remained. Reviewing all of the data which they'd accumulated.

One piece continued to mystify him. What reason could the idol have for pushing him out of the rooms? It had told him he'd missed something. Had it been meant as a taunt? Or had the idea truly come from his own inner thoughts?

No answers, only questions running in a circle.

Enough clarity remained to wonder on that encounter with Kosminski. Should he have let Singh chase the man? No. He'd seen enough people unwell in their minds to know when it was time to back away. As he'd said, no more information would have been coming from the man that night. They would see Kosminski again ... but did he want to? That man had knowledge, of that there was no doubt, but where did that end and delusion made up by his feverish mind begin?

Did he have any right to judge the mental stability of another?

A ring at the bell drew Shaw from his ponderings, as it drew his gaze toward the door. In works of fiction this would be the very person he'd been thinking of, but coincidences like that didn't happen in real life. Not often in any case.

He considered ignoring it. That trip to Whitechapel had restored some previous sense of self, drawn him back up that spiral of despair by a couple of turns, but he still hadn't acquired any desire to interact with others unless necessary. The thought of seeing a patient, to listen to them prattle on about their ordinary, everyday problems was a struggle. In truth he envied them those mundane problems.

A second ring told him the person would not abandon it. With resignation he rose to his feet, a deed he would not have done yesterday, and gritted his teeth against the journey to the door.

Singh came from his bedroom where he'd at least had some few hours' sleep. He rubbed at his eyes and stifled a yawn, heading for the door.

"I've got it," Shaw said, waving the lad back while berating himself for committing to get the door in the first place. More self-recriminations came for not being more diligent in exercising his leg and allowing it to lose what strength it had. "I'm fine."

Fine? No. He was far from fine. Not even in a state of mind where he could pretend at being fine. Best he could do was force himself to continue acting *fine* until the idol sunk its talons back in.

Could he allow himself reprieves? To get out of their rooms and release the pressure which came from the idol? A stroll up the street to the park. Would that allow him to hold on to who he was a while longer?

A third ring. Persistent.

Annoying.

"I'm coming!" Shaw said, hoping his irritation carried through to the bell ringer.

Perhaps it would be Harrison Willoughby, with further dreams to tell about, or with some of his stories. Did he care? He concluded that it was much more interesting than the problems of the usual hypochondriacs.

Singh watched his progress, knowing how far Shaw was from fine, in both the physical and mental sense. It both irked and touched him that the lad felt a need to watch out for him.

His thoughts rode a manic carousel. He hoped to see Willoughby and hear about his dreams, but he didn't truly want to interact with the man. A lead toward the location of the book, this Necronomicon—Shaw shuddered—would be a boon, but he had limited desire to leave these rooms already. Would the day come when he could throw that damn idol in the ocean? Or throw himself from the window? Up and down, up and down.

Shaw pulled the door toward him. "Oh!"

It wasn't Willoughby or any other patient.

"Inspector Abberline," Shaw said, stepping back to allow the man entry. "Come in."

Abberline's jaw hung open a moment. Shaw being up and about was one step, being sociable enough to answer the door was another. It was rare to surprise this man but he recovered quick enough, his surprise changing to good humour in a moment.

"Good morning, Doctor." Abberline stepped into their rooms, depositing his bowler on the rack before shifting back to his usual seriousness.

"Is the prince with you?" Singh asked. Sometime in the moments it took Shaw to usher Abberline inside the lad had left, dressed and returned, as if he'd been awake for hours.

Abberline shook his head. "Visiting with Her Majesty I'm afraid. She gets preference."

Shaw made his way toward the sitting room, following Abberline. The man moved as if this were his home, resting on the couch and looking around as if to say *have a seat, you two*. He placed the same folder of photographs and papers on their coffee table.

Shaw raised one eyebrow. The mystery of these missing men was enough to keep his attention, at least for the short-term. As long as that interest maintained he could force the impending stupor back. Push the idol back, back! He needed to leave these rooms again before succumbing too much.

Abberline cleared his throat. "I have to tell you ..." He tapped the folder with the fingers of one hand and gave a nod, as much to himself as either of them. "Well, firstly, one of the missing men has returned."

"Alive?" Singh asked.

"Yes, though completely raving."

"Which one?" Shaw asked.

"The musician. He was found shambling along the Thames, heading east."

Yes, it didn't surprise Shaw that the artist was the one to have the damaged mind. Had the man been forced to read the book?

"It took four bobbies to subdue the man and get him into a carriage. I believe he would have continued on until he hit ocean."

"Bedlam?" Shaw asked.

The inspector made a noise of agreement and Singh cocked his head to one side in question.

"The asylum," Shaw explained. "Bethlem hospital, better known as Bedlam."

Abberline continued to tap the folder. It was a common tactic for him to give one piece of information to delay on another, more difficult, piece. Whatever he held back it was some news which he didn't want to share. Shaw hadn't slept since yesterday and felt his patience waning.

"Come, Abberline," Shaw huffed. "Out with it."

"Hmph." One last tap on the folder and the inspector opened it, pulling out a face-down photograph. "Yes, well, several more men have gone missing, and one is known to you. Reported missing by his wife after not returning home these past two nights."

Shaw glanced at Singh then back again. Known to him? Who could it possibly be? The only person he cared for was Singh.

"Your father," Abberline said, flipping over the man's picture.

It was a needless gesture. Shaw knew what his father looked like. He probed himself for some sadness or concern on this but still found no love for the man.

"I haven't seen him in roughly a year," Shaw explained, "and even then I would have been happy not to. We are ... estranged is the correct word, I suppose. Still, I don't wish him ill, which is a step up."

Abberline nodded, back to business. "I wonder on the choice of your father. I've said before I do not believe in coincidence."

Shaw glanced at the picture then to Abberline. "He doesn't match the profile of these other men, does he? My father has been to school, but he's a businessman, not a scholar or artist."

Singh cleared his throat and both turned. "These holders of

the book. They know your history with it. They know you have resisted."

"You think they've taken my father to see if there is a"— he waved his hand, searching for a term—"a hereditary consistency?"

"Just so."

That made a certain amount of sense. Start over with one who has not been damaged by the book yet. Then that would make his father's abduction his doing, at least to some degree. The three sat in silence, staring at the table, the mood descending into gloominess.

"We also have news," Singh said.

Shaw glanced at him, one eyebrow raised. News? What ... Oh! "Our new acquaintance."

They took time to fill Abberline in on this man who may or may not be some sort of lunatic, Shaw presenting one side while Singh took the other. Both agreed that Kosminski has provided useful information. Abberline grunted and shook his head, not liking the sounds of the man.

"Where did you meet this Kosminski?"

"In Whitechapel, last night."

Abberline was on his feet. "Whitechapel! Are you barmy? That is not a place to just wander through, much less at night." He started to pace. "Anything, *anything*, can happen there. Why you could disappear like that." He snapped his fingers.

"Well, I ..."

"Singh, did you think this was a good idea?"

Singh stared back at the man, meeting his gaze. "Yes."

"Wh—" Abberline was taken aback. Obviously not the response he expected. "Why?"

"Doctor Shaw has not been out of these rooms for two years." He stated it as if the answer were obvious.

It was enough to slow Abberline. He let out a slow breath. "Yes, well ... couldn't you wander around Kensington instead?"

"We did that too."

Abberline emitted one short huff of air that passed for his

laugh, and which was only half humorous. "Look, if you're planning to go on some risky, ill-advised exploit like this you call me for support, understand?"

Shaw and Singh glanced at each other then back. Explaining how they didn't want to waste the inspector's time on some half-baked idea wouldn't mollify the man. Instead they agreed.

"I'm delighted to see you up and about, Doctor, but that doesn't mean you should be rushing into danger. Don't do anything foolish without me in the future."

"You would prefer to be a part of any foolish plans," Singh stated, earning him a narrow-eyed gaze from Abberline. His moustache twitched in what could have been either an expression of humour or an annoyed grimace.

"Aaron Kosminski?"

"Yes," Shaw agreed.

"I shall inquire into the man, see if there is any mention of him in the books." Abberline gave a shrug and retrieved his hat, placing it on his head. "I'll be back within a few days, probably with the prince." He went to the door and placed one hand on the knob. "Stay out of Whitechapel, gentlemen."

With that he was gone. A scowl crossed Shaw's face at being ordered about like a schoolboy. His father used to issue such statements, expecting blind compliance.

His father.

How much responsibility did he feel for dragging that man into this? No, he had more empathy for his father's wife, Emily, and how she must be worrying.

"Did you sleep at all?" Singh asked.

"No."

Singh considered, understanding the thoughts behind his refusal to sleep. "You will need to sleep at some point. I suggest a short nap. I will get the morning paper then make breakfast." He turned to leave.

"Singh."

The lad turned back, a quizzical expression on his face.

"I hope I don't in any way treat you the way some of my countrymen do. I don't ever want you to feel less than my equal."

That brought an actual smile to Singh's face. "Doctor Shaw, we each have our strengths, and I am a far better cook than you."

It caught Shaw by surprise, pulling a small grin from him. "That is true."

"I have never felt like anything but an equal partner," Singh said, then turned and departed.

For a full minute Shaw stared at the door where the lad, *his* lad, had disappeared. He felt a fierce sense of protection and pride toward him, and love as well. Yes, he loved the boy with a deep paternal instinct and wished the world were a better place, for Singh.

With a sigh he stood, noting Abberline's folder had been left behind on their table. It could stay there until the man returned. Staring down the hall toward his room, he resisted the call of his bed, knowing it was inevitable. Singh was correct, he had to sleep sometime. It was the one process he couldn't put off forever, and once succumbing he would give up all control.

Sleep.

He was so, so tired.

Perhaps a short nap would keep the idol's influence at bay.

"I do need to sleep some time," he muttered.

JULY 31, 1888

"Where is it?" he demanded.

The woman, Martha Tabram, turned toward him, a condescending expression plastered across her face. "Oh, you'd like to know, wouldn't you?"

"Tell me!"

It was meant to sound commanding and reached halfway there. The woman laughed at his assumed authority. It had been two years since he'd met Tabram and her two friends, but he remembered them all well.

Why was he here? What would this accomplish? This woman had no idea of the book's location, did she? No, of course not. Then why—

"Doctor Shaw."

Martha Tabram's mouth hadn't moved. Who had spoken? That sounded like Singh, but he wasn't here. Was he?

"Hmm?"

Shaw turned a full circle taking in his surroundings and wondering where Singh had gone. He stood in the main room of a tavern. The floor was dirty, rough wood worn somewhat smooth by foot traffic, covered in sawdust to control inevitable spills. Tables sat all around the room, people with drinks in hand at every one of them. It was silent. Eerie. Every patron and even the bartender had stopped in their activity to stare at him. Malicious stares. Judging stares. Hateful stares. As if he were some kind of monster.

"Doctor Shaw?"

"Wha ...? Singh?"

His eyes slid halfway open.

With effort he surfaced. A deep sleep had claimed him the moment his head landed on the pillow.

Memories of the dream lingered, as did his confusion. Was this the real world? Or was the other?

No. This one.

"What time is it, Singh?" His voice was raspy, dry.

"Not yet noon."

"I'll skip breakfast. Let me sleep."

It was a dangerous request. Too familiar. Words he'd spoken often over the past two years. So quickly any changes had been abandoned, bad habits returned to.

"We have a visitor."

Shaw groaned.

"One I believe you will want to see."

The words sank in and Shaw opened one eye. Who would he possibly care to see? With another groan and a momentous effort he forced his legs from under the sheets. He still wore last night's clothing, having decided it was too much effort to change for a nap.

"Lead the way, Singh."

Shaw followed him down the hallway and into their sitting room where a man stood. Even as Shaw entered the room the man glanced at the clock on the mantel, turning the expensive top hat in his hands. A man not accustomed to being kept waiting. Far too important for that.

"Good morning," Shaw said, also glancing at the clock. A few minutes before eleven. He'd been allowed to sleep for three hours and now that he was up and moving felt remarkably rested despite the odd dream. "I'm Doctor Archibald Shaw."

The man somehow made it necessary to use his full name, though it would still be judged as lacking. This man wore the richest of clothes, silk tie and shoes which shone despite the fact that coal dust coated the London streets. The man was shorter than Shaw but stood with an air that added a foot of attitude.

"Willoughby," the man said. "Richard Willoughby."

Shaw showed his surprise. "Harrison's brother?"

"Yes."

Not only Harrison's brother but a member of the Hellfire Club. This was the man Abberline had questioned after the affair with Butterfly and his cronies, and the subsequent massacre at the museum.

"I—Won't you come in and sit?"

Richard Willoughby looked past Shaw at their furniture and sniffed. "I think not."

Shaw's eyes narrowed. So, this man didn't want to be here any more than Shaw wanted him to be. A common ground. "You are here for some reason, I assume."

"Harrison has been committed," he said, voice softening.

"Committed? I saw him a few days ago."

"He became dangerous, to himself, to others. Alternating between suicidal and violent."

Shaw remembered the Harrison Willoughby who had left his office, at the haunted quality to those eyes. "The dreams?"

"He could no longer ignore them."

Poor Willoughby. He'd only wanted to write his stories and be left alone. "Thank you for coming to let me know."

Richard Willoughby stood as close to the exit and still say he was inside the room. It was obvious he wanted to leave; instead he scrutinized Shaw, once again rotating the hat in his hands. "Harrison always had high praise for you, Shaw."

Not Doctor Shaw, or even Mister Shaw. Just Shaw.

Self-important *and* rude. Shaw gritted his teeth, glad he had foregone the use of morphine for his nap.

Willoughby lowered his gaze a fraction, throwing his hands out to either side. "What is happening to poor Harrison? Where did these dreams and madness come from?"

Shaw reminded himself that this Willoughby brother had no real knowledge of what was happening. How to explain Harrison's state of mind without sounding like a madman himself? "It is … complicated."

Richard Willoughby's jaw set in a determined way. "Is it anything to do with this book?"

"You *do* know about it. I didn't get the impression you were that high up in the Hellfire Club."

Willoughby stared back, eyes set on Shaw's own. No response.

"Very well," Shaw said. "Yes, I believe that book is the cause of your brother's and many other people's madness. It affects artists and sensitive types of people."

Richard Willoughby grunted. "Harrison was always too sensitive for his own good, but calm and friendly. Now …" The man took a deep breath, turning the hat in his hands a half circle, then another. "Will you visit Harrison? See if he is beyond hope? I have no right to ask it, but I do anyway."

Shaw huffed out a breath, equal parts humour and exasperation. He turned to Singh, who stood on the edge of the room between them and the front door, watching the entire exchange. The lad raised both eyebrows in an expression of interest in this turn of events. Shaw focused on the younger Willoughby once again. "Is the Hellfire Club still searching for the book?"

Willoughby's eyes narrowed. After a moment he gritted his teeth and spoke as if it pained him. "They know you continue to do so as well."

"One more question."

"No." An unspoken implication that the answered question was payment enough for Shaw's services.

Shaw was close to telling this man to go visit his own brother and diagnose him.

"We have taken a vow of secrecy, Doctor, and for the sake of my brother I have already told you more than I should."

The two stood, at an impasse. Willoughby cocked his head to one side. Curious?

"Hmm, how is this, Shaw—You may ask your question and I will answer if I can without betraying my brotherhood."

"Brotherhood? You are a mob of hedonists."

"Your choice. I promise nothing."

So Willoughby gets to satisfy his curiosity but not give an answer. Shaw considered the information he'd already received from the man. It could be of value. "What happened to the man in the butterfly mask?"

Richard Willoughby gave a derisive snort and thought about it for a moment before responding. "Ejected from the club, along with his remaining friend." With that he turned and headed for the door. "Harrison is in Bethlem Hospital. When you have information send it by messenger. We shall not meet again in person."

The room was quiet a full minute as Shaw considered the information. Willoughby. The book. The Hellfire Club. Butterfly.

"We can have breakfast in the carriage," Singh said. "Pastries."

"Carriage?"

"To this Bedlam Hospital."

Shaw had no desire to visit Bedlam. All he wanted was to return to bed and get more sleep. It was comfortable here, and the call of his bed came from the opposite direction. So simple to just slip back between the sheets.

No.

The ability to resist still remained in him, like a dying fire in desperate need of fanning. Could he regain that full sensation by leaving again? Bedlam was further than Whitechapel. Would the increased distance help? Maybe. Maybe.

Though rested he still felt a draw to return to bed.

"I ... believe we should leave while I am still able."

July 31, 1888

B edlam's head doctor, Theophilus Hyslop, welcomed Shaw with professional amiability. Once Shaw explained that he had been Harrison Willoughby's doctor before the breakdown it wasn't difficult to secure a brief visit. Singh was accepted as part of Shaw's entourage and the other doctor barely spared him a glance, except perhaps to wish for orderlies with such build for unruly patients. Hyslop himself escorted them through the hospital, talking of the work being done in Bedlam.

The sharp scent of alcohol followed them as they passed down corridors, covering underlying smells of stale sweat, urine, and feces. The hospital was remarkably clean.

"We see all manner of mental problems here, Doctor Shaw. Delusions. Paranoid ravings. Extreme depression. I am quite used to patients believing their own babblings."

"Yes?"

Shaw was quite aware he was listening to a monologue, and one that was undoubtedly rehearsed, but he wanted to encourage the man, show an interest. After Willoughby he hoped to see the musician who had returned. He would need to have built up an amount of goodwill for that. He could have arranged it through

Abberline, or had the inspector join them, but for that Shaw would have needed to know he would be coming to this place.

"Quite progressive here these days," Hyslop continued. "Using hypnosis as a method of treatment and making some headway with certain patients."

"Most interesting."

"This man Willoughby, he hasn't been here long but has already proven interesting. The other patients are drawn to him, listening to every word he has to say. Even ..." With that Hyslop glanced at Shaw then back to eyes forward.

"Yes, Doctor?" Shaw prompted.

"I believe I can count on your discretion in this?" Hyslop said.

"Of course."

Hyslop cleared his throat and forged ahead. "The staff, too, find themselves drawn into his ravings. The first doctor to treat him came out of his room and leaned against one wall for ten minutes before an orderly came along to help him. He'd forgotten where he was or why he was even there."

"Indeed?" That was a new development.

"What was Willoughby like before?"

Shaw was quiet a moment, remembering the man. "I didn't know him socially, only in a doctor to patient relationship. He impressed me as quiet but amiable, introspective."

"Hmm," Hyslop considered that, filing it away for later. "The rule now is that no one goes in alone. I'm glad you brought your own help with you."

Shaw grimaced at the use of the word "help." "Singh is a great help in my practice. He is also my ward."

"Oh?"

The response had the same type of inflection as if Shaw had said he wore dresses on Sunday. Had he lost some of the goodwill he had built? Damn the man if that were the case.

They continued on, Hyslop filling in the silence with details on the changes in treatment since he became head doctor, emphasizing his progressiveness. They passed door after door, all of strong metal and lock. Each one held a barred window at the top for viewing inside before opening the door. As they passed these rooms they heard whimperings from behind some, mutters from others. Shouts. Cries. Rapid chatter. At one window a man's deformed face pressed against the bars, bulbous eyes and puckered, rubbery lips, fishlike. That grotesque mouth worked at words only the man himself could hear.

A flash of recollection. The sailor they'd seen in Limehouse.

"This is the room." Hyslop pulled a key from a chain at his side and slid it into the lock. "I warn you that Willoughby is restrained so he won't cause any problems." Doctor Hyslop muttered the next part but Shaw caught it anyway. "Not physically, at least."

The door was opened and Hyslop entered first. Shaw followed with Singh stopping at the door and crossing his arms. In the room sat Harrison Willoughby, dressed in a straitjacket which had been secured to the wall. The man had pressed himself in tight to one corner of the room. He appeared calm, though gave no indication that he recognized Shaw at all.

"I say, Doctor. Is all that necessary?"

"I did warn you he was restrained."

"Yes, but—"

"I don't come to Kensington and tell you how to treat your patients, Shaw."

Shaw held up both hands. "No, no. Of course not. I ..." He glanced at Harrison Willoughby then back again. "I saw him only a few days ago."

"And he was fine at that time?"

"No, though by no means was he at this state yet."

"Hmm, there must be some catalyst in those few days. Some cause for his further breakdown." With a shake of his head he refocused on the man in the room. "Do not come within reach of him, Doctor."

"Yes, I understand."

"Do you? Don't confuse this man with the one you knew. Don't expect the same reactions or disposition."

A glance at Willoughby then back to Hyslop. "Yes, I do understand."

Hyslop stared at him a moment before turning and heading for the door. He slowed passing Singh to give a jerk of his head back at Shaw, as if to say watch out for him. "I'll be just outside."

The door clicked as it sealed them into the room.

It was hard to tell through the straitjacket but Willoughby seemed even thinner than the last time they'd met. His cheeks had sunken inward. Part of his scalp showed through where his hair had either fallen out or been ripped free.

"The nightmares," Willoughby muttered, a moment after the door closed. "The nightmares."

The man pressed in tighter to the corner of his room, turning his head to expose an angry purple bruise on the right-hand side. Willoughby looked like he'd taken a length of wood across the head.

"Willoughby," Shaw said, taking a step forward.

Singh caught one arm in great gentle fingers and held him back. When Shaw turned, the lad gave his head a shake, a reminder of the parting words Hyslop had given. He gave the lad a nod, going no closer. Instead he crouched, with some effort, coming to eye level with the man.

"The nightmares." Willoughby chuckled, turning his head, slowly, without so much as a twitch to his body, as if head and body were separate entities. The eyes bored into Shaw. "They're worse."

A tear ran from each eye.

"So much worse." Another whisper.

Shaw found himself at a loss for any reaction. "Willoughby."

"Willoughby," Harrison repeated, his gaze sliding away. "Willoughby. Willoughby. Willoughby. Willoughby."

"Tell me about the dreams."

Willoughby spun back to Shaw, eyes wild, huge. Spittle flung from his mouth with the motion. "Dreams?"

"Yes, Harrison. Tell me about your dreams."

"Dreams!" Willoughby said through gritted teeth. He gave his head a rough shake. "Dreams. Dreams. Dreams."

Once again his attention disintegrated, speech degenerating into a mutter.

Shaw shook his head. Willoughby was so much worse than he'd been only a few days earlier. That day he'd been erratic, but Shaw had still been able to speak with him. He couldn't help but believe that if he'd chosen his words with more care he might have reached through that gathering madness.

"Dreams," Willoughby said, then spun his head back again, his eyes vibrant but crazed. "In my dreams it is awake and it watches me. In the waking world it sleeps ... but not for long. When I am awake it speaks inside my mind, whispering to me. Preparing me."

"Harrison, I—"

"Leave."

"I'm sorry I couldn't—"

"Leave!" Willoughby drew his legs up tight, knees reaching his chin. "Leave me to my dreams."

Shaw got back to his feet with Singh's assistance. He would regret that gesture later, no doubt.

"It." Willoughby punctuated the word with a strike of his head against the wall. *Whap!* "Is." *Whap!* "Always!" *Whap!* "Watching!"

Whap!

Whap!

Whap!

"Harrison." Shaw took a step toward the man, concern on his face.

Singh held him back again.

The two stared at the self-punishing man across the room.

Whap!

Whap!

Whap!

Shaw knocked on the door with his cane and a moment later it opened to reveal Hyslop's face. They stepped from the room, glancing back.

"He is—"

Hyslop nodded in understanding and gestured for two orderlies to enter the room. It was a sad turn of events but Shaw had an answer for Richard Willoughby, and it wouldn't be the one either had been hoping for. Would it be enough to convince the man to give up his insane chase of the book, and doing so convince the Hellfire Club?

Doubtful.

Perhaps then he could convince Richard Willoughby that his brother's only hope would be in retrieving that book and destroying it.

Equally doubtful.

Hyslop started up the hallway, back the way they'd come. They passed the same cell of the deformed man, staring at them with his fishlike expression. His words had gained volume.

"Father Dagon!" he said. "Father Dagon! Come for me, father. I beseech thee!"

Shaw came to a stop. "Dagon?"

"One of the other elder gods Kosminski mentioned," Singh said from just behind.

The lad stared with a furrowed brow of his own toward the sealed door. Shaw stepped toward the man. As he neared an odor of fish and salt water came from within the cell. The man's bulging eyes turned toward Shaw.

"You are not of Dagon!"

"No. No, I—"

"This way please, Doctor." Hyslop gestured from up the hall, having realized his visitors were no longer with him.

Shaw looked to Singh, who shrugged. Nothing more to be learned here, his face said.

As they made their way toward Hyslop the man gestured toward the cell. "A sad case, that one. Not only insane but hideously deformed. Most call him the fish man."

"I ... see why."

Hyslop waved the thought aside, continuing on while speaking over one shoulder. "I hope you got what you needed from Willoughby."

"Not what I'd hoped for," Shaw said, "but an answer in any case."

"Yes, I see." The man continued back toward his office or the front door. "The nightmares he complains of are a common affliction."

"Oh?"

"Many patients suffer from the same, undoubtedly influencing one another with their comments. I have certain theories I am currently considering for a paper."

"Hmm," Shaw muttered. "Most interesting."

Any theories this man had would be far from the mark, they would have to be. If not Hyslop would be ready for one of his own cells. As far as theories went Shaw had started to formulate one of his own in the past few minutes. Artists and insanity. It appeared the two were of closer relation than he'd previously considered. While artists were unquestionably affected by the influence of that book, perhaps those already mad were even more afflicted. Was creativity and madness so closely related then?

"Doctor Hyslop," Shaw said, pushing that thought aside for now. "I have a second request if convenient."

The other doctor slowed, turned his head. "Another request?"

"I am working with Inspector Abberline and he informed me of another man who'd been brought here recently. The man found wandering along the river."

"Oh, you must mean the pianist. Sebastian Maynard."

"Yes, that's the man."

Hyslop stopped and scrutinized Shaw, followed by a less respectful glance at Singh. "Since you're working with Scotland

Yard I will naturally arrange that. Normal protocol is to bring a letter of request from the inspector in question, but since Maynard is unresponsive I doubt you'll get much from him. He hasn't said one word since arriving."

Shaw acknowledged the irregularity of the situation and thanked the man. In truth he would accept any admonition from Hyslop if it got them in to see this man Maynard.

"He's in the next section." Hyslop changed direction at the corner. "Same rules for this patient. Don't get close to him."

"Is he violent?" Singh asked, the first words he'd spoken in several minutes.

Hyslop shook his head, looking at Shaw as if he were the one who had spoken. "Worse. He is an unknown quantity. He could have any reaction at this point and I wouldn't like to explain to Inspector Abberline why his doctor friend got attacked by a kidnapping victim."

"Understood."

After a few steps Hyslop took a breath. "I will say this. Maynard must have suffered considerably. To change that much over a few days. What he must have been put through."

Hyslop sounded almost admiring. Professional fascination? Shaw had a guess on what this man had gone through. Shaw's exposure to the book had been over a matter of minutes, he couldn't imagine what a span of days would be like.

"This one," Hyslop muttered, stopping at a door and pulling his ring of keys free again.

With a clank the door opened and they entered the modest cell. Sebastian Maynard sat on his bed, as if he'd been placed there by someone. The pillow had not been disturbed by a head placed against it and most likely Maynard was in the same position he had had since arrival.

The man was stout to the point of being overweight. A thin beard and moustache were ruffled and uneven now, but judging from the picture in Abberline's folder this man would have been immaculately styled not so long ago. Both hands lay forgotten in his lap, slender fingers disappearing between his knees.

"Ten minutes," Hyslop said, backing from the room and closing it behind him.

"Mister Maynard," Shaw said. "Good afternoon."

No reaction.

"My name is Doctor Shaw, and this is my friend Singh."

No reaction. Not even a blink.

"We are here to aid the police in finding those who kidnapped you."

A twitch of the left eye. An involuntary reaction or an acknowledgment?

"Can you tell us who took you?"

Back to no reaction.

Shaw rubbed his chin with one hand. He didn't have all the finer skills in dealing with those who were mentally damaged. All he could do was go by instinct. No time for subtlety with only ten minutes.

"I know about the book."

The eyes shifted, a quick twitch to Shaw before sliding back to center again.

"Fair enough. I shall speak then. I know of the book. I too escaped from people like those who took you, demanding I read the book. I know what ... madness is in those pages."

No reaction but Shaw felt the man's attention. Had his breathing rate increased?

"When they took me, back in India, these people wanted my help raising an ancient god."

"The sleeping god," Maynard rasped.

"Yes. That's correct."

Shaw waited, expecting more, but was disappointed at the man's attention, his actual presence, dissipating.

"Mister Maynard," he tried again. "Sebastian. Where are they? Can you tell me?"

One shake of his head. An answer that he didn't know, or that he wouldn't tell? Either way ...

"What are their plans?"

No reaction.

Not the correct question then.

Shaw gritted his teeth. Hyslop had warned him he would get no reaction, but that wasn't the case. One phrase *had* elicited a response.

"The sleeping god,." Shaw repeated.

"The sleep is nearly done."

Shaw moved a step closer, stopped at that point once again by Singh's strong yet gentle grip. Shaw shook his head at the lad to say he had no intention of going any closer. He shuffled sideways to peer into Sebastian Maynard's face.

"The sleeping god," Shaw repeated.

"It comes. For me. For you. For everyone here, doctor and lunatics."

So Maynard was aware of his current residence.

"It comes for all," Maynard continued. "Coming. Coming. Coming."

"Yes, but where are—"

"Cthulhu."

A shiver coursed through him, starting at his toes. His legs went to jelly and threatened to spill him to the floor, would have if not for Singh's grip. Maynard drew his feet up and stood upon his bed, back sliding up the wall. Once upright his gaze snapped upward with such force it must have hurt, though the man gave no sign of pain. He stared into Shaw's eyes without changing that neutral, emotionless expression.

"Cthulhu."

"Stop!" Shaw said. "Stop it!"

"CTHULHU!" A shout now. "CTHULHU!"

"No, stop! Tell me where to find them, damn it!"

"CTHULHU!"

Maynard's face had split into a wide grin, the lunatic humour not reaching the man's eyes. No, the eyes merely held mortal terror.

"CTHULHU!"

Every utterance was a gut punch. The word hurt, on both a physical and mental level. It scarred him on the level of his immortal soul. Outside the cell other voices were raised in shouts and screams and cries, joining Maynard, echoing off the walls. Behind them the metal door opened, Hyslop returning.

"Not yet!" Shaw spat, turning toward the other doctor.

"Now see here, Doctor!"

Hyslop started forward, eyes narrowed. Singh moved into his path, blocking the head doctor with a scowl of his own. An unspoken promise of violence in his stature. Outside the now-open door more screams joined Maynard's.

Hyslop backed to the door. "Orderlies!"

Shaw spun toward Maynard. "Tell me where they are and we can stop them, damn it."

"The sleeping is nearly done," Maynard repeated, his gaze leaving Shaw. The man slid back down the wall to sit on his bed.

The sleeping is nearly done. No, Shaw refused to accept that as definite prophecy. Destiny can be changed with some foreknowledge. Like Scrooge receiving warning from the ghosts.

"Cthulhu," Maynard whispered.

Outside the screaming stopped as if some frenzied conductor had gestured to quit. The silence which filled the vacuum was that much worse. Eerie.

Two strong orderlies entered through the door and set their attention on Singh. The lad flexed his muscles, leaning forward. The other men looked unsure of their actions, the thought of facing a Sikh's mystical powers influencing their thoughts.

"Stop!" Shaw said. "We are leaving."

"Too right you are," Hyslop said.

Shaw hobbled forward, once again making more of a show to his lameness than was fact. "I apologize, Doctor Hyslop. I felt on the verge of a breakthrough there."

Hyslop scrutinized him then glanced over at the patient. There was no denying a man who had not spoken since coming had done so within minutes of Shaw's arrival.

"Sounded more like the patient screaming nonsense," Hyslop said, though his demeanour had relaxed. He understood the drive behind an impending breakthrough. He motioned toward the door in an *after you* gesture.

Shaw made his way through and into the hallway outside, Singh close behind. Hyslop dismissed the orderlies as he relocked the door to Maynard's room.

"Cthulhu." A whisper from across the hall. Sweaty face pressed against the bars, watching them.

"Cthulhu." From another cell, farther along.

Then another. And another. All whispered, filling the air like crickets. The air felt heavy, oppressive. A thickness to it.

"Cthulhu!"

"Cthulhu!"

"Cthulhu!"

All whispered.

The head doctor's eyes darted, lips pressed together. A rabbit cornered by the fox.

"This ... happens from time to time. One will pick up the verbal ramblings of another until they are all repeating it. Most disquieting." Hyslop returned to business, remembering that Shaw was not in his good books. "Follow me to the front door."

July 31, 1888

Passing through their front door Shaw wobbled and leaned against the door jamb, putting more weight onto his cane.

"Doctor?"

"Yes." It was a low sound, barely audible.

"The idol?"

Shaw groaned. Its presence and influence came down on him like a hammer. How had he considered that he would be free of it, even for a short time?

Leaving again would not be so easy.

Singh took his arm, ready to guide him into the sitting room or wherever he wanted to go. Shaw shook it off. He wasn't in the mood to be treated like an invalid, not even by Singh.

"I'm not *that* tired, Singh! I think I can manage to make it to bed on my own."

It was the idol's influence making him short-tempered, or the exhaustion. In the past twenty-four hours he had slept three at most, and not restful ones at that with the strange scenes he'd witnessed in his dreams. Little wonder he'd fallen asleep in the carriage, rocked by the rough motions.

A deep breath in then a slow release. He patted Singh on the arm. "Thank you."

"Very well, Doctor. I shall get the evening paper while you nap."

"Yes," he agreed, barely registering the words. "Excellent idea."

Shaw stomped into the sitting room then turned back to stare at Singh. Both waited for the other to act first. Being in a petulant, irritable mood Shaw was prepared to remain there as long as necessary. With a sigh the lad surrendered and headed back out the door, closing it behind him. Did he listen on the far side for the thud of a body hitting the floor?

With a grunt of annoyance Shaw turned, his only thought on reaching his room and bed. Yes, sleep was all he—

Off to the right a shape registered on the edge of his vision. Something out of place. A cold sweat broke over his body as he turned his head and saw the visitor.

"No! Damn it, no!"

A portly man stood to one side of the couch, closer to the dining room. Brown suit, brown tie, brown hair. He stared, eyes wide, lips muttering.

Shaw gritted his teeth and looked over his shoulder toward the bedroom. Damn this apparition for coming now. He should continue on and leave the man standing here. If it was still there when he woke then ... Once again he stomped into the sitting room, returning to photographs Abberline had left behind.

"Come on, come on," he muttered, scattering the photos across the table and sifting through them. "Here!"

The librarian.

"Mr. Eames?"

The man remained at the same spot, disoriented and muttering. At the sound of his name the focus shifted.

"Marcus Eames," Shaw said, moving toward the man, though in truth he wanted to do the opposite. He tried his best for an agreeable demeanor. "What's the last you remember, sir?"

The man started to weep. Phantom tears made their way down his face. "Dorothy? Where are you?"

Dorothy? The man's wife?

"She's not here," Shaw said. "Can I—?"

"DOROTHY!"

"Shh, it's ..."

It's what, Shaw? Fine? Not for this man. The man was dead. Murdered. He could see the slit in Eames's neck, just like Professor Moore.

"Oh, Dorothy! It's so dark. Where ... where am I?"

"Mr. Eames. I ... I can bring Dorothy a message. What shall I tell her?"

Eames started to weep again, building into a wail which rose in pitch with each second. The man brought his slightly transparent hands up to grab his hair in two great fistfuls, pulling at it as if trying to separate it from his head.

"DOROTHY!"

"DOROTHY!"

The final syllable rose to a screech, Eames becoming more transparent.

"DOROTHHHHHYYYYYYYY!"

Then he was gone, leaving no sign he'd ever been there. That final call to his wife tapered into nothingness as his body did.

A second visit from a dead man. It left his knees week and his mind agitated. He could not endure this as a regular occurrence.

Not this.

Shaw continued the journey to his room, sitting on the bed's edge for several minutes before laying his head against the dense feather pillow.

Without a doubt sleep would be elusive, if it arrived at all.

Shaw groaned. Morphine. He'd forgotten to administer some before laying down. He would rest a moment before rising to take care of that.

Between two thoughts he drifted off to sleep.

AUGUST 7, 1888

Days passed in a blur of overwhelming sameness. One day was like the next to the point that Shaw was unsure of the date, and cared even less.

The weight of that hideous idol was on him, like a thumb crushing an insect. Inch by inch he was dragged deeper under the sway of it. Singh had tried encouraging him to leave the flat for a short stroll up one side of the street and down the next. Shaw refused. It would make no difference. Even as far as the corner the idol would still be there.

How far would he need to go to be free of the influence?

It didn't matter.

Nothing mattered.

Within days Shaw found himself back where he'd been before their excursion to Whitechapel. Getting out of bed was a chore of epic proportions. When he could muster it he would go from bed to couch and back again as if in a dream.

Depression sunk its black talons into his soul.

Despair.

The idea of having missed something, it *had* come from the idol. It was intended to rouse him from his lethargy so that he could sink even lower. Had he ever truly been out of the idol's influence? In Whitechapel? At Bedlam?

Interest in the idea slid away.

Head on his pillow Shaw stared at the ceiling and thought of Bedlam, of the poor inmates there. How long until he joined Willoughby? Would he become violent? A danger to others?

A message had been sent to Richard Willoughby on their return home. In his opinion Harrison was too far gone, but if the book could be taken out of the equation then a miracle might happen. His brother's insanity was external and without that perhaps ... perhaps ...

Richard Willoughby never responded.

Never.

Never.

Never.

What had he been thinking of?

Drifting. Darkness falling.

Shaw found himself on the street.

Whitechapel.

How had he gotten here this time?

Angry shouts from behind, many voices raised. "He went this way!"

They were approaching and Shaw knew it was he they searched for, though he couldn't say why.

"Singh?" he said, in a low soft voice. "Singh, where are you?"

He started forward, using the cane as his second leg in a loping, skipping motion. His approximation of a slow run. The pain was incredible, shooting through muscle and bone until reaching his ankle.

He couldn't be caught. Too much was depending on him.

Too much. Like ... like ...

Another blast of pain. Shaw glanced down to find that his pants were covered in blood. As was his shirt and jacket. He held the scalpel in his right hand this time, also coated in a layer of thick, dripping gore, spattering against the cobblestones.

Was this a continuation of his previous dream?

Dream?

Yes! This must be a dream.

Shaw found himself still terrified of those voices catching up with him. Closer. Closer. Shouldn't the awareness of his dreaming state be enough to wake him? That made perfect sense and yet he still could not wake. Not this time.

What could he do? What would happen to him if he were caught and killed in a dream? He would like to say it would make no difference, but ...

Better to hide.

There. A fence. Shaw squeezed into the gap where two boards were missing into a dim yard lit only by moonlight. A yard he'd been in earlier that night.

In one corner lay a mound of rags.

No. Not rags. Clothing. And under all of that, a person.

"Are ... are you injured?" he asked, inching closer.

On the fence's other side the crowd passed, shouting and baying for blood.

His blood.

No doubt existed that he would be torn apart if this mob caught him.

With all the silence he could muster Shaw crossed toward the shape. As he came nearer he discovered it was a woman, though she lay face down. From the clothing she was one of the working ladies of this area. He reached out, touching her arm. She was as cold as stone. Shaw pulled on the arm, turning the woman onto her back, and let out a gasp. He knew her. One of the three he'd met at Ananya's the day of her murder.

Martha Tabram.

She had been stabbed, multiple times, in the body and neck until she was a bloody mess. This hadn't been done by anything so tiny as a scalpel. Shaw looked to his right hand again and this time found a butcher's knife. He dropped it, stepping back from the weapon and dead woman.

"I'm dreaming. I'm dreaming. Wake up. Wake up. Wake up."

A sound from off to the right. Shaw spun, sure that the mob had caught him and equally sure he deserved it.

Nothing there.

He opened his eyes to the sunlight of early morning. Had he slept through the—

"No!"

He was outside, standing on the pavement and staring at their front door.

Was this still part of the dream? No. This was reality, he was sure of it. His sleepwalking hadn't taken him outside their home before. He'd not only risen, he'd dressed, gone down the stairs and out the front door. All without alerting Singh.

"No," he repeated, more of a plea.

The street was mostly empty, early as it was. In the distance a newsboy called that day's headline. One vendor trundled past with his cart, on his way to whatever corner was his place of business.

He stepped forward and climbed the three steps to their front door. Climbing the inside stairs took longer. He watched his feet rising and falling, step after step. It was some small piece of his life which gave him a sense of control and normalcy. Halfway up, watching those shoes rise and fall, Shaw came to a realization. His shoes had mud around the edges, and coal dust on top.

Just how far had he travelled?

The dream of Whitechapel wormed its way back to the front of his mind. What had he been doing while sleepwalking? He shoved it aside as something to contemplate later.

Shaw passed through the front door to find Singh in one of the sitting room's chairs, sipping a cup of tea and perusing the paper. The lad looked at Shaw a moment, then down the hall toward his room and back again. Such was the outward display of Singh's surprise.

"Good morning, Doctor."

Shaw grunted, then cleared his throat and tried again. "Good morning."

"Where did you go?"

"I—Downstairs. The office."

Why had he lied, and to Singh of all people ... No, he knew why. Embarrassment from the sleepwalking tinged with a bit of fear. First impulse had been to lash out at the lad but he'd managed to rein that in.

The lie was an improvement.

The truth obvious.

"Downstairs?"

Shaw was unable to maintain eye contact. Singh's expression showed concern as well as understanding, acceptance.

"It is good that you get out of these rooms."

Shaw nodded, grateful for Singh not probing further. One thought returned, bubbling up through all else: What *had* he been doing while sleepwalking?

AUGUST 18, 1888

M isery.
A living hell.
Shaw couldn't exist this way any longer.

Ten days since he'd sleepwalked from their rooms and out to who knows where. At least, he thought it was ten days. The passage of time was uncertain, filled with hazy recollections of sleeping and waking, sleeping and waking. Several more attempts to leave in the night were thwarted by the gentle redirections of Singh. The lad had gone so far as to have another lock installed, this one with a key facing inward and out of Shaw's easy reach.

Each day was much the same as the last. He slept too much, ate too little, and wallowed in misery and self-pity.

This couldn't continue. The idol would not lead them to the book, no matter what Kosminski had declared. He must have been delusional to hold it this long in hopes that it would. No. It had to go.

Where?

In an iron box, buried deep beneath the earth? Would it still come back? Yes, of course it would. All the idol needed was to influence some poor soul and entice them to dig it up.

The ocean then. It had to be dropped somewhere deep, where

no one could retrieve it. It would still come back. Of course it would, no preventing it. In time the ocean currents would push it back, but not for some time. A century if they were lucky and he could be blissfully dead when it returned.

Returned to be someone else's problem.

While contemplating the horror he wanted to pass on to another generation Shaw felt the fist of sleep grasping at him. Soon he would be attempting to leave the flat yet again ...

Soon.

Soon.

A noise.

His eyes fluttered open, wondering if he'd truly heard it?

A grunt. Then a hollow thud.

Yes. It was real.

At least as far as he could tell. Who was he to judge reality?

Staring at the ceiling of his room Shaw lay, listening to the semidarkness. All was silent now. Another trick of the idol then? He ran one hand down his face, suppressing a shudder and a sob.

"Why?" he whispered. "Why can't you leave me alone?"

Did it want him to sleep or not?

Neither. It wanted him to go mad.

Shaw refused to examine that thought too closely. An ache accompanied it similar to how a person's tongue could find that sore tooth again and again. Each brought jolts of sudden, fresh agony.

Another sound from the hallway. Slight but undeniable. He wanted to call for Singh but feared someone, some*thing*, else would answer. Was that so irrational? He reached for the night table and retrieved his service revolver from the drawer. Was it an intelligent idea for him to still have this in his present state? It had rested mostly forgotten in that drawer since their return from India, though it would have certainly been of value on their trips to Whitechapel and Limehouse, and even the museum.

Shaw made his way to the door, congratulating himself for opening it without a sound. Remembering the Hellfire Club he vowed to not be taken by surprise a second time. With as much silence and care as could be mustered, cane in one hand, revolver in the other, Shaw made his way down the hall. Pointing the weapon ahead of him he entered the sitting room.

There he stopped.

"What ...?"

In the room Singh wrapped a length of rope around an unconscious Aaron Kosminski, securing him to one of their dining room chairs. It was reminiscent of how he'd been tied to the same chair by Butterfly and his two men.

Was this actually happening? Shaw lowered his weapon.

"Singh?"

The lad finished securing the ropes. "I was away longer than expected, talking to the newsboys while out."

Shaw nodded, coming closer. He was astounded to find it was early evening now ... though he had a tough time placing what the date was, or the day of the week.

"I returned to find Kosminski in our rooms, headed toward the office. He'd gone through the drawers of this room already."

The two end tables had their drawers open, the contents a jumble.

"You knocked him unconscious?"

"With the pommel end of my knife. I assumed you wanted him alive."

"Yes, thank you, Singh."

Shaw crossed the room and returned with his medical bag. Once in front of Kosminski he pulled out the smelling salts kept inside and waved them under the man's nose. Kosminski jerked, eyes bolting open, still unfocused. Shaw moved to return them, then raised the salts to his own nose. The sharp tang assaulted him, jerking his attention back to here and now. A temporary clearing of his mind, but it would not last. Shaw squinted his eyes, blinking back the tears and bringing his focus back to their prisoner.

Kosminski's acrid unwashed smell warred with the ammonia

for dominance. His eyes focused, showing a lucidity which was missing when they'd first met. The man stared, silent.

"Why have you broken into our home?" Shaw asked.

Shifting in his seat Kosminski glanced behind him at Singh, then at the ropes which bound him. The gaze returned to Shaw with a smile of uneven teeth.

"We parted on friendly terms, I thought," Shaw continued, "but this is not the act of a friend."

"I need it."

It. Shaw glanced at Singh then back. "The idol?"

"Yessss."

"To find the book?"

Kosminski hesitated before responding. "You should not have it."

Singh came around to stand beside Shaw, arms crossed. The two waited for more.

Kosminski took a deep breath and let it out in a foul cloud which reached them five feet away. "It will destroy your mind and your soul. Slowly. Inexorably."

Shaw understood all too well what Kosminski meant.

"I am already ... What is the term?" Kosminski chuckled "Not right in the head? I am aware of this. It is not too late for you."

Shaw considered the dreams, the visitations, the sleepwalking and wondered on that.

"Certain times I am fine, like now. Most times I am not. Better one person goes mad than two."

A tempting proposition. This man *wanted* the cursed idol, and understood what he asked for. The thought of being freed with such ease, and without guilt, got Shaw's heart beating faster, his palms sweaty. Hadn't he been thinking about how best to be rid of this curse? Could Kosminski be trusted with it though, would he be strong enough to resist the idol's influence? Shaw recalled the morning he'd woken outside of their home, still unsure of what he'd done. What could this man be forced to do?

No.

"I thank you for your concern, Aaron, but the idol is my burden. I shall carry it until we have found the book."

"Hmm. Yes. The book." Kosminski's head bobbed back in time to his words. "The book. The book. The book. Oh, yes, the book is the true danger. That which will destroy us all when it returns—"

"Do *not* say their names again."

Kosminski giggled but closed his mouth.

"The missing men," Kosminski said, "they are reading the book. I have felt it."

"Yes, and at least two of those men have died."

"More to come." Kosminski's grin faded. "More to come."

Shaw had a sense of circumstances speeding out of control, like a train with a dead man at the brake. "The idol can lead to the book?"

A hesitation, then a nod.

"Singh, release Mr. Kosminski, please."

Singh levelled his gaze on Shaw, a questioning expression on his face. "Are you certain, Doctor? The man who first woke was more worthy of release."

It was true. That Kosminski was more lucid and rational, but this was the one they had to deal with. "I am sure, Singh. He will not be violent toward us."

"Very well." Singh was able to put all his misgivings into those three syllables. He withdrew his knife, making sure Kosminski was aware of it before moving behind to sever the bonds.

"You are ready to help us find the book?" Shaw asked.

"Ready. Ready. Ready." Kosminski rubbed at his now free arms. "Yes. Yes. I can help. I believe."

"You believe?" Singh asked.

"Believe. Think. Hope." Kosminski shook his head. "Tonight in Whitechapel. Same place. Same time."

"Tonight?" Singh demanded. "Why not now?"

Kosminski turned toward Singh, stepping close. The lad winced at the foul breath but kept his eyes on the man.

"Because," he said in a low voice, as if imparting a secret. "We must have darkness to chase darkness."

Singh made a disgusted noise and backed away, though whether from the man's mental condition or odour was unclear.

"Bring the idol."

"What?" Shaw started at the idea, shaking his head. He hadn't considered yet how he would leave the rooms. The idol would not allow it, but to open the drawer and touch it ... "No."

"Give it to me then. Allow me to be the holder."

Shaw stared at the man, then glanced down the hallway toward the office. Bring the idol. He doubted he would be allowed to leave its presence again. It was either bring the idol or stay here with it. "No. No, I ... I'll bring it."

"Hmm, yes," Kosminski mused. "The idol. The book. The book. The idol." He backed toward and out of the door repeating words in an absurd singsong as he went. "The book is the hook to land a fish."

It faded into indistinct murmurings as Kosminski descended the stairs and passed through their downstairs door.

"This man should be in Bedlam as much as any," Singh said.

Shaw nodded.

"I don't trust the man, Doctor."

"No."

"As he said, he is not right in the head."

"No," Shaw said, then took a deep breath. "Neither am I though."

"Kosminski is mad without an idol."

Shaw shrugged, unsure that it was enough of a distinction.

"He wavers between madness and lucidity."

Shaw had noticed the same. An effect from exposure to the book? Better complete unhinged than to come back to your right mind and know the circumstances of your life.

"Will we invite the inspector this time?" Singh asked.

"The inspector?" Shaw tried to hold on to his focus. Any

clarity from the smelling salts had departed and the hazy fog seeped in again. "I ... I ... What do you think?"

"I believe it would be recommended."

Abberline *had* been adamant about being contacted in regards to any such endeavors. To be honest it would be comforting to have the protection of a man from Scotland Yard along. Another perspective on Kosminski.

"Send him a message. Please."

The doctor's bag, still on the table, would do to transport the idol. The same way they'd brought it home. Shaw refused to have it in his pocket. Too close to his body. Too much like Lassiter.

"Should we consider giving the idol to Kosminski?"

"I did. Would you trust him with it?"

"No."

The day's paper lay on their coffee table, folded in half so only part of the main headline was exposed.

WHITECHA—

The woman murdered in White—

Doctor Killeen placed the—

Shaw reached out and unfolded the paper, exposing the full article and accompanying illustration of the deceased. Eyes closed, lips parted enough to show teeth, dead but still recognizable as the woman he'd met two years earlier.

WHITECHAPEL MYSTERY

The woman murdered in Whitechapel, one Martha Tabram, was stabbed a total of 39 times.

Doctor Killeen placed the time of death between 2:00 and 3:30 am.

"No."

"You remember her?" Singh asked.

He glanced at the boy then back at the paper. The article continued with gruesome details. Tabram was stabbed in the chest and neck, in the genital area. The body had been found on its back.

Just as in his dream after he turned her over.

August the seventh. The morning he'd woken outside on the walk.

"No," he repeated, almost inaudible.

August 17, 1888

I do not like this, Doctor."

Shaw shook his head, less in answer and more in an effort to clear his thinking. They stood on the streets of Whitechapel as they had not so long ago when Shaw had found himself free of the idol. Tonight it was with them, clouding his thinking.

"No ... I know you don't, Singh." A deep breath and even deeper effort. "I understand. Imagine if tonight we could secure both idol and book? We could be free of this nightmare by morning."

"Hmm."

Shaw did not believe it either, but Singh was too young to become pessimistic. The lad closed his eyes, teeth gritted, and stood this way a moment before giving his head one hard shake. An assault by the idol? Shaw felt envy at Singh's ability to resist its influence.

"At least I am out of the rooms."

"It is not the rooms which need to be left behind." Singh glanced at the doctor's black bag.

Inside was a cargo that neither wanted to be so near to, though in truth both had lived in close proximity to the idol for the past two years. It was a distinct experience to carry the thing. Shaw felt like a slave attending its master. Singh glanced at their surroundings. Across the way was the building where Ananya had died.

"Where is the inspector?" Singh asked.

Shaw had no answer. In truth Abberline should already have been here. Had he not received their message?

Singh let out an uncharacteristic sigh.

"Kosminski knows more about this book than we do," Shaw reminded.

"Kosminski is a madman."

"You are both correct."

They both jumped and turned toward the voice. The man stood no more than a foot or so away. It was incredible that they'd neither heard nor smelled the man approaching. Kosminski giggled and winked at them.

"I am indeed mad, but one with knowledge." At this Kosminski tapped one temple as he had the night they'd first met.

Singh's eyes narrowed on the man but had no response to Kosminski agreeing with him.

"Are you ready?" Kosminski grinned, showing teeth with bits of food stuck between them.

Singh peered left and right.

"You are expecting your inspector friend?"

"We are."

The man nodded, looking into the distance as if for the missing inspector. They waited but Abberline still did not arrive. Already twenty minutes late when Kosminski arrived, at half an hour Shaw called an end to it.

"Something must have happened."

Singh's lips pressed into a grim line. He glanced in each direction for the inspector, finding no one. A moment of silence, of uncertainty, broken by Kosminski.

"The idol is in there?" he asked, gesturing toward the bag.

Shaw nodded.

"Can I see it?" Kosminski rubbed his hands together like the villain from some Shakespearean play.

Shaw glanced to Singh for confirmation and received a resigned shrug. Numb, Shaw lifted the bag, undoing the clasp and pulling it open. They'd emptied out all of the other contents so the idol travelled alone. Shaw stared inside, wondering if the poisonous, green shimmer emanating from the bag was truly there or just in his mind. He had no idea anymore and cared even less.

The crazed man gasped, raised his hands to cover his mouth then reached out. One hand dipped into the bag, fingers wrapping around the idol and pulling it free. It was wrapped in the same blue cloth which had covered it in the museum. Kosminski pulled it away and brought the idol to his eyes, nodding.

Then he screamed.

Shaw staggered back, one hand rising at the sudden pain in his head. Singh glared at Kosminski, grabbing the bag and holding it out for the idol's return.

"What was that?" Singh demanded. "Was that from you touching the idol?"

"No," Kosminski gasped. "No."

"Someone read from the book," Shaw said. "Didn't they?"

"Nearby. Not simply one word this time."

"That is it then?" Singh said. "We've lost?"

Kosminski showed his ugly teeth again. "Don't be so pessimistic, Mr. Singh. If it were over a gigantic god would tower over London as we speak."

All three turned their eyes skyward for reassurance.

"No. No. No. The reading has stopped. Another has lost their mind, or their life."

"Or their soul," Shaw added.

Kosminski's focus was drawn back to the idol in his hands. A shake of his head, then another. Already it assaulted the man's mind. Was it worse for him or did his alienation provide a buffer?

"This way," Kosminski said, pointing up the street. He started off at a manageable pace. "This way."

Neither Shaw nor Singh were pleased with the idea of wandering through Whitechapel. They agreed with Abberline that they shouldn't be taking such chances, but what other options did they have? Call it off for another night? Each hesitation was the loss of another person's life.

They fell into step behind Kosminski.

"Other people are being murdered," Kosminski said over one shoulder. "Not just these missing educated men. Prostitutes. Sailors and dock workers in Limehouse. Those who will not be missed."

Prostitutes? The memory of Martha Tabram, his dream and her subsequent murder. Was it coincidence? Shaw pushed the uncomfortable idea aside, latching onto another.

"The night gaunt?" Shaw asked.

"Doubtful. Doubtful. Doubtful. A monster like that cannot exist for long in the waking world."

Kosminski led them a winding route, up one street, through an alley, down another. Ten minutes until they came to a stop outside a building, the Monument Tavern. Kosminski held the idol in both hands, pointed toward the building. Across the way a couple entered and from the open door came the scents of roasted meat and cheap ale.

"There?" Singh asked, incredulous.

Kosminski stared at the idol, then across to the pub. A bob of his head and a worried expression crossed his face. "If we go in the front door they could escape out the back."

"And you wish for me to leave you here alone with Doctor Shaw and the idol."

Kosminski continued to stare at the tavern across the street, not saying a word.

Shaw placed one hand on Singh's shoulder to attract his attention. "It could be worth seeing if there even is a back exit."

Singh's eyes narrowed, glaring at the unbalanced man who paid no attention to anything other than the building.

"I will be fine for the few minutes that takes," Shaw said, tapping his cane with meaning. When Singh glanced down Shaw raised one eyebrow.

"Fine," Singh said. "I shall go, but do not go anywhere without me."

"Upon my word."

A final warning glare at Kosminski and Singh rushed off.

"He is an admirable boy," Kosminski said. "Loyal. Caring."

"Yes."

"Sane."

"Yes." Shaw's eyes flitted to where Singh had disappeared into the night.

"I would see him stay that way, and so would you."

Shaw shifted his attention toward Kosminski.

"This is why he could not hear what I have to say next."

Shaw's hand closed around the head of his cane, ready for whatever might come. He considered that Kosminski might try to rush off with the idol. No! The idol was his. His! The hand around his cane gripped tighter, ready to draw. And he ... he ... was sounding like Kinkaid. Shaw drew in a deep breath and eased his grip.

"What do you have to say, Aaron?"

Kosminski had turned toward the pub, alert for Singh's return, then refocused on Shaw. The idol was once again wrapped inside the blue cloth, held tight in his hands.

"I do not need this," Kosminski said, holding it toward Shaw. "I need you."

"Me? But you asked me to bring this—"

"Would you have come without it?"

No. He would not have left the flat, not this time. Maybe never again.

Kosminski gestured with the idol and Shaw held out the opened doctor's bag, unwilling to touch it with his flesh as the other man had. Kosminski placed the wrapped idol inside the bag and took a step back.

"Then ... this idol in unimportant?" Shaw asked.

"Oh, no! Far from that. It is an item of great power. Great power and great corruption. Not so much as the book, but it wears down the walls of the holder's mind."

Holder, not owner. Shaw nodded.

"It wears the mind. Wears it. Wears it. Making the holder susceptible to the call of those elder gods. More willing to do their bidding."

"As Ananya told me."

"Yes. Yes. Exactly! But it reorders the mind too. Corrupts the thinking, bringing it more in parallel with these *other* alien thoughts."

Corrupting his thoughts. Was it possible that all the idol had done was intended to pervert his thinking rather than drive him insane? Or were they one and the same?

"I broke into your home to see you. I needed to speak with you alone. Couldn't have Singh listening. Oh, no."

"Why?"

"We can destroy the book."

"Yes, that's what—"

"We need to read a certain page. One page. One spell."

Shaw stared back at the man, a prickling, sweaty sensation coursing up his back. "Go on."

"I can find the page but I cannot read it."

"Why?"

Kosminski looked back toward the pub then again at Shaw. He shrugged. "My mind will be spent in finding the page."

"Someone else needs to read it."

"Yes! Someone strong enough. Someone who has been exposed to the book and survived. When we find the book, I will give what is left of my mind and find the page. Will you read it?"

Shaw retreated a step, the trapped animal. There had to be a better solution. "Can't it be burned?"

"No."

No, of course it couldn't. Not this book. "Well, you ... you ... you ... did what was needed before. You read the page. You destroyed that copy. Can't you do this from memory?"

"No."

No. Kosminski had said as much the first night they met. "The words leave the mind after."

"Yes."

"But the madness remains."

"Yes."

This wasn't fair. He'd already given so much and now was being asked to give even more. To become unhinged, like Kosminski. Shaw stared across the street, wanting to cry.

"Singh is returning, Doctor."

Singh. Wouldn't he do it to keep Singh safe? His son in all but blood.

"Yes." Shaw said in a soft, defeated whisper.

"Yes?"

"You find that page and I will read it."

"There is no back way in," Singh said, returning. "It is not a place to be in a fire."

"Ah, well," Kosminski said. "It is not the correct location in any case."

"What?" Singh rounded on the man.

Kosminski gave a shrug and a giggle.

"Doctor, may we go home now? This lunatic has wasted enough of our time."

Shaw looked up from his contemplations. "Hmm? Oh, yes, Singh. We can go home now."

Singh turned, muttering about wasted time and madmen, and started to lead them back the way they'd come. Shaw glanced at Kosminski, who nodded. An acknowledgment of their pact.

Together they would destroy the book, and lose their minds.

AUGUST 18, 1888

Outside of Whitechapel Shaw abandoned his shallow breaths and took one much deeper, enjoying the steady breeze which pushed all noxious odors back into the neighbourhood. Another block and Singh was able to wave to a passing cab.

"Lucky," Shaw said with a sigh.

Lucky for the cab to be passing by. Luckier still that the cabbie should stop once he saw Singh. The lad helped him inside then handed him the doctor's bag, the heft of the idol inside shifting as it exchanged hands. Shaw placed it at his feet, not wanting to touch it more than necessary.

Singh gave their address then climbed into the cab himself, sitting across from Shaw with concern on his face.

"I'm fine, Singh."

Both eyebrows raised in question.

"No, I suppose *fine* is too optimistic. I am coping."

Singh considered. "It is the best we can expect."

"This excursion helped. It is odd but I find myself somewhat refreshed, despite this." He nudged the bag with one foot.

"Hmm."

The cab had still not moved and Shaw gave a questioning

glance toward where the driver would be. A window showed the man up on his perch but making no effort to have his horse get underway. Singh leaned forward and reached for the door handle but before he could go further the opposite door opened. A man jumped in to sit beside Shaw. His head was inclined forward so that the hat's brim obscured his face.

"I beg your pardon," Shaw said, "but this is our cab, sir."

The man's head lifted, exposing the butterfly mask.

"You!"

"Yes," the man said dryly, cultured tone coming through. "We meet again."

Singh twitched, ready to leap.

"I wouldn't do that," Butterfly said, showing the pistol he held, concealed up his sleeve until then. The gun was pointed at Shaw's torso. "At this distance it would be an effort to miss."

The man reached his free hand back and knocked three times on the window. The carriage jerked forward in response. Singh settled into his seat, though he seethed at the impasse. His eyes burned with the desire to attack.

"Quite the dilemma, hmm?" Butterfly said. "The gun is not levelled on you, yet you dare not act."

"What do you want this time?" Singh demanded.

"I come as a friend, believe it or not."

"I do not."

"Let us say friendly then."

Shaw said, "I hear you and your remaining friend were ejected from the Hellfire Club."

The other man didn't react but clenched and unclenched one hand, giving a distinct impression of holding back on the desire to strike out. He swallowed, then continued with what sounded like gritted teeth behind his mask. "This is true, but not the reason I am here." Butterfly withdrew an envelope from his jacket and placed it on the seat between them.

"What is this?"

"An address and a date."

"Why would this be of interest to us?" Singh asked.

"There will be a meeting at the address noted which you will not want to miss."

"The Hellfire Club?" Shaw said.

"That and more."

"The book?"

Butterfly glanced to one side, more toward Singh. "I believe so."

"You're not sure."

"Circumstances are coming together and something will happen soon which will be monumental."

"Why should we trust you?" Singh demanded.

"Trust me? Oh, you shouldn't, not if you're smart. However in this case the information is true and of value to you. Share it with your inspector friend."

"You're giving this to us out of the kindness of your heart?" Shaw said. "Is that what you expect us to believe?"

"No."

"Why tell us then?"

The man gave one quick laugh, devoid of all humour, the bitterness coming through. "Let us say I do not like being rejected. As repayment I seek to derail their plans."

Both Shaw and Singh stared at the paper with distrust as if it might bite them.

"I assure you that no danger will leap from the envelope." When still neither man made a move to take the envelope Butterfly shrugged.

"Why not take advantage of this information yourself?" Shaw asked.

"Let us say I currently lack the resources."

"You wish us to do the work for you." Singh said.

"Let us say that by giving this information to you I am taking advantage of it in my own way. Trust me when I say our goals run in similar directions at the moment."

"How did you get this?"

"By all the gods, do you want this information or not?" A deep breath and another shrug. "I still have one friend inside of the club. Is that satisfactory?"

"No."

"Unfortunately it is all you get." The carriage rolled to a stop and Butterfly gestured toward the door with his free hand. Outside was their front door. Mere steps to the safety of their home. "This is where you get out."

Shaw stared at the envelope a moment longer before taking it, sliding it into one pocket without comment. Singh glanced at the door then back. He would need to get out first to help Shaw descend but that would leave the two alone.

"Quite the dilemma, hmm?" Butterfly chuckled.

Singh eyed Butterfly and the gun levelled at Shaw's chest, then the door.

"I don't see we have a choice, Singh." Shaw reached for his doctor's bag.

"Here is the second part of our exchange," Butterfly said, his pistol following Shaw's movements. "Leave the bag, Doctor."

"What? No."

The door jerked open and a second gun was aimed through the opening at Singh. On the other end stood the man in the comedy mask.

"Fair trade, Doctor," Butterfly said. "You get a chance to retrieve the book in exchange for the idol."

"No charge for the cab ride," Comedy said, his Russian accent coming through.

Shaw shook his head. "It won't be any benefit to you."

"Then all the more reason to hand it over."

"No."

"Shoot the Indian."

The revolver's report was deafening in the closed space.

"No! Singh!"

A bullet hole had appeared in the seat next to Singh's chest. A foot or so to the left would have put it into his heart.

"Slide the bag over or the next shot will *not* miss."

"Do not worry about me," Singh said.

"Oh, you should most definitely worry about him, Shaw. My man is a crack shot."

Shaw's grip twisted on the head of his cane. The cramped cab didn't leave much space to withdraw a sword, much less thrust it, but could it be enough?

"Don't try it." The man's eyes glanced at the cane, informing Shaw that he knew about the concealed weapon. "I have one like it at home."

With gritted teeth and a look of pure loathing Shaw pushed the doctor's bag across the carriage floor.

Butterfly grabbed the bag by both handles, lifting it into his lap. With one hand he undid the clasp and opened the bag, with the demeanor of a child on Christmas morning. He reached inside and grabbed the weight of the idol, gasping. It was deceptively heavy, Shaw knew from experience.

"If either moves, shoot the other one," Butterfly ordered.

He placed the wrapped idol in his lap, knocking the bag to the floor. One-handed and eyes chiefly on his treasure Butterfly unrolled the blue cloth covering it. He peered down into his lap, eyes narrowing.

"Is this some sort of joke?"

Shaw looked at Singh then back, focussing on what Butterfly held in his hand.

A small brick.

The man glared at them, taking in their surprised faces. Understanding dawned on Shaw. Kosminski had done some sleight of hand when placing the idol back into the bag, switched it for this brick which explained the sensation Shaw had of being refreshed. It wasn't solely renewed vigor, it was relief from a heavy burden.

"Very well," Butterfly said, rubbing his hand down his face. "Your expressions tell me you didn't expect this either. That means your shabby friend in Whitechapel took it."

"I—" Shaw began.

"What is his name?"

"I—" The gun was pointed at his midsection with meaning, the other man's eyes not wavering. "Aaron. Aaron ... Kemp."

He cursed himself for giving Kosminski's first name. It had jumped into his mind without thought. At least he'd had the presence of mind to change the family name.

Butterfly's eyes narrowed, about to speak.

"There's a bobby on his rounds," Comedy said low. "Up the street but coming this way."

The policeman couldn't have heard the gunshot or he would have rushed them already. Another carriage clopped past headed in the opposite direction.

"Make no mistake, Doctor. I will find him, whether his name is truly Kemp or not."

Shaw doubted that. Just one more disheveled, dirty man on the streets of Whitechapel. Kosminski fit the description of half the men there.

"Get out."

Comedy gestured with his revolver for Singh to exit the carriage, taking a step back to put space between them while facing away from the approaching bobby. Singh stepped out onto the walk, one hand still gripped against the edge of the cab as if it might gallop away without a driver. He held his other hand toward Shaw while both eyes remained on the man in the butterfly mask. Shaw retrieved his doctor's bag and shifted toward the door, descending to stand beside Singh.

He could call for the bobby, bring him running, but the two men held guns and the best Shaw could expect would be the policeman to be shot. In the end Butterfly had come away with nothing.

Comedy jumped back into the driver's seat and urged the horses forward, giving a quick tip of his hat toward Shaw as the carriage started forward again.

They watched the carriage disappear around the following corner and paused several more seconds before heading into their home.

The idol was gone.

The idol was *gone*.

Shaw tried to wrap his mind around the idea that the ugly oppressive thing was out of their home. He also tried to decide if he was upset by the fact.

Yes and no.

Mostly no.

For it to be away from him and out of his mind was a blessing, a godsend. He wanted to shout it from the roof! But why would Kosminski have stolen it from them? Unless it held more hidden power than he'd let on.

You should not have that idol. Kosminski's words came back to him. *It will destroy your mind and your soul. Slowly. Inexorably.*

Had he taken it to spare Shaw?

Better to be stolen by Kosminski than Butterfly.

Beside him Singh snorted and Shaw turned. Had he spoken aloud?

"Butterfly is not an honorable man," Singh said, "but Kosminski is unwell. The one will use it for unknown evil, the other for unknown lunacy."

Shaw gave a sound of agreement as they continued up the stairs and into their sitting room.

"I would have been happy to drop that idol in the river," Singh said. "I am uncomfortable with either man holding it. There is too much unknown power to it."

Singh was correct, but what could be done? Only one idea would come to his mind, and he was loathe to suggest for fear of it succeeding.

"We could wander the streets of Whitechapel until I perceive the idol's presence."

Singh turned toward him, considering the idea. The lad knew

the likelihood of it succeeding but shook his head. "Butterfly will be in Whitechapel tonight, searching. We would only make his task easier if he could follow us to Kosminski."

Shaw nodded.

The night was late, or the morning early, whichever perspective it was considered from. The two retired to their rooms to get some much-needed sleep. Shaw knew with the uncertainty of this occurrence his mind would be too active to allow sleep. He was wrong. It only took a matter of minutes.

And he slept through what remained of the night.

August 19, 1888

No nightmare had disturbed his sleep, and he had not sleepwalked. For this first time in two years Shaw awoke refreshed. Gone were the despair and depression which had plagued him.

They had breakfast, Shaw eating more than he had in any four recent sittings. The delicious smell of bacon, eggs, and pastries a treat to his senses. He tried to control his expression but the great, crushing weight removed from his soul was too wonderful a sensation and a smile repeatedly crept back to his face. Singh had also relaxed, enjoying Shaw's rediscovered disposition. Both knew they would need to return to Whitechapel to search for the idol, but at the moment Shaw enjoyed the reprieve all the more for knowing it would prove to be temporary.

Butterfly's paper with the information rested in Shaw's pocket, afraid to lose it though he'd committed it to memory. Shaw had studied the scrap of paper twenty times or more since last night, and would double that before the day ended.

"I do not trust this information," Singh said.

"No," Shaw agreed.

"But we will follow it nonetheless."

"I fear we must."

Shaw glanced at the paper once again. Three simple lines which read:

August 30th at 7:30 pm
South Quay Warehouse #6
St. Katharine Docks

"Will the book be there?" Singh asked.

"It has to be."

Once again that impression of the ticking clock returned. A sense that time was running out, not just for them, or for this situation, but for all of humanity. With the idol gone the urgency had returned. Shaw realized he had been numb for far too long, leaving all to rest on Singh's shoulders. Years.

The bell rang and Shaw's pleasant sentiment departed. Another patient or visitor to demand his time ... but that was the remnant of his previous outlook. The true dread of seeing another person wasn't present when he searched for it. Whoever stood on the far side of that door would be welcome. Patient or visitor. He would even have accepted a visit from his father.

His father who was missing.

Was the man still alive? Shaw found himself hoping so, not because he held out hope for a tearful reunion, but because he didn't wish ill upon the man.

They made their way from dining room to sitting room, Singh continuing on to open the door. He stepped back to allow space and Abberline stepped forward to fill it. This was his third visit in ... Shaw found it impossible to determine how many days had passed. The first had been the morning of—

"Oh!"

Following Abberline, his mere presence commanding attention, came Prince Albert Victor, Duke of Clarence and Avondale. Eldest child of the Prince and Princess of Wales, and second in line for the throne after his father.

The man was youthful yet his presence and personality was magnetic. Commanding. At the same time he was affable and attentive in conversation and hardly interacted with them as one would expect high-born royalty to. His eyes bulged slightly but that minor imperfection only added to his relatability. He smiled warmly at Singh, giving the lad a nod of greeting.

The man was dressed in a simple jacket and vest which would have cost more than Shaw's entire wardrobe ... and which would put Richard Willoughby's to shame.

"Your Royal Highness," Shaw said.

The smile faltered, becoming a grimace. "Oh, please, none of that. I get enough subservience at home. Please allow me to be Eddy for a short while."

"I ... I ..." Shaw had no idea how to respond. Had the prince made the same request on his last visit? He couldn't recall. This was against all he had been taught in regard to the royal family.

"How are you, Singh?" the prince said, shaking the lad's hand as if they were equals.

"Good morning, Eddy."

"Yes! Thank you for that. There will be enough time for all the *your majesty*s when I am king." He spun toward Shaw, smoothing his thin, neatly trimmed moustache. "I must say, Doctor, you look much more healthy than last time I visited. More colour to your complexion and more life in your disposition. I'd been led to believe you spent most of your time abed lately."

"There have been some recent changes."

"Splendid! It is excellent to see you up, and sociable. Now, tell me of these changes."

"Ah. Yes." Shaw gestured toward the sitting room, inviting the prince and inspector into their home. He took a deep breath and started.

Shaw glossed over all that had occurred since the prince's last visit. Not much to tell in that period of Shaw lying in bed and wishing for death. That surprised him. *Had* he truly been wishing for an end? On some level he must have been. He jumped to their first meeting with Kosminski, telling of that man's encounter with another copy of the book in Poland, and his assertion that this book was the original.

"More than one," the prince exhaled through gritted teeth. "I had found similar rumours in my travels ... what mention of it I could find."

"The Necronomicon is its name," Shaw said, a brief shudder at uttering the word.

"A ghastly name. Fitting."

Shaw moved on to their Bedlam visit. The afflicted Willoughby. The words spoken by that poor musician who had returned. Then Kosminski's return to these rooms.

"I investigated this man," Abberline said. "Works as a barber or hairdresser, though only when it suits him. Relies on his brother and sister's goodwill to survive. From a moderately successful family of tailors but Aaron Kosminski has chosen not to join them in business. He apparently suffers from hallucinations." Abberline's nose wrinkled at this point. "And has chosen to stop bathing."

"Yes," Singh agreed. "That is the same man."

"Disappears for days or weeks on end—"

"Where?" Shaw asked.

Abberline shrugged. "No idea and neither does his family. I wouldn't place much trust in him. The man is at best a layabout, and at worst dangerously unbalanced."

"I agree." Singh turned to Shaw then back towards the inspector. "I said as much when we saw him last night—"

"Saw him? Where?"

"Whitechapel."

"What?" Abberline leapt to his feet, an explosion of movement. "I thought we agreed against taking foolish, dangerous actions like this without me."

"We sent word," Shaw said. "At Scotland Yard. You didn't respond or appear at the meeting time."

"I didn't see any message."

"That is my fault," the prince interjected. "I had the inspector with me most of the evening and he wouldn't have returned to the yard until late."

Abberline glanced to the prince who stared back with a calm expression. The inspector couldn't allow his prince to take the blame. There was a deep, ingrained respect behind the gaze whenever he looked in the man's direction. "I ... My fault. I should have checked in for messages last night before heading home."

The prince turned his attention back toward Shaw and Singh, gesturing to continue. Shaw told of this second visit to Whitechapel and seeing Kosminski again.

"A waste of time," Singh added.

Shaw moved on to their subsequent encounter with Butterfly and the discovery that they had lost the idol. Abberline dropped back onto the couch.

"That would be the change you referred to," he said.

"I'm afraid so," Shaw said.

The prince's easy grin disappeared into a scowl, rapping his knuckles against the arm of the couch. "This is a blow."

Shaw was afraid that any words he might say would betray how glad he was the damn thing was gone. Yes, it was his responsibility to keep it from the wrong hands but ... but ... No. There was no but. He'd failed in his charge. Better for it to be on the bottom of the Thames to be retrieved by a random person one day than in the hands of Butterfly or Kosminski.

"You say the younger Willoughby admitted to this man being expelled from the Hellfire Club?" the prince asked.

"Yes," Shaw said. "And he admitted as much himself last night. Telling us this information was his petty revenge."

"Hmm, I see. If he is no longer a member then his identity may not be protected any longer. Leave this with me."

Again Shaw nodded, numb. Was it possible to discover the man's identity? They'd tried every resource two years earlier, but as Albert Victor said, the man had been a member of the Hellfire Club then.

"Yes, Your Maj—" Shaw fell silent at a scowl from the prince. He swallowed it down and forged onward. "Yes, Eddy."

The prince relaxed, giving a grateful nod to continue.

"Butterfly seems to think that the information he gave would have been fair trade for the idol."

Shaw showed the note with the warehouse address and date on it.

"He gave no details on what would happen?" Abberline asked.

"No."

"Very well, I will gather all the forces of Scotland Yard for that night." Abberline hopped to his feet, starting to pace. "Whatever is set to happen won't go far."

"No." The prince spoke in a low voice, introspective. "No. You mustn't do that."

"But ... why?"

"Think about it, my dear Inspector. There is no guarantee that every man at Scotland Yard is honest. It is easy for any man to be a source of information for another, even one of those in the Hellfire Club."

Abberline shook his head. It was the closest the man had ever come to outright contradicting the prince.

"I make no accusation of criminality," Eddy said. "Are you not a source of information for myself?"

"That is different. You are my prince. A member of the royal family."

"And certain men in the Hellfire Club are gentlemen and lords."

Abberline considered this a full minute before letting his breath out in a regretful sigh. "I concede your point."

"We need a group of men who can be trusted without any reservation. Do you know any who match that description at Scotland Yard?"

"A few. I can think of four ... no, five whom I would trust in such a way. Two of them recent additions to the Yard."

"Excellent. While I have a half dozen men in my service whom I consider in the same light. Honest men who protect myself and my family." The four looked from one to another until the prince clapped his hands and stood. "Gentlemen, it appears that we have a plan."

"In the meantime," Shaw said, wanting to suggest anything else, "we can search through Whitechapel for an awareness of the idol."

"You have that much connection?" the prince asked.

Shaw nodded, a miserable mood descending on him at the idea of retrieving the idol. Eddy gripped one shoulder in his hand, giving Shaw an expression of commiseration and deep compassion, almost sadness.

"Inspector, go with them on this pursuit. I will take the carriage back and start the hunt for this man in the butterfly mask."

AUGUST 25 TO 28, 1888

In five days, events would come to a head at this warehouse, assuming Butterfly's information was to be trusted. Shaw thought it was. That didn't mean plans wouldn't change in those five days and everything fall apart, but—with luck and hope—five days until the book was retrieved and destroyed.

The book. Destroyed.

Shaw thought of the promise he had made to Kosminski. If that man could find the correct page before going mad, then Shaw would read it. Which meant there were five days until he lost his mind, like Kosminski. Only ... now that the idol was gone and his mind clear of that outside influence the prospect was less and less appealing. Hadn't he come close enough to losing his mind already?

We do what is right, not what is easy.

It was one of his mother's favorite sayings, and one he could find no argument against. Not without admitting to complete selfishness. What was the cost of his life and mind compared to that of every life on earth? Compared to Singh's life?

His life and soul were only of value to himself.

After the prince had left they spent the rest of yesterday going up one Whitechapel street and down the next until Shaw's leg was screaming an opera. All for nothing. He felt no impression of the idol being close by. They saw no sign of Kosminski, and no denizen of Whitechapel would give them the time of day, much less the whereabouts of some poor soul being sought by a police inspector and two men from outside of the neighbourhood.

All through the search Shaw's mind whirled like a child riding the carousel, starting with his duty toward the idol and retrieving it, but ending with his relief at being free and not wanting to return. In the end relief came out the victor and they returned home empty-handed. Shaw probed for some regret on the matter and found it short-lived.

Abberline came to the bitter conclusion that Butterfly had indeed found Kosminski and stolen the idol, but Shaw couldn't bring himself to agree. The inspector shifted focus to finding the identity behind that mask.

Two days later Shaw had steeled himself for the inevitable, certain that they would gain the book. A moroseness returned as he hobbled around the rooms, distinct from that which came from the idol but no less definite.

Shaw passed between dining and sitting rooms, thoughts turning to his time in India. All he'd wanted was to be a doctor, to make a difference. All had gone wrong and his life headed in a different direction. His eyes had been opened to the world's unseen horrors. Ignorance is indeed bliss, but it's unappreciated until that bliss has been destroyed.

A few steps into the next room and he shuffled to a stop, all thoughts of self-pity chased away with ones of terror. Horror.

Cold sweat trickled down the small of his back.

A man stood at the juncture between sitting room and the hallway leading to their bedrooms. He faced toward the room and Shaw, though his attention was anywhere but. An expression of utter grief covered the man's face.

The man was dead, as the librarian who'd stood in this same room a few days earlier had been. If the man's countenance didn't give that away then the fact that Shaw could see through him to the hallway beyond removed any doubt.

"No!" Shaw spat. "You can't be here. The idol is gone!"

No need for Abberline's photographs to realize this man wasn't among them. This was someone else, someone new. Judging by the style of dress he wasn't of the same social station as those others. Cheap fabric over solid muscles, and hands which were no stranger to physical tasks. This man was working class.

Shaw ground his teeth. Why was he even there? With the idol gone these haunting visitations should have ended. The idol couldn't be close by ... No, he would know if it was. He would be aware if it had reached back out to sink its claws into him, even if he couldn't have done anything to stop it. Was this some leftover effect then, some unwanted, loathsome ability from his possession of the idol?

A permanent effect?

"No! No, no, no, no, no!"

Damn it, no! Wasn't giving up his sanity enough? Did he have to suffer from now to then as well? Where did the sacrifice end? When he had nothing more to give? When he'd lost every facet of himself to this other, shadowed word of idol, book, and damned ancient god.

When he'd lost his soul.

"Hurry!" the ghostly visitor shouted, jerking Shaw's attention back to here and now. The man's attention now bored into Shaw, lips peeled back in an angry scowl. The grief was gone from the man, replaced with determination.

"Hurry where?" Shaw stepped toward the man. "Tell me where you are!"

The man shook his head. He didn't know, or it wasn't important?

"Hurry," he repeated. "He's huntin' for it."

"Hunting for what? The book?" If so then whoever killed this man wasn't the same as the ones who had the book. "Who is *he*? What do you—?"

"Hurry," the man repeated.

"Yes, I understand but—"

"Tell him I'm sorry. I did my best."

"I ... Yes, but tell who?"

"Hurry. Hurry. Hurry." With each successive word his voice became more vehement.

The ghost's eyes grew wider even as he became more transparent. The eyes of panic, and this was not the sort of man given to panicking ... not while alive in any case.

"HURRY!"

This last was a shout which hit Shaw with physical force, knocking him backward into the wall. On the coffee table yesterday's newspaper ripped apart and flew in two separate directions. A teacup and saucer catapulted from the same to shatter against the far wall. Both end tables tipped and fell. Couches and chairs all shifted a foot away from the apparition. As that final word tapered off the man faded away, eyes remaining on Shaw's to the last.

"Damn."

Shaw leaned against the wall, knees trembling, needing to sit or else fall to the floor. He made it to the nearest chair and collapsed into it, raising one shaking hand to comb through his hair. After several minutes he looked about at the chaos of the room. The newspaper and pieces of cup and saucer were easy enough to clean up, as were the two end tables. Shaw opened and closed the drawers to confirm no items inside had broken. The chairs took more muscle to put back in their proper place, but the couch was beyond his ability. He would need Singh's help with that. He hadn't told the lad about these visitations, never sure enough of their reality. Now he would need to—

The doorbell rang.

"Go to hell," he muttered.

Before that experience he would have been happy to see

another person. Now ... no, now he found it to be a need. Any distraction to not be quite so alone. Anything.

He rose to his feet and rushed, as much as he was able to rush, to the door and opened it. There stood Abberline, rumpled coat and scuffed bowler completing his usual style.

"Montague John Druitt."

Another missing man? The one he had just encountered? "Who?"

"He's a barrister and a teacher," Abberline continued, "*and he's the man behind the butterfly mask.*"

"Oh!"

"Oh, indeed. The prince discovered his identity, don't ask me how. Now I have his name and address. On my way there now."

"Ah, very good ..."

"Get Singh and come along. Hurry."

Hurry! He heard the dead man echo.

"Us—?"

Abberline nodded, sheepish. "Hate to ask it of you, Doctor, but if Druitt got the idol then you need to be there too, to retake possession."

Shaw retreated a step at the words.

Retake possession. No, for the idol to retake possession of him.

"Singh is not home."

"Well, leave him a note then."

"No need," Singh said, coming up behind Abberline. "I am here."

It was somehow a comfort to see the inspector startled. Small comfort. Shaw found he was not at all ready for this in the least, but as usual that made absolutely no difference. He grabbed his hat from the rack. The revolver already rested in his right-hand coat pocket, had been there, loaded and ready for use since the night Butterfly held them at gunpoint.

"Ready," Shaw confirmed to both.

"Butterfly ... I mean, Druitt, had a gun," Shaw said. "So did his man."

Abberline grunted, the carriage bouncing its three passengers left and right as they rolled along, rushing toward Druitt's address. "Doctor, I always assume the other man has a weapon."

What more could be said? Shaw watched the scenery passing, wondering on whether the idol would be at Druitt's or still with Kosminski somewhere in Whitechapel.

A sense of resignation had crept up on him. After a couple days' rest—recovering some of who he had been—he found himself hurtling through the city, hoping to recover the one item which he hoped to never see again.

Oh, shut up, he told himself. *You had plenty of opportunity to turn away from this. After Lassiter died. When we saw the cultist in the market that day. Again in Bombay after Ananya had fled from India. Once home in London you could have left all of this madness to the next poor fool who stumbled on it.*

No. No, he couldn't. Leaving demanding times for others to face was not a part of who he was.

"Is it far?" Singh asked.

"Hammersmith."

Not far at all.

"I sent one of my men ahead to keep an eye on the place, in case Druitt should happen to leave."

The carriage rocked on for some few minutes before rolling to a halt. Abberline had told the driver to stop up the block from their destination. After descending from the carriage the inspector exhaled an annoyed breath.

"Problem?" Shaw asked.

"He should have been here," Abberline said. "The man I sent here."

Shaw felt a prickling of fear.

"He must be off tailing Druitt."

The three walked up one side of the street, a more conspicuous trio this neighbourhood had never seen. One man in a shabby bowler with a walrus moustache, another needing a cane to move around, and the third a wide-shouldered Indian in a turban. If they were committing a crime any witness would identify them without effort.

Abberline came to a halt two houses away, watching the front door for any activity. The entire street remained silent. With a grunt he started forward again.

"Not much to be done for it." Abberline rang the bell, one hand inside his pocket, expecting trouble. After a minute he rang again.

No answer.

Another grunt and the inspector headed around one side of the house, Shaw and Singh following in his wake, until arriving at the back door. He rapped on it with one knuckle. Still no sign of life inside.

"Not home," Shaw said needlessly while peering through the glass over Abberline's shoulder. Inside it appeared to be an average home though what else could they have expected?

With a shrug Abberline removed his hat and pressed it against the glass pane nearest the door handle. "Desperate times and all that."

He punched his hat, muffling the sound of breaking glass, then reached through to unlock the door. It swung in with ease and silence. Abberline followed it, drawing his gun, shoes crunching against glass shards. Singh's muscles were tensed and ready for attack as they followed the policeman in. The entry was a meagre kitchen with nothing of interest. Smells of fried food and tea hung in the air. One cup sat on the table, half-empty. Abberline felt it with his left hand.

"Cold." He looked toward the doorway leading into the house.

"The idol is not here," Shaw said.

Both Abberline and Singh turned toward him.

"Come now fellows. If it was here I would know it. Probably would have known on the street."

Abberline considered this then lifted his revolver again. "The man is still a criminal, guilty of assault, attempted theft and lord knows what else. Wait here."

Abberline disappeared into the next room while Shaw and Singh searched the kitchen for some evidence to prove Druitt was indeed the man in the butterfly mask. Shaw had trouble reconciling this home with the persona of that masked man. One was common, drab, while the other was cultured, educated.

Singh had opened a wide pantry door when the inspector returned.

"Seems safe enough. Come on."

They made a slower route with the inspector, through a sitting room, dining room and hallway. Not so dissimilar to their own flat of rooms. This house held no sign of Druitt, or his activities as Butterfly, nothing of interest lay hidden in any drawer they opened. A normal house. Abberline headed upstairs and returned in less than five minutes.

"Obvious that Druitt isn't here," Abberline said.

Shaw wondered if this was the correct man at all. "What next?"

They returned to the kitchen where Singh pointed at the wide pantry door.

"The basement?" he said.

"Basement?" Abberline said, already headed for the door.

It looked like every other cabinet in the room but when the inspector pulled it toward him it revealed a dark opening. A basement. Where all the worst situations happened in stories.

Poe's story "The Cask of Amontillado" jumped to Shaw's mind. *For the love of God, Montresor,* the character pleaded as he was bricked up inside a wall.

After a moment of peering down the dark stairs Abberline grabbed an oil lamp from the counter, lit it, and descended, not bothering to suggest the other two wait upstairs. Shaw withdrew his own revolver as they descended.

The stairs themselves were a rougher wood, and the floor at the bottom stone. It was several degrees cooler and an earthy smell filled the air. Abberline continued forward, lamp in one hand, revolver in the other. They passed through an opening into a separate room and came to a stop.

The rich coppery smell of blood filled this area.

"No doubt to his identity now," Abberline said.

Shaw glanced around. "None."

Strange sigils had been carved into the stone floor and surrounding walls. Other marks, added with care, were made in chalk and what could only be blood. At center was a star of sorts, inside a circle of smaller symbols. They made Shaw's head ache with the desire to look anywhere else.

Arranged on one entire wall, separate from the markings, were photographs and sketches. Pictures of Ananya, confident and comfortable in her European fashions. Pictures of several of Ananya's prostitute friends from the lodging house. Richard Willoughby. Each of the missing men whose pictures were in a drawer back at their home. A sketch of the idol from each side. Another of the book, front and back. Lastly they came to a floor plan of a warehouse with all the dimensions marked off.

"The warehouse we've been directed to?" Abberline guessed, pulling the sketch from the wall. "Various entrances have been marked off."

A picture of his father was separate from the other missing men, as if of greater importance than the rest. Druitt wasn't the one who'd kidnapped these people, that much was certain. Why keep pictures if you had the men? The same logic applied to the idol. Why sketch it if you have the actual item?

A map of London was separate from the other pictures. A red circle had been drawn around Whitechapel, another around Limehouse, and a third around the dock area. Handwritten X's dotted the map with the most recognizable being the lodging house where Ananya had been murdered.

"Damn it!" Abberline cursed.

Shaw turned in time to see the inspector disappear through a low opening. Singh was a step behind, glancing back to ensure no danger crept up from behind. Shaw crossed the open room, following the other two into a third area. There a man sat tied to a chair.

Hurry!

It was the dead man from earlier, the burly man. Even without seeing the face Shaw could recognize him from the clothing, and the muscles underneath. It was the fear he'd felt outside become fact.

"Your man?" Shaw asked.

Abberline nodded, teeth gritted.

Tell him I'm sorry. I did my best. A message for Abberline? How was he to deliver that without sounding mad?

Under the chair were markings which matched the ones in the previous room. These were smaller though, and made in chalk rather than carved. Blood seeped through the man's shirt and Abberline reached out, gently opening it.

"Good God!" the inspector muttered, taking a step back.

More markings had been carved into the man's flesh.

Hurry! He's huntin' for it.

Was that what all of this was for? To locate the book?

On the wall beside the dead man was a page with more strange markings, all of which reminded Shaw of those from the book. He averted his eyes. A moment later his focus had slid back, the symbols and markings on it shifted inside his mind, joining in places, resolving into legibility. It was as if the page itself was alive.

"A sacrifice," Shaw said, tracing the page with one hand.

"Sacrifice?" Abberline said. "For what?"

Shaw's head pounded, like an animal inside fought to escape. "I ... think an attempt to locate ... something."

"The book?" Singh suggested. "Or the idol?"

It was impossible to tell. No, he couldn't look any longer. Shaw staggered to one side, sagging against the wall in a wave of dizziness, head pounding. He leaned forward and vomited. Singh moved to his side, giving one arm for support.

"Sacrifice," Shaw repeated.

"Druitt won't return," Abberline said through gritted teeth. "Not now."

Shaw shook his head. No.

"Man like that can't help but watch his handiwork," Abberline added, lifting his gun for emphasis. "He'll be at the warehouse and I'll have him."

AUGUST 30, 1888

Between the efforts of Inspector Abberline and the prince they had commandeered a nearby warehouse with windows facing towards their target. They arrived early, hours before the appointed time, and once inside no one was permitted to leave for fear of being spotted. Of course, no one there had the authority to tell Prince Albert Victor to stay put. Luckily the prince saw it all in the same light.

In addition to Abberline and the prince a dozen men milled about inside of the warehouse, those trusted men the prince had advised on using. Each were chosen with great care and confidence from among the prince's own protection or from Scotland Yard's finest. Shaw wondered if he would have been able to choose someone he could trust with such ease, other than Singh of course. It was a sad state that one of the people he thought of first was Kosminski. True, the man had broken into their home, tricked them and stolen the idol, but on some level Shaw believed the man's actions were born from necessity as much as madness.

"We wait inside until evening?" Shaw asked.

Abberline nodded. "We've more than plenty of sandwiches and tea to keep us going."

Shaw glanced at several of the men who sat at a table playing at cards.

"The men will rotate through shifts at the upper windows," Abberline said, seeing Shaw's attention. "Watching for activity in the other warehouse."

"What if we should need ..." Shaw waved one hand in a vague way which Abberline understood without a need for embellishment.

"There are pails in the far corner. Not pleasant, but functional."

"Ah."

The prince, Eddy, stared toward this other end of the warehouse as if he might need the facilities sooner rather than later. A shrug and the man turned away, taking one of the aforementioned sandwiches as he went. Shaw steeled himself. If a prince of the royal family could relieve himself in a pail then so could he. It might distract him from the ache in his leg caused by the dampness of being so close to the water.

"Tea?" Singh suggested.

"A lovely idea, but let me get it for a change."

He made his way to the table, absorbing the warring scents of various spices stored in the warehouse. It was pleasant though confusing. Each blended with the next until it was impossible to tell where cinnamon ended and nutmeg began.

Standing at the table and waiting for water to boil Shaw realized why Singh always made the tea. Using a cane cut down on how much he was able to carry at any time. Singh was more cognizant of this than he was and appeared at his side, surreptitiously inspecting what sandwiches were available and taking the cup from Shaw.

A sense of hope and optimism filled Shaw. Whatever would happen tonight Druitt considered it important enough to disrupt and had said he believed the book would be here. After seeing his handiwork in Hammersmith it was obvious Druitt was as much a lunatic as Kosminski, though much more dangerous. The man could not be trusted, and yet Shaw did trust this information.

"You have your revolver?" Singh asked.

Shaw patted the pocket of his jacket. "Confirmed it was loaded and ready to use before leaving home."

Abberline made his way over, doing rounds to ensure everyone was keeping any noise to a minimum, and monitoring whoever was on watch duty to confirm they were being vigilant.

"You still believe Druitt doesn't have your idol?"

Shaw wanted to object at the idol being characterized as *his*, but let it go. "No. Kosminski has it, I am sure of it."

Abberline grunted.

"I didn't get a sense of the idol at Druitt's house. I could be wrong, but ..."

"No." Abberline held one hand up. "When it comes to that idol I trust your judgement. What the devil was that business with my man at his house though?"

"A sacrifice, that much is certain."

Shaw had tried to study the ritual on that paper more, but the harder he tried the more it pushed him away. In the end the world had gone grey as he came close to passing out. Abberline called an end to his attempts at that point.

Druitt had enough in his basement to prove he was no mere dabbler in all of this. The extent of what he knew compared to what he thought he understood was impossible to say though. Whatever the case he had left in a hurry, leaving valuable items behind.

"I will have Druitt," Abberline said. "One way or another."

The inspector had been in a foul mood since losing his man days earlier. Abberline may be rough around the edges and not have the best outlook toward some people, but he was a loyal friend. When misfortune happened to a person in his charge or under his protection it was taken personally.

Would Druitt be in the warehouse though? Yes, he would want to see the effect his sabotage had. How close would he come? He had given the information knowing full well that Shaw would get Abberline and the police involved. Not for the first time Shaw wondered if this might be a decoy, or a trap. To what end? Shaw no longer held anything which Druitt wanted.

What if *they* were the distraction though? Could Druitt be hoping that the police would cause enough trouble inside the warehouse that he could perform some action? Like stealing the book for himself?

Yes, that was possible. Quite possible.

The initial thrill of the operation wore thin after hours of waiting. A person could only eat so many sandwiches, drink so many cups of tea, and Shaw had no interest in playing cards.

He made his way upstairs to look out the window. More for some change of scenery than to monitor outside activity. The sun was low, leaving grasping shadows thrown across the area. No lamps would be left burning at the docks for fear of fire. Once the sun was set the only light would be from personal lanterns.

Across the way and up the passage was the warehouse, its appearance much like every other one around it. Insignificant differences set them apart from each other. The one they watched was enormous, about a hundred and fifty yards in length, and half that wide. One man-sized door was set in the shorted wall facing toward them, and another in the long wall which faced the street.

"A wide sliding door on the side facing toward the water which can't be seen from here," Abberline said from beside him. "And another man door on the upper level."

"Upper level?" Shaw had seen the sketch but hadn't committed it to memory.

"If anything like this one it leads to an upper landing for storage."

"Movement outside, Inspector," the man at the window said.

Abberline moved forward and took one set of binoculars on the window's ledge. Shaw grabbed another. Outside a group of twelve men moved with purpose, heading for the door in the side of the warehouse at a brisk pace. Each of them wore black clothing and a mask, much as Butterfly ... Druitt ... had worn when he'd attacked them in their home.

"Now we have them!" Abberline said, withdrawing his gun and ready to give chase.

"Inspector, wait," Shaw said. "These men haven't done any illegal acts yet. One of them may well own that warehouse."

Abberline lowered the revolver to his side, staring back at Shaw.

"Besides," the prince said, coming up beside them both. "We will need to know the book is inside before we attack, no?"

"Yes, exactly." Shaw was grateful for the calming influence of the prince. He was the one person Abberline wouldn't tell off.

"Yes, yes, yes," Abberline said, replacing his gun back into his pocket and watching the men disappearing through the warehouse door. He pulled from his other pocket the sketch of the warehouse, taken from Druitt's home, and placed it on the nearest table, pointing to the outside stairs and upper door he'd mentioned earlier. "If we mean to see whether that book is inside I will need to get in to observe."

"*We* will," Singh said.

Abberline looked at the Indian lad then to Shaw.

"I am coming as well," Shaw said.

"No, you bloody well are not."

"Abberline, you know I need to be there," Shaw said. "To take that book."

"And you can do that after the danger is finished."

"Damn it, Inspector. This isn't the time to dig in your heels."

The man crossed his arms and glared at Shaw.

"I know this book better than anyone else here."

Abberline conceded that point.

"I need to be on hand to take that book. We can't chance it getting away. I *am* coming."

Abberline looked past them and Shaw followed his gaze to the prince.

"I agree with them, Inspector."

Abberline rolled his eyes and threw up his hands in surrender. "Just so long as you're not planning to come too."

"We are wasting time," Singh said, turning for the door. "After you, Doctor."

Abberline wore an expression of annoyance and spun back toward the room. "You men be ready. I'll blow the whistle when it's time."

He followed Shaw and Singh out the door. Dressed in black, as everyone was, the three blended into the shadows and made their way along the path. Two-story warehouses lined either side, like a city's version of canyon walls. It took a few minutes to get around to the stairs and climb them in silence. By the time they reached the top Shaw's leg was once again screaming at him. *Focus past the pain,* he told himself. A lesson from Singh.

"Oh, no," Shaw whispered.

A thick padlock rested in place, holding the upper door secure. Panic gripped Shaw for a moment before Abberline pulled out a short iron bar from his coat. The inspector had considered this potential problem and came prepared. Placing the bar through the hasp he pulled, snapping the lock in two and catching each piece before it could hit the stairs. He pulled the door toward him then stepped into the darkness beyond.

Only, it wasn't all that dark once their eyes adjusted. Ambient light spilled onto the upper section from below, creating flickering shadows. The smell of alcohol filled the warehouse with an intoxicating aroma. The three moved with all the care and silence they could muster, keeping to the shadows until reaching the overhang. There they were able to see much of the picture below, in better detail than those they spied on could see though many lanterns hung from support posts.

The Hellfire Club, an even dozen men in expensive black top hats, overcoats, and decorated porcelain masks, stood in a group not far from where they'd entered. Some looked to either side, as if someone should have been there to meet them. Their leader, standing at the front of their procession, was the only man in a featureless mask of purest white. He stared straight ahead, continuing deeper into the warehouse.

At just about center, in a wide clearing among the crates, was a table, one end resting on a low box to give it an incline. Fastened to this table was a man, tied at wrists and ankles. His mouth was gagged, the eyes were wild, unfocused. The man's hair was mussed and his glasses were missing but he was still recognizable.

"The vicar," Shaw whispered.

Abberline nodded. "So the Hellfire Club *is* behind all this."

The men in masks stood, casting glances in each direction. Shaw was sure from his stance that one of them was Richard Willoughby. Abberline had drawn his revolver and looked left and right for the stairs.

"The book," Shaw whispered.

Abberline gritted his teeth and jerked his head toward the man on the table. "I won't allow harm to come to that man."

Shaw withdrew his own weapon. "Understood. Can you get a clear shot from here?"

Abberline gauged the distance and gave one quick nod.

"Let's wait a little while longer."

"For the book to appear?"

"Yes."

"And if it doesn't come?"

"It has to."

A noise from below and the wide sliding door opened. The Hellfire Club turned as one toward the sound. From the opening another dozen men entered. These were all dressed in the slickers and caps of sailors. Not the sort that had accosted them in Limehouse two years earlier, but those who had grudgingly given directions from behind obscured features. These had the facial features of that man from the cell in Bedlam, the one who'd been calling for Father Dagon. Each was deformed, fishlike, and displaying these features proudly. Grotesque mutations ... but what could be the cause?

"Fish men." The Hellfire Club's leader stepped forward, his

plain mask glinting in the light from a nearby lantern. At his side stood the presumed Willoughby next to another man. "What are you doing here?"

"You call us here?" one sailor demanded. "Pretty boys playin' dress up."

"If this is a trap," the man in the white mask said, "you will regret it."

"Ia!" the sailor spat. "Now you threaten us?"

The sailors pulled handles ending in wicked, rusty hooks from concealment, brandishing them. Others pulled curved knives with etchings on the blade, and an eye on the handle. The Hellfire Club each started to reach inside of their coats for whatever concealed weapons they held.

"What are you doing here?" a voice called from their right. "You're all trespassing."

"No," Shaw whispered, leaning forward to get a better view. "It can't be!"

"Who is it?" Singh asked.

A man emerged from the shadows and into the clearing, creating a triangle between himself, the Hellfire Club, and the fishlike sailors.

"Your father?" Abberline said. "But ..."

Shaw well understood the inspector's confusion.

"Speak up," his father demanded of the two groups. "What are you doing here?"

The Hellfire Club leader turned his attention toward this new target, looking the man up and down, dismissing him with a sniff as below his own station. With disdain in his voice he spoke. "If you must know we received an anonymous letter suggesting we come here."

"Ia! Us as well," the lead sailor said, scowling at Shaw's father.

"You come to my warehouse after nightfall, just like that? From receiving a letter?"

Both groups hesitated, neither wishing to be the first to give information. White Mask cocked his head to one side and spoke first.

"The letter told us we would find answers here."

"Answers, letters," Shaw's father spat. "You're not making sense."

"Answer about a certain book's location," the lead sailor said.

His father took one step back, eyes narrowing. "Well, I did not invite you and don't know who did. You can get the hell out now."

White Mask came a step closer to the elder Shaw. "Can we? If we left, why shouldn't we let the police know about this missing man?"

He gestured toward the inclined table. The man on it cast his glance in every direction, not appearing able to focus on any one individual.

"Now, now," Shaw's father chuckled, somewhat forced. "Let's not be too hasty here."

"Indeed, let us not," another voice said, from the direction Shaw's father had appeared. "We all have similar interests."

Shaw gripped his revolver tighter, ready to fire at the owner of that voice, ready to command Abberline do the same.

"Ananya," he whispered.

She stood, inside the light cast by the nearest lantern, an Indian princess dressed in English clothes. From her stance and the expression on her face she was still every bit the royal princess. A woman stood to either side of her. The one on her right was Mary Ann "Polly" Nichols whom they'd met at the lodging house.

"Impossible!" Abberline said. "She was dead. I may not be a doctor but I can tell when a body has no pulse, no heartbeat. Can this book bring life back to the dead?"

"The book," Singh said, "takes, it does not give."

"Which means the dead woman was not Ananya," Shaw added.

"We are all one people," Ananya said, voice rising to the rafters. "The people of the elder gods."

Shaw gritted his teeth, right hand clenched into a tight fist that he bounced against his leg. Of course she wasn't dead. The body had been a decoy, some other poor soul beaten to death to throw the wolves off her trail.

What has she been doing these past two years?

"She was Indian," Abberline said, "and she'd been beaten to death. If I'd known her I would have still found her difficult to identify."

"Yet Miss Nichols did so with ease," Singh said.

"She was so certain, but couldn't have been," Abberline said. "Why didn't I see that?"

"She was a dead Indian woman," Singh said without any hint of irony. "Not someone important."

Abberline opened his mouth with a retort, then shut it and looked toward the people talking below. He took a deep breath. "This is no longer the case of a murdered cultist, but a murdered innocent."

It didn't seem prudent to point out that, as far as Abberline or the police were aware, this was always the case of a murdered innocent ... or was until that night at the museum when he heard Ananya's true story.

"Yes! People of the book! You devotees of the elder gods!" Ananya said, and looked away upward. "Unlike those spying on us."

All three wore matching shocked reactions. Had one of them made a noise? How—?

"Come out, Doctor Shaw."

So not a stray noise, then. She *knew*. With a setting of his jaw Shaw stepped into the ambient light of the lamps below.

"And the others."

Singh stepped forward as well, then Abberline on Shaw's other side. He held his revolver in one hand and the whistle in the other. Shaw placed one hand over Abberline's, giving the message of *don't blow that whistle just yet.*

Shaw shifted his focus from Ananya. "You are aiding evil, Father."

The older man scoffed. "This is business, Son. Princess Ananya required a place to hide, where she could make her preparations. She needed resources and paid handsomely for them."

"Resources? Like these men?" Shaw gestured at the unfortunate soul who cowered on the table.

"That was always your problem, Archibald. Can't see the forest for the trees." He shrugged, glancing at the Hellfire Club. "These men understand. It's about the profit."

Several of the masked men nodded, but not White Mask or Willoughby.

"Where will you spend your profit when the world is in flames?"

"So melodramatic. Ananya assures me I shall be looked after once all is said and done."

"And Emily? She waits for word on whether her husband is dead or simply disappeared."

He chuckled. "I am neither. I merely stopped returning home. More important things to occupy my time."

"You played me for a sap." Abberline pointed at Ananya, then to Nichols. "You and your friend."

"We did."

Through gritted teeth. "Who died in your place?"

"An unfit follower. No one who will be missed." She moved closer to the center of those gathered. "We are at a slight impasse here. We cannot go up there without being shot, and you cannot come down for fear of a similar fate."

Abberline raised the whistle to his lips.

"I wouldn't do that, Inspector Abberline." She gestured toward the man on the table and the unknown woman rushed over, withdrawing a curved knife to place against the man's throat. "Not unless you want his death on your conscience."

Ananya waited, staring upward. Abberline looked as if he were gauging the distance once again, deciding if he could shoot the woman without hitting the person he wanted to save. The hand holding the whistle dropped back to his side.

"Unfit," Ananya repeated, turning back toward those assembled, as if those above were inconsequential now. "I praise the followers of Dagon for removing those less than pure from their ranks."

The men Kosminski said were disappearing from the streets of Limehouse.

"And you." She turned to White Mask. "For removing incompetents within your organization."

"Sticks and stones," a voice said, coming from over to the right, near where Ananya had first appeared. "I am not incompetent. I merely needed a chance."

Druitt. His revolver pointed toward those in the room.

Abberline gripped his gun, ready to shoot though he would need to circle the landing to be in a better position. He held off, prepared to see if those below would resolve that problem first.

"You had ample chance," the man to White Mask's side said, definitely Richard Willoughby. "When you heard of the book you attempted to go it alone rather than bring the information to the club. You are not fit to wear that mask."

"Oh, I see." Ananya focused on Druitt. "You called all of these people here."

"I did."

"Shaw and friends as well?"

A quick nod. "I received the time and location from Martha Tabram, seeing this possibility in an instant."

"Martha Tabram," Ananya said, as if the name left a sour taste. "I suppose you were also the instrument of her death."

Druitt shrugged. "The less people knowing a secret, the more value to that secret."

Druitt had killed her! Relief flooded Shaw. Up to now he still half believed it had been his doing but he'd merely been a witness to her final minutes. Another trick from the idol?

"To what end?" Ananya asked. "Why call these people here?"

"In truth I had hopes of taking the book while everyone was distracted."

"Ambitious. There may be a place among my group for you after all."

"Thank you, no. As I explained when we first met, I am not interested in being a follower."

"Unfortunate."

"Where is the book?" Druitt's revolver was pointed directly at Ananya.

She didn't give the impression of worry. "It is here, in this warehouse. Would you like to see it?"

"Yes." Druitt's voice came out low and far away. Several of those in the other groups echoed their own agreement.

Ananya gestured with one straight finger, drawing a strange shape in the air which remained on the eyes afterwards. Then the book was in her hands, as if it always had been. The room was dumbstruck except for her own followers.

The Hellfire Club and the sailors both sighed in ecstasy of the book's presence.

"Two years in hiding," she said. "Raising my group of followers from the women of Whitechapel, so tired of abuse. Two years of taking whatever men I could to read the book. I had come to realize how little I knew before then. One of those men read the spell which brought forth the night gaunt."

Shaw shuddered at the memory.

"Only one was called forward, and luckier still it followed directions. It was a creature of dreams and shadows and soon returned there."

"After it killed Director Kinkaid," Shaw said.

"Kinkaid. Yes. He refused to join us."

The same simple reason Lassiter and Middlemarch had been

murdered. Ananya may have realized this god was not Kali, but she still clung to their basic thoughts.

Nothing changed.

"We were unable to summon another," she said.

"Good!" Abberline said, one hand slapping the rail in front of him.

"For the best perhaps." Ananya shrugged. "Two years of experimenting, of discovering which pages were the history of our gods and safe to read, and which pages call up creatures that may or may not do my bidding. I discovered more about the cosmic cycle. How planets so far out of our knowledge and ability to see had to align. Now I know which pages will summon our elder gods, and when to read them."

"But you do not know which page summons which god," Singh said.

Ananya's eyes narrowed on the lad and she glared at him for several moments before giving a low throaty chuckle. "A detail. Once that is resolved I only need one strong enough to read."

Ananya placed one hand on the shoulder of Shaw's father who grinned up at him.

"You're insane," Shaw said. "Both of you."

"Not at all, Son. The princess told me how you resisted. The way I see it I am a superior specimen of manhood than you, both physically and mentally. I will survive just fine. In two months—"

"I believe that is enough information for your son."

"Ah, quite right." He gave a sheepish grin.

"Indeed it is," White Mask said. "It is enough information for us as well."

Ananya's attention was drawn back to the Hellfire Club and the Dagon worshippers. She stood her ground, staring all the men down, book grasped with both hands. White Mask gestured and three of his men started forward, each having only their mask to differentiate them. Not to be left behind the lead sailor also gestured and three on that side did the same. Druitt stood still, sparing the occasional glance behind but content to watch what unfolded. His gaze returned to the book over and over, while his gun faced out and away from him. Would even a cad such as Druitt do the unthinkable and shoot a woman in the back ... with a woman such as Ananya was it truly so unthinkable?

Each group of three approaching men kept their eyes more on each other than any of the three women. Ananya's follower at the table rushed away from the bound man and flashed out with her knife toward a Hellfire Club member with a red heart on his mask. It took him across the throat and dropped him like a cow, his blood flowing across the floor. She had already spun and slashed across one sailor's abdomen, sending him staggering back, holding his stomach. The knife was wickedly sharp, reminding Shaw of those he'd seen back in India. Three of those remaining stopped, uncertain of this wild woman. The fourth refused to be intimidated and lost three fingers in reaching for her.

"Hey!" White Mask said, as if rules had been broken.

Others started forward from the two groups, while six other women came from the shadows on all sides of those gathered. Each held a similar knife in her hand and a dead look in her eyes. One sailor rushed forward, swiping out with his hook. In less than a second he was face down, blood pooling from his slit throat.

The leaders on both sides gestured for their followers to retreat, bringing them all back together for a regrouping and replanning. White Mask and Willoughby both reached inside their coats.

"Well done," Druitt said. "I suspect your ladies will have more trouble with this." He waved the gun, being careful to keep his back to a crate so none could sneak up on him.

White Mask withdrew his own gun but gestured for Willoughby to wait. Ananya turned back toward Druitt, book in her arms like a lover, an unsettling grin on her face.

"Hand over the book," Druitt said, raising the gun and aiming at Ananya.

"I think not."

He cocked the gun.

"Don't you think there are more of my women in the shadows? One coming up on you right now."

"Perhaps." Druitt raised his voice. "The blonde on the left."

A shot rang out and one woman fell, a perfect circle in her forehead. The remaining jumped and glanced around before disappearing back into the shadows.

"Move you fool," Druitt yelled to his unseen partner. "They're coming for you."

"Or for you," Ananya said.

"I doubt that. None will attack me when I could put a bullet in their leader with such ease."

"Hmm," Ananya stepped forward, opening the book. It glowed a sickly green, then a pale purple. She advanced on the man.

Without hesitation Druitt squeezed the trigger, aiming for Ananya's midsection, just above the book. She came to a stop, as did everyone within the warehouse. The silence surrounding them helped all hear the bullet, crumpled flat, fall to the ground.

"Impossible!" Druitt brought the gun higher, aiming at her head.

Another shot, and another, and a third. All bullets falling to the ground at Ananya's feet.

"Do you think the book will allow me to come to harm? It serves me!"

Druitt took another step back, uncertain. He spun and grabbed the nearest lantern. "Fine, burn then!"

He threw it at Ananya who didn't halt her advance or so much as flinch. Steps away from her the lantern exploded, raining fire in every direction except toward her.

"Idiot!" the elder Shaw hissed, stepping toward Druitt. "Do you realize what is in these crates? Gin and brandy. Highly flammable."

"I did *not* realize," Druitt admitted, "but that fits my current plan."

Druitt jerked the gun to one side and fired, catching Shaw's father in the stomach with a bullet. The man went down like a sack of flour. Druitt then shot his remaining two bullets into the nearest crates, sending alcohol spraying from within. Rushing to the next post he grabbed two lanterns, pivoted and launched them toward the damaged crates. The lanterns shattered, coating their targets in flames which rapidly jumped to their neighbours.

Abberline tried a shot at Druitt before the man could disappear into the shadows he'd come from. The bullet missed. "Damn it!"

Now the inspector blew his whistle. One shrill blast after another on it while the fire below spread like fog.

Below, the prostitutes came to Ananya, providing a wall of protection and hustling their leader out the far side. The two groups, seeing the book getting away, rushed forward and were met by four women with their sharp blades.

From there it descended into madness.

The police burst in through the same door where the Hellfire Club had entered. They took in the situation and started swiping about with their truncheons, their own revolvers in their free hands.

The sweetish smell of burning alcohol drifted up to them.

"Get that man off the table," Abberline ordered, "then get the hell out of here." He turned away from the opening and toward Shaw and Singh. "Come on, we are leaving too."

"The book!" Shaw hissed.

"It's not down there anymore. If we're lucky we can catch them coming out the back."

Shaw could see the inspector didn't believe that at all. It was a convenient excuse to hurry them from the burning warehouse. Shaw headed for the door, Singh a step behind him. At the top of the stairs he cast a look about for Ananya but saw no movement.

She was gone. Again.

"So close," he said. "So damn close."

AUGUST 30, 1888

The steamers arrived at a few minutes past nine, with more called for from all corners of London. The firemen worked to gain entry and allow the boats a chance to pump their water inside. Great tongues of flame, bluish and yellow, reached toward the sky, lighting the dock like noon. Not until eleven o'clock was the fire brought under some semblance of control, and the flames were diminished.

"We won't be sure who managed to escape and who perished," Abberline stood with Shaw, Singh and the prince, among a great group of onlookers gathered to watch the spectacle. "Not until the fire is completely out."

"The man on the table?" Shaw asked.

"Yes, one of our men freed him. Out of his head. Whatever they'd been planning with him they'd already done it."

Ananya had made it out of the warehouse, that much was certain, and her minions with her. In all probability Druitt and his man had escaped too. Met with the choice of chasing the Hellfire Club and sailors or stopping the blaze from spreading, the police officers had chosen the latter and summoned the fire brigade. If there had been any hesitation it hadn't been obvious. Those who had escaped had gotten away free and clear.

"Your father mentioned two months," Singh added.

"Yes."

Two months until what? There had to be an assumption of the worst possible circumstance. Ananya had insinuated his father was to read the book. Would the planets, this cosmic cycle Ananya mentioned, be aligned at that time?

How did one fight on such a level? It was an ant trying to thwart the plans of a human. No, an ant at least could hope to disturb a picnic, and a swarm could devour something much greater than itself. This was more akin to an ant wishing to reach the moon.

Impossible.

All they could hope for was to find Ananya and destroy the book.

"Two months to track her down then," Shaw said. He turned to Abberline. "My father's properties?"

"You are thinking they have a second place to hide."

Shaw shrugged. He had no idea if all of his father's properties were even documented.

"I shall investigate," Abberline said.

The four men stood, staring at each other. This night was to be their great victory; instead, they were lower than before. Ananya knew they searched for her and would be even more careful.

"I believe it is time to return you two home," the prince suggested.

Shaw glanced at the carnage and destruction that had taken hold of the docks. He realized the prince would have felt powerless here, a sensation he was unaccustomed to. This was beyond the ability of a single prince. Fire neither bowed nor served.

The ride home was a quiet one. None of the men inside were interested in conversation. Shaw was tired and sore, a weariness which reached deep into his soul, yet he didn't have any desire to sleep.

Shaw followed Singh through the door to their rooms and

into the sitting room. He made his way across to the couch and allowed himself to slump into it.

"Some tea, Doctor?"

"No, thank you, Singh. I believe I need some time alone."

"Doctor?" Singh hesitated.

"You go on to bed, my boy. I need some time to think."

"I understand. Good night."

"Good night, Singh."

He tried to clear his mind the way Singh had taught him but it was no use. Too many thoughts whirling around. He'd gone to the warehouse in hopes of ending this; instead, he had seen and lost the book. He still didn't have the idol. His father had been involved, and much deeper than he ever would have thought possible. The evil of greed and indifference.

Ananya was alive.

Somehow that last piece was the worst. His mind would go to other topics but always return. He'd assumed there'd been another unknown person holding the book, but now he found it had been Ananya all along. And she'd had the time to study the book and learn.

Did she truly know the correct page to read?

Had his father escaped the warehouse as well, or died in the flames? Or from the gunshot wound? If dead Ananya would be searching for another to read the book. Could they use him as bait in that case?

Two months.

It took several minutes to acknowledge the smell of smoke and burned meat.

Shaw turned to find his father standing a few paces from the couch. The man's clothing had been burned, and the wound in his stomach seeped blood. Shaw's first reaction was to jump up, ready to treat this unexpected patient. Then he realized his father was far beyond any help.

"You were always a disappointment," his father said.

No preamble this time. This spirit had no doubt or confusion on where he was, or whom he was in front of. No difficulty in speaking. His father moved closer, one ethereal hand drifting through the chair unnoticed.

Was this his father's unfinished business? One final harangue for a son he'd always regretted.

"You should have kept your nose out of it. I warned you when you came to see me."

Shaw shrugged, willing the spirit to be done its business and be on its way.

"Your interference got me killed."

"Your greed got you killed."

The dead man harumphed. "I was embarrassed, ashamed, when Ananya told me you couldn't see the potential of allying yourself with her. Typical."

"Yes? Did your partner pull you from the fire? Or leave you to die?"

"Bah! Business."

Even in death they couldn't agree.

"Is that all you came to say, father?" Shaw crossed the room, heading toward his bed. "Go to your rest, and I will go to mine. I'm tired."

Shaw had almost reached the hallway. He turned back. "Where has she gone? Where is she hiding now?"

A dry chuckle raised the hairs on Shaw's neck. "You've only foiled her plans for the moment. Do you truly think you can stop Cthulhu from returning?"

Shaw stepped back at the name, teeth gritted.

"You won't find her. She is beyond you."

His father had lost some of his solidity. Shaw could see through him now, like a painting on glass.

"The princess has her ladies to help carry out the plan."

Her ladies. Like Polly Nichols.

"You were always a disappointment," his father repeated as he faded.

Shaw was alone again.

Alone, except for the ghost of an idea. Something his father had said twigged it in his mind and Shaw considered this as he headed for his bedroom.

In all likelihood Ananya was too well hidden, beyond their grasp. But ... what if he could find Nichols instead?

PART THREE

WHITECHAPEL

THE LONDON EVENING NEWS
No. 243
London, Friday, August 31, 1888
Price one penny

In which Shaw slides further into madness

AUGUST 31, 1888

S haw stood in the wan dimness of a dirty street. The windows around him were all shadowed, their inhabitants asleep. Shaw reached for his pocket watch to see just how late the hour was.

He stopped.

Once again he was covered in blood. A knife like those of Ananya's women was gripped in his right fist, knuckles turning white.

Where was he?

Whitechapel? Yes, it must be.

Dreaming. Again.

He moved forward, the stickiness of the blood on his hands, soaking through his clothing to lay against his skin. The coppery scent of it stayed in his nostrils. His leg screeched at him and he wasn't able to move a step before needing to lean against the nearest wall.

At least he held his cane.

Why was he dreaming this again?

The last he remembered ... Yes, he'd seen his father, and gone to bed thinking of how he needed to find Polly Nichols. Was this what he dreamt of now?

He searched for any avenue of escape from this nightmare. Why couldn't he wake up?

With a sigh he shifted weight to lean more against the wall. Setting the cane against his leg he reached into his inner pocket, thinking once again of seeing the time. Instead a heavy weight pulled down on his outer pocket, demanding attention. He reached inside and grasped what was there, pulling the chunky shape out to see.

"Noooooo."

The idol stared back at him, the ugly squat figure of Cthulhu hunkered on its pedestal. The script around the edge of that block wormed into his mind, resolving into comprehensible script.

In his house at R'lyeh dead Cthulhu waits dreaming.

He wanted to drop the damned thing, to throw it away, but his fingers refused to work.

"No," he whispered, the sound of a man who was losing his soul.

No, he was finally free of it. Why should it continue to haunt his nightmares?

"Doctor Shaw!" He spun to see Kosminski rushing toward him. "Found you, finally!"

"I want to wake up."

Kosminski shook his head. "You are not sleeping, Doctor."

A sob caught in Shaw's throat. He would have stepped back but that simple act would have spilled him into the street.

It wasn't true. It couldn't be true.

He felt …

He …

He … he … felt as he did after sleepwalking, not as he did while dreaming.

It *was* true.

"Come, let's go where you can rest."

Rest. Rest. Rest. Was there any hope for such a goal? Still, he allowed Kosminski to slide one arm below his left and take the weight as they started forward. The man's rank body odor was barely noticed.

"Time?"

"Almost four. It will be light soon and you need to be off the street before then."

If Kosminski had any question about why he was covered in blood, why he was carrying the curved knife, or indeed, why he was even in Whitechapel, the man didn't voice them.

"The idol," Shaw said.

"You have it?"

"Yes, but why?"

Kosminski didn't answer, continuing to guide Shaw forward. Another block. Around a corner.

"I can't." Shaw stopped.

"You can. You must." Kosminski gestured with a jut of his chin. "A few more doors."

Shaw looked at where the man had gestured and forced himself on. In truth, Kosminski did most of the work.

"You said, 'Found me, finally.' How did you know I was here?"

"Knew you were here? You came to Whitechapel with me a few hours ago."

"I ...?" He found no recollection of any memory after lying in his bed. "I ..."

"We are here."

Kosminski opened a door and helped Shaw inside. The stairs almost forced him to surrender. He could lie on these steps and sleep as easily as in any bed. His guide forced him forward, helping with each step which felt like a full journey of its own. At the top he was surprised to find they had arrived.

Inside was a cramped one room flat not so different from those of the shabby lodging house where Ananya had died. No.

"Ananya is alive."

Kosminski helped Shaw across the room and into the one chair. One of each in the room. One chair. One bed. One tiny table, scuffed and scratched. The violin on that table was out of place, a relic and well cared for. Shaw wanted to ask about it but didn't have the energy for it. He sagged in the chair.

The smell of this flat slapped Shaw, like Kosminski's own odor but amplified, multiplied.

For a moment Kosminski left his side and returned with a basin of water and a cloth. He began the process of helping Shaw from his bloody, ruined clothing, taking the knife still clenched in his fist and placing it beside the basin.

It was one of the blades Ananya's ladies carried.

"I came here with you?"

"Yes."

"Why?"

"I came to your rooms last night and watched for the lights to be dimmed, when I knew Singh would be asleep, to enter."

"You ... you broke in again?"

"Yes." Kosminski removed Shaw's shirt and wiped the remaining blood from his arms. He rinsed the cloth in the basin again. "I heard of the warehouse fire and knew what had happened."

"You ... knew?"

Kosminski nodded. He gestured at the pocket of Shaw's coat, now waiting to one side, a ruined bloody mess. The meaning was clear.

"The idol told you?"

Kosminski grinned wide, revealing his uneven, yellowed teeth.

"Why would I leave with you? Without Singh? Why don't I remember any of this?"

Another glance toward the idol. Shaw had never seen Kosminski so ill at ease.

"You brought the idol with you, to my home."

"Yes."

"Why?"

A shrug. The idea had not been Kosminski's. "You were insistent that we leave and come to Whitechapel. Insistent that we find Polly Nichols."

"Nichols?"

Yes. That part he remembered. It was on his mind as he fell asleep last night. Find Polly Nichols and they would find Ananya.

"I left you here and went searching for her as you demanded."

Shaw remembered none of this ... though, this room was familiar wasn't it? Familiar in the way only a place one had visited could be.

"While I was away you left with the idol. You didn't get that knife here though."

Another glance at the knife and the basin full of red water. Blood. So much blood. Whose was it though?

"Do you remember anything, Shaw?"

A quick memory of sliding the idol into his coat pocket.

"No ... No, I ..."

Making his way down the stairs.

"No ..."

Stalking through Whitechapel, peering into the windows of taverns.

Then nothing from there.

Shaw's eyes drooped and Kosminski helped him across to the bed.

"I need to get home."

"Sleep. Time for that later."

Shaw wanted to protest, to insist Kosminski take him home but once his head hit the mattress any thought of resistance was banished.

And he dreamt.

Dreams of Polly Nichols occupied his sleep, searching for her, finding her, questioning her. The dreams turned blood red, as if looking through a tinted bottle at the scenes. She drew her knife, and Shaw lashed out with his cane, disarming her. He took the knife then, holding it gripped in his fist. It flashed upward, then the scene changed to him on the street, wandering until Kosminski found him.

Then it all restarted.

Again and again and again.

Some variations inserted themselves into the dream. At times he would be at the warehouse, looking down at each of Ananya's acolytes, committing each face to his memory.

Then the scene would shift once again, bringing him face to face with Polly Nichols.

"I knows ya," she said with a mocking laugh, as if there were no threat from Shaw finding her.

"Where is she?"

"Miss Ananya? Oh, you'll be seein' her right soon enough."

And again the blood red curtain would fall.

September 3, 1888

Shaw's eyes fluttered open. He tried to rasp out a word.

Kosminski appeared at his side with water. Shaw sipped at it, appreciating the moisture as it coated his throat, then he sucked at it greedily until the glass was empty. He could care less on the drinking vessel's lack of cleanliness, cared even less at the quality of the water or where it had come from.

Finished, he sagged back against the mattress, one arm up to cover his eyes. His forehead against the inside of his arm was hot, feverish.

"Two days," Kosminski said, answering the unspoken question.

"Two ..."

"You dreamt of blood and knives, didn't you?"

Shaw dropped the arm.

"Oh, you yelled and raved. Had whole conversations even."

"I have to get home." Shaw struggled to roll to one side and get his feet under him, get upright. No such luck.

Kosminski made no move to help Shaw or move aside. "Are you sure you want to involve Singh in all this?"

Shaw stopped in his efforts, looking toward his caretaker.

Kosminski turned and lifted a newspaper from the table. He held it up for Shaw to read the headline.

GHASTLY MURDER IN THE EAST END!
Dreadful mutilation of a woman!

It was dated September 1st. Two days ago now?

Shaw didn't want to read any further than he had.

"Think about what needs to be done, Doctor," Kosminski said. "You want Singh involved in that?"

"What needs to be done?"

"We made a deal."

"Yes, yes. You find the page and I read it. I remember, damn it."

"When I came to you in your rooms you were raving about finding Polly Nichols. Saying we needed to find her to know where Ananya is, and we need to find the princess to get the book."

Shaw said nothing.

"I'd say you found Polly Nichols." Kosminski tossed the paper back onto the table. "You were covered in her blood."

"No." It came out as a whisper. A shake of his head. "No."

Miss Ananya? Oh, you'll be seein' her right soon enough.

Polly Nichols hadn't died by accident. She hadn't fallen down the stairs during a struggle or staggered in front of a carriage to get away. Her throat had been cut—

"No!"

He couldn't have committed such a heinous act.

Shaw looked away. His clothes from that night lay in a pile to one corner, the evidence of blood plain on the ruined fabric. Why hadn't Kosminski disposed of them? As a reminder? As proof for Shaw when he denied the possibility? Shaw looked away from this as well.

"Where is the princess?" Kosminski asked.

"I don't know."

"No. No, of course not. If you knew you wouldn't have returned here. Who do we find next?"

"Annie Chapman."

"Yes." Kosminski's head bobbed like a child's toy.

Shaw had said the name without hesitation. He'd known. How? Miss Mary Ann "Polly" Nichols had told him.

Shaw sank back against the mattress again, any vigor he'd accumulated in sleep had been spent. His brain pounded inside of his skull, fit to burst the sides and escape. Dizziness swelled around him like a cocoon. A fever raged inside his brain.

He forced his eyes to remain open. "No," he mumbled. "Not a fever."

There! Beside the bed, on a nightstand, was the damned thing, no longer in his pocket. The idol. He reached one hand toward it, wanting to bat it onto the floor but lacking both strength and coordination. Through sheer luck his flailing hand connected, knocking it onto one side.

Kosminski reached for it with a grimace and held it toward Shaw.

"No!"

With a shrug the other man placed it back onto the nightstand, where the idol stared at Shaw, keeping watch over him like a malevolent master.

"I was free," he said with a weak sob. "Free."

"No. Never free."

A sudden thought sprang to mind and Shaw forced his head back up, scanning the room. No. She wasn't here. He collapsed back again.

"You were looking for Polly Nichols?"

"Yes! Where is she?"

Kosminski opened his mouth to reply but Shaw's eyes were already closing as sleep reclaimed him.

When he awoke next his head felt less feverish though no more clear. Kosminski was there with some broth to drink from a cup. Chicken, salt and spices filled Shaw's nostrils in a heavenly cloud and he tried to remember the last time he'd had any nourishment.

It wasn't the only question he wondered about.

"Why was I seeing dead people?"

Kosminski glanced at the idol then back.

"Yes, yes," Shaw rasped between sips of broth. "I understand that! Why was I *still* seeing them after you took it?"

"Never free," Kosminski said, echoing what he'd said before Shaw fell asleep. "No. No. Never free."

Shaw stared at the man, waiting.

"You touched evil, lived with it. Some part of that evil will always be with you."

"No."

"Oh, yes. Yes, yes, yes."

"Al ... always?"

The man nodded.

"Like your music?"

Kosminski started, listened to sounds only he could hear, then nodded again.

Shaw felt a great sympathy for the man. If Kosminski had not been driven out of his mind from reading the book he would surely have been from the effects afterward. How long until he was as unbalanced as Kosminski?

"Why don't I see Nichols's ghost?"

Kosminski shook his head, brows knitted. "Perhaps ghosts are only innocents taken too soon."

Shaw only considered that a moment before seeing the flaw. "I saw my father and he was no innocent."

"Hmm, yes. Yes. Those with unfinished business then? Did your father have a message?"

You were always a disappointment.

"He did."

Kosminski refilled the cup and helped him drink more broth.

This soup was the single most delicious meal he'd had in recent memory, rich and salty. His stomach rumbled with a desire for more.

Since the last time he'd woken his strength had increased. Now he could remain upright long enough to drink, though both legs and arms ached as if he'd struggled through a lengthy illness. His ruined clothing was gone now and a set of folded clothes sat on the room's only chair, presumably from Kosminski's own wardrobe. Shaw's cane rested across them.

"Was the book there," Kosminski asked, "at the warehouse?"

Shaw returned attention to his caretaker and gave a nod. How much had he already told the man that night before leaving home? With a sigh he lay back against the mattress and started from the beginning. Waiting in the warehouse. Sneaking into the other one. Ananya. Druitt. His father. The Hellfire Club and those hideous sailors.

"The Order of Dagon," Kosminski said.

Shaw shuddered. A simple but fitting name.

"They pretend at being helping the poor people in Whitechapel and Limehouse."

Shaw remembered seeing a charity house, providing food in exchange for listening to a sermon.

"They're not trying to help. What they want is new recruits."

"Recruits?" Shaw thought of the deformity each of those men wore. "Recruited for what?"

"To become like them."

A horrific thought, to willingly choose that. After a few moments Shaw pushed the Order of Dagon aside. He continued with his tale, telling how Ananya pulled the book from nowhere, of how it had stopped bullets and fire from harming her.

"She boasted that the book serves her."

Kosminski jumped to his feet. "Serves her? Serves her?" He paced the cramped room, outrage clear on his face. "The book does *not* serve her. The book serves none except the elder gods.

Oh, it will protect one who does their bidding but only so far. She considers herself the master. Hah!"

He continued to pace, raving about Ananya's effrontery. It was the most lucid and focused the man had been in all the short time Shaw known him. In time he calmed himself and returned to Shaw, giving more broth.

"What happened next?" Kosminski asked, as if he hadn't been the one who interrupted the telling.

Shaw continued with the warehouse fire and Ananya's escape with the book, which earned another angered expression from Kosminski. He concluded with the subsequent visit from his father, glossing over the message he'd had for Shaw.

"His final words gave me the idea ..." His eyes flitted to the newspaper laying discarded on the table "The idea to track down Miss Nichols."

Track down Miss Nichols. Yes. He'd done that. He—

"Enough!"

Kosminski raised one eyebrow and Shaw shook his head, looking down at the bed. No. He just couldn't examine that ... Couldn't ...

"We may have only two months to find her," he mumbled, eyes starting to droop as sleep grasped at him.

"Two months. Yes. Yes. Yes. The cosmic cycle. The alignment of planets."

Shaw struggled back to awareness. "You knew?"

"Know of it. Know the concept. Not the details though, not the timing."

"Running ... out ... of ... time."

Shaw's head sunk deeper into the mattress. Was this true fatigue or the idol? Either way it felt as if there couldn't ever be enough sleep. Certainly not enough to return him to who he had been.

"Annie Chapman," Kosminski said, once again drawing Shaw back from the depths of slumber. "I will locate her."

"Take ... take ... the idol."

Kosminski's sympathy was clear ... no, not sympathy. Pity. "No."

A whimper as Shaw's gaze went to the idol. Then his lids slid shut.

The idol had its own agenda, and its own plans.

Did ... did it want them to find Ananya?

Why?

SEPTEMBER ? TO 9, 1888

Days of drifting in and out of a perpetual dreaming. Nights of Kosminski rambling on about the book, telling Shaw about the elder god's history. The man would continue to speak after Shaw had fallen back to sleep, the words penetrating his dreams. Several times Shaw awoke to Kosminski playing haunting melodies on his violin. The tunes itched at his brain like an infection. Was this what the poor man heard in his head all day?

Dreams replayed that horrific night with Polly Nichols, with merciful gaps in the memories. Over and over and over until he was awoken by the sound of his own sobbing, and the sure knowledge of one clear fact.

He was a monster.

Sometimes Kosminski would be there when he woke with warm broth, or some more substantial food. The man himself never seemed to eat and the one time Shaw offered to share Kosminski jumped to his feet and backed away, suspicion and anger plain on his face. Shaw didn't offer again.

Thoughts of returning home to Singh warred with his deeper desire to keep the lad safe. A hollow ache filled his heart whenever he thought of Singh. He wished fervently for them to be reunited, but he would not have Singh anywhere near this evil. The choices made. What he had done. This was his own evil, his own aberration, and he would not allow that to descend on Singh the way it had on him, and on Kosminski.

"I have found Annie Chapman."

Shaw's gaze drifted across the room to land on Kosminski. Was he awake or was this another facet of a dream? Perhaps this was replaying an earlier memory of the man telling him this same news, in which case any response would be without value. He shook his head, wishing he'd never started down this path.

"These are her acolytes, Doctor. They are not worthy of your sympathy."

"They are human beings."

"Barely."

"*I* am barely human."

Shaw closed his eyes. Kosminski held the same outlook that other men in society did. That these women, indeed, that all women, were somehow lesser beings. Shaw thought of his own mother, treated shabbily by his father their entire married life. It was vile.

Is the human race worth saving?

Singh.

Yes. One person was worth it all. He would sacrifice what was left of his soul for that boy.

Shaw opened his eyes, expecting Kosminski to have left, or for him to have not been there in the first place. He remained, dark staring eyes levelled on Shaw.

"There are certain items we will need for this final spell to destroy the book."

"Items? What items?"

Kosminski told him and Shaw tried his best to retreat from the man and his words.

"No! No, no, no, no."

The night of Annie Chapman's murder Kosminski helped him from the bed and into a standing position. He dressed Shaw in the set of his own clothes, slipping him into a black coat and placing a felt hat onto his head.

"What day is it?" Shaw asked.

"September eighth."

Could that be true? Had he been here a full week?

Kosminski handed him the knife taken from Nichols, which Shaw tucked into his belt. After a moment's inspection the other man sighed, the sound of someone with an inevitable task. He lifted the idol from the nightstand and slipped it into the pocket of Shaw's borrowed coat.

"No. Please."

"I am sorry, Doctor."

They left together, Kosminski leading him through the gloomy streets of Whitechapel. The two roamed from one pub to another until Kosminski was able to point Annie Chapman out to Shaw.

Yes.

Shaw knew her.

One of the women from the warehouse.

Darkness.

SEPTEMBER ? TO NOVEMBER ?, 1888

D o we know Ananya's location?"

"No."

"Who do we search for next?"

"No," Shaw whispered, half sobbed. "Please, no."

Kosminski continued to stare, waiting for the words. Shaw scanned the room for distractions. His clothes once again lay in a heap on the floor. Were they less soiled this time?

A vague memory of the knife at work, and he felt his gorge rise.

No. They would not be less soiled.

On the table were two jars filled with liquid and ... and ... the items Kosminski needed for the final spell. Needed to destroy the book. Collected and brought back by Shaw. They reminded him of the specimens in medical school, grim displays for educational purposes. He closed his eyes against the sight.

Against the memory.

"Doctor?"

"We can't continue with this, Kosminski."

"We must."

"You don't understand! I swore as a doctor to do no harm."

"And if more harm is done through inaction?"

An argument he'd made to himself more than once, several times since Kosminski had brought him back here. What value his moral code if it doomed everyone he ever knew? Logic, or self-justification?

Both?

The idol once again influenced and pushed him, kept his brain in a fog. Had this been the plan the entire time? Let him rise up a few steps, only to crash that much further, then do it again and again until he was numb. Yes, the idol influenced him but it was his hand which held the knife.

McCready, the head doctor in Hyderabad, jumped forward in his mind, repeating words he had said after that horrible day at the cave when Shaw had caused another man's death.

There are times when we must remove a limb for a patient to survive. Think of this death as the removal of some greater disease.

The removal of some greater disease.

A smaller evil to prevent a greater one.

Justification for his own heinous acts, but it was either that or lose his mind. Had he already done so? Would he know?

The way he knew what a monster he had become.

The way he knew the clock continued ticking for finding Ananya and the book. A clock which would end, not with a ringing alarm, but with Armageddon.

Smaller evil to prevent a greater one.

Yes.

"Elizabeth Stride."

"I killed *two* women last night!" Shaw wailed. "Two!"

They'd gone out again after Kosminski had found the location of Elizabeth Stride. It had taken some time, some hunting on the other man's part. At least Shaw thought it had ... all other days and nights blended together. They'd been interrupted this time while ... questioning ... Elizabeth Stride. A Jewish man had been passing and became suspicious. Kosminski had called the man Lipski and chased him off, playing into London's anti-Jewish paranoia. Meanwhile Shaw had obtained the name and location of their next target. Catherine Eddowes.

A fair march for him but they'd found her where Stride had suggested.

No interruption this time.

Two in one night.

"Two!" he repeated.

"Remember that these women are evil, Doctor. Followers of the book and Ananya."

"Followers, or pawns the way I am a pawn of the idol?" There was no reply to that so Shaw forged on. "No. No more. No more."

The idol had forced this violence, but that something so abhorrent could exist in him in any way was shocking. He wished to be allowed to die. Jars on Kosminski's table had increased. Shaw identified a kidney before he forced his eyes away.

Had he done that?

"No more," Shaw repeated.

"Where is Ananya?"

"I don't know. I don't know. I don't know."

"Who does know?"

"Mary Jane Kelly."

The name had slipped out. He hadn't wanted to say it, had wanted to take the name to his grave, but it had leapt from his mouth like a living thing. Mary Jane Kelly. The third woman he'd met in Ananya's lodging house with Polly Nichols and Martha Tabram. She had not been at the warehouse the night of the fire.

Yet Catherine Eddowes had given her name.

"I will locate her."

"No. Please no. Please don't. Kosminski, it isn't too late."

"No?"

"There must be another way."

"One month has passed since that night in the warehouse."

Shaw looked away.

"At that time you said we only had two months."

Two months. Two months. Two months until what? For all he knew it was an unimportant date thrown out by his father. A trick. A joke. Some misdirection. A ... a ...

No. He didn't believe that.

And wasn't it just as possible that his father had rounded the time up? Seven weeks into two months. Six? How much time did they *actually* have? How long until this cosmic cycle and all circumstances aligned?

When this was done would he then be allowed to die?

Shaw prayed that would be so.

"Mary Jane Kelly," Kosminski repeated, turning to leave.

Shaw's eyes closed again, ready to be drowned in repeating dreams of what he'd done. His punishment. His penance.

A mere fraction of what he deserved.

November ? 1888

S he was innocent!" Shaw wailed at Kosminski, tears streaming down his face. "Innocent!"

Even once he'd known that for sure the idol would not allow him to stop, he'd continued, and continued, and continued. If he had the strength of will Shaw would pluck the idol from his pocket and throw the damn thing away, throw it as far as his malnourished arms would allow. Likely not far at all.

His legs shook with each step back toward Kosminski's home. One step. Another. A stumble. He needed sleep, and was petrified of doing so. What awaited him this time? His too-thin arms leaned on the cane for support. Thinner than he'd been in years.

Not so thin and weak that he couldn't use a knife though.

Kosminski! He wanted to push that man away from him, cursed the day that they'd ever met. He and the idol could have each other, burn in hell together.

"Where is Ananya?"

Shaw shook his head. It was one thing to find these other women, to ... to ... do what was done. But ... "An innocent woman!"

"No woman is innocent!" Kosminski spat out, seething. "We will discuss our next steps once we are off of the street, Doctor."

"All done. No more."

"Oh, no, there is always some other step to take."

"Done. Done. Done."

Down the street. Through the door. Up the stairs, with effort. Through the door at the top. Shaw staggered into the shabby room, his gaze on the floor to hide his shame.

"What ...?" Kosminski said, before expelling all his air in one quick exhale.

Then Kosminski was thrown across the room, crashing through his table, smashing the jars of organs. The sharp tang of vinegar filled the room. They were under attack.

Shaw twisted, hand going to the head of his cane then dropping as quickly.

"Singh?"

The lad rushed over to his side, grasping him in both arms. "Doctor, we found you."

We?

Yes. Abberline was there as well, and the prince just behind him. The inspector stood over Kosminski, placing handcuffs around his wrists without any great gentleness. He left the man lying in the glass and gore and stench of vinegar.

"Singh," he whispered, raising his arms to hug the young man. "Is it you?"

Then darkness reached up and Shaw collapsed.

November 9, 1888

S haw surfaced again without knowing how much time had passed.

He was weak and miserable, but his mind was clear. He rolled to one side, clawing at his pocket. Ridiculous to think he wouldn't know if he lay on a chunk of stone. As if he didn't know in the first moment of waking that the idol was ... not quite gone, but more distant.

"It has been disposed of," Singh said.

The mattress under him was the same worn, filthy bedding he'd slept on these past ... weeks? Kosminski's flat. Singh must have placed him here when he'd collapsed, meaning his unconsciousness had only been a matter of minutes. Shaw struggled to rise and found he lacked the strength. Singh helped him to lean against the wall.

"You've been wanting," Shaw gasped, "to dispose of it for some time."

"Just so."

"Where?"

"In your doctor's bag for now, in the carriage."

In his bag. Shaw's heart fell as he realized this was just a reprieve. The idol waited for him where he would take possession of it once again and have it worm through his mind, pushing him to still greater heights of depravity. He wanted to beg Singh to throw it in the river.

"It shall be disposed of more permanently," the prince added. "In a place where no other will be affected for some time."

No! The idol was his. His! He ... he ...

Hadn't he just been thinking about asking Singh to throw it in the river?

Shaw gritted his teeth and forced those thoughts aside as much as he could.

"Where?"

The prince shook his head. His message was clear: It was better that Shaw didn't know where.

"How did you find us?"

Abberline came forward. "We've been scouring Whitechapel for more than a month. Since the night you disappeared."

"A month? What ... what day is this?"

"November the ninth."

"November ...?" So much time lost.

"Your friend Kosminski there, was sending letters to the papers from Jack the Ripper." Abberline added.

"Who?"

Singh caught the inspector's eye and shook his head. Abberline waved the question aside. "I reasoned someone had to know where he was holed up. At the very least he was going out to mail his letters. We found this place tonight, while you were away."

A misery hit Shaw like galloping horses. Memories of *why* they had been out, what he had done. Mary Jane Kelly. When these men saw his handiwork they would lock him up. As he should be!

A piercing scream came from within the room. A cry of utter anguish. Shaw jolted, almost toppling back to the mattress. He drew his hands up to cover his ears while turning toward the source, noticing as he did that he was the only one to react. What greeted him was the most horrendous sight he'd ever seen. A woman, her abdomen and lower body a mass of blood, parts of her body and face missing. Her dress had once been white, and the only way Shaw knew this was from seeing it earlier, before she'd been mutilated.

Mary Jane Kelly.

"No!"

He tried to retreat as she leapt onto the bed, crawling toward Shaw like a frenzied crab until her nose—where her nose should be—almost touched his. "You killed me, you bastard!"

"I'm so—"

"You killed me and now that ... that ... horror downstairs is drivin' me mad. It's whisperin' to me, tellin' me horrid stuff, givin' me information I don't want."

"The idol."

"The idol?" Singh said, glancing toward the door then back. "It's still too close."

The prince sprung into action. "Abberline, tell my driver to leave and have another carriage sent back." The inspector was halfway out the still open door when the prince added, "Make sure he knows not to touch that bag."

"Ananya!" Kelly wailed.

Shaw stopped in his efforts to retreat. "Ananya? Yes."

"Ananya!" she shrieked.

"Yes, what of her?"

"Tomorrow. Midnight."

"Tomorrow at midnight?" So soon. Too soon. Did they have time to prepare?

Kelly screamed, sounding like the mythical banshee of her own Ireland. "Ah, God! It hurts. It hurts!"

"Who is he talking to?" the prince asked Singh.

"I ... believe the doctor sees someone we do not."

Both men wanted to help but it was just as clear that neither had any idea how.

"I told you I knew nothin' about Ananya, Doctor. I told you and still you did not stop!"

Shaw choked back another sob, shaking his head. What could he say? That it wasn't him? It most certainly was, and with the idol gone those memories of all he'd done were starting to flood back in. Soon he would remember every inhuman detail. Telling Mary Jane Kelly that he was sorry was nowhere near how he felt, and nowhere near to what she deserved.

This innocent woman had suffered at his hands, unable to give what was demanded.

And now he must demand more.

Ananya. Tomorrow. Midnight.

Mary Jane Kelly had died innocent, but now she *did* know something. Whether that information came in death or simply from what the idol pushed at her ... she knew.

"Where?" he repeated. "Please. Tell me where."

She spun, eyes blazing. "Why should I give you anythin'?"

"You shouldn't. I don't deserve it." Shaw forced his eyes to remain on hers. "But there are millions in London who will die, and more around the world."

She stopped. Glaring at him. Seething. Her ruined mouth opened and shut.

Shaw kept his own mouth shut and waited.

"So many."

Shaw nodded.

"That book?"

Shaw nodded again.

A deep sigh. "An' you'll stop this if you know where?"

"We ... will do our best. Yes."

Eyes still blazing hatred at Shaw she considered, then with a deep breath that she no longer needed Kelly told Shaw, through gritted teeth, where Ananya would be.

Shaw repeated the address to himself, then again to Singh. "I ... I know this place. It was my father's first factory. East End, of course, close to cheap labour."

A memory of being separated from his father. The terror only a young child can appreciate.

"That's where Ananya will be. Tomorrow at midnight."

"Doctor—"

That was as far as Singh got. On mention of the address Kosminski exploded up from the floor and plowed his head into the lad's stomach, driving all air from him. Taken by surprise Singh went over backwards, stumbling over the chair and coming up against the far wall. He rolled to prevent further attack. A wild kick caught the prince across his chest and knocked him onto the bed, tangling him with Shaw. Both Singh and the prince struggled to rise but Kosminski was already gone. Moments later Singh got enough wits about him and took off in pursuit while Eddy stayed with Shaw.

The prince rubbed at the spot where he'd taken the kick while righting the room's one chair. He sat, leaning toward Shaw. "Who were you talking to?"

"I ..." Shaw cleared his throat. "Mary Jane Kelly."

"Another victim?"

"Yes. The last." Shaw felt the world starting to recede again. Whatever strength he'd regained was now spent. Before consciousness deserted him once again he managed three words, more relevant than any others. "She was innocent."

November 9, 1888

S haw awoke in his bed, clean and wearing his own
nightclothes. Gone were the sharp tangs of vinegar, body
odor and unwashed clothing. He was comfortable and safe
and the damned idol was gone. Without it he found himself physically more rested, but misery and guilt squeezed at his soul, if he
still had one. He stifled a sob.

"You are awake."

Shaw shifted to see Singh in the chair, where he'd probably
been since they'd returned home.

"How long?"

It was a question he tired of asking. So many days and nights
merging into one inseparable nightmare, ever since that night at
the warehouse. It all melted together with too many instances of
slipping into unconsciousness to escape the facts of the waking
world, then awaking to escape his dreams. Shaw jolted, remembering Ananya, the date and time.

"How long?" he repeated, more frantic.

"We returned home this morning. It is now six in the
evening."

Twelve hours gone, and a few hours more than a day until
they confronted Ananya at his father's factory. Without that

information, thwarting Ananya would be impossible. That information. Provided by Mary Jane Kelly without hesitation even though ... even though he ... he ...

"Oh, Singh." He shook his head. Wretched. "I did abominable, unforgiveable acts."

Singh leaned forward, full attention on him. Shaw took a deep breath and told every detail he remembered from his time with Kosminski. Shame forced his gaze to his hands while he talked. Would the lad leave once the story was told? Storm out the door never to return? He would understand. It was no less than he deserved. Once Shaw rambled to a close Singh did not leave. Instead he filled in the few missing details he was privy to through the inspector and other sources.

All of London was in a panic, but none so much as the inhabitants of Whitechapel. The police hunted for Jack the Ripper, as did the Whitechapel Vigilance Committee. This last a group of Whitechapel citizens. There'd been some apparent close calls where the Ripper had come close to being caught. If someone had gone left instead of right. If a policeman had gone a bit further on his route.

He should have been caught. Incarcerated. Hung.

Stopped.

Those poor women. Yes, they were servants of Ananya, but they were also disaffected, abused people, discarded and ignored by their "betters." They wanted something more from life and hoped to find that in Ananya. Instead they found death. Whatever terrible acts they had done, it paled compared to what was done *to* them.

"As I see it, Doctor, you were influenced by the idol."

A convenient excuse. How easy to say it was the idol and wash his hands of it, set that guilt aside and be done with it. The fact that even an item as loathsome as that idol steering him to such evil acts meant that inhuman violence was inside him somewhere. He never would have suspected himself capable of such things.

"That is no excuse."

"I recall you telling me that my acts in India were the fault of the cult's corruption."

"You were just a child!"

"That excuses the actions?"

Shaw had no answer to that. What was the difference between those influences? The difference between Singh and himself? They both needed to carry their guilt with them, whatever the outside influence which guided them.

"Inspector Abberline believes Kosminski is guilty of those murders."

"No," Shaw responded, voice low, ashamed. "It was me. All me."

"All you? Hmm ... You sent those letters to the papers?"

"I ..." Shaw shook his head.

"You sent that package with a human kidney to the Whitechapel Vigilance Committee? Did you give yourself the title of Jack the Ripper, or place those writings on the wall in Whitechapel?"

"I ... I know nothing of that."

"Of course not. Those were Kosminski. The inspector believes he was the Ripper and I agree. From all you've said he was as much an influence as the idol."

No. It was too easy an excuse. Like blaming the idol.

"If Abberline knew any differently he would have to arrest you."

"That would be such a bad thing?"

"Yes."

"I see no reason why."

"We must still find Ananya and stop her, Doctor."

"That is what Kosminski is doing, looking for the book to destroy it."

"You still believe this?"

"Yes, of course. He destroyed that copy in Poland. He's searching to destroy this one now, the original."

"We have the unreliable word of a lunatic on what he's done

or intends to do. The only verifiable fact is that he came from Poland. His own family knows him to be unwell. He disappears for weeks, and when he is with them he refuses to bathe or take food anyone else has prepared."

"You never did trust him."

"And you trust him too freely. He fights to destroy the book, and keep these gods asleep? Then why did he take the idol? Why did he keep it?"

Shaw opened his mouth to speak but Singh continued on.

"Why keep it in front of you the whole time, and force you to carry it? Why allow it to affect and influence you? Is there any reason other than to keep you under his control?"

Shaw closed his mouth, having no explanation.

"Where is the idol?"

Had he said that aloud? Judging by the look on Singh's face he had.

"Eddy has hidden it away. His family has many places where even such items as this can disappear."

Shaw grunted. "Mention to Abberline that he should keep an eye on the prince for erratic behaviour. Just in case."

Singh nodded. "Would you like some food?"

Food. Yes! He found himself ravenous. "Yes! Anything, please."

Singh stood and crossed to the door, stopping with one hand against the frame. He turned back to Shaw, no change of expression. "Why did you leave me behind?"

Shaw shook his head, not understanding.

"The night of the fire, after we came back. Kosminski came for you. You left me here. I departed India and all I knew to come here and fight this evil with you. You cast me aside for Kosminski."

"Oh, Singh. I don't even remember leaving. Once I was there in Whitechapel, well ... I told myself I was protecting you."

"I do not want or need protection. I want to be the equal you said I was."

Shaw stared at the young man, half expecting him to leave without another word. That would have been easier, and again better than he deserved. Could he have insisted that Kosminski wake the lad as well? Or come back after that first night? He could have gotten word to Singh in some way ... but he hadn't. He'd purposely chosen to exclude Singh from what was happening.

"Quite right, Singh. I treated you like a child, not as an equal, and I apologize."

A crossing of the arms while he considered Shaw's words.

"If I do this again, please tell me at once."

"I shall."

"Good. Good." He paused, unsure how to ask the next part. On some level he felt self-conscious. "I was wondering ... would you try teaching me meditation again?"

The corner of Singh's mouth curved for a moment in his almost smile. "After you eat." Then he was gone to prepare the promised food.

"He's a fine lad."

The Irish lilt so close to his ear startled Shaw. He spun to see Mary Jane Kelly, as she had appeared last night, after he had visited her. He looked away again.

"Aw, poor wee baby. Can't look on yer own work?"

"I'm sorry."

"Yes, well, that's sure to bring me back ta life then, isn't it?"

"I ... I will turn myself in. Confess to the murders."

"Hmph, yes, by all means. Make my death more meanin'less."

"What do you mean?"

"You have a job ta finish, Doctor."

A job. Yes. They needed to find Ananya and the book, to put an end to all of this damned business forever.

"After then."

"Fine. Fine."

Kosminski had been correct. Some part of that idol had become a permanent part of himself. To be visited by the dead! How long before that led to madness?

"Why are you still here?" he asked.

"What d'you mean?"

"My own father only visited me the once after he died. He took care of the unfinished business of telling me what a disappointment I was, then he was gone."

"Ah, I take yer meaning." She mulled over this thought before responding. "Perhaps I still have unfinished business then."

"I see."

"Do you? I doubt that." She rested on the edge of his bed, staring at him. "I believe I will tell you all about my life."

"Why?"

"So you'll know all about the poor innocent woman you murdered." She hesitated, looking toward the window and back. "And maybe so I won't be completely forgotten."

Shaw took a deep breath and forced himself into a sitting position, determined to keep his attention on the woman, no matter how distressing he found it.

She shook her head, one flap of skin waving with the motion. "Oh, not now. Singh will be comin' back any minute. Don't you worry none, I ain't goin' anywhere."

Little time was available for convalescing. As a doctor he would have prescribed rest for a week or longer to any patient in a similar state. Shaw had a day. One day to build up his weakened body and recover some much-needed sleep. Each time he woke Shaw forced himself a step further. To sit up without help. Then to shuffle to the edge of his bed. To stand.

Mary Jane stayed with him, telling the story of her life as promised, doling it out in portioned amounts. She came from a sizable family with too many mouths to feed. At the age of sixteen she married a coal miner, who died soon enough in an explosion.

Shaw found he liked the woman, and empathized with all she'd been through.

On one of his waking periods he heard talking from the sitting room and tried to rise and see who was visiting at that late hour. Through the closed door it was difficult to tell for sure, but he thought it was Abberline's voice, the prince's as well. Sure enough the two men came through his bedroom door, led by Singh, just as he'd managed to get his feet into the waiting slippers.

"You're looking better, Doctor," Abberline said, as Singh ushered Shaw back to bed.

"I feel better."

Abberline glanced down at the bed and Shaw, not making eye contact. "You know, Scotland Yard can take care of this business tomorrow night. You don't need to be there."

"You know better than that, Inspector."

"Do I?" His gaze bore into Shaw.

"I *do* need to be there."

"Why?"

"To destroy the ..."

"Without Kosminski there's no way to destroy it." Abberline spoke in a brusque, businesslike tone, much like he'd used at Ananya's lodging house. He looked toward Singh for confirmation. "If ever there was one."

Yes. They all knew about Kosminski's insisting that he could destroy the book, but none knew of the deal Shaw had struck with the man. That one piece he had held back in telling the story to Singh ... But, had that all been a deluded fantasy? Or was it manipulation as Singh had suggested?

"I need to be there, at the end of it all."

"Very well, Doctor. But you won't be at the front of the charge. Not this time. After the action is over you three can come in. Not before."

Shaw opened his mouth to protest, but what could he say? That he should be at the front with veteran policemen? That he was every bit as fit and able as those men? No. "You've organized your men? The same as last time?"

"Oh no, I learned from our time at the warehouse." Abberline shook his head. "Mobilizing the whole of Scotland Yard, or as many as they'll allow me."

"What did you tell them?"

"Only reason I could to get that many men involved." Abberline's eyes bore into Shaw. "Told my superiors I had a line on catching the Ripper."

Shaw's mouth opened then shut. The Ripper. Was that why Abberline stared at him in such a way? The inspector had his doubts on just how much innocent captive Shaw had been. Maybe he'd put all the pieces together and knew who had held the Ripper's knife.

Shaw responded in a low voice. "Ah, good thinking."

"Luckily I'm the man in charge of the Ripper case," Abberline said, turning toward Singh again. "The men only know that we hunt for the Ripper. I will spring the location on them last minute so there can be no reporting back to other interested parties. I trust them but ..." Another shrug.

"The stakes are too high," Singh said.

"Yes. Exactly. Only we four know the location."

"Kosminski knows too," Shaw said. "He heard before rushing off."

"Escaping, more like it," Abberline said. "Fine, I hope he does show his face. Maybe we'll catch the Ripper after all."

"Maybe," Shaw said, voice low.

"You have the factory under watch, I'm assuming?" the prince asked.

"No!" Shaw spun back toward the conversation. "You'll frighten Ananya off."

"I think we know how to watch people without being seen, Doctor," Abberline said in a soothing tone. "We don't want to lose her or the book."

"We won't. They will be there at midnight. That much is confirmed."

"Confirmed."

"Yes."

"By your ghost lady?"

Shaw said nothing, hearing how ridiculous that would sound to a man like Abberline. He'd seen strange, unexplainable happenings but was still a simple copper at his core.

"Calm yourself, Doctor," Abberline said. "I have one man in the area, dressed as a wandering beggar. He knows no detail except that we are hunting the Ripper."

It didn't matter what Shaw said to the man, he would not win this argument. He prayed that this wasn't a foolish chance taken by the inspector. Conversation turned to the plan, which was simple enough, formulated between the others while Shaw slept. They would arrive at the factory close to eleven-thirty and storm it with the police Abberline had been assigned. The idea was to come in from every entrance and overwhelm any possible opposition. After that, get to Ananya and remove the book from her possession by any means necessary. The book protected her, they'd all seen that, but there must be some limit. If they could get to her before she could use it ... If Shaw could wrestle it from her grip. They had no protection from the book's power. All they had were guns, determination, muscle, and—hopefully—superior numbers.

Could they keep her trapped inside and bring the building down around her with explosives as a last desperate measure? Was that possible?

Then ... once he had the book Shaw would find Kosminski again. Together they would destroy it, if at all possible. If Kosminski could be trusted. Too much of what Singh said about the man bothered him. Too much he couldn't find logical answers for.

November 10, 1888

With little to do in way of personal preparations the following day passed with agonizing slowness. Shaw napped often to ensure he was rested for that night, and out of a need for something to do. He awoke in early evening, the sun close to fully set. He'd sunk into a deep sleep despite all of the worries and fears crowding his thoughts.

Tonight was their last possible chance to defeat Ananya and take possession of the book. If they failed all of humanity would pay the price. Everyone. Everywhere. All would die screaming without knowing whose name to curse as they did.

Not much longer now. The prince would come at ten-thirty and bring them to Abberline. The force would then travel to the factory together in silence until ready for the attack. Even for a simple plan there were far too many places where it could go wrong.

Shaw had come to another conclusion. After all was done and if they were successful—No! Not if. When, damn it. *When!*—then he would turn himself in as the Ripper to take his just punishment. Hanging most likely.

It was the right thing—

A slight cough startled Shaw, not a true cough but an expression to gain attention. He turned, more startled by who it was. In the chair beside his bed was Montague John Druitt. No butterfly mask hiding his features. No gun either.

"You!" Shaw spat. "Singh!"

"Your ward is not available."

"If you've hurt him—"

Druitt held up both hands in a calming gesture. The man's impeccably neat attire was somewhat rumpled, and circles lay under his eyes. He was haggard, tired. Had he finally realized just how much in over his head he was? "What I mean is Singh is not here."

"He isn't, Doctor," Mary Jane Kelly said from the other side of his bed. "He left two hours ago."

"Two hours?"

That wasn't like Singh to leave, not while Shaw was in the midst of recovering in any case, not while he was asleep and defenseless. Shaw turned back to Druitt to find the man staring toward Mary Jane Kelly, brows knitted.

Let him stay confused. "What do you want?"

Druitt uncrossed his legs and leaned forward. "Singh has been taken by Ananya. She's taken Michael as well," Druitt said.

"Michael?"

"My ... partner. He—"

"Why?"

"To influence me, I suppose, and keep me out of her business. I've been following her since the night at the warehouse. I've lost the scent, but she's not taking any chances. Same with you."

"You're lying."

"I can understand why you wouldn't trust me."

"That is an understatement."

"Last time we met I gave you valuable information."

"For your own ends. Then you tried to steal the idol."

Druitt looked around at mention of the idol.

"It's gone."

"Ah." Druitt brought his gaze back around to Shaw. "*This* is for my own ends as well. I admit that."

Of course it was. Shaw expected nothing less. He crossed his arms, ready to hear and disbelieve whatever self-serving explanation the man had. Without the mask it was easier to get a sense of what he was thinking.

Druitt took a deep breath and let it out. "Michael is ... important to me, Shaw. Just as Singh is important to you, though in an obviously different sense. Help me get him back, please, and I'll make sure you get Singh back."

"Why should I trust you?"

"You shouldn't. I've given you no reason." He leaned closer to Shaw. "Can you take the chance where Singh is concerned?"

Singh.

Could he take that chance? All he had was Druitt's word that Singh had been taken at all. The lad could be getting some groceries ... No. Any other day, but not tonight. Some other reason then.

"Ah, the poor lad," Kelly said.

Shaw turned toward her, one eyebrow raised.

"What? You expect me ta hate him? He's ain't the one that murdered me."

Shaw flinched and looked away, back to Druitt. The man stared at him as if he'd gone delirious. Maybe he had, talking to people only he could see. Miss Kelly moved across the room to stand before the window, viewing the world outside.

"I ... overheard the boy talkin' with that inspector friend of yers, last night just before he left."

"Yes?"

She turned back toward Shaw. "He, the inspector not Singh, was sayin' he wasn't sure one man in the area was enough. He wished he had another ta send. Someone who knew what was truly goin' on."

"Abberline sent Singh there?"

"No." She shook her head. "Singh volunteered, but the copper was against it."

He saw her meaning. Just because Abberline was against it didn't mean Singh hadn't taken it on himself to go. They couldn't chance Ananya slipping away again and the lad would choose that over coming back to watch him sleep, or over his own safety.

Damn it.

Memories of Lassiter and Walsh, and what had happened to them at Ananya's orders, wormed into Shaw's thoughts.

No. Not Singh.

"There is ... someone else here?" Druitt asked.

Shaw waved it aside. "A long story."

He glared at Druitt. If Singh was indeed in Ananya's hands then he needed to go to the lad's aid. If not ... well, what would happen if this were a trick and he was incapacitated or killed? Nothing. The raid would continue as scheduled.

"What do you want from me, Druitt?"

"Tell me where she is."

Shaw scoffed. "Why not use that vicious ritual you performed at your house?"

At first Shaw interpreted the regretful expression as shame or remorse at the taking of that officer's life. Druitt sighed. "No, that is far too difficult. It takes much preparation and various uncommon ingredients. To rush it would be certain death."

"Was it worth it the first time? What information did you get?"

"Information? The depth of your knowledge astounds me. Yes, I received information that tonight at midnight was when all this would end."

"All ...?" Shaw bolted upright. "Everything?"

"No, no." Druitt made a calming gesture then thought better of it and shrugged. "Well, perhaps ... No, I mean tonight is Ananya's final chance as much as it is yours."

Shaw eased back. That wasn't a perspective he'd considered.

This was the last chance for both sides. "You knew this at the warehouse?"

"I did. I wanted to get the book before tonight."

"So you can be the one to end the world?"

"No! Do I impress you as a lunatic?"

He did not. "What *do* you want?"

"Power!"

"Power?"

"Yes! The book doesn't have to end the world. It can grant untold power."

This poor fool still had no idea of the nightmare he was chasing.

Druitt cleared his throat. "For now though, I only want Michael back."

Michael? No. Shaw didn't believe that for a moment. Once he had his friend back then the attention would shift again. Shaw couldn't allow this man to have the book any more than he could allow Ananya to have it.

"You can't take a chance that he's lyin'," Kelly said.

"No, I can't."

"Fine!" Druitt stood, thinking this last was aimed toward him. "You can stay here or waste time going to the police. By the time they take action this will all be done. Please, Shaw, you of all people know what she's capable of. Tell me where she is and I'll go myself."

Shaw pushed his legs from under the sheets and stood. He was no fool ... or not as great a one as Druitt believed. He didn't trust the man, but as it had been pointed out he couldn't take the chance.

Had he actually been worried that Abberline's actions were foolish?

Shaw's stance held no sway this time and he turned back toward Druitt. "Give me time to dress."

"Of course. I'll be in your sitting room."

Shaw dressed quickly, with Mary Jane Kelly staring out the window again.

"Will you come with us?" he asked, making sure the revolver was in his jacket pocket, loaded and ready for use.

"No!" The sound of horror in that one word was enough. Kelly wrapped her arms tighter around herself. Considering how adversely she'd been affected by the brief experience with the idol he could only imagine what the book would do to her spirit. Death, it appeared, held no end to an ability for suffering and Miss Mary Jane Kelly had suffered enough.

Shaw left the bedroom and ghostly woman behind. Now that he was dressed and moving Shaw felt more like his true self, the self he had been before the idol came into their lives.

Druitt was ready to leave, overcoat and hat back on. "I have a carriage waiting."

The last time he'd been in a carriage with this man had not been a pleasant experience. He gave the driver directions as they were needed, refusing to give a final destination.

"That is not my man," Druitt said.

Shaw didn't reply. A short ride into the East End section of Mile End, followed by an equally short walk brought them to the building where Ananya hid. Though hiding insinuated fear. No, this was where Ananya made her preparations.

The factory appeared much as it had when Shaw was a boy, immense and industrial though a bit more run down now. This was not a happy place. Not for him. Not then and not now. He and Druitt stood in the shadows across the street, watching a building which gave every indication of being abandoned.

"You're sure?" Druitt asked.

"I—"

The factory door opened and a sailor passed into the chilly night air, also sticking to the shadows. Inside, windows had been blacked out to prevent any light or signs of life from escaping to the outside world. Yes, he was sure. The sailor performed some unknown action, moving with caution, before turning and heading back inside.

From where they stood Shaw couldn't tell more than the man's style of dress, but he was certain there would be some fish-like deformity there. The Order of Dagon. They'd allied themselves with Ananya.

"Around back," Druitt said.

This door was more conspicuously guarded with two men standing outside. They made a show of looking casual, waiting in the night, but a promise of untold violence existed in the way each moved. No one was getting past them.

Shaw had his revolver but couldn't go in with gun blazing, like some dime novel cowboy. He may get to kill these two men before they reacted but more would be inside. How long until the bullets were gone and he was reduced to his cane for defense? No, that wouldn't save Singh and doing anything so foolish would upset all the plans that were in place as well. This needed stealth.

A sudden gasp escaped him with the memory that sprang to mind. He hooked a finger over one shoulder, pointing down the slope leading to a muddy waterfront. The terrain and night together were not his friends. Shaw stumbled, almost falling, but Druitt caught him by one arm, stopping his descent. Moving with more care Shaw led them to what he hoped was real and not a trick of memory.

Yes. There it was. A metal door leading into the factory, built into the slope itself. A door he'd last seen through the tears of a child. This one was not guarded, or at least didn't appear to be.

"I hope it isn't locked," Druitt said low.

Locked? Yes, surely it would be.

The gate swung open and Druitt stepped inside, Shaw once again following. The musty smell of an area long unused filled his senses. Druitt took a small hand lantern, the sort bobbies carried, from inside his coat and lit it. A scan of the area showed their one option of straight ahead.

Locked. That one word swirled inside his mind. Locked.

Was it because of the gate? Sure it should have been locked or guarded.

No. Something else.

Locked.

Locks. Door locks.

"After Kosminski's last visit Singh had the locks changed," Shaw said. "Replaced them with much better ones."

"Yes?"

"How did you get in tonight?"

"I just—"

"Used Singh's key?"

The gun was in Druitt's hand that quick, as if it had always been there. Shaw had no chance to go for his own. Instead he stood there cursing himself for a fool and following Druitt. Cursing himself for not drawing his own revolver before accusing the man.

"Yes," Druitt said.

"*You* have Singh, not Ananya."

"Yes again. Let's go."

"No. I don't think so. You can shoot me here."

"Don't be a fool. Singh will be allowed to go free when this is done."

"I don't believe you."

Uncertainty creased Druitt's face. He looked the way he'd been headed then back toward Shaw, lowering his weapon. "Leave."

"What?"

"Go home. All I wanted from you was to be led here."

"No! Druitt, you will ruin everything."

He turned, gun aimed toward Shaw's midsection. "I *will* have that book."

"For God's sake, why?"

"God!" Druitt spat the word like a fly had landed in his mouth. "Our god of love and forgiveness who routinely rewards others. Is that the god you mean?"

Shaw said nothing, hardly able to argue in favour of a god he didn't himself believe in.

Druitt nodded, as if his point had been made, then continued on. "I seek an honest god. One which is only concerned about its own interests but perhaps will reward one of the livestock who serves him well."

With that Druitt backed away, lantern lighting the path. Shaw watched him. One step. Two. Now that Shaw was more in shadows could he draw his own revolver? Would Druitt react in time? Any shots would alert Ananya and her protectors more than them skulking through the factory.

What could he do?

Druitt could destroy it all. If he was caught Ananya would realize her location was known. She could relocate without Abberline and his men having any idea. Plus Druitt was the only person who could tell him where Singh was; he was not trusting in this man's assertion that Singh would be set free.

Shaw shuffled after him. Could he lash out with the cane, knock Druitt unconscious? That wouldn't rescue Singh. The other man came to a stop, allowing Shaw the chance to catch up. He kept the revolver pointed towards Shaw's chest. Impossible to miss at this distance.

"Don't think of swinging that cane at me."

Shaw grunted a reply and continued on when Druitt waved him forward. Several passages branched off from the one they followed. It would be quite easy to get disoriented, as he knew from experience, but ahead lay another light source which guided them forward.

They came out into a wide room, lit by several lanterns. The smell of dust and dirt—and blood?—filled the air. On the left stairs led to a landing and a door twenty feet up. More passages led off on the other side. At center was a great stone altar, reminiscent of what he'd been tied to back in Hyderabad, after he'd fallen down the stairs. That first time he'd seen the book and his entire world had flipped.

That had not been here when he was a child.

"Would the book be down here?" Druitt wondered, approaching the altar, circling it.

Shaw knew it would be wherever Ananya was, and both would be well guarded.

A door was set in the wall across from them, on the far side of the altar. Impossible that Ananya would be so careless as to leave the book in there.

"Druitt—"

The sound of a revolver being cocked was distinct against the backdrop of silence. Then another. More. Both men turned slowly, Druitt careful to have his weapon pointed toward the ground. From all sides came men in delicate white masks, each with a distinguishing decoration.

So, not only the Order of Dagon. The Hellfire Club had thrown in with Ananya as well.

Each held a gun pointed at the pair. Seven in all. Eight with their leader who came from the shadows to join the rest. The man in the plain white mask, his amusement somehow carried through the expressionless mask. He gestured toward the altar and Druitt took the direction, placing both gun and lantern there.

He raised both hands in surrender. "I came to see Ananya."

"Undoubtedly," White Mask said. "But why should *she* want to see *you*?"

Druitt turned toward his former leader. "Because I brought her a present."

White Mask chuckled and Shaw felt a prickle of icy fear. "Ah, yes. The resourceful Doctor Archibald Shaw."

"Yes," Druitt agreed. "Surely that is enough to grant me an audience."

"Perhaps." White Mask gestured toward the closed door in the other way. "Move toward that room."

Shaw and Druitt crossed the open area toward the door. One of the armed men arrived first to open it ahead of them. He made a mocking *after you* gesture. Shaw recognized the man's build and stature.

"Richard Willoughby," Shaw said.

The eyes behind the mask darted to his leader, then the man shrugged. "Doctor."

Willoughby leaned forward and checked Shaw's pockets, taking the hidden revolver.

"Inside, please," White Mask commanded them.

The room was lengthy, but only about half as wide. It had the same scents of dirt and dust, but also stale sweat and something unclean. White Mask gestured and one of his men placed Druitt's lantern inside with them. At least they would have light. The door closed with a soft click. Shaw didn't try the knob. Either it would be locked or one of those men would be waiting with a gun outside to convince him it was a bad idea.

"So, I am a gift to Ananya, am I?"

"I had to say something."

"I'm sure."

"I didn't warn them about your cane, did I?"

Shaw glanced down, admitting this was true. He still had his cane, and the sword inside it. "That does not mean I trust you."

"I told you not to."

"No trust. No trust. No. No. No."

The voice came from deeper into the room, inside the shadows. Shaw knew the voice.

"Kosminski?"

"Yes. Yes."

Shaw worked his way along the rough wall, coming across heavy metal loops every few feet, until he reached the other man. Kosminski's hands had been bound and tied through one of the loops.

"You remember your promise," Kosminski whispered.

"Yes. Of course."

Druitt turned up the flame on their lantern and opened the baffles on each side. The light exposed the stone walls, the metal loops and Kosminski, who was the same disheveled mess he'd been last time they'd seen each other.

Shaw tried to push all doubts aside that he had for this man. He needed the faith that this man could help destroy the book when the time came.

"What are you doing here?"

"Been here since yesterday. I came after I heard the address back in my flat."

"No!" Shaw whispered. "So they've known we had their location for a full day?"

"No. No. No." Kosminski shook his head. "They think I'm some vagrant. They don't realize I have the *knowledge*. I know the book. I knooooowwww it."

He winked at Shaw then fell silent. Shaw had to wonder if Abberline's man, dressed this same way, would have been similarly ignored. There must be more vagrants like that wandering through the area.

Minutes later the door opened again. Ananya stepped in, accompanied by two of her prostitute followers, each brandishing one of those wicked knives; a knife which Shaw could not see without remembering his time in Whitechapel. Two others had followed, standing near the door. White Mask and a sailor who must lead the Order of Dagon.

"You have brought me a gift," Ananya began without so much as a greeting.

"Yes," Druitt said, gesturing toward Shaw. "I—"

"The true gift is the knowledge that somehow this place is known to our enemies."

Shaw gritted his teeth. Exactly as he'd feared. Now she could change her plans. Ananya turned toward the two men at the door.

"Ensure your men know we will have company."

"Company?" the sailor asked.

"Inspector Abberline and the police."

The man fidgeted, as if the police were already outside the door. "Shouldn't we go somewhere else?"

"Far too late for that. No, put extra men at each entry and tell them to stay out of sight." She looked back to Druitt, then to Shaw and back to the other men. "Make sure that metal gate is guarded too, and find the man who was assigned to guard it and have him killed."

"Yes, princess," both men said without hesitation.

She stepped over to Druitt and stood before him, arms crossed. Though shorter than either man, she showed no worry at all. It wasn't because of the men at the door, or the women with their knives either. No, none of them were the real threat. The book then. She was protected by the book.

"What do you want?" she asked of Druitt.

"To be part of this."

"That offer was made before. You rejected it."

"Yes, I wanted the book to myself," Druitt said, "but I admit defeat. It is almost time."

"Is it?"

"Tonight at midnight?"

"So that is known as well."

Shaw wanted to slap Druitt, to tell him to shut up.

Now she spoke over one shoulder to the other men. "They know the location and time."

"They'll want to know for certain the book is here," White Mask said.

"They will be watching. Not too many in case they should alert us. No, I think, one man."

"I can have my men search the nearby buildings," the man of Dagon said.

Ananya considered. "There is nothing they can do to stop us, but do so in any case."

The man gave a short bow and left to pass on the orders.

"You may leave," she said to White Mask. "Take my ladies with you."

"Princess Ananya?"

"I will be fine. They know better than to attack me. Don't

you, Doctor Shaw?"

Shaw gave one quick nod.

"Before you go, do take the doctor's cane though."

White Mask came forward and took it. Shaw leaned against the wall, shooting the man a venomous glare. Ananya couldn't know about the concealed sword, but the cane had too much potential as a weapon on its own. Once White Mask and the two women had gone Ananya stood before them, as if daring an attack. Without the cane Shaw was no true threat, not a physical one for certain. Druitt stood with arms crossed, a statement that he had no intention of attacking. Ananya gave a shrug, disappointed.

"You are prepared to be a loyal follower?"

Druitt nodded. "Yes, princess."

She considered him a moment before turning to Shaw. "I am pleased you are here, Doctor. It provides a poetic ending to this."

"How so?"

"I could read the final spell myself. I've found the correct page and the book will not harm me."

"You seem certain of that."

"If you mean about the page, I am. A symbol of the tentacle adorns the top, a sign of our dread lord Cthulhu." Shaw flinched at the word. Mean-spirited humour danced behind Ananya's eyes. "And if you mean about the book harming me I am equally sure. It serves me and will cause me no harm."

"HA!" Kosminski spat from his place on the far wall.

Ananya turned toward the man as if seeing him for the first time. A look of interest crossed her face. "You disagree?"

"Yes! The book serves no one except the elder gods. You are merely the holder of the book."

"So, you are more than some wandering vagabond then." Her gaze narrowed for a moment before refocusing on Shaw. "In any case, it pleases me to have *you* read the final spell."

"No."

"Oh, Doctor. You are not being given a choice in the matter."

As if on cue the door opened again and two shapes were propelled inside, followed by two Hellfire Club members with guns levelled.

"Singh!" Shaw said, shocked.

"Michael?" Druitt said.

"Yes, Singh and Michael," Ananya said. "Tell me again of your loyalty, Mister Druitt."

"Sorry, Monty," Michael said, embarrassed, his Russian accent coming through. "The Indian tricked me. Once he had the upper hand he forced me to come with him."

Druitt raised a hand to stop his friend, looking Ananya in the face. "We had Singh under guard to force Shaw's cooperation."

"Then you promise your loyalty."

"I do."

"No matter what."

"Yes."

"Very well." She turned to the men at the door and gestured toward Michael. "Shoot this man dead."

"No!" Druitt shouted, stepping toward Ananya.

A flash of purple light and Druitt was thrown several feet, landing on his back with a groan.

"As I thought."

"Please," Druitt croaked from the floor.

Ananya waved a hand toward the men with guns. They retreated toward the door.

"Not to worry, Mister Druitt," Ananya said, heading for the door. "Loyal or not, you will be permitted to see our lord rise again. Then you may pledge loyalty to Cthulhu."

Michael rushed over and helped Druitt to his feet while Singh came and acted as support for Shaw, easing him to the floor since there were no chairs.

"I am surprised to see you," Shaw said. "What are you doing here?"

"Rescuing you."

"Hmm, I thought I was rescuing you."

NOVEMBER 10, 1888

S ailors returned with lengths of rope and secured each of
their hands together, then through a loop in the same style
as Kosminski's bonds. One man at the door with gun in
hand kept them docile while his fellows did the work.

"That will hold you," one said through rubbery lips. "We
know our knots."

The sailors filed from the room.

Shaw and Singh each took turns filling the other in on how
they'd come to be there. Singh had gone to get the paper, for
something to do, and had been struck from behind on his way
back. He'd woken to find Druitt and his man standing over him.

"Singh was harder to trick," Druitt said from their spot on the
floor.

"A touching reunion."

Singh spun toward the voice, squinting into the dimness.
"You! What are you doing here?"

He started for the man, forgetting he was also bound to the
wall.

Kosminski howled with mad laughter, then fell to muttering
unintelligible words to himself. They all ignored the man and he
returned the favour.

Shaw gave a quick glance at his watch, at least that hadn't been taken. Not quite eleven.

"The prince will have come by now and realized we are gone."

"He'll go to Abberline."

Yes, if the prince went directly to Abberline and they mobilized without delay they would be here soon. Abberline would be expecting trouble of course which would help prevent an ambush. More than an hour.

The door swung open with a squeak of one hinge. Not even locked, that was how confident Ananya was. Three of the Hellfire Club stepped inside, followed by Ananya and then three of the followers of Dagon.

"This is nostalgic, isn't it, Doctor Shaw?"

Shaw said nothing. Ananya gestured toward the prisoners and four of the men approached. Each untied one from the wall and started to lead them away. Shaw's eyes went to them then back again. This couldn't be right. More than an hour remained until midnight.

"One moment," Ananya said. "Singh, if you struggle, as I know you are considering, Doctor Shaw will be shot in his other leg. Right around the knee should give the best damage."

She gestured and their captors continued on, leading Singh who moved without resistance except for his gritted teeth and clenched fists. Ananya led Shaw herself, moving at a slower pace since he had no cane for assistance. They crossed the floor to stand in front of the altar. On either side of the room, against the walls, were dazed, vacant-eyed men, chained at the wrists through similar loops in the wall. Shaw recognized some as the educated men who had been abducted. Others must have been recent abductees, or people who hadn't been missed yet. At least ten stood on either side, the vacant faraway stares of soldiers who had seen battle. Some were covered in blood. Others twitched. None looked toward Ananya.

A simple wooden armchair waited to one side of the altar, the sort from a poorer family's kitchen. Ananya led Shaw to this and pushed him into it. The arms stopped him from toppling out and onto the floor. Shaw took in the altar, swallowing involuntarily.

One prisoner was tied to each side of the stone block, Singh to his right with Druitt to the left. On the farthest end stood Kosminski, grinning like a child about to receive cake. Around the periphery of the altar, in a perfect circle, stood men of the Hellfire Club and those from the Order of Dagon, intermingled. Twenty of each stood at the ready with more further back in the shadows. Others would be upstairs, guarding the entrances. A dozen or so women stood around the room, their wicked knives held at the ready in one fist. They shot warning scowls at every man nearby.

Shaw took a deep shuddering breath and let it loose.

"You will be reading the spell tonight," she said.

"No." It's still too early. Surely she is getting prepared. Could he distract her? "Is your own faith not strong enough?"

"Faith is one thing, but why take chances when a disposable resource is available."

Disposable resource. Him.

"Beside the fact, Doctor. You are the only person I've met who has been able to resist. Your father may have been able but ..."

"But you abandoned him to burn to death?"

"He was already dying. So sad."

If she thought the idea of his father's death would affect him Ananya was barking up the wrong tree. Shaw glanced at Kosminski who stared back. His eyes appeared lucid, planning. Yes, Shaw had survived a glimpse into that book, but so had Kosminski.

Ananya moved away from Shaw, nearing the altar where she retrieved the book—had that been there the entire time? Shaw expected her to come in his direction, ready to close his eyes. Instead she headed for Singh. She drew a sister blade to the ones her followers carried and placed it against Singh's throat.

"Shall we jump to where I threaten to cut Singh's throat if you won't read?"

Shaw said nothing, his eyes going to the lad. Singh didn't appear concerned in the least.

"Doctor, if you do not read it I am dead and if you do we are *all* dead."

Shaw nodded.

"A smaller evil to prevent a greater one," Singh said. "Remember."

Yes. He remembered.

Where the hell was Abberline?

"Have you seen this tentacle pictograph with your own eyes?" he said to Ananya, grasping at distractions.

"I have." She chuckled. "One within the Order of Dagon sacrificed himself to confirm it as well, though I'll allow you to do the same."

A noise, distant. Was that the bang of a police revolver?

Shaw listened, praying.

There it was again. Ananya had heard it too.

A sense of relief filled him. "You don't have as much time as you thought."

"I have all the time I need."

She said it with such confidence, such surety that Shaw found his own confidence shaken. The fact that the lair had been found and police were drawing closer didn't matter in the least to Ananya. She did however lower the knife from Singh's throat, considering the lad.

"I find your argument logical, Singh. Threatening you won't work this time. Very well." With one fluid motion she came around the altar, opening the book and holding it toward Shaw.

"Close your eyes," Singh yelled.

Shaw did, clenching them so tight his temples throbbed. She had almost taken him by surprise with her sudden change of action but nothing would get him to open his eyes now. He recalled back in Hyderabad when he had considered chewing out his own tongue to prevent—

THUNK!

Unimaginable pain flared through his body, starting at his left leg. His eyes shot open and stared disbelieving at the knife protruding from the meat of his leg. It had sunk halfway in, until the tip had halted against bone.

He screamed.

The book was placed between his gaze and the knife.

Yes. Yes! Shaw saw the pictograph she'd mentioned. Tentacle. Water. Words swirled within his view, becoming legible.

"Shaw!" Singh yelled.

No!

He tore his eyes from the book. Had he already started reading the words? Yes, he could feel them on his tongue, the way a burn could be felt for days afterwards. Now that he was aware he would guard against looking back ... at the ... book.

He could hear the words!

Who was reading now?

No! His eyes were back on the page. *He* was reading the words. He was screaming the words.

Singh was screaming too, screaming his name.

Somewhere more gunshots went off. Shouts. All distant. Too distant.

The book sucked words from his mouth, spurring him on and on and on.

Shaw forced his eyes shut.

It made no difference.

BANG! BANG!

More gunshots. Closer. Closer.

A great commotion erupted behind him. The door at the top of those stairs bursting open. Shots fired. Men's screams. Shouts. Threats. The Hellfire Club down there drew their guns while the sailors pulled knives out. They moved towards the dazed prisoners on the walls. The interruption was enough. Shaw pushed with his stronger leg, toppling the chair over backwards. His head slammed against the floor and the world before his eyes went white.

The spell had been broken. Shaw no longer had the words bouncing inside his head. His skull pounded from hitting it against the floor and dizziness threatened to consume him, but free of the book's words. Ananya's eyes narrowed.

Where was Abberline and the police? They should be swarming down the stairs and into this area by now. He could hear gunshots. Ananya's men of the Hellfire Club and the Order of Dagon were doing their jobs, delaying the police from arriving.

Shaw's gaze returned to Ananya. She glared a moment longer as he backpedaled, then turned the book toward herself. Ananya's eyes widened and she screamed, a high sound that filled the entire room and echoed off the ceiling. It went on and on, her face a mask of terror. A shake of her head in the midst of that scream, then it just petered out, resolving itself into a single word.

"No!"

She gave her head a shake, then a second. Frantic determination filled her face as she continued the words from where Shaw had left off.

"No!" Shaw said. "No!"

Screaming with each movement Shaw forced his way to Singh. One shuffle. Two. Three. Any more and he would have passed out, and surely would after his next action. Shaw grabbed the hilt of the knife protruding from his leg and pulled it free, howling with pain.

The world wavered. White to grey to black.

No! He could *not* pass out now.

When his focus returned he found Singh had already taken the knife from his hands and finished cutting through his bonds.

"Stop her, Singh. Stop her, stop her, stop her."

He was asking Singh to kill once again and the lad stood, ready to do it. The room wavered around Shaw, receded into white. He pressed both thumbs into his wound, partially to staunch the flow of blood but mostly to force his attention back.

Singh pivoted while raising the knife, took a step.

In the space between two breaths the temperature plummeted

ten degrees, fifteen. Static energy surged through the room and the lanterns all glowed a baleful green.

They were too late.

It was done.

They'd lost.

A foot behind where he'd sat a moment earlier a hole no bigger than a dinner plate opened in the floor, glowing a wan yellow. It expanded, growing larger with each passing second. The chair disappeared, swallowed up by the circle. Ananya's followers retreated step by step. Hellfire Club, Order of Dagon, and prostitute warriors, all bordering on a wild-eyed desire to turn and flee as the hole reached where they stood. The Russian, Michael, still tied to the altar, scrambled on top to avoid falling in. The edge neared Ananya who made no move to back away, the expansion coming to a stop at her foot. In all the hole had grown to the size of two large carriages. Foul, stagnant water rushed to fill it from some unknown source. Frosty emanations shot from the liquid in waves which could be felt across the room, fit to freeze a person body and soul.

The door at the top of the stairs was hammered against. Once. Twice. Then it broke inward. Abberline and his men forced their way through the splintered opening to stare at the scene below. The woman. The altar. The glowing circle filled with water. From here Shaw could pick out Abberline at the front and Prince Eddy to one side, not quite waiting for everything to be clear after all. The prince held a bloody sabre in one hand.

"Too late!" Ananya shouted. "I've won!"

She *had* won, and kept her mind while doing so.

A wind built in the room, swirling among those assembled, pushing some back.

"Great Cthulhu," she screamed, her voice rapturous, "come forth to this world!"

From the jagged edged hole rose a figure. A great, horrible, unthinkable deity. A god which towered above the tallest of insignificant humans. A salty smell of ocean water and rotted fish wafted through the room, pushed by the wind.

"Who. Calls. Dagon?" it rumbled.

The voice was cold, like the ocean's bottom, where drowned men settle after their ships are destroyed. It was the sound of every hideous, alien thing swimming through the waters, of every uncaring beast with teeth waiting to consume men stupid enough to enter their domain. The sound of jagged reefs tearing through wooden planks.

Dagon!

This god wore the same features which defined its worshippers. The blubbery lips. The unblinking, silvery eyes. More! A ridge down the back. Fins. Gills.

And the teeth!

"Father Dagon," one sailor muttered.

Then another. And another. The room was filled with the low, reverent whispers, almost a hymn.

"No!" Ananya shrieked, a sound of pure outrage as she looked up at Dagon. "No! This was my planning, my scheming, my sacrifices! I orchestrated this and I didn't do it to summon some minor fish god!"

The room went silent. The Order of Dagon halted their chants. No one moved. Even the police, grouped together on the top landing with weapons drawn stared agog at what transpired below in the center of the room.

Father Dagon narrowed his terrible gaze on Ananya, his lips retracting to show every pointed sharklike tooth. "Indeed," he rumbled.

One hand shot out, grasping Ananya in its webbed fingers. She screamed in agony, dropping the book as she was jerked upward. Dagon's mouth opened in a vicious rictus.

Senses returned to the room as shock was replaced by determination. The Hellfire Club turned their guns on the immense god, firing off shots while Ananya's female minions brandished their knives, ready to attack. Abberline gave the order to his stunned men to start forward.

"Father Dagon!" the lead sailor shouted.

The Order turned on Ananya's loyal followers, attacking the better-armed men, burying knives into sides, necks and backs. The women fought back with like weapons, felling some of the Dagon worshippers. The room filled with gunshots and screams. Bullets ricocheted off the altar.

Singh dropped the knife into Shaw's lap and scooped him up, heading for the far side of the room.

"Shaw!" Druitt called, glancing from him, to Dagon, to Michael and back. Both still tied. "For God's sake, Shaw."

With a quick flick Shaw threw the knife toward Druitt. He didn't see where it landed. For all he knew it had landed far outside the man's reach. Singh didn't stop until he reached an alcove leading toward another passage. There he took the opportunity to rip a strip from his robe and wind it around Shaw's leg as a bandage. It hurt like hell but would slow the bleeding for now. Druitt and Michael were fleeing to the opposite side, for the room they'd been held in earlier. Kosminski, still tied to the far side of the altar, stood watching the great god Dagon with fascination.

"I called you here," Ananya screamed. "I command you to release me."

"No one commands Father Dagon," the god answered, not focusing on the woman in his fist. "You presume too much."

"Help me!" she shrieked.

"Enough!" Dagon shouted, laying his baleful gaze on Shaw. On Singh. On all those in the room. It had the effect of once again bringing all to a halt. "Return home, my children. Take your place among the Deep Ones."

Not one sailor hesitated in their immediate rush for the portal, pushing those they battled aside to get there and dive in headfirst. When the last disappeared beneath the frigid water, the elder god pulled himself to full height and sunk back below the water himself, Ananya still held in one great fist.

"No!" she shrieked, water filling her mouth.

Then they were gone.

The portal closed rapidly with a high audible *pop*, leaving confusion behind. A moment's hesitation as the balance of power shifted and every officer continued their rush forward, guns drawn. The Hellfire Club retreated, looking to their leaders for direction. These men were no warriors for battle. Ananya's female minions hesitated a moment before stepping back into the shadows.

A second passed before White Mask and Richard Willoughby both rushed for the book, which had been dropped near the altar. A shot rang out and Willoughby fell, a perfect circle through the forehead of his mask, cracks radiating from it. Inspector Abberline positioned himself in front of the book, revolver trailing a wisp of smoke, daring the man in the white mask to come forward and take it. Hellfire Club and police all held their breath, waiting for the actions of their leaders. All attention was focused on these two men while Kosminski scrambled around the other side of the altar, hands untied now from some discarded knife.

"Abberline!" Shaw called across the open room.

Too late. Kosminski leapt for the book, grasping it while he rolled to his feet. A few policemen started to turn, a couple of the Hellfire Club. Abberline turned his head, trying to keep an eye on White Mask at the same time.

"Protect me so I may do your bidding!" Kosminski cried.

A concussive blast, like that of an artillery shell but without the shrapnel, blasted through the room, sending people in every direction. Hellfire Club and police officers alike were scattered like a child's toys. Singh was thrown against the wall, Shaw just after him. The lad acted as a cushion for him and Shaw prayed he wasn't hurt. Abberline impacted the wall next to the door, sliding down to rest against the cold floor, eyes closed.

"What ...?" Shaw said, spinning back toward Kosminski, forcing his legs under him. "What the ...?"

"Shaw. Come. Come. This is our chance." Kosminski flipped through the book, eyes flashing, until coming to a page. "This is it! This is the page. This will destroy the book. Come. Read it quick!"

Shaw staggered toward the man, hopping on his right leg. Kosminski flipped the book toward him. The displayed page made his head ache. The words resolved—

"No!" Shaw threw one hand over his eyes. He wouldn't look. He. Would. Not.

"Shaw! This is our chance!"

"I heard what you said, Kosminski. Begging to do the book's bidding."

Kosminski squinted one eye and nodded.

"Singh was right about you all along."

"He was." Kosminski turned the book back toward himself.

"Whitechapel. Everything—"

"Hah! The idol kept you under control, while each murder brought you deeper into depravity. I was amazed when you started to bring back the organs I asked for."

"Your goal was never to destroy the book."

"Of course not. *I* wanted to be the one to bring forth great Cthulhu."

"I'm a fool."

"On that we agree."

No one had recovered yet, each of those thrown across the room struggled to get their wits back. Shaw continued to hop. Somehow he had to stop this man. He fell to the floor, grasping at a dropped revolver, then jerked it up level with Kosminski and fired.

The recoil and his own lack of strength knocked him over backward, the shot going wide and missing Kosminski by several feet. By the time he'd managed to return to a sitting position Shaw saw movement behind the other man.

"Don't—" he started.

Too late.

Druitt rushed up from behind Kosminski. He'd been in the room with Michael and was the only one not hit by that blast. Druitt launched himself forward, grabbing at the book. His fingers grasped one edge, locking into claws, tugging on the book.

"No!" Kosminski screamed.

Each man held one side of the great leather book while Shaw did his best to get closer, unsure what to do if he did. Who did he shoot? Both of them?

"It is mine!" Kosminski said.

"No! No!"

The two men's eyes flicked from each other to the pages of the book and back again. The page, then back. The page, then back. Each time their eyes would remain longer on the book, struggling to pull their gaze away at all.

"M ...Mine!" Kosminski repeated, more of a whisper.

Druitt shook his head, eyes glazing. Another shake.

Each pull on the book was slower, weaker, more of an effort. Druitt, stared at the book a full ten seconds, eyes growing wide and terrified, before Kosminski tugged it back.

"It's ... It's ..." Druitt tried. "M-m-mine."

"Monty! Let it go!" Michael rushed forward and rammed him with a shoulder, knocking his hands free from the book.

"Who?" Druitt turned to his friend, viewing him with haunted eyes. The eyes of a man who couldn't ever be the same. His fingers slackened and he staggered backward, collapsing heavily to the floor.

"It's me. Michael."

"Michael ...? Yes."

Michael looked around at all the police and Hellfire Club starting to recover and did some quick calculations. "We need to leave. Now."

"Leave?"

Shaw whipped his focus over to Kosminski, sure that he

would have continued his reading after coming out sole holder of the book. The man's face had slackened, jaw hanging open.

"Cthu ... Cthu ..." The words came in mutters until his lips stopped moving.

Kosminski slumped to the floor, clutching the book, but no longer seeing it.

Shaw continued to crawl. "Kosminski! Let go of the book."

No reaction.

Druitt and Michael had fled while Shaw's focus was on Kosminski. A sad shake of the head. Montague John Druitt was not a man he ever expected to have pity for, but he did. That man had looked on the forbidden and his mind paid the price for it.

"Doctor," Abberline said, coming up beside him. A gash ran across his forehead and a second along one cheek. He gestured at Kosminski and the book. "How do we ...?"

"We ... we need some gloves."

Abberline called to his men about the room, "Who has gloves?"

Singh came forward and helped Shaw to stand, bringing him across the room to where Kosminski lay curled into a ball. The prince appeared on his other side, a pair of white leather gloves held toward Shaw.

He was numb, knowing he was expected to pry the book from Kosminski's hands but not wanting to touch it. Shaw glanced at Abberline, the prince, both staring at the madman on the floor. Neither would volunteer to take that book. He refused to look at Singh, knowing the lad *would* take that burden without hesitation. With a deep sigh Shaw crouched before Kosminski.

The gloves fit nicely, so soft. The best quality pair of gloves he would ever wear.

"Kosminski," he said. "Aaron."

No response. No sign of recognition. Was the man breathing?

Shaw reached out and touched the book. Even through the gloves he could recognize the waves of evil, the probing, questing sensation of that which wanted to know him better. Shaw let go and drew one arm up to cover his eyes.

"Doctor?" Singh said from beside him, one hand on his shoulder in support.

Shaw nodded and took hold of the book with one hand. With the other he peeled each of Kosminski's fingers away. Once a finger was removed it stayed as it was placed, as if the man had become an immense doll. Finally done, Shaw retreated with the book and threw it onto the altar, backing away from it. He focused on the carnage around him.

Abberline and his fellow policemen had seen horrible circumstances in the line of their duty, but nothing like this. The men had all the signs of shock, yet still they pushed forward with their jobs, starting with freeing the prisoners from the rings on the wall. The prince too had seen enough strangeness in his lifetime, but this would be the strangest, if he was lucky.

"I am pleased you are both well," Prince Eddy said, clapping Singh on the shoulder. Even through the words the man was wild-eyed and disbelieving.

Shaw knew how he felt.

The words he'd read today and in the past floated inside his mind. It was as Kosminski had said: Some evil would fade in time and others would be with him forever. Why? Why should he have to live with such knowledge? Why couldn't he be allowed to forget? Why was he able to survive such close contact when others lost their minds on the reading of a word or two? Was it the previous exposure to the book in India? The idol's influence? Or was it the strength of Singh's unconditional support?

All three?

NOVEMBER 10, 1888

The policemen not tending the kidnapping victims, gathered the surviving members of the Hellfire Club—before any could make their escape—and brought them to the waiting police carriages. The Order of Dagon had all departed with their god, except those too wounded who were left behind. Dead from both groups littered the floor but they would come last. Those needing medical treatment would get it at the station, though it was doubtful any of the club would remain there for any length of time. Kosminski left in handcuffs, to be returned to a family which would commit him to Bedlam for the rest of his days.

Shaw's leg had been wrapped in a clean bandage and his cane had been located. It was enough for the moment. Now he, Singh, Abberline, and the prince remained behind, standing at the altar and staring at the book, surrounded by the dead.

"It doesn't sit well with me that Kosminski gets away with it," Abberline said, watching the man being led out. "Him and Druitt both."

"Actually—" Shaw began, but stopped when Singh's hand landed on his shoulder giving it a warning squeeze.

It was time to confess, it had to be. Shaw turned toward his friend, hoping to convey that sentiment in a look and instead saw the pain in Singh's own expression. It took his breath away, the words dying on his tongue. What would his confession and execution mean to Singh? Perhaps they should talk this over at home first. He could put things in place so the lad would be taken care of once he was gone.

"Actually?" Abberline prompted.

"Hmm? Oh, um ... actually Druitt looked like he had lost his mind, too."

"Oh yes? Well, we'll see when I track him down."

They were avoiding the real topic.

"What do we do next?" the prince asked. "What can we do? Can we burn it?"

"I doubt it," Abberline said. "We saw that book stop bullets and a lantern with flaming oil."

"According to Kosminski there was a spell inside the book to destroy itself."

"You still believe him?" Abberline asked. "That man had his own agenda and would have told you anything."

Shaw shrugged. The point was moot. If a spell did indeed exist inside of the book they wouldn't find it, not without going insane. Kosminski's mind was gone, and even if it weren't he couldn't be trusted to help. "Can the book be hidden the way the idol is?"

"No." Prince Eddy shook his head. "I do not believe this book will stay hidden so easily."

"Others will come searching," Abberline said, "and it will call to those people."

"It's calling to me right now," the prince said in a wondering voice before shaking his head. He took another step back from the altar.

"Yes," Shaw agreed. "That book, unsupervised in Prince Kanwar's private library, had resulted in the Cult of Kali being reborn, the mauts being called up, and the murders of several people."

"The book needs a caretaker," Abberline said, looking point-edly at Shaw. "Someone to watch over it."

"No!" Shaw stepped back. "I've given enough of my life and sanity on all of this from the day I arrived in India until this moment. I've given enough! You can't ask me for more!"

"Who else is there?"

"I shall be its caretaker," Singh said.

"No! Singh, you can't!"

"This is why I left India, Doctor. I left to protect people from this evil. This is my purpose. My ... redemption."

"Redemption?" The word caught Shaw by surprise and he covered his face with both hands. He didn't want this for himself, but doubly so for Singh. The bloated tumor of a book would be a chain around the lad's neck, the way the idol had been for Shaw but more so. It already poked at the edges of their individual psyches.

Singh did not speak, nor did the others.

Shaw let out a sigh, bordering on a sob. "I am sorry, Singh. You are correct. I will watch over it with you."

Somewhere a clock chimed midnight.

Shaw didn't know if he was worthy of redemption but he would accept this book as penance for all he had done in Whitechapel. He would live with the guilt of that the rest of his days, and likely with this book as well.

Once again the solution was as horrible as the problem.

A smaller evil to prevent a greater one.

"This is not a task for one person," the prince said. "You will need to support each other."

"And keep an eye on one another?" Singh suggested.

The prince nodded. "You must leave London. Go where there are no people within the book's radius other than you two. I shall arrange a house in the countryside for you, Cambridge perhaps."

"Thank you, Eddy," Singh said.

"For the good of England," the prince added. "Once I am

king we will find a better solution. When I have all the resources of the crown."

The three looked at the prince. Shaw raised an eyebrow and Eddy shrugged.

"I can't bring this to my grandmother, she would think me unbalanced. As would my parents, and then I would never be king. No one wants another madman on the throne."

THE YEARS TO COME

Prince Albert Victor never became king. He died of influenza less than five years after their adventure with the book.

Inspector Abberline would rise to the rank of Chief Inspector before retiring in 1892.

Druitt's body was found later that year in the Thames. Suicide. He'd loaded his pockets with rocks and jumped in. A letter found in his room held one simple sentence: *Since Friday I felt that I was going to be like Mother, and the best thing for me was to die.* His mother had been institutionalized when Druitt was young.

Michael's last name was Ostroh, a swindler and con man born in Russia who had an extensive police record. After Druitt's death he disappeared.

Kosminski was committed to Bedlam, believed by several to be Jack the Ripper. A fact which was only half correct.

Shaw and Singh found themselves in a Cambridge house, funded by the prince even after his death. They were accompanied by Miss Mary Jane Kelly who haunted Shaw for several years, telling him her life story over and over before finally moving on to the afterlife.

ACKNOWLEDGMENTS

It seems my attention to detail is sometimes lacking. Because of this I missed adding acknowledgments in my previous book, *Cults of Death and Madness*. I will attempt to make up for that here.

Where to start, where to start ...

My two sons, Jack and Oliver, are an important part of my life. They are my motivation and make me want to do better. On top of motivating me they also read my work, come to book launches, and just generally believe in me. That is the highest praise as far as I'm concerned, and I thank you both.

A great big thank you to my buddy Greg Neill. He kept asking me to write a Lovecraft inspired story until I finally said: Okay, sure, why not, then sat down to do it. That story was "Damned Voyage" which took third place in *Writers of the Future Volume 35* (4th quarter). From there the rest is history ... or maybe literature. One of those subjects.

Speaking of WotF. The people at Galaxy Press have done so much for me since the publication of *Writers of the Future 35*. Thanks to John Goodwin, Emily Goodwin, Joni Labaqui, the late great David Farland, and every judge of the contest who thought my story had what it took.

First readers are an essential part of the writing process. Those first few readers who point out all the mistakes and typos are invaluable. I have a few who have been with me through many stories and I give a big thank you to Allison Batoff, Jack Haas (yep, my son), Kevin Quirt and Julie Lee (did I forget someone? I hope not).

There was research on this book as well, and a big thank you to Karen Hale, David Cleden, Christina Anderson, and Lauren Mastrogiacomo for all the info about London.

Thank you to the lovely Michelle Lacroix who not only holds my heart but has taken on the daunting task of looking after my website, and finding new ways to promote and market my work. I couldn't do it without you.

Lastly I need to thank the amazing people at WordFire Press. Thanks to Kevin J. Anderson and Rebecca Moesta for taking a chance on me. Thanks to Marie Whittaker for working with me and patiently responding to all my emails. And another thank you to all the editing staff for fixing those errors and anachronisms.

About the Author

John Haas is an award-winning Canadian author living in the nation's capital of Ottawa, Ontario. He grew up in Montreal, Quebec, and also lived for many years in Calgary, Alberta, and misses each of those cities for different reasons.

Since his early days John has been a storyteller, always making up the plots to whatever games he played with the other kids in the neighborhood. Now he focuses on getting those stories written down and published. In the last decade or so he has seen around twenty of his stories published in various excellent publications, including *Writers of the Future Volume 35*.

This book in your hands is his fifth to see publication. If you haven't read *Cults of Death and Madness* yet you may want to start there, then come back to this one. It will make more sense.

Currently he is hard at work on the next novel of Shaw and Singh's struggles against the forces of darkness.

His goal is to become a full-time writer (every writer's dream). Rich and famous would be nice, but one step at a time.

When not writing John enjoys time with his two wonderful sons, doing all sorts of family stuff. He enjoys collecting action figures, reading comic book collections, as well as all things science-fiction, fantasy, or horror related. Once an active gamer, these days he saves gaming (video and board) for family time with his boys.

IF YOU LIKED ...

If you liked *BOOK OF DEATH AND MADNESS*, YOU MIGHT ALSO ENJOY:

Banshees
by Mike Baron

Harmony in Light
by Walter H. Hunt

Mr. Menace
by R. Michael Burns

OTHER WORDFIRE PRESS TITLES
BY JOHN HAAS

Cults of Death and Madness

Our list of other WordFire Press authors and titles is always growing. To find out more and to shop our selection of titles, visit us at:

wordfirepress.com

 facebook.com/WordfireIncWordfirePress

twitter.com/WordFirePress

instagram.com/WordFirePress

 bookbub.com/profile/4109784512